Number 10 Affair

The Banks Book 1

Joanna Maz

Copyright © 2024 by Joanna Maz

All rights reserved.

No part of this book may be reproduced in any form or by any electronic or mechanical means, including information storage and retrieval systems, without written permission from the author, except for the use of brief quotations in a book review.

To the whole of Booktok that wants to be pushed against the wall by an obnoxious and intimidating politician with a filthy mouth, who Googled STFUATTDLAGG for you all.

Roses are red
Unhinged characters are born
This book I am reading is practically slow burn porn

The following story contains mature themes, strong language and explicit scenes, and is intended for mature readers.

Bear in mind that the vocabulary, grammar, and spelling of Number 10 Affair are written in British English. Some of the phrases and words might not be familiar to other English speaking audiences.

Chapter One

Spencer

Why couldn't the Prime Minister of the fucking United Kingdom get laid?

It had been weeks since I'd had sex. If I didn't get some soon, my staff would suffer. They knew me for my impatience and sometimes explosive temper—a flaw I acknowledged—and this dry spell didn't help any. I was in a terrible state. After too many weeks without a decent lay, I was aware my behaviour had worsened, and people had avoided me. I recognised the caged look in their eyes as fear to approach me.

Bloody hell.

At least, what I lacked in personal charm, I made up for in

political life. I cared for my people and dealt with challenging situations head-on. Perhaps that was why most turned a blind eye to my shortcomings.

Tonight, though, was all about me. I planned to put an end to this frustration so that tomorrow I could return to my office and act like my usual annoying self.

Tonight, my blue balls would go back to their normal shade.

I released a frustrated growl and checked my watch. It was seven forty-five, and my escort was fifteen minutes late, which had never happened before. This girl was going to pay the price for her mistake. I expected professionalism, punctuality, and discretion.

I wiped the sweat off my brow, straightening my posture. It was Wednesday, the beginning of May, and I wasn't used to the warmth that had been blazing through Britain in the past few days, although forecasts were even more optimistic. For a change, the month of May would bring lots of sunshine rather than rain, and I reminded myself that this was a good change.

Cursing under my breath, I recalled the last woman who'd shown up at my door. Tanya. She was great in bed and obedient, but the whole experience still felt underwhelming. Maybe I was growing tired of these women who always worked hard to keep me satisfied.

The Emperor VIP Club, an exclusive agency providing high-end escorts, always catered to my requests, but it'd been eighteen months now. Perhaps this entire arrangement had run its course.

The owner, Matthew, and my brother, James, were discreet.

Number 10 Affair

Matthew had a credible reputation in London, and he preferred the company of affluent people. My brother had recently invested in the business, and word had spread around quickly. It wasn't a secret that politicians and businessmen used escorts, but this was an exclusive club. The membership fee was expensive for that very reason.

My muscles tightened, and I exhaled. As the leader of the country, I needed discretion. This week had been stressful as fuck, and I was physically drained. The new policy aimed at increasing funding for social housing had kept me up all night. My party was reluctant to push it, but more people needed access to affordable housing, especially in London.

Tonight, I needed to blow off some steam and spend a few hot hours with a woman without thinking about logistics. I wanted to push boundaries, to dominate and punish her. Vanilla sex didn't interest me.

A loud knock pulled me from my intrusive thoughts. I was at my private home in central London. My daughter was with my mother tonight, so I didn't have to worry about her. Only a few trusted people and my security detail had this address. I walked to the door of my study and opened it. Jason, the head of security, greeted me.

"Sir, Miss Laura Watkins is here to see you," he said, and at my nod, he stepped aside, allowing me to greet my new guest.

A tall and slender woman stood at the bottom of the first flight of stairs, clutching her bag against her stomach. She gazed around uncertainly, and when she saw me, she paled.

She was taller than any of the other women I had been with

before. Dressed in a caramel fitted summer dress and flat shoes, she gave off a teacher's vibe. Was this a joke? A game? Had Matthews forgotten the type of woman I typically asked for? Perhaps it was some roleplaying shit.

Impressive, Matthews. Very impressive.

"Come on in, Miss Watkins," I snapped, wondering what she was waiting for.

Her eyes widened, and she surveyed the space once again, as if unsure whether she wanted to go farther into my home.

I decided not to wait for her and walked back inside. She finally climbed up the stairs and entered the room, scanning the walls. I spun to face her. The air was heavy, thick with tension, as I listened to her erratic breathing. This was fucking turning me on. This woman was so much in her character, and in the dim lighting, she appeared completely lost. I didn't care at this point. I was so fucking hard.

"Go upstairs, Miss Watkins, and wait for me in the first bedroom to your right. Take your clothes off," I commanded her.

"But—"

"There are no buts. Do as I say, or you will face consequences," I cut her off, then strode past her to go to the living room.

I heard her go upstairs. I tried to get my cock to fucking relax, but it was almost impossible. This woman appeared young, but I hoped she was experienced. Judging from her acting skills, she knew exactly what to do. I poured a glass of whiskey and downed it. The alcohol burned my throat but took the edge off my bad mood. Tonight, after I'd fucked her ten ways until Sunday, I would be more than satisfied. My position had limitations, but I still could enjoy no-strings-attached sex.

I headed upstairs, picturing several ways I could fuck her—on all fours, straddle saddle, missionary, hands-on, and my favourite, the reverse cowgirl. The possibilities were endless. As long as it was intense, I was happy with it. I pushed the door handle and went up to the bedroom. Miss Watkins sat on the bed, still fully dressed, but she quickly stood when I entered.

She parted her lips slightly as if wanting to say something but changed her mind. Hell, she was young, so innocent. She was beautiful, slender, blonde, and a green-eyed babe, the girl next door. I continued staring at her, observing that she didn't have the typical features of a British woman, and although I didn't detect any accent, I recognised a slightly curved nose, high cheekbones, and very fair skin, which indicated that she originated from somewhere in Eastern Europe. She was the kind of woman I would have gone for in the past ... but I didn't want to go there right now.

My cock hardened even more at the thought of enjoying this game.

"You should be on your knees and not looking at me at all. I didn't give you permission to stare at me," I snapped, unbuttoning my shirt.

She seemed shocked. Her innocent face flushed.

Obeying my command, she knelt on the floor, her gaze downcast.

I got into her space. I never really liked blondes because of my daughter's mother, but tonight I didn't mind.

"You should know the rules, but maybe you don't, so I'll let it slide this time," I said, already imagining her red lips wrapped around my cock.

Warmth rippled from her body. Lust coursed through my veins, and my temperature soared.

I lifted her chin. Fuck, a pair of incredible green eyes stared back, and my breath hitched. This woman was not what I was expecting. She was so damn stunning. Something in her eyes tipped me over the edge—uncertainty, fear, and also desire. Her eyes widened, and thousands of unspoken words passed between us.

I wanted her more than usual, but this was her job. Pleasing me was her goal. I paid for her submission.

First, she needed to suck my cock.

"I think there's been some mistake, sir," she mumbled, her voice so sultry my heart pounded.

She seemed like a forbidden temptation I wanted to explore.

"Trust me, little one, I don't make mistakes. Now be a good girl and release my cock. I want it in your mouth."

Fear flickered across her features. She was really in the zone here.

The seconds dragged, but she didn't move.

"I hate repeating myself. You're here to serve your prime minister," I growled, ready to rip the clothes off her body.

My damn cock pulsed, and intense pressure flooded my groin. With trembling hands, she undid my pants, and I helped her slide them down to my knees. Something didn't add up here, but I pushed that thought aside because I was too turned on to stop now. When her fingers met my skin, an inferno took over my body. Her touch was so soft, silky, and perfect. She tugged my boxers down, and my erection was right in front of her face. Laura stared at the glistening pre-cum on my tip, transfixed.

"I really shouldn't be doing this, sir," she choked out.

I glanced at her, overwhelmed with lust.

"Why the hell not? It's your job."

"I thought I came here to be interviewed for the nanny position," she finally blurted out.

I laughed.

This woman was so fucking hilarious.

Laura stared at me with a mix of confusion and anger. My pulse drummed in my ears, and suddenly, everything clicked into place. I hastily pulled my boxers and pants up, realising I had made a fucking huge mistake.

"I thought Matthews sent you? You work for Emperor VIP Club, right?"

She frowned, clearly perplexed.

"No, I don't. I am here for the nanny position. Someone called me earlier, and they said they'd send a car for the interview."

What the fuck had I just done?

"Stand up now!"

The nanny. This woman was here for Maja. She wasn't a fucking escort.

"Matthews doesn't make mistakes either," I snapped, glaring at her. "So what the fuck are you doing here?"

She closed her eyes and continued to breathe, while I was losing my mind here.

"I'm really sorry ... I didn't mean to. This was a terrible misunderstanding. My roommate works for an exclusive club, and she must have—"

"Quiet! Just be quiet for a moment and let me think." I paced. I was still painfully hard, and this whole situation had put me in a difficult position. Discretion was important—I couldn't afford to lose my credibility and reputation. This woman could cost me my career because I had dangled my cock right in front of her mouth. Christ, what a fuck-up!

I turned to her. "So you're telling me that you got a call earlier this evening? Someone asked you to get in the car. Why didn't you question any of it?"

Chapter Two

Laura

I saw the Prime Minister's cock. I saw the Prime Minister's cock. I saw the Prime—

Did I just say that out loud?

Stop it, you idiot. It's a misunderstanding. Pull yourself together!

Oh my God. I wanted the ground to open up and swallow me whole. I felt paralysed, rooted to the floor, unable to speak or move. Each passing minute felt like an eternity. My throat was dry, and my knees shook as if I had been running for miles. My heart pounded, and I was sure he could hear it. God, I was such an idiot for thinking getting on my knees would help my chances of securing this job.

My phone had rung, and I'd answered it. The man had informed me that someone was interested in hiring me and I just had to go to that specific address on time. He'd hung up before I could ask questions, and that should have alerted me enough.

Damn, this man—no, Prime Minister Spencer Banks—was even more attractive in person than on the screen. Tall, jet-black hair, square jaw, perfect symmetry, great shape, and these incredible blue eyes that burned through my skin. He was every woman's dream. Veronica would always call me over whenever he gave a press conference, commenting on his good looks.

"Well, the man on the phone told me it was urgent." My voice quivered, and I fought back tears. His cock was huge and beautiful, possibly the most impressive I had ever seen in my twenty-seven years. I bit my lip, berating myself for such thoughts. Moisture pooled between my legs. I imagined how it would feel to have him in my mouth.

"Fuck," he swore, his piercing gaze fixed on me. "Get up. What the hell is wrong with you?"

"There's nothing wrong with me, Mr Prime Minister." I attempted to sound sarcastic but sounding desperate instead. This entire situation was so humiliating.

He strode forward, getting dangerously close. Dammit, why did he smell so good? His cologne was masculine. How old was this guy? I didn't know, but I would have to find out later.

"Do you kneel during every interview?" His muscles tensed.

A wave of heat coursed through my body. The azure hue of his eyes blazed even brighter.

"Why did you even do it?" he asked.

"No," I replied and tried to contain my desperation, "but this is my fifth interview this week, and I can't bear to mess it up. Can we start over?" I bit my bottom lip.

His gaze zeroed in on my lips, and the tension between us grew heavy. I felt an inexplicable attraction—deep and powerful—towards him. A man like him had no need for a nanny, so why was I even suggesting it?

The heat emanating from his body stirred something deep within me. How long had it been since I last had sex or experienced desire this intense? A very long time—years ago, since my heart was broken and I couldn't find the willingness to start sleeping with other men.

"Start over? You want to be my escort for tonight?" he asked, with a hint of amusement in his voice.

I averted my gaze, since he was distracting me.

Being an escort was my roommate, Veronica's, job. She played the role of a seductive mistress and occasionally slept with wealthy men. I could only ever be a nanny, like my ex claimed.

"No, I mean, I came here for the nanny position," I repeated in a mumbling tone. Things had surely turned on their head. How could I tell him I was fantasising about him already, and he thought I was here to fuck him? How was that even possible? He was too attractive and powerful for me—the Prime Minister of the United Kingdom—while I usually settled for quiet guys, no matter how pathetic they were.

I took in his pecs, his defined jawline, and those intense blue eyes. My mind raced as I realised it was time for me to leave, so I headed to the door. There was no point in embarrassing myself further.

"Sorry, Miss Watkins, this just won't work," he said, firmly.

His irritation boiled my blood. I didn't need his charity and certainly wasn't planning to be his escort, even for one night.

"Fine," I retorted, made eye contact, then turned around.

We'd never see each other again anyway.

But ... how would I pay the rent this month? I couldn't rely on Veronica, always bailing me out. She had already done enough.

I exited the room and walked downstairs as fast as I could, then took the wrong turn, forgetting the second flight as I tried to find the door out of this house. I looked around nervously, itching to find my way out of this labyrinth.

Footsteps sounded behind me, and a heartbeat later, he spoke again in a sultry voice. "Miss Watkins, wait ... I hope I won't regret this."

The lights came on, and I could finally see him clearly. This man was breathtaking, handsome, dark, and just totally knickers-melting hot, but the truth was that he acted like a total arsehole. Still, TV appearances didn't do him justice.

You already said that. Yes, he is hot, just not for you.

"Yes?" I couldn't even make eye contact with him without blushing. His presence intimidated me so much.

"Be at Number 10 in Downing Street tomorrow morning, and we will conduct the interview with my daughter. She's a handful, and I really need a decent nanny," he breathed.

I was stunned, processing what he meant, while my body still buzzed with arousal from our earlier interaction.

Oh right, he had a daughter—it was common knowledge I remembered, even though I didn't keep up with the news.

"All right, yes, thank you, Mr Prime Minister," I said uncertainly.

"You'll need to call me Spencer from now on, especially when Maja is around." Now that was an unusual request. "I can't promise anything. Just come tomorrow and we'll see how it goes." Then he disappeared into another room.

Part of me wanted to follow him and tell him I'd do anything, and the other part was angry at his insinuation that I was a whore. I left the room and finally found my way out, stepping out into the night.

"Ma'am," the security agent said, standing by the door.

I gave him a smile, then got into the car. We drove away, and I tried to calm my racing heart while questioning my actions.

I awoke before the sun, my eyes still heavy from lack of sleep. Besides, it was hot in my room. It seemed that the summer in London had already begun; the temperature was rising every day. I hurried to get ready, wanting to make a good impression on the little human I would eventually care for. I also needed to tell Veronica about last night since she was due home from her night shift.

I descended the stairs, the clanking of pots and pans chiming up to me. Veronica must have finished her shift earlier than planned. I yawned and stretched my arms above my head as I entered. While she stood there, tall and radiant, as always. Her long, tan legs seemed to go on forever, and her curly red hair was neatly styled atop her head. Even after working all night, she still looked gorgeous.

"You're up early," she said, slurping a mouthful of noodles up from a pot on the worktop, barefoot.

I made my way over to the kettle, taking a deep breath, and prepared to tell her what had happened the previous night.

"Did you finally decide to go on a date with Danny boy?" she teased.

I sighed, thinking about Spencer Banks's beautiful and veiny cock once again. God, I needed to get laid.

"No, I don't even know where to start, but you're going to freak out once I tell you what happened to me last night," I said. I explained about the weird call that had come in the day before. Despite my recent streak of bad luck, I told myself this could not possibly be a coincidence.

"I barely slept last night thinking about today," I said. "What if that little girl doesn't even like me? Maybe I'm doomed to stay jobless forever."

Veronica stared at me with her jaw wide open and noodles falling from her fork. She swallowed and put the dish aside.

"Fuck ... you can't be serious, Laura!"

"Serious? Absolutely! It all happened exactly as I described it. I got the call, hopped into the limo, and then found myself in that house or whatever it was ... and his cock was massive and the most beautiful thing I'd ever seen." I leaned in close as if someone might overhear me, then added quietly, "It was a sight to behold."

Chapter Three

Spencer

Today, all I could think about was Laura Watkins. I wanked off in the shower, imagining her on her knees in my bedroom. None of it made any sense. Yes, it was clearly a misunderstanding, but still, the shy and innocent girl had got under my skin.

As soon as I left the shower, I contemplated all the reasons why I shouldn't hire her, but none of them were convincing enough. Later on, when I saw her résumé in the bedroom, I realised she was more than qualified to be a nanny. She had worked for the same family for over five years. There were no red flags while I vetted her.

I wondered if she'd be able to satisfy me if she were an

escort. Her smile, her scent ... when she'd stared at my cock and her eyes widened, I'd lost my mind.

"Spencer, are you even listening to me?" Jeremy, my advisor, asked.

Laura was due to arrive in twenty minutes, and I was already semi-aroused.

"What were you talking about?" I asked him.

Jeremy gave me a typical look. He was a good friend, and we'd known each other since secondary school, but there was no way I was going to tell him that I'd accidentally wiggled my cock in my future nanny's face last night. He was married and had two beautiful girls.

He tossed a piercing stare at me.

"You have a phone call with the US President at ten o'clock and then the cabinet meeting. I thought we could go through the agenda this morning," he reminded me, raising his eyebrow as if trying to figure out why I was so distracted today.

"I'm not in the mood. I'll just wing it as usual," I snapped. "Maja will be here shortly. I need to get ready for this nanny interview."

"Whoa, hold on a second. Why are you preparing yourself for this? Maja either likes her or she doesn't. Let her decide," he suggested.

I felt the urge to punch him square in the face. My daughter was nine and had already driven away six nannies because of her mischievous pranks. She had been too naughty lately, and I wondered if it had something to do with her mother being absent from her life. Even though I'd told myself that it was probably good that Maja had never known her.

"No, I'd rather not let her pick this time. I need to speak with the woman myself, so if you'll excuse me, I've somewhere to be." My heart raced whenever I thought of those green eyes so desperate to please me. And that was my problem; I needed to keep my composure and act professional if this was going to work.

"What's going on with you, Spencer? You're not being yourself," Jeremy prodded.

I didn't want to look at him because he would figure it all out and I wasn't ready to talk about it yet.

"Nothing, it's fucking nothing. Just give me the list for the phone call with Boden later." I avoided his gaze.

Jeremy knew me better than I knew myself, so I hurried away from the room before he could bombard me with questions.

People greeted me in the hallway. I entered one parlour and furtively glanced at my reflection in a mirror, making sure everything was in order. My pulse pounded in my ears. Was I nervous? It seemed that way.

The beautiful, innocent, and mouthy nanny intrigued me. I planned to call another escort for this evening regardless of how today went. She didn't matter to me, and if she was going to be my employee, I would avoid her as much as possible. I had already instructed Cath, my assistant, to poke into Laura, so this was going to be interesting. Besides, I really did need a nanny who was reliable and professional. I had travelled a lot over the last few months for diplomatic reasons to various countries, and although some of these trips were short, it didn't change the fact that I didn't like leaving Maja behind. Our relationship had gone downhill since I'd been appointed to run this country, so I had to make sure Maja would like her next nanny.

Exhaling, I opened the door to a quiet and airy room. Laura Watkins was already there, seated on the sofa and waiting for me. The image of her kneeling in front of me from last night turned me on again. She stood when I walked in, appearing flustered. My fucking cock twitched in my trousers once more as I took in her slender frame. Her light-blue dress fitted her perfectly, and her hair was down, like last night. What had I done?

"Miss Watkins, please take a seat. Let's not waste time. My schedule is tight today," I said curtly.

"Of course, I understand. Let me get you my CV." She grabbed the folder next to her.

I sat opposite her, then immediately regretted it—I could see her incredible legs.

"It's fine. You left it at my home last night, and I've already gone through it," I said.

"Oh ... right." She sounded surprised.

Her green eyes were fixed upon me, and for a moment, I thought I was looking at Samantha—Maja's mother—but I banished that ridiculous thought as quickly as it came to me. The past was dead to me now. No point in resurrecting old memories.

"Tell me, why do you think you will be a good fit for the

Banks family? My daughter has had a lot of nannies. They all quit because she has a bit of a snarky attitude and a fiery personality."

My daughter was exceptionally confident for her age, very popular at school, and she clearly had problems with authority. I had been called up to the school multiple times, which embarrassed me because I didn't raise her to be entitled or snobbish, but something must have gone wrong somewhere.

Laura stared at me uncertainly, as if uncomfortable.

"I was with the Forresters for years, taking care of their three kids. Mum and Dad were doctors, so they were always busy. We got along really well."

"Can you tell me why you left? Or did they kick you out?" I shifted in my seat.

Her brows creased as if she didn't appreciate my comment, and I wanted to spank her for being daring enough to judge me.

"No, they didn't let me go. Mr Forrester received a job offer in Philadelphia, and the family moved away." She answered and gave me an irritated look.

Miss Watkins hadn't responded to me as expected. I thought she'd be more submissive, but she was so confident, so defiant.

"How convenient."

"Excuse me, sir? Are you implying that I'm lying? Maybe your opinion is biased because of what happened last night? You can call the Forresters for a reference if you'd like. Honestly, I'm not sure why I'm even here if you aren't willing to give me a chance anyway. I thought this interview was for your daughter," she stated firmly while giving me a heated glare.

My cock stiffened again.

I sucked in a sharp breath and told myself not to lose control around this woman.

"I'm impartial. I'm only offering you an opportunity." I ran my fingertips along my jaw.

Laura followed the movement of my hand and inhaled. It seemed like she was just as affected by me as I was by her. The atmosphere in the room grew heavy and oppressive with the tension.

"What else would you like to know about me?"

Everything. I wanted to discover every detail of her life and know if she was ready to obey my commands.

She shifted on the sofa, showing more of her thigh.

"Why do you think you were called last night?"

"I don't know, but it was likely because of my roommate, Veronica. She works as an escort, and maybe that call was intended for her."

"Your flatmate works for an exclusive escort service?" I wondered why this woman wasn't involved in the same line of work. It was strange—a nanny and a prostitute under one roof?

Laura bit her bottom lip, and a rush of pre-cum beaded on my cock.. She had me captivated. What the fuck?

She glanced at me in horror, as if she'd said too much.

"My big mouth." She sighed. "Please, Spencer, I don't want to get Veronica into any trouble. She's been covering my rent ever since—"

She paused. I assumed Veronica was the one who was supposed to show up last night. Before I could think of something appropriate to say and ease her nerves, there was a knock at the door, followed by Jeremy and an annoyed-looking Maja entering the room. It was still early, but she was ready for school. Jeremy's nanny had been helping me out by getting her ready in the mornings.

"I apologise for interrupting." Jeremy eyed Laura curiously. "But here's Maja, and you must be the potential new nanny."

"Nice to meet you." Laura shook his hand.

As soon as Maja stepped in front of her, Laura's face brightened with a radiant smile. Even the grumpiest person couldn't resist it.

"No way, Dad! I don't need a new nanny. I can take care of myself." Maja scowled.

"Watch that attitude, young lady, and no, you cannot take care of yourself, and that's why you need an adult who can make sure you're not getting yourself into trouble. Besides, we have already talked about this. Addison can't look after you all the time, and sometimes I've to be away abroad. Now, I'd like you to meet Laura." I quickly stood and buttoned my suit.

My daughter rolled her eyes, but I followed Jeremy out, who kept staring back at Laura.

"Be back in five."

"So this is who had you so flustered earlier on, Prime Minister? Interesting," Jeremy said with a hint of amusement.

I wanted to wipe the smug smile off his face.

"I don't know what you're talking about. She's just a nanny, and I wasn't flustered. Besides, I haven't even vetted her yet. I don't think she's a good fit for Maja."

"Why? Because she has already met you and decided that you're too obnoxious to work with? Well, no surprise there, Sherlock." He patted me on the back while I glowered at him. "You might be lucky if she lasts two days, but personally, I don't see it. She seems a little fragile."

"You may be right, but I don't think Laura would take any nonsense from me or Maja. I need someone who can commit, because you know yourself how hectic my schedule is these days, so that's why I'm giving her this chance," I grumbled.

"That's why you should hire her straight away. You need someone who will keep you in line when I'm not around," Jeremy stated.

I had been cold with all my staff, particularly the previous nannies, so that had to change. Otherwise, I was setting a poor example for my own daughter.

"I've a lot to do before the meeting this morning, Spence. Just give her the job and don't be an arsehole. That shouldn't be too hard, right?"

"Fuck off," I barked.

"Love you, too. Gotta run," he said.

Then he was gone before I could argue that I wasn't difficult, I just had high expectations from people.

I made my way back into the room. Maja appeared bored, while Laura tried to engage her.

"Have you ladies got to know each other better?" I asked with a small smile.

"Maja is such a sweet little girl." Laura smiled at my daughter.

I was a little surprised that this was going so well.

"However, she also called me an uneducated snob and then decided it was a good idea to stick her chewing gum under the coffee table." Laura gave my daughter one of those scalding looks.

Maja's jaw dropped, and for a split second, she just stared at Laura, seemingly unable to believe that her nanny would rat her out like that. I was equally astonished.

"Laura, could I've a word with you for a second?" I asked.

As she moved past me, I smelled her shampoo or soap—either way, the aroma stirred something in me.

"What do you think you're doing?"

Laura tossed her hair behind her shoulders and folded her arms. "Trying to get along with your daughter. What do you think?"

"Well, it doesn't seem to be working, so you may not be a good fit," I sniped, though my mind raced with how well her body would fit into the curves of mine.

"I think you're underestimating me, Prime Minister." She flashed a smile. "I need more time to win her over, so let me try this again." She opened the door wider and called out for Maja, but then stopped.

Maja was already gone.

Chapter Four

Laura

Damn it! Where did she go?

"She must have used the other door." Spencer walked to the other side of the room.

Maja was smart and sassy, more than I had expected.

"Let me help you look for her." I trailed after him into the long hallway.

"No, stay put and wait until I find her. She can't have gone far," Spencer said curtly, without glancing at me.

His tone irked me.

"I'm not a dog, sir, so don't order me around like one," I snapped, still following him closely.

Spencer shot me a deadly glare and continued to give orders to his staff to find his daughter and bring her back immediately, should they catch sight of her.

It appeared this wasn't the first time Maja had done something like this. I was sceptical about how I'd fit in here, if I got hired. But based on how things were going right now, this was highly improbable anyway.

The agent disappeared, indicating this was more serious than I'd initially thought. Spencer kept on walking, and I suggested for us to split up, with me heading right and him going left. He seemed tense, but also more annoyed than concerned for his daughter's safety.

"This is what Maja does," he bit out. "She likes to play games. She knows the area well from her old nanny, who let her wander around for hours. And before you ask, I got rid of her as soon as I learnt how incompetent she was."

Excitement filled me at this challenge. It seemed like Maja was exactly the kind of child I'd been looking for. We needed to find her, so I reiterated that splitting up would work best.

Spencer ignored me, continuing up the stairs. By the time we reached the second floor, I was out of breath and freaking out a little, worried about her. Working out was definitely in my future if I ever wanted to keep up with Spencer or Maja.

After checking several rooms, we came to a dead end with no progress.

"Sir, Prime Minister, please, can we just take a moment?" I called out as he ascended to the third floor.

He turned to face me. His infuriated expression resembled a

beast's, and I quickly dropped my hands to my knees, trying to catch a breath.

"It's all your fault, Miss Watkins. And call me Spencer here." He got into my personal space. He had a habit of doing that.

The cedar scent of his cologne filled me with an intense sensation. His gaze travelled down to my lips. My heart pounded in response to his hard stare. I attempted to ignore his tall, muscular body and husky voice. I couldn't let him distract me again.

Placing my hands on my hips, I met his gaze. He needed to know I wasn't scared of him. His vibrant blue eyes oozed heat and lust, though I pretended not to notice the clench of his jaw.

"Are you out of your mind, Spencer? You rushed me out of that room so we could talk and Maja wasn't even under my care, so how exactly is this my fault?"

The scent of his cologne was overwhelming and impossible to ignore. I wanted to run away as fast as I could, but my legs felt like lead, sinking me closer to him. Despite all my efforts to push away our obvious chemistry, an electric charge pulsed through the air, drawing us closer.

"Watch the way you talk to me, Miss Watkins," he growled, his breath fanning my face.

I didn't know why, but his harsh tone was affecting me deeply, stirring something within. I was itching to fire back with a defiant 'or what?' Yet, I restrained myself, realising I was stepping into dangerous territory.

His eyes burned with fire, and I swallowed hard.

"You're the one who needs to watch out. I may be no one significant, but I know when I'm in the wrong, and this time, it wasn't my fault." I wondered how it would feel if I kissed him right then. His lips were just inches away from mine, and I knew he was thinking about it, too.

He smirked, and his eyes twinkled mischievously. He still didn't move an inch. He seemed to be enjoying playing the intimidating role. He wanted to see if I would back away, but I had no intention to do so. His scent, a tender wisp akin to the subtle dance of fire pit smoke, wrapped around me, sensually igniting every fibre of my being.

"People don't speak to me like that," he said.

Someone cleared their throat behind us, reminding us we were no longer alone.

I spun around. A dark-haired woman in a black skirt suit, her expression stoic, stared at Spencer while gripping a tablet in her arms.

"I'm sorry, Mr Prime Minister," she began, "but Jeremy has found your daughter."

"She's been messing with us," Spencer muttered, finally moving away so I could breathe. "Thank you, Catherine. I'll be there shortly."

The woman nodded and gave me a brief look before disappearing, leaving us alone again. Spencer was eyeing me with his dark-blue eyes. He wasn't mad anymore and appeared amused, which for some reason made me even more angry.

"Am I amusing you?" I asked, still irritated that he had blamed me for his daughter's decision to take off.

He moved beyond me without saying a word and walked downstairs again. I rolled my eyes. This man was infuriating.

"On the contrary, Miss Watkins, you're not humorous at all." He sounded annoyed again.

I wasn't certain how to even respond, so I simply followed him back.

He led me into another large open-plan room. Maja was sprawled on the couch, eating something resembling an apple. She shot her father a glare and then grinned at me.

"I need a word with you, Jeremy. Miss Watkins, please stay with Maja and don't let her leave this room," Spencer commanded in a stern tone.

I nodded, restraining myself from rolling my eyes.

The moment the door closed behind the two men, I sat next to Maja. It was time to make her like me, or at least tolerate me.

"Why did you run away? Your father was really worried about you," I said.

She continued to eat her apple, and I thought she was a beautiful girl—blonde hair, blue eyes, dressed in her school uniform. She'd probably inherited her looks from her mother, because her father was dark-haired. I had researched Spencer Banks last night but couldn't find much information about his personal life. One website stated he was a single father, and the mother had never been in Maja's life. She didn't stop eating her apple.

"He didn't care, like always, and I was hungry, so I went to look for some food," Maja said, nonchalantly.

She hadn't told me much, but she had given me enough to understand that she craved attention from her father.

"Do you think your dad doesn't care much about you because now he has this very important job and his time is limited?" I pressed.

"He wasn't like that before. He sucks now," she said.

I smiled. This was it. I finally understood why this little girl had been behaving so badly. It seemed that no one had ever taken the time to sit down with her and listen to what she really wanted.

"Yeah, I've to agree with you on that—your father sucks, and he's rude and obnoxious, too," I said.

She turned her wide eyes on me.

"You shouldn't talk about Dad like that," she said.

"You're right, but he hasn't been very nice to me." I added quickly, "but I think we can change him if you let me take care of you."

Maja frowned. Spencer was probably too busy with work to spend much time with her, and she obviously yearned for his attention.

"How are you going to do it?" she asked.

"I'll tell you, but first, let's make a deal?"

"What kind of deal? You don't have to be nice to me. I know you'll leave soon because I drive everyone away," Maja said with a hint of sadness.

My heart broke at the loneliness in her voice. Nine-year-olds should not feel so isolated.

"How about we become a team—me and you?" I extended my little finger in a pinky promise.

"Fine, we have a deal," she said.

We interlocked our fingers. I grinned, excited. This was a small breakthrough, but my strategy worked.

Soon, the Prime Minister and Jeremy re-entered the room.

"Miss Watkins, can you please take Maja to school? The other nanny is unavailable. Catherine will inform you of her schedule. I'll likely see you this evening," Spencer stated.

I raised my brows, confused. Then I stepped towards him.

"Yes, but you have yet to give me the chance to accept the job, Prime Minister." I crossed my arms over my chest and glared at him. He had some nerve assuming that he'd ask me to jump and I'd say how high.

"I like her!" Jeremy chuckled.

Spencer glowered.

He had to accept that I wouldn't stand for any nonsense from him if I was going to look after his daughter properly. He had to work on his attitude before I'd even consider it.

Jeremy mirrored my stance, observing us with curiosity. Spencer was probably accustomed to people obeying him all the time, but if I was going to work for him, I needed him to know that I wouldn't be a pushover, and if he wanted me to take care of Maja, then it would have to be on my terms.

"I need a nanny, Miss Watkins, and I don't have time for your attitude." He was a piece of work.

Jeremy chuckled. I could hardly contain a smile. This guy

was acting like an dickhead, and it was about time someone called him out on it.

I glanced at Maja, who was watching us as if she wasn't sure the deal I'd just made with her would stand.

"You'd best get off your high horse, Prime Minister, and ask me nicely, or I might accidentally tell my roommate to take this job off my hands," I suggested innocently.

Something dangerous uncurled inside me as I warned him not to test me. His eyes snapped back to me, turning darker. He then glanced at his daughter.

"What is sh—"

"Fine," Spencer cut Jeremy off instantly. "Miss Watkins, would you please accept the position as Maja's new nanny?"

"Of course, sir. Just to let you know, Maja and I are already best friends, aren't we, sweetheart?" I asked.

"Yes, she can stay, and you still suck, Dad."

Chapter Five

Spencer

After Laura left with Maja, I had a long and intense day. Jeremy wouldn't stop drilling me about Laura Watkins and her roommate's involvement with my hiring her.

The conversation with the American President was challenging enough to put me in a bad mood, though I couldn't make much sense of what the man was rambling about half of the time. At the cabinet meeting, MPs posed numerous questions until lunchtime, and I had a splitting headache by then. The opposition party had hounded me because of my housing reform.

Amidst everything, Laura Watkins was still on my mind.

She infuriated me so much that all I wanted to do was put her over my knee and spank her for talking back to me. When she'd arrived that night, she'd looked so innocent and shy, pretending she didn't find me attractive, but I could tell she'd secretly wanted to take my cock into her mouth.

My stomach growled for food, but I couldn't hide from Jeremy forever. Besides, on Thursdays, I went out for a pint with a few MPs, but this evening, the local pub felt unappealing, and I wasn't in the mood for social gatherings. I needed to spend some time with Maja because I had been neglecting her lately.

I also needed to discuss Laura's contract. She didn't seem too impressed by my social standing or charming personality, which wasn't surprising since I rarely made a good first impression. But she was undeniably attractive, although off-limits.

My pants tightened as visions of my hands on her arse flooded my brain. I no longer wanted simply to fuck or make love—rough sex was now my preference.

The sound of an email coming through jolted me away from my thoughts. I needed to pull myself together and forget about the nanny. The report had pictures of her with Jake Marlow, an international pop star who looked like a total wanker. What was Laura even doing with him?

They'd apparently met at a party and were together for two years before a scandal broke out after a video emerged showing him having sex with two women backstage and snorting cocaine. I remembered that incident.

Laura had a master's degree in International Relations and

had worked for Steven Roberts MP for about six months before she got a job as a marketing executive for another CEO in the city. After her split with Marlow, she'd retreated from political and corporate life and started working as a nanny. She also had a degree in Childhood Psychology, which made her more than qualified to take care of children. My blood pressure increased as I read on. Marlow had irrevocably damaged Laura's reputation and career prospects. She had the skill set to become a politician.

I was right about her roots, because as I scanned the text further, the report told me that Laura had been born in Poland, but she was adopted when she was a toddler by a North London couple who couldn't have children on their own, and they'd given her a standard middle-class upbringing. It was no surprise that she didn't have an accent, because she had been brought up in the UK.

After her relationship with the pop star ended, she was hired as a nanny straight after. She had chosen the role as it provided safety after the drama with Jake Marlow—who was now in rehab.

It was safe to assume that Laura would make an ideal nanny for my daughter, although I wondered if she'd stay for long. Maja and I used to be very close before I'd taken on the role of Prime Minister, but things had changed since then. This job came with a set of unique challenges, and it often required me to prioritise other things over my time with Maja, which wasn't ideal.

The email also contained another file: Veronica Micelli, the roommate. It appeared my guy had done his work well. This girl was wild. I scrolled to the bottom of the screen and gazed at the image of an attractive and petite red-haired woman. She was exquisite, with curly, fiery hair and a cheerful smile, but sadly, she wasn't my type either. Veronica had begun as a stripper after she'd moved back to London. That was her last job before she'd accepted Matthew's position and became an escort with Emperor. I had no idea how Laura ended up rooming with her, but I was certain last night couldn't have been coincidental.

I shook my head as I scanned through Veronica's list of clients. Many of them were people I knew personally; some were even married with children. The knowledge that they'd strayed didn't particularly surprise me, nor did it make me angry, but cheating was wrong.

I closed the folder and leaned over in my chair, taking in the view outside my window. The fact that Laura lived with Veronica posed a hazard for me. Her housemate had slept with most of the politicians in my cabinet, and she'd likely know many of their secrets. To me, that was a huge risk. This was too close to home, so tonight, we would have to have another long conversation about moving into Number 10 Downing Street.

"Ah! There you are. I thought we were going to have dinner together."

I cursed under my breath when Jeremy walked into my office.

"Let's talk about this tomorrow instead, yeah? I've to get home. Maja and the nanny are waiting for me," I said.

He gave me that knowing glance he sported when he knew I was avoiding him.

"You mean Maja and the *attractive* nanny are waiting for you. Now tell me what's going on with her. How did you even meet her?" he asked, settling himself into a chair.

I ran my hands through my hair in frustration and released an exasperated sigh. No way could I hide this from him.

"We'll need some scotch for this story," I grumbled and got up from my seat.

"You should keep her around. She's not intimidated by you or swayed by your looks. Have I mentioned how much I love her already?"

"We'll talk about it over some alcohol," I said gruffly and walked to the decanter set on a cabinet and poured us a few measures into crystal tumblers.

Jeremy laughed and talked about a proposal from one of his colleagues. That man never switched off. Work was his one true obsession.

I handed him a glass and sat on the couch near my desk, knowing he wouldn't like what I was about to tell him. Still, I tried to explain how I'd met Laura Watkins. I took a sip of the drink, if only to push aside any mental image of her kneeling before me.

"Last night, I was horny, so I called Matthew for the regular girl. And before you say anything, I wasn't here. Maja was with my mother at the Elm Street residence while I ..."

Jeremy nodded. I shifted uncomfortably, knowing that this story sounded unbelievable even for me.

"Around half past seven, the girl showed up. Although she wasn't what I asked for, I instantly liked her. So, I told her to go upstairs and get undressed, then wait for me. I was amped up. She was stunning, so I went to the room. She was still seated on the bed, fully dressed, uncertain. That should have clued me in, but I'm an idiot. I instructed her to remove her clothes. Despite that, she didn't move an inch. So I stepped up to her and unzipped my pants, hoping she would take the hint and start sucking my cock."

"I bet she loved this dominant Banks," Jeremy muttered. He didn't like my lifestyle, but he had learnt to accept it. He knew that after Samantha, I'd trust no other woman.

"Well, not really," I continued. "She didn't act like a regular girl. She was all shy and scared. I thought it was just an act and that it would turn me on until she said she was there to interview for the nanny's job."

He nearly choked on his glass of scotch. I took his glass and placed it on the coffee table.

"You're kidding me!" he said, shocked and wide-eyed.

I took a generous sip of my drink, which burned my throat on its way down. If only it could also burn away my growing attraction towards Laura, but that would not happen anytime soon.

"No, I freaked out, zipped up my jeans, and asked her how she ended up in my house," I said, then added, "Apparently, a guy on the phone told her to get in the limo sent to her residence for the job."

"What the heck, Spencer? Are you telling me that your new nanny is an escort?"

"No, don't be ridiculous. Of course she's no escort, but her roommate works for Matthews. It must have been a mix-up, the call was meant for her roommate and Laura assumed it was an interview for the nanny's position," I explained, desperate to end this discussion.

"So, her roommate works for Matthews and she was supposed to be entertaining you last evening? Not your usual girl, but still ..."

"Yeah. Laura confirmed that said roommate is an upscale whore. After this whole mess, I felt sorry for her when she told me she had been applying for nanny roles without success and told her to come back here in the morning. Then Maja disappeared—"

"Good thing I found her," he muttered, but he looked a bit flustered.

I needed to take care. Jeremy had high blood pressure. He should avoid stress.

"I asked Laura to come outside so that I could speak with her privately, and when we came back into the room, Maja had gone into hiding. Then you brought her back, so the crisis was quickly averted."

Chapter Six

Laura

"When do you expect to be back?" Veronica asked on the phone as I tidied up the kitchen.

Maja was in her room, doing her homework after I'd promised her that tomorrow I would arrange for her to have a movie marathon with her father—a reasonable bribe. But if Spencer said no, it could come back to bite me in the arse.

"No idea. It's been hours since I saw Spencer. He's a workaholic. How about you? Busy tonight?"

Veronica was an upscale sex worker. She wanted to quit and become a full-time content creator, but she didn't have that many followers on TikTok yet. She knew she couldn't earn that kind of money working in the corporate world.

"I don't think so, but there's something going on in the club, some big changes are coming." She sighed.

"Really, so what's going on?" I asked. She piqued my curiosity; her life seemed so much more interesting than mine.

"I don't know, but Rowan has been rather cryptic, but I'll figure it out. I just don't like this tense atmosphere," she mused. "Anyway, enough about me, tell me more about Spencer Banks? The hot PM."

"He's a complete dickhead, but his heart seems to be in the right place."

She laughed, and I smiled to myself.

"I heard rumours that he walks around barking at people," she said, still giggling, and after a long pause, she added, "Don't worry about the situation in the club. Rowan Matthews would never get rid of me. I'm great at my job, and I know too many clients and even more secrets. They'd have to kill me first before they let me go."

Deep down, I felt like a failure because I should have had an amazing career in politics after graduation, if it hadn't been for my short affair with Jake Marlow—an international pop star. Veronica was making money, but I couldn't expect her to keep supporting me whilst I was unemployed.

"Don't say that. Anyway, I better go. Don't want him to hear us talking." I lowered my voice again. Damn, I needed to get it together. Spencer Banks was probably still in his office or meeting another woman—whatever it may be, it was none of my business as long as he came home on time, so I could finish up work. I still had to catch the train home.

"Why not? Plenty of ladies frequent the club. I just have to figure out which ones will talk about him," she added.

Though curious about him, I didn't want to cross any boundaries.

"You don't need to do that. Anyway I'm not interested in him that way. This job is too important for both of us, you know that," I said.

"Laura, don't be a twat. The man clearly has an interest in you, and you've seen his bloody cock. Do you know how many women in London would cut off their arms to see the Prime Minister's massive, hard cock?" she asked.

I chuckled.

"Spencer Banks doesn't want me, silly." I wiped the worktop with a cloth.

Spencer's home was rather large, and the kitchen was huge. He seemed to be a neat man with a taste for order.

"Girl, I'm telling you this man may appear to be doing this out of concern for his daughter, but he only hired you because he wants to get in your knickers. And from what you told me, there's a mutual attraction," Veronica teased.

"He may wish to get into my knickers as much as he pleases, but I'm just not interested in arrogant, obnoxious snobs who think the world revolves around them," I snapped into the phone as I scrubbed even harder at a worktop stain that wouldn't come off.

"I believe it's clean," a voice echoed behind me.

I jumped in surprise. My phone slipped from my grasp, falling in excruciatingly slow motion. By the time it hit the floor, my brand-new iPhone 13 was shattered.

I glanced at Spencer, who was standing in his kitchen with an annoyed expression. I couldn't move; his gaze kept me pinned. Meanwhile, I could still faintly hear Veronica talking in the background. She must not have realised that I had dropped my phone ... but Spencer had obviously heard my insults.

I reached for the device at the same time that Spencer was trying to grab it for me, and our fingers accidentally brushed. A jolt of static electricity rushed through me, and I lifted my eyes to meet his—they were like the water in the Adriatic Sea, so deep and inviting I could've easily drowned in them. I pulled my hand away as if his touch burned me before he put my smashed phone to his ear and said, "Laura will call you back."

My jaw dropped, and I just gaped at him, unable to say anything. God, why did I always have to embarrass myself like that?

"I'm sorry. I was distracted and didn't hear you come in," I mumbled, sweaty from the summer heat. Damn the month of May!

"Obnoxious, snobby arsehole ... That mouth of yours is going to get you into a lot of trouble, Laura," he said with a hint of amusement.

"Can I've my phone back, please?" I tried to ignore his remark.

He was too gorgeous for his own good, and it took all my strength not to admire him. It should be illegal to be this perfect

—Veronica was right. He was so handsome, and I doubted that I'd ever seen a man who could compete with his looks, because Spencer must have been shaped and moulded by a god in Heaven himself. He was walking sex on legs, but if anyone ever asked about my opinion on this matter, I'd deny it instantly.

"The screen is smashed." He showed me the broken device.

I groaned inwardly, knowing this repair job was going to be expensive.

"Thanks, but there's no need for you to help. I've got a phone insurance policy," I lied through my teeth, without really knowing why. Spencer didn't need to know that money was tight, and I couldn't actually afford to repair this phone.

"But as an obnoxious and snobby arsehole, I insist on it," he jibed, "since it was my fault for startling you earlier."

"Once again, I apologise for calling you that, sir, but you really don't need to do that. I need the phone," I argued.

"I've a spare one, Miss Watkins," he said. "If you need to contact someone, feel free to use the house phone. We really should discuss your job, though. Why don't you take a seat?"

"I'd rather stand, thank you," I answered without thinking about why I had so much difficulty following his orders. Until now, at least.

Spencer took an audible breath, obviously attempting to stay composed.

He moved closer, and I stepped back, only to hit the edge of the kitchen worktop behind me as he loomed over me. He was wearing his usual suit and looking irresistible.

"You're making this harder on yourself than it needs to be,

Miss Watkins," he murmured after a few moments of stillness. His ocean-blue gaze zoomed in on my lips. Spencer's presence pushed all other thoughts away.

"L-Laura," I stuttered. "You can call me Laura."

"Why do you keep defying me, Laura? You should try to impress your boss if you want to keep your job," he said.

The smell of his cologne clogged my senses, and why did he have to sound so sexy while discussing simple subjects like what I should call him? Suddenly, I was aroused again. This job wasn't good for me. I had to get out of here and put some distance between me and this man who'd dangled his magnificent cock at me.

"I came home earlier because I needed to talk with you," he continued. "As much as you infuriate me, I checked into your background, and you seem honest enough. You need employment, and I need someone trustworthy to take care of my daughter. She's driven away many nannies in the past and has been misbehaving a lot lately. If you can turn this around, then you can stay as long as you like, but you must move in, because I often have to travel for diplomatic reasons and I know Maja doesn't like it when I'm gone for too long, but it's the nature of this job. Unfortunately our flat has only two bedrooms, but we will find you a room in another part of Number 10. However, if I'm away, then you could sleep in my room. It will be safer this way."

I didn't answer right away because I was still processing the way he'd said my name. I liked how it rolled over his tongue, and damn it, I shouldn't.

"How often would you need to travel?" I asked.

He went to the fridge, and I took in a much-needed breath. This space was good.

"That depends. A lot of the time these kinds of trips are hard to predict, but I'll ask Cath to share my future plans with you, so you won't be surprised. Maja takes riding lessons twice a week and tennis lessons on Thursdays. Sometimes I'm forced to work late, so I need you to stay until I get back. We have plenty of guest rooms. You could take any one you please," he explained. He retrieved food and started putting things on the worktop. Didn't he have a chef or something?

"All right, but could I go back to my flat in Camden on the weekends?" I asked, knowing Veronica didn't like staying home alone, especially during the weekend.

He stared at me so intensely then, as if I'd told him I lived in a cave.

"You live in Camden? How are you going to get home now?" he questioned. He reached for a large pan from the cupboard.

Seeing him so domesticated turned me on even more.

Stop it! There is no you and him. This will never happen! my inner voice screamed at me.

"Tube."

"It's late, and some parts of Camden Market are unsafe. That's why I want you to move in, so you don't put yourself in any unnecessary danger," he said, his voice tinged with annoyance.

Damn it, maybe there was more to Spencer Banks than just being a dickhead.

"I went home late almost every night when I used to work for the Forresters. I can take care of myself," I said.

He paused while taking a steak out of its wrapper and setting it on the sizzling pan. His eyes moved to study me momentarily, and I shivered.

"I know you're able to take care of yourself. When you work for me, though, I want to make sure you get home safely, so I'll arrange a car for you," he said, focusing on his steak. "And don't even try to argue with me. This isn't open for discussion."

My stomach growled as he cooked his steak. I hadn't eaten much today, I'd been too busy trying to make a good impression with Maja. Spencer must have heard it because he looked at me with a deep frown.

"There's really no—"

"Sit your arse down, Laura," he interrupted me.

His tone sent a wave of heat through my body. I couldn't believe this was happening. I was having dinner with Spencer Banks, Prime Minister of the UK!

Chapter Seven

Spencer

Jeremy was not convinced by the situation and demanded that I dismiss Laura because of her roommate's affiliation with Matthews. That created a potential security risk.

Despite his objections, I had already come to my own conclusion. Laura was trustworthy. There were no secrets hidden in her past, and I believed she could be good for Maja. To escape Jeremy's questions, I made my way back to the residential part of Number 10.

When I entered my kitchen, Laura was diligently cleaning the worktops and looking exquisite whilst doing it. Her dress hugged her curves perfectly as she bent over the worktop, exposing her toned legs. Blood rushed to my groin.

"He may wish to get into my knickers as much as he pleases, but I'm just not interested in arrogant, obnoxious snobs who think the world revolves around them."

I hadn't misunderstood what she'd said. Laura had felt our mutual attraction, and after what had happened the previous night, she assumed I wanted to fuck her. But while that wasn't a lie, she remained off-limits, and I didn't want to ruin the only good thing in my life—the prospect of some stability with Maja.

I'd stepped behind her before she could say something else that she might later regret, and that's when she'd dropped her phone, startled.

"'I'm not really hungry, and you don't have to get anyone to drive me. I've a pass for the Tube. I'm going to be fine." She avoided eye contact.

She was obviously hungry, and her phone had broken because of me. Besides, I wasn't planning to let her leave this flat alone and take the Tube so late. If she wanted to work for me, then she'd better abide by my rules.

"Where is Maja?" I grabbed another plate from the cupboard. I took the potatoes Phoebe had left for me and another container from the fridge, placing the first in the microwave.

"She's in her room doing her homework, but let me just check—"

"For Christ's sake, just sit down for five minutes! I won't bite." I banged my fist on the table. The woman infuriated me so easily. All I could envision now was throwing her over my lap and spanking her arse hard enough to leave marks.

Laura finally sat, sighing loudly. She was fucking beautiful, and I wanted her badly. No, I wanted her to submit to me, but this would never happen.

I grabbed the steak knife and sliced the steak in half, then placed it on her plate. I added some potatoes and grilled vegetables on both our plates, then uncorked a bottle of red wine.

"Thank you. This looks delicious, Spencer." She selected a fork.

"So, how did you make Maja do her homework? She typically refuses, and then the school calls my assistant and we argue over it for days." I felt calm being in her company. This had never happened before, since most women made me uneasy.

Laura took a sip, whereas I took a bite out of my steak, which actually tasted amazing.

"If I'm going to work for you, Spencer, then I've some rules of my own," she said. She cut into her steak, stabbed it along with a piece of grilled pepper, and put it in her mouth. She closed her eyes and moaned.

I dropped my fork because that fucking sound made my cock so damn hard it was almost painful. I was already picturing her screaming for God and moaning my name while she rode my face.

"This is delicious!" she exclaimed.

I got up to get a clean fork. Jesus, I really needed to have an ice-cold shower to keep myself in line when I was near her.

Luckily, I had on black pants, although I was certain my erection was visible enough.

"I'll say first off that I raised Maja myself. My mother and brothers helped, but I had to learn a lot of things early on," I said, careful not to bring up Sam, her mother, because this subject would ruin my appetite. "Now, what are your rules, Laura?"

I continued eating, silently praying she wouldn't moan again. She swallowed her food before smiling at me, and it felt as if the room got instantly brighter.

"Maja is desperate for your love, Spencer. She's missing her father, and that's why she's been acting out lately. I can't understand why you stopped spending time with her like you used to," she said softly.

I paused mid-bite.

I hadn't expected to hear that.

"I'm giving her as much attention as possible, Laura, and I really don't want to talk about this right now," I said, taken aback by her insinuation that I was a bad father.

"I'm sorry; I didn't mean it in an offensive way. It's just apparent why she's been misbehaving and why there have been so many nannies in the past. I don't really follow the news, but you have only just started your term as Prime Minister of this country, right? Everybody knows that."

"You couldn't have missed it even if you didn't watch the news. You must have seen snippets of me on social media because you recognised me right away the first time we met." I coughed into my fist. I didn't know where this conversation was going, but I didn't like it one bit.

"I stay away from politics and all that stuff. I've my reasons." She popped another piece of steak in her mouth.

When she swallowed the last bite and moaned again, I wondered if she would make noises like that if she sat on my face. *Of course she would*, my inner voice answered.

"I've been at Number 10 for around eighteen months," I answered. I really needed to call Matthews again and arrange for him to get me a new girl. I desperately wanted to get laid and relieve this sexual frustration.

Her emerald eyes were piercing me—as if they could see past the brokenness of my dark soul. I didn't want her to see the vulnerable part of me, so I glanced away.

"And when did these problems start? No, don't answer that ... about eighteen months ago, right, or maybe a little after?" She cocked her head to the side. "Maja said she's missing you. Those were her exact words, Spencer, and she's acting out because she wants your attention."

I glared at her, irate that she was pointing these facts out as we both continued to eat our meal. We both finished in tense silence, while I thought about what she'd said about Maja. My mother had told me the same thing several weeks ago. Laura was very perceptive and intelligent, but she didn't know me well enough to understand fully why Maja seemed so different now, though it brought a smirk to my face. I loved Maja very much, more than anything else in my life.

"Your phone will be fixed by tomorrow. Go and say goodbye to Maja. The car is waiting outside."

She let out a loud sigh but didn't argue again.

I made my way to the office part of the building, gave the phone to one of my agents, and texted Cath to get the car ready. When I came back, Laura was nowhere to be found and all the dishes were put away. I finished my glass of wine and dragged my hand through my hair. Since I was home early tonight, I realised Maja didn't have any late evening classes, so I could spend some time with her. Our relationship had been difficult lately, and we barely talked anymore. I would have to try if anything was going to change.

Five minutes later, Maja and Laura appeared together.

"Hey, Dad," Maja said upon seeing me leaning against the worktops.

Her smile caught me off guard. Usually, she would ignore me when I got home early.

"Ladies," I replied gruffly.

Laura bent down and kissed Maja on the cheek, displaying her stunning cleavage.

"So, do I get any Daddy points for finding such a good and fun nanny?" I attempted to lighten up the atmosphere a bit.

Maja rolled her eyes. "No, but she can stay for now."

She then winked at Laura, who responded with a sly smirk, only adding to my already uneasy feeling.

"I'll take Laura out and be back soon to read you a bedtime story," I muttered.

"Dad, stop babying me. We both know you never read me a bedtime story," she said.

Laura chuckled.

"Just go to your room and I'll be right there. If you're good tonight, we can watch your favourite show together." I tried to rectify the situation and prove myself a decent father.

"All right. Don't take too long," Maja said, then walked away.

I pressed my hand against Laura's back in an encouraging gesture. An electric jolt shot through my palm, and she recoiled ever so slightly.

We walked in silence until eventually reaching the door. Laura stopped and bit on her bottom lip—so damn distracting.

"Thank you for this opportunity, Spencer," she said. "I won't let you down. Maja is such a sweet girl. She just needs to come out of her shell a bit."

"I'm certain you won't. Just don't argue with me when it comes to safety, all right? I'll meet you tomorrow at seven on the dot with your suitcase," I said, and before she had a chance to respond, I softly placed my finger upon her lips, hushing her.

Fuck, why did I do that? A wave of heat coursed through my body as our eyes locked. Laura stared at me with dilated pupils and parted lips.

"Please, don't argue with me. The car will wait outside your flat at six-thirty precisely. Goodbye, Laura."

I hastily pulled away my hand, as if it had been scorched by a flame, and her breath hitched.

"Good night, Prime Minister," she whispered.

Chapter Eight

Laura

Veronica wasn't too keen when I told her that Spencer had asked me to move in, but she knew that my financial situation was terrible, and this way I could save some money because I didn't have to commute as much. I told her that this was probably only temporary and I would be back home every weekend, so we could spend time together. I also needed to call my parents and let them know that I'd got a new job. My dad probably wasn't going to believe me when I told him that I was looking after the Prime Minister's daughter.

My parents went all the way to Poland to adopt me when I was only a toddler. Apparently, my mum's mother was Polish, so my mother was familiar with the culture, and since my parents couldn't have any children of their own, they'd both decided that they wanted to adopt a child from Eastern Europe. I knew I had a sister somewhere in the world, but I didn't know what had happened to her. We were separated when I was adopted. I wasn't sure if she'd stayed back in Poland, and since I only knew a few words, it was difficult for me to communicate with anyone there to find out what had happened. After I'd graduated, my career took off. I'd travelled there a few times but never got anywhere with the local authorities. I wasn't willing to give up just yet, though. I hoped someday I would find her again.

In the past month, Veronica had been paying for everything, and I wanted to make it up to her. Spencer's assistant had sent me my new contract, and when I'd seen the salary, I just about lost my mind. It was seventy thousand pounds a year! This would have been an impossible sum to make before, not to mention inclusions of all the other luxuries, such as accommodation and travel expenses and other perks.

Veronica usually worked every other weekend, but she attended to her exclusive clientele throughout the week, so whenever I worked, we would rarely see each other. Maybe Spencer wanted me to distance myself from her because she worked for the Emperor VIP Club. I was discreet, but he was probably apprehensive, especially after what had happened during the first night we'd met.

The next morning, a car took me back to Number 10 with Cath, one of Spencer's assistants, greeting me at the door.

"Are you sure this is the correct salary?" I asked Cath upon my arrival, whilst she waited for me to finish reading the contract and the NDA.

She glanced at the sum I pointed out and nodded.

"Yes, it's correct," she said and smiled. "You're working for the head of state, so it's only fair that you should be compensated well. Mr Banks also asked me to send you an advance payment for any other expenses. Will that suffice?"

As a notification of a five-thousand-pound transfer popped up on my temporary phone, my jaw dropped. Damn! This job was paying more than I could've imagined, I no longer had to stress about bills.

"Yes, that's more than enough. Thank you," I said after recovering from my mini heart attack.

We completed all the paperwork, and Catherine took me back to the residential part of Number 10.

"I've been waiting for you, Laura," Maja said as I walked into the kitchen. "Tell Phoebe she needs to make me pancakes for breakfast."

"Well then, I'll leave you to it," Cath said, giving me an encouraging smile.

Phoebe had already started tidying up the kitchen.

"Good morning, Maja," I said with a warm smile. She was so cute in her school uniform. "Did you sleep well last night?"

She gave me an inquisitive stare before responding, "Yes, thank you."

"I said to Miss Maja that I've already made waffles for her. We don't want to throw any food away. There are a lot of kids out there who are starving and would be very grateful for such a tasty breakfast," the woman grumbled in a thick Scottish accent. She was much shorter than me, with thick, dark hair pulled back in a bun, and even thicker eyebrows.

"Phoebe, please, my dad likes pancakes, and I think he'll have breakfast with us if you make them," Maja whined.

Just then, Cath walked into the kitchen and handed me my phone. The screen had been fixed, and it also had a new case on it.

"One of my assistants just brought it in," she said.

"Oh, really? Thank you so much. How much do I owe you?" I asked.

"Don't worry about it. Now, I've to run. Good to see you both," she chirped before exiting the kitchen.

I ran my hand over the brand-new screen. It was so nice of him to do this, but I needed to tell him to deduct the repair cost from my salary.

I turned around and took a step towards the housekeeper. "I'm sorry, we haven't been introduced. My name is Laura—"

"Laura Watkins, this is Phoebe, our housekeeper, who we very much adore. Laura is my new nanny," Spencer's deep voice interjected. He looked so damn handsome in a grey suit and crisp white shirt, accompanied by a dashing smile.

My mind screamed at me to keep it together, but my ovaries were having none of it.

"Oh, another new nanny," Phoebe commented. "I hope she isn't going to be chased away like the others were."

Maja seemed distressed, and unfortunately, Spencer had

already declared that he had to leave for an important conference call and turned to make his way back out of the kitchen.

"What about the pancakes?" Maja muttered to Phoebe.

"Your father probably has a million things to do and, as usual, no time for breakfast," she replied.

"A word, Spencer." I hurried after him as he left the kitchen and then stopped, turning to face me.

"Why are you following me?"

"You need to go back to the kitchen and eat breakfast with your daughter. Also, pretend that you love waffles." I moved around to get in his way.

He appeared amused, eyeing me up and down like I was his breakfast.

"Are you telling me what to do again, Laura?" He stared at my lips.

"Yes, make time for your daughter. She really needs this today. It's a small request." Before he could say another word, I spun around and headed back to the kitchen. If he would not prioritise his own flesh and blood, then no amount of money could keep me in this dysfunctional situation.

I entered the kitchen. Maja was already at the table, awaiting breakfast. Although I normally skipped the first meal of the day, I pulled out a chair and sat with them. All the while, I counted to five in my head. If Spencer didn't budge within that small timeframe, then I would be done.

Just as I was about to rise from my seat, he said, "Phoebe! Bring us those waffles and that syrup I like!" before sinking into the chair beside me.

Maja's face lit up with excitement, and Phoebe rushed over with a plate piled high with waffles. I gave Spencer a half-hearted smile, standing again.

"Where are you going, Laura? Aren't you having breakfast with us?"

"I don't eat breakfast. I normally just have some coffee," I said.

But Phoebe was already pushing me back down on my seat.

"Don't worry, child," she said with a gentle smile. "I make the best coffee. Now, eat. You need to put on some weight. You're all skin and bones."

Maja snickered then ate from her plate, while Spencer stared at me once more as though I was going to be his dessert.

No, get that thought out of your head immediately.

He was my boss, and he only hired luxury escort so he could satisfy his needs. Not a good combination.

"I think she's perfect as is," he said then stuffed an entire waffle into his mouth.

I glanced at him in shock, flustered.

"I wanted to thank you for my phone." I tried to change the subject. "Cath brought it over earlier today. Please deduct the cost of repairs from my salary."

I gave Phoebe a grateful smile when she handed me my coffee.

Just then, Maja asked him about the TV show they'd watched last night, so he didn't continue with the subject of my smashed phone. I put some waffles on my plate, adding fruit and syrup. Everything tasted great, like last night, but what got me going was the fact that I was seeing Spencer interacting with Maja.

"All right, Maja. It's time for school," he said, bringing me back from my daydreams.

She protested a bit, though inside, I was thankful he'd made time for her this morning.

"Addison will be here shortly to run through Maja's schedule with you and show you where she goes to school, so good luck," he said and stood close enough for me to catch the scent of his cologne. He leaned down to kiss Maja goodbye. "And you, young lady, be on your best behaviour. Laura has only just started looking after you, and I don't want any trouble."

"I pinky promise that I'll be good," she replied.

He just shook his head and left the kitchen. Phoebe must have finished breakfast by now and gone off to clean other parts of the flat, so I helped with some tidying. I had to unpack and get familiar with Maja's schedule.

"Did you tell him to have breakfast with me?" Maja eyed me suspiciously.

She had maple syrup all over her chin, and in that moment, she was the spitting image of Spencer. I wondered what had happened to her mother.

"Don't be silly. Your father had the time, and he really wanted to have breakfast with you," I said.

She seemed happier when he was around.

Just then, another woman walked in.

"Oh, hey! You must be Laura. I've heard such wonderful

things about you from Jeremy!" The woman approached me and took my hand, shaking it vigorously. "I'm his nanny, and I was supposed to show you around today."

"Great." I gave her eccentric self—bleached-blonde hair and twenty or more bracelets on her wrists—a quick once-over. "But I think first we need to get this little munchkin off to school."

"Come on then," she exclaimed. "I'm so glad Spencer finally hired someone. This one is quite a handful!"

Chapter Nine

Spencer

Since meeting Laura, my only release had been wanking in the shower. Then later on that morning, I saw her in the kitchen, and my cock was semi-hard again already. I needed to get my head straight because this wasn't fucking normal. It was Friday, this was supposed to be a busy day, but after breakfast, I spent all morning signing papers while Jeremy talked about a few other MPs from the opposite party who were being investigated for fraud.

By the time the afternoon rolled in, I'd had enough, so I sent most of my staff home. Jeremy wanted to argue, but the summer holidays were right around the corner, and he needed to spend some time with his family.

I had booked and planned out a trip to Sicily for the entire six weeks, hoping that it would bring Maja and I closer together. Since my father was half Italian, my brother and I had spent almost every summer in Sicily. I'd fallen in love with the island, and even after all this time, I continued to spend holidays there, year after year. This year, I had spent much less time with her than she deserved and I felt guilty. Maybe Laura was right: she was acting up because she was missing me.

"So, what are your plans for Friday night? Is your nanny staying in or going home?" Jeremy asked, being a nosy bastard.

"She's probably going home," I said. "See you at the tennis tournament this weekend."

"Just behave, Spence, and don't do anything I wouldn't do," he said, then finally left me alone.

I poured myself a strong drink. I hadn't felt this way about any woman since Maja's mother, although that was a long time ago. I needed to have sex soon. After the disaster with Laura two nights ago, I was gagging for it. In the past, there had been a few women I'd slept with, but working in the office made things complicated. The press mainly focused on my political career, but occasionally, magazines speculated whether there was a woman in my life, though I never gave them any evidence either way.

I ran my hand through my hair, considering arranging an escort for tonight, but an odd sense of guilt stopped me. I didn't owe Laura anything; she was only a nanny. There was curiosity and attraction between us—which we were both aware of—but it wasn't something I planned to act on. Wanting to give Maja a good life, I worked hard and thought deeply before making any significant decisions. Maja didn't need a mother, and being a single father suited me.

As usual, when desperation struck, I sent a text message to someone who could help ease my frustration, then waited for their reply. Yes, it was reckless. It would come back to haunt me eventually, but I needed to clear Laura from my mind before she drove me insane.

As if on cue, their response chimed in.

Tanya should be with you just after half past eight. She's looking forward to seeing you, Spencer.

Emperor VIP CLUB

My rational side whispered that this wasn't wise, maybe a colossal mistake even, yet the pulse of desire surged through me. Laura was off-limits. I couldn't risk anything jeopardising my relationship with my daughter. Turning to Tanya seemed like the least disruptive scenario.

Remaining in my office, I attempted to lose myself in a crime thriller, a futile effort to distract me from Laura and Maja being at home together. I needed to spend time with my daughter, but this forced proximity to Laura would eventually drive me insane.

If I didn't get laid tonight, I was going to be irritable all weekend. I knew I should have gone back to the apartment, so Laura could go home, but since she'd only just started, she could stay until Saturday morning. I didn't have to explain myself to her.

Sam's face flashed through my head. Maja kept asking about her mother. She knew I didn't like talking about her, so she talked to my mother instead. Mum had told her a few things about Samantha, it was only natural that my daughter was curious.

I wasn't supposed to feel guilty about my decision, but here I was, wondering why I had such a huge issue starting another relationship with a woman. I was too afraid of being burned again.

Around eight, I changed into more casual clothes and then jumped in my car. Laura knew I had to work late. Later on, when I got home, I would talk to her for a bit, and then she would go home none the wiser that I'd fucked someone else tonight whilst she'd stayed home with my child.

Jason drove me to Elm Street. Tonight felt uncomfortable and unfamiliar. This had been my routine for months, and yet I couldn't stop thinking about Laura. Maybe Tanya could help me forget about my little almost-encounter with the nanny.

"Sir, Miss Johnson is here to see you," Jason informed me as I waited in the living room.

I flexed my knuckles and took a deep breath.

"Let her in. Thank you, Jason," I replied.

He nodded.

Tanya approached, looking stunning in a fitted red dress and high heels. I ushered her in, and Jason closed the door behind her.

"Hello, Prime Minister. I'm glad you called. I thought you might have grown tired of me." She entered my place that felt more like a dark realm. Tanya exuded beauty and seduction, her chocolate-brown hair cascading down her bare arms. She oozed sophistication, too. Women working for the Emperor were never cheap. Her scrutinising dark eyes met mine as I released a ragged breath.

"Let's skip the small talk. Go upstairs and get naked, Tanya," I commanded, oddly on edge.

She ran her hand over my shoulder, flashing a smile before swiftly walking up the stairs. I flexed my fingers, recalling Laura's deep-green eyes that had stared right through my soul.

"She's your fucking nanny, nothing else and nothing more," I reminded my pathetic self, even when I desperately wanted Tanya to become Laura.

Several minutes later, I rushed to the bedroom, opened the door, and stepped inside. My pulse drummed, and I studied this stunning woman, who was ready to do anything I wanted. She was already on her knees. I noticed that her thin thong covered barely anything. Her tits were perky, nipples hard and ready to be sucked on. She had her hands clasped, and her gaze was fixed on the floor.

My cock got hard, so clearly, I wasn't that unhinged by my innocent nanny. I could still fuck someone else.

"You're such a good girl, Tanya, but you were two minutes late, so I need to punish you." I walked up to her.

I unbuttoned my shirt, and Tanya lifted her head, fire in her brown eyes, biting on her lower lip at the same time. That triggered me, and before I could stop myself, I wrapped my palm around her throat. She gasped for air. Dragging her to the bed, I hovered over her, squeezing her throat tighter and tighter.

"I didn't like that look you just gave me, so do you want me to fuck your face until you choke on my cock?" I rasped, thinking how much she'd loved deep-throating me the last time we were together. I normally didn't see the same woman more than once, but tonight I needed to make an exception to that rule.

"I'm sorry, Prime Minister. I'll be good. I'm already drenched for you," she said, even when I was clearly cutting off her airways. Her face was bright red, and she seemed to be struggling for air.

"On all fours," I commanded, then stopped squeezing her throat so she could take a breath and calm down.

Tanya obeyed me, facing the wall, exposing her dripping cunt. When her arse was up in the air, she gazed at me, and a seductive smile played on her lips.

I quickly took off my jeans and boxers. My cock sprang free, and I wrapped my hand around it. I was going to spank that stunning arse so hard, until Tanya couldn't take it anymore.

Just then, I was hit with the flashback of Laura on her knees, right in front of me. She'd gnawed on her bottom lip, and I shuddered, releasing a ragged breath. Her eyes drifted down to my hard cock, and she licked her lips.

The flashback was gone in a split second, and I was back in the room with Tanya.

"Come on, Prime Minister, I've been bad. I need you to punish me." Tanya's voice softened my erection.

I stopped stroking it and cursed under my breath. Something was seriously fucking wrong with me. I don't know how long I stood there, furious and distraught, trying to get turned on again, but nothing worked. Tanya must have noticed because she sat back on the bed, staring at me inquisitively.

"What's wrong, Spencer? You're not yourself tonight."

"Obviously," I replied, pulling my boxers and jeans back up.

I had a bad taste in my mouth. This was fucking humiliating. She was spread on the bed, so fucking delicious and ready to be fucked, while I couldn't even get it up. I told myself that if I spanked her a few times, then my erection would eventually roar back to life.

"Come on, we both know I'm discreet." She crawled towards me. She smelled incredible, looked even better, and yet, she wasn't turning me on.

"It's none of your fucking business," I snapped, then immediately regretted it because she appeared hurt.

Her face brightened up again when I dragged my hand through my hair and released a shaky breath.

"Oh my, dear Lord, you like someone else? Is there another woman in the picture?" She brought her hands to her mouth.

I turned around and walked to the window, forcing myself not to say anything offensive.

"No, I don't like her. I can't fucking stand her." I knew that this was a lie, because although Laura had a bit of an attitude, she was really quite sweet.

"Spencer Banks, are you telling me that this woman somehow hasn't started worshipping you yet?" Tanya sounded amused.

I glared at her.

"Normally, all you have to do is smile and women fall madly in love with you, so this one must be immune, and your ego can't take it. Am I right?"

"I suggest you to leave now. The money will be deposited into your account as usual," I growled, irritated that Tanya could see right through me. It was a crappy thing to say, but I couldn't help myself. I needed to be alone tonight.

"I'm not going anywhere, and you can keep saying awful things, but I can see you need to talk. So, come on, spill the beans and tell me more about her." She wrapped her hands around me.

I exhaled sharply and faced her, then I started talking, because what other choice did I have? Tanya was right—I needed to talk to someone, because sooner or later, these thoughts about my nanny would drive me insane. I needed to get her permanently out of my head.

Chapter Ten

Laura

It was Monday evening. Maja was already asleep, and Spencer wasn't home yet. He'd come back on Friday late and in a bad mood. We didn't say much to each other, and after Maja was asleep, I hurried home. I was glad I'd had a weekend off. I could really recharge my batteries again for Monday.

Maja and I were getting on well, but tonight, she had barely listened to me and hadn't even touched her dinner, likely because of Spencer's absence.

We'd both had a long day, and this little girl was exhausted when we got home from horse riding. Last week, I'd taken one of the spare bedrooms in another part of Downing Street, because unfortunately Spencer's apartment on the third floor only had two bedrooms. In a way I was glad that I wasn't going to sleep next to Spencer, because he was very overwhelming and intense. He'd mentioned that I could take his bedroom if he was away from the residence as his room was next to Maja's, and I thought it would be good to keep an extra close eye on her, especially when her father was away. Then I unpacked and went through Maja's schedule that seemed awfully busy for a nine-year-old. She really didn't need to attend all these extra classes.

I started reading my contemporary romance novel, trying to ignore the fact it was really late and Spencer still wasn't home yet. He couldn't possibly be working that long, although he clearly was a workaholic. Something else had to be keeping him away from his daughter this evening—possibly me, but I doubted he would go to this extreme just to avoid me.

Veronica was still seeking information on my behalf. I wanted to know if Spencer had been using the agency regularly or ever dated anyone from the Emperor. I'd told her to forget about it, because I was not interested in him that way, but she obviously didn't want to listen. She had made it her mission to find out if beneath that cold, heartless man there was another loveable person. I shouldn't really care, but he'd got under my skin because he seemed so guarded.

My inner voice kept warning me to stay away and keep our interaction strictly professional.

Spencer Banks didn't differ from Jake, my cheating ex, and I refused to be fooled by his good looks. He had a reputation for using women, and since winning the election, he hadn't been seen with anyone on a date. I had a good thing going on here, and Maja was sweet. It was still early days, but if Spencer just spent time with her, I knew she would stop acting up.

After I checked on Maja and made sure she was fast asleep, I went back to my own room. I tried to focus on my book, but my thoughts kept wandering to Spencer. Later that night, I took a shower, changed into my nightgown, and put on a thick robe, because I felt that it would be inappropriate if I walked around in my skimpy nightgown, especially when security agents were always around.

Then before I went back to my own bedroom, I headed to the flat's kitchen to get some water. With only the sound of my bare feet padding across the floor, I entered the kitchen and filled a glass with tap water, reaching into the fridge for some cubes of ice. I didn't know if Maja had spilled something earlier on but I didn't notice the wet floor and I slipped. Luckily, I managed to regain my balance but I spilled the water all over my robe, so I took it off because it was all wet. Besides, the kitchen felt so humid and I was boiling hot. I refilled the water again and then finally added several cubes of ice. It was an old habit of mine—chewing on ice when it was hot outside—but one I couldn't resist.

I went to the window and stood quietly staring out at the clouded sky, my feet taking me up onto my tippy toes as I crunched the ice between my teeth. Even after a shower, my body felt like it was on fire, sweat rolling down my back in heavy lines.

"What the hell are you doing?"

The deep, sultry voice came from nowhere, and I nearly dropped the glass on the floor. I spun around so abruptly that I splashed water all over my chest.

"Shit." My nightgown was soaked now, too. I glanced up to find Spencer standing close to me, inches away from touching me in dozens of places. Two of his shirt buttons were undone, revealing his unusually tanned and muscular chest that drew my gaze down. His colouring wasn't from British blood, for sure. My heart beat faster, and I imagined running my hands over his smooth body, feeling every contour of his perfect shape. "God, you scared the crap out of me." I placed a hand over my racing heart.

Tension grew between us. It was such a shame that he had to be so rude most of the time. His blue-eyed gaze travelled from my face slowly, lingering on my lips until it settled on my chest. In the dim kitchen light, his pupils dilated as he looked at me through the thin material of my nightgown that barely reached my arse. I gasped at the realisation that he could see my nipples hardening beneath the wet fabric.

"You shouldn't be walking around the apartment like this, Laura. I don't want any of my security men eyeing you up besides me," Spencer growled, his voice barely above a whisper, and yet, every syllable seemed to drip with lust.

"I didn't know you were home for dinner. You were supposed to be at work late tonight," I said, not daring to move an inch.

He slowly dragged his eyes away from my body and replied,

"I used another door so I wouldn't wake up Maja. I just wanted something to drink after a long day."

The summer holidays were approaching, and he should have tried hard to be at home at a more reasonable time. I didn't really care if he had been out drinking or doing who knows what else late at night, but this was not acceptable. I was too furious to stop myself from saying what was on my mind, even if my inner voice kept saying that this was a bad idea.

"Is this how it's going to be from now on?" I snapped. "You're always coming home late—pretending that you're working, but you're taking care of your needs instead. What about Maja?" I shook my head in disgust. "Shame on you, Prime Minister."

Spencer stepped closer, and I held my breath. I could smell a masculine scent mixed with something citrusy—possibly another woman's perfume—but maybe I was being paranoid.

"I don't need to explain myself to my new nanny," he snarled.

"I'm not forgetting anything." I jabbed my finger into his chest. "The only person who forgets their responsibilities is you! You didn't tell me when I took the job that I'd have to stay late every single night. I don't care what you do in your free time. What I do care about is this little girl crying herself to sleep daily because her father can't be bothered to come home on time."

He didn't give me a chance to finish my sentence before he roughly grabbed me by the hair and violently pushed me against the fridge. He snatched the glass of water I had been holding before it crashed onto the floor and set it on the worktop.

I couldn't move, couldn't breathe. His dark eyes filled with rage, and in that moment, I knew this would be it: he was going to fire me for having spoken out when I shouldn't have. His grip burned into my flesh, creating an unbreakable connection between us. Lust surged through my veins, and a drop of my arousal trickled down my thigh. I stared back at him.

"You're fucking unbelievable, woman," he growled and crushed his lips against mine, yanking my hair even harder.

The moment our lips met, I was overcome with a powerful and alluring heat. His cock pressed against my body, and his tongue forced its way into my mouth with unrestrained passion. A low rumble escaped his throat, and the vibrations reverberated through my nipples that were now painfully hard. He refused to let me pull away and held my face in place, feverishly exploring every inch of my mouth. His other hand snaked up inside my clothing, sending unexpected ripples of pleasure cascading down my spine.

My entire world spun out of control as Spencer's kiss intensified. I dragged my hands over his ripped muscles. Every gasp and groan of mine seemed to fuel him further, and he fought to possess my lips, body, and spirit. When he finally released me, I was out of breath and utterly dazed by this beautiful man who had just tilted my world on its axis. Spencer took several steps back, looking equally disorientated yet completely wild. My heart raced, and my body ached for more of him while we stared at each other.

"Fuck, I don't know what came over me. This wasn't supposed to happen," he muttered.

And then my gaze fell upon the bulge that I had been so desperate to touch just moments before.

I didn't know what to say or do, so I did the only thing that felt right: I bolted out from his apartment, completely forgetting my robe, and quickly ran back to my room. I slammed the door behind me, my chest heaving. My entire body throbbed with need. I was soaked for him, and if he touched me again, I would combust.

I crawled beneath the covers. My nightgown was still damp, and my nipples were painfully erect. No other man had ever kissed me like that—he might as well have seared his lips into mine.

I waited silently and wondered whether he would go to his room. I turned off the lights and grabbed my phone, attempting to distract myself, but I was too wound up, too aroused. My fingers slid of their own volition between my legs. I needed to find some relief before I could rest tonight. Within two minutes, a fleeting orgasm rushed through me, but it gave no release, as all I wanted was him. I craved him between my thighs. Oh God!

At some point later, sleep finally came. That night, I vowed to myself that whatever had happened in that kitchen would never happen again. He'd made it clear that it was a mistake, and I wanted nothing more than to forget this had ever happened and go back to being his employee. I knew I was fooling myself, thinking we could stay away from each other, because after one taste, I was hooked.

Chapter Eleven

Spencer

The next couple of weeks flew by, and I was like a ticking bomb, so everyone stayed out of my path. During a meeting, Jeremy mentioned that I'd made Dolores from public affairs cry the other day.

I tried to keep my distance from Laura as much as possible, but since I was coming home for dinner every night, for Maja's sake, this was unavoidable. We never talked about the kiss. Hell, we never even spoke.

I hadn't called Tanya or any other girl afterwards because that disastrous night had taught me not to pay for sex anymore.

For the first time, I couldn't get aroused, and it was all because of Laura.

Every time I thought I had my sexual urges under control, the memory of Laura's lips on mine had my body reacting all over again. I was so pathetic and realised that my constant wanking in the shower wasn't helping. I'd never been attracted to anyone who disrespected my authority so fucking much. And after the way she'd spoken to me in the kitchen, I wasn't sure if I wanted to fire her or fuck her until she apologised for how she'd spoken to me.

I was happy that Laura was getting along well with Maja. This was the one thing that kept me sane.

After the kiss, I tried being home at a reasonable time, so Maja and I had dinner together. Laura cooked every now and then, but our conversations at the dining table were strained. Often, I noticed her glancing in my direction, and I appreciated the flush that spread across her cheeks when our eyes met. This attraction between us was dangerous, and the kiss had only proved it.

My schedule was already packed before the summer officially started. I was busy all the time, while Jeremy held the fort.

Luckily for me, Laura spent most of her weekends back in her flat in Camden with her roommate. She took Maja out a few times on the weekend while I had to go away for short trips. I was a politician through and through, but I also ran an investment company. When I'd been elected and took the post as Prime Minister, I paused my investment activities so I could focus on this role. However, since Laura had moved in, I kept myself busy with stocks and shares during any free moment, just so I didn't have to think about her.

On Friday evening, my phone rang. When I saw my mother's smiling photo, I wanted to let it go to voicemail but knew she would just show up at my door if I did that, so I answered.

"Hello, Mother, how are you?"

"Always so polite," she said.

I passed people in the corridor and gave them all a curt nod before continuing our conversation.

"I'm very well, thank you, darling," she said. "How have you been? I heard you've had a tough week."

"I'm managing it all," I replied.

She rarely just chatted unless it was about Maja.

"Of course you are, darling, so I'm hosting a family dinner this Sunday and would like you to come over with Maja."

"We have plans on Sunday, Mum. Maja might have another birthday party she has to attend," I lied.

My mother tried to be supportive, but she was also trying to control me. As I was the oldest of us four, she was always on my case.

"Spencer Banks, don't lie to me. Cath told me your schedule is clear; Maja doesn't have any birthday parties. She also mentioned that you have a new nanny, and I took the liberty to introduce myself to her, after Cath gave me her number. It's just a family dinner—all your brothers will be there as well as your new nanny, of course," she continued.

It didn't surprise me that Mum already knew about my new nanny. She and Cath spoke regularly. Damn it.

"That's short notice, Mum. Laura won't come for dinner. I wouldn't expect her to. She doesn't work weekends, only when she needs to take Maja to tennis," I explained, wiping away the sweat from my forehead as I walked into the living room and undid my tie.

Giggles came from the kitchen.

"It's not, Spencer. I asked Laura to have dinner with us the other day, and she said yes. Maja was very pleased, too. Laura is beautiful and so affectionate. I should introduce her to Rupert. Is she still single?"

A wave of envy cascaded through my abdomen, and I clenched the phone hard. Rupert, my youngest brother, was a ladies' man. Laura deserved better than him, and if I couldn't have her, then nobody else could!

"You aren't introducing my nanny to any of my brothers and that's final," I snapped into the phone, still remembering our kiss all too well. "But all right, I suppose we must come to dinner."

Now, I had to persuade Laura to find an escape route. There was no way I'd drag her to a family gathering. She wouldn't be comfortable in their company, especially with all my brothers in attendance.

"Why not? She's intelligent, single, and beautiful. Your brother needs to settle down, unless you want this girl for yourself, of course. I don't even know why I haven't thought about this before. She would make a great wife, but the press would ruin you unless you do it discreetly."

Mum was an eternal romantic who still kept her feet firmly planted in reality. She never paid much attention to social status when it came to relationships. She had long tried to fix me up with women, regardless of how badly those dates typically ended. It didn't matter if I chose a nanny or a cleaner as my partner—she just wanted me to be happy. She knew Samantha had really screwed me over, which explained why I was so guarded when it came to new relationships. I wasn't ready to trust anyone else yet.

"I'm not getting involved with my nanny, Mum! That would destroy my career anyway, and she's not like other women," I added, convinced that Laura wouldn't be easily impressed by me, since we'd had such a poor track record so far.

Mum chuckled. "Spencer, are you telling me your nanny isn't falling for your good looks? That's impossible, darling, unless she's a lesbian?"

"Christ, Mum! She's just picky, I guess." I didn't understand why we were even having this conversation. "See you Sunday," I said and hung up.

I'd promised Laura I'd finish early so she could go home, but I didn't know what she was planning. I told myself that it was just a simple conversation and I had to get it over with. I raked my hand through my hair, unsure of how to even begin.

"Just be nice," I muttered to myself before walking into the residential part of Number 10. I headed upstairs and changed into some jeans and a T-shirt. This would be our first official talk since I'd kissed her that night.

Coward. You're a fucking coward, Spencer Banks. She is your nanny, and you're the fucking Prime Minister.

My inner voice kept reminding me I wouldn't change my

ways because of this woman. As I walked into the kitchen, I was dumbstruck. Laura and my daughter were baking, laughing and giggling. My heart swelled at the adorable sight.

"What are you two up to?" I asked, my gaze fixed on Laura.

She looked stunning in her red dress with white flowers that showed off her slender figure. Her skin glowed, and there was something about her laugh that instantly put me at ease. All the stress and worries vanished when she was around.

"We're making cupcakes," Maja replied excitedly. "Do you wanna help us, Daddy?"

I shook my head. "I've to talk to Laura," I replied.

My daughter's face dropped.

"We are busy, and if you have anything to say, you can do that in front of Maja. We have no secrets, right, cupcake?" Laura asked, smiling at my daughter, ignoring me.

Fuck her attitude!

"Yeah, Daddy, Laura is the best, and these cupcakes will be delicious, with sprinkles and smiley faces. You can talk while you're helping us," Maja said while attempting to clean the mixture off her fingers.

I really didn't want to do this in front of my daughter.

"Talk, Spencer." Laura stirred the ingredients without so much as a glance at me.

I clenched my fists and reminded myself to stay in control.

"My mother just called me and invited us for dinner on Sunday. It's a family thing, and she wanted me to bring you with us, but I said that you would be busy because it's your weekend off," I said.

Maja frowned. "I told Granny to invite her, and Laura said it would be fun," my daughter interrupted.

Of course this was her idea.

"Darling, Laura only agreed to it to be polite. She probably has plans, and you know how Granny is sometimes," I replied.

Laura finally lifted her head to look at me with narrowed eyes. That kiss kept playing on my mind like a fucking pianoforte, spiking my body temperature.

Laura raised the giant spoon to her mouth and slowly licked the base.

My cock hardened as she moved her tongue over the spoon. I was already picturing those lips around the tip of my cock.

Fuck, focus, but I couldn't.

Chapter Twelve

Laura

I was having fun with Maja until my boss walked in and opened his mouth. The last few weeks had been tough because we were both avoiding each other. Veronica told me I should have insisted on talking to him about it, but honestly, I was too hurt even to try. That arsehole made me feel tiny and unimportant, just like Jake had.

The memory of our kiss blazed through my mind. How his tongue dominated mine, the feel of his rock-hard chest beneath my fingertips. I knew he wanted me then—his body language screamed loud and clear that this hadn't been a mistake, and the intense attraction would continue to drive us both up the wall.

"The Prime Minister is hot for his nanny," Veronica had kept singing when I'd told her everything. "You two are going to bang, and soon. God, I'm so jealous. All the girls who went out with him said that he is a beast in the bedroom. He's so domineering, you will have a hell of a ride, girl," she'd added.

I grew flustered. How sad and pitiful.

"We aren't. We both know that he's more suited for you, not me. I wouldn't know what to do. I'm not that sexually experienced," I'd replied, while still wondering how it would be if we had gone all the way that night on the kitchen worktop. How it would have been to feel him against me, inside me … taking me to that special place … Damn, my imagination was running wild again. My roommate was so loud, outgoing, and confident. She had slept with plenty of guys and always took what she wanted. She was the complete opposite of me.

Anyone who'd taken even one look at Spencer would figure he must be incredible at sex.

"He's attractive, sure, and I would love to bang him, but that one time I met him, there was absolutely no attraction between us, no spark," she'd admitted.

I'd turned to face her. "You met him?"

"Yes, but I don't think he remembers me. It was at a gala I attended with another politician. There were lots of people there, men and women," she'd explained.

Friday afternoon rolled in, so Maja and I made cupcakes.

When Maja had asked me to do this activity together the other day, I'd said yes without thinking. A week before, I had finally met Sue Banks, Spencer's mother. She'd showed up at the flat unexpectedly when Spencer was at work. I was so shocked at first and really didn't know how to act, but she turned out to be a sweet and completely down-to-earth lady. She was nothing like I'd imagined, and we'd chatted like we had known each other for ages. I felt comfortable in her company.

There was no way I was going to miss this family dinner. I knew Spencer was very private, but I was curious to know more about him. His mother had said he was guarded, but he hadn't always been like that, and after what had happened between us, I wanted to become his business.

God, he looked so good in simple jeans and a white t-shirt which outlined his muscular chest that I'd rubbed weeks back. I lifted the spoon to my lips and unintentionally licked the mixture. Damn, this was unbelievably delicious.

"No, I don't have any plans," I said as I tasted the sweet, delicious mix. "I would love to attend this dinner. It's been a long time since I've had a proper Sunday roast."

"Yay. Daddy, you assumed too much. Laura is going to meet all my uncles," Maja said with a sidelong glance at him.

Spencer let out a growl. Judging by his uncomfortable and stiff demeanour, this plan was not as appealing to him as it was to her.

"You really don't have to go," he insisted hoarsely. "All my brothers will be there, and they'll give you hell. Trust me—my family can be overbearing."

He didn't know how lucky he was. My adopted parents were great and supportive, but I had no siblings in my life, or many friends at school because of being seen as an introvert.

I finally put the spoon down and grinned at him. That mouth, I wanted it on me again. No ... what the hell?

This would not happen. I walked to the cupboard and pulled out the cupcake moulds I'd bought the other day.

Spencer kept his eyes on me, and I could tell me licking the spoon had him in a state.

"Oh, Spencer, I really have no plans for Sunday, and I look forward to meeting your family," I said sweetly, then poured the mixture into the cupcake moulds, ignoring his hard stare.

When I glanced back at him, he seemed totally furious, and I couldn't help feeling a certain satisfaction at that.

"Do you think the cupcakes will be delicious?" Maja asked when I put them in the oven.

Spencer didn't move, and I could sense the anger rippling out of his body in waves.

"Of course, but I think your daddy needs to take over from me now. I've to rush. Need to get home," I said, barely leaning over the oven to make sure I didn't show off too much of my legs, as this dress was just a tad short. The June heatwave was overwhelming in London, and I wanted to be comfortable around Maja, while still appearing professional.

I washed my hands and turned to face Spencer. His expression was twisted, and he seemed troubled.

"I'm going to the toilet, Daddy. Don't touch anything. I've to be the first to taste the cupcakes," Maja chirped, jumping off the stool and bolting from the kitchen.

I grabbed my bag, hoping to leave before the man decided to stop me.

"I know exactly what you're doing, Laura, and so far, your plan to drive me fucking insane is working well," he growled.

I flinched when he caged me between the kitchen cabinets with his muscular arms. My breath caught. So close ... and then he leaned over, bringing his mouth only inches from mine.

"I've no idea what you're talking about. Let me go. I'm going out with my roommate tonight," I informed him, although my heart was hammering deep in my chest and the familiar wetness pooled between my legs.

His eyes darkened into a deeper shape of blue.

"You're not leaving until we talk. We need to discuss Maja, ideally when she isn't listening," he said firmly.

My confidence was slowly slipping away because I wanted him to devour my mouth again.

"No, my workday has ended, and I really have to leave, so please let go of me." I summoned a sweet smile, just in time, because Maja returned to the kitchen, and he had no other choice but to step back.

"Your daddy agreed to keep an eye on the oven. I need to go, cupcake, but I'll see you on Sunday, right?" I said, giving her a kiss on the cheek.

She nodded.

"Laura, wait. We really need—"

"Daddy, look at the colour. I think this needs a higher ..."

I quickly slipped out the front door. My palms were damp with sweat, and my pulse must have been going a million miles an hour, but at least I'd left him without causing drama.

He had been ignoring me for weeks and now he suddenly

wanted to talk. There was no way I was going to dance to his tune.

I ran to the Tube and got the train that took me straight to Camden Market. Veronica had been planning this night out for as long as I remembered. Apparently, one of the girls from the Emperor Club had gained VIP tickets for the opening night at some fancy new club. I'd initially planned to skip it and instead go to the late hot yoga class, but my roommate had kept insisting, so I'd given in.

The relationship between Spencer and Maja was improving, but sometimes, he still acted cold and distant. I didn't know what his issues were, but that man needed a therapist because this wasn't normal behaviour.

I got home an hour later, and we ate some Thai food I'd grabbed on the way.

"I'm so excited about this. Maybe I'll meet the guy of my dreams tonight and I'll finally be able to forget about that one-night stand." Veronica smoothed her stunning silver dress. She'd styled her red hair in waves and put perfect makeup on.

Her phone kept pinging, but she ignored it.

"Are you still thinking about that guy from your holiday in Greece?" I questioned.

She raised her left eyebrow.

"Of course. It was the best sex of my life. I should have bloody stayed with him, but no, I got scared and snuck out before he woke up. I didn't even give him my real name. I told him my name was Valerie," she complained. "Well, I had my flight and Clara with me ... Anyway, enough about me. What's wrong with you?"

"Nothing, it was just Spencer again." I pulled out my dress from the deepest recesses of my closet. It was red and slutty and everything I was not, but Veronica had bought it for me and insisted I wear it. Again, I gave in—a moment of weakness. I already knew this was a bad idea. I could hardly move in the club the last time I'd worn it because every guy there wanted to get my number.

Veronica snatched the dress from me before I could protest.

"You're wearing this tonight because you're hot and you're going to fuck some hotshot to get that prick out of your system." She gave me 'the look'.

"I don't need to get him out of my system. It was one kiss that meant nothing. You know I can't just sleep with random guys. That just isn't my thing!" I grabbed her phone. "Are you going to check your notifications? It says here that you have over one thousand of them. This pinging is driving me crazy."

Veronica frowned and took her phone off me. She scrolled, and her eyes went wide.

"Oh my God, I think I might faint." She sat on the sofa.

"Why? What happened?" I stared at her screen.

"Clara sent me this video from Greece. I sort of knew she was recording me when I was dancing in that club. I started editing it, before I posted it on TikTok, asking people to locate this guy," she explained. "Anyway, I'd forgotten about it, ignoring the notifications, and now look ... this video has five million views already! People are going crazy over it, and I don't know what to do. Oh Lord, I've gained over fifty thousand followers."

I took the phone off her and clicked on the video. She was dancing in the club when this guy passed her, staring at her with so much love—yes, love, sheer adoration—that one would think they'd known each other their entire lives. She'd edited it, so the look was shown in slow motion, making it seem even more dramatic. People on the app were going mad, everyone commenting that it was love at first sight.

"What are you going to do?"

"Have her take it down, of course. I can't be recognised—this is too risky," she said sadly.

"No, don't take it down. Leave it for a bit. Maybe someone will find him, and you said it yourself ... It was the best sex of your life!"

"Yes, but what are the chances?" she asked. "Anyway, put that dress on and get ready or we'll be late."

Chapter Thirteen

Spencer

The cupcakes turned out delicious. Maja was in heaven, but my bad mood wouldn't go away. After dinner and dessert, we played a few board games together. Around close to eight, Maja passed out in my bed while her favourite TV show droned on in the background.

Switching the TV off, I went down to the kitchen, itching to smash something, because now that I had nothing to do, I kept obsessing over that kiss. I just couldn't get it out of my head. Technically, I could call Laura because I had her personal number from Cath, but since we had never communicated that way, it would come across as odd.

"Hello? Anyone home?" The door opened, and my mother and brother entered the kitchen.

My family had clearance to visit me whenever they wanted, but now I was wondering whether I needed to have a word with them about coming in unannounced.

"What are you two doing here?" I asked.

"Oh, Spence, Rupert suggested you go out and let your hair down a bit." Mum looked radiant. "You've been cooped up in this flat for months!"

"Yeah, bro, I'm taking you out. Mum agreed to babysit since your nanny took off for the weekend." Rupert slapped me on the back.

"Are you nuts? You know I can't just go clubbing. My security detail would flip out, and the press would have a field day." I stared at my youngest brother like he had grown two heads.

Rupert was about my height, and he favoured me in looks, but his hair was chestnut brown, and he was in much better shape than me. He was also out of his damn mind.

"Nonsense. I normally don't approve of this, but Rupert is right. Stick to private, VIP areas, use private entrances, you know, go somewhere exclusive. And of course, you have your detail accompanying you—you'll be fine. You need to relax for once. The summer holidays are coming, and you will be away most of August. Maja is going to take all your time and attention." Mum made herself comfortable as she put the kettle on.

I dragged my hand through my hair, wondering how to get out of this, but it seemed they'd both made their minds up.

"Fine, but we won't be staying long. Maja wants to do something tomorrow," I said.

"Whatever, bro, just get ready. Range Rover Sentinel is waiting outside. Your muscle is already in there." He plonked himself down on the chair next to Mum.

My brother was wild, untamed, and he fucked anyone with a vagina and a pulse. The bastard knew he was good-looking, too, and women were naturally drawn to him. He used to work as a model, but that was a while ago; he had left that industry to start his own business.

I rushed back to my room and had a quick shower, then changed into a white cotton shirt and pastel trousers.

Twenty minutes later, the Range Rover dropped us outside some exclusive new club in one of the best parts of London. Rupert insisted we get dropped at the back, because of me, and I also made sure he arranged we'd be allowed into a secluded, separate and lockable VIP section for privacy. I had four bodyguards with me who would not leave my side. That was my life.

The back door opened, and a bouncer let us through. If he recognised me, he said nothing. They would be used to celebrities walking through, and I was well aware of several MPs and other prime ministers before me going out to clubs like this—so I wasn't the first.

The private area was pretty appealing, with its décor in black and gold. The biggest flat-screen TV I'd ever seen was mounted on a wall, taking up almost all the space. I had no clue such a size even existed. On it I could observe the main club area from several angles in a split screen.

The place was already packed, everyone clearly having fun, dancing, and sipping cocktails and other drinks at the bar.

I sat on the black velvet sofa, Rupert following suit.

"Only the most lucrative and affluent pussy will be here tonight, so pay attention, and maybe you'll get lucky, big brother," Rupert teased.

"I get laid regularly. I thought James told you. It's not like I'm celibate," I muttered, even though I hadn't been able to fuck like I used to, all because of my mouthy nanny. "Also, you know I can't hang out in the main area. You can do whatever you please, of course."

He studied me for a long moment, his lips curving in a lazy smile.

"Yes, he told me you like using Emperor. Famous head of state uses an escort," he mocked, then glanced at his phone.

I wanted to laugh when I noticed he was browsing through TikTok. But then, at one point, his expression changed, his brows furrowed as he narrowed his eyes at the screen.

"What the fuck?"

"What? What's going on?"

"It's this girl from two years ago, the one I fucked in Greece. Valerie. She posted the video of us dancing. Shit, it's definitely her," he explained. "I think her real name is Veronica, not Valerie."

I glanced at the video. Indeed, a red-haired girl seemed oddly familiar. Rupert was walking past her then stopped and stared at her, positively smitten. He'd mentioned her before, telling everyone that it had been the best lay of his life, but then the girl vanished. Apparently, he never knew her full name.

"So, is she looking for you or something?" I asked.

His face turned suddenly angry.

"Doesn't fucking matter. I need to get in there and fuck a blonde tonight to get a certain redhead out of my head."

"You don't look so good. Are you sure you want to go in?" I asked, wondering what had scared him off. As far as I knew, he didn't date, just like me, and everyone in London knew him as a notorious womaniser.

"Yes, come on. Let's have fun, brother," he stated.

"I don't think so," I insisted.

"Oh, come on. These brick walls here will be with you at all times." He motioned at my security guys, who kept on impassive expressions. "Put on those sunglasses I gave you," he added.

"That would make me look like an idiot."

"Well, what's new, brother?" He guffawed, the arsehole.

Sighing, I motioned to my bodyguards, and we all strode down a long corridor, the loud music heavy in the background.

The space was impressive. Everything screamed luxury. There were people everywhere, but it wasn't too crowded. I put on those damned stupid sunglasses, hoping I wasn't doing the most asinine thing ever.

Rupert headed straight to the first floor where another VIP section was located, this one not completely secluded. James and Matthews were already seated on the large leather sofa, talking when we approached.

"Whoa, I think my eyes are misleading me. This can't be the

one and only Spencer Banks." Matthews grinned as I sat next to him.

An attractive blonde showed up by our table. "What can I get you?" she asked.

"The best whiskey you have for all of us," I said.

She smiled and then walked away to get my order. A minute later, I glanced at my phone. Laura was calling me, which was strange, because she never had before.

"What's wrong with you, Laura?" I asked, the second the call connected.

"Spencer, I'm sorry, I didn't mean to call youuu."

She slurred down her words, and I could barely hear her. She must have been out in a club.

"Are you fucking drunk, Laura?" I asked, not hiding my anger.

"A little. I'm a bit sad that Veronica is dancing with a cute guy and I'm all alone."

I gripped the phone tighter while my brothers were talking to Matthews.

"Let me send the driver for you," I said. "Where are you?"

"No. Spencer, I'm not leaving and I want to dance!"

Christ, she was clearly drunk, but that didn't seem like her. She'd told me she didn't drink often.

"Tell me exactly where you are?" I ordered, because I was going to lose my patience soon.

"Uh ... I'm in the club," she responded.

"Laura," I warned her. We weren't going to get anywhere if she didn't send me her location.

"Try to lighten up, Spencer, although I do like when you're serious, because you make me feel all kinds of things," she confessed breathlessly.

"I can't help you if you don't tell me where you are. I want your location. Now!"

"Are you going to come rescue me yourself, Prime Minister?"

"Laura. I'm losing my patience." We were wasting time.

"I want to hear you moan in my ear while you—"

"Where the fuck are you?" I spat, and I was furious. Where the hell was her roommate? "Hello?"

The line went dead, and I swore under my breath again. Then the waitress came back, and the timing couldn't have been more perfect because James was glaring at me. He could probably sense my anger. I finished my whiskey and then tried to forget about Laura while Matthews talked about his latest trip to Thailand. An hour later, I felt a little tipsy, I'd drunk more than I should have because of Laura. I was worried about her safety. I kept rehearsing that phone call in my head, and I was fucking frustrated that I couldn't do anything to find her.

"What's wrong? Who was that earlier on the phone?" Rupert eyed me with curiosity.

"No one, don't worry about it." I knew full well there was no way I could track her down. She was out and she was clearly out of control.

My detail sat close by, always on the alert. They wouldn't be drinking tonight. Besides, I couldn't just leave, but after this phone call, I didn't plan to stay long.

I removed the sunglasses as I could barely see anything in them and they made me feel like those guys from *Men in Black*.

"Rupert dragged me here tonight. Totally unplanned, of course, and maybe not the best idea." I stared at my brother, James.

He was the complete opposite of all of us, quiet, down to earth, and discreet. All four of us had always been close, but lately, James had been distancing himself from the rest of the family. Something was going on with him.

He had the same dark hair and build as the rest of us, but his close-cropped haircut and posture made him look like an MI5 agent. He had a private security firm that protected high-calibre people, including our other brother, Andrew, who was a famous actor. I found out a few months ago that James provided security agents for royals, too, not only in the UK, but also abroad.

"Fuck me, that's an occasion. In that case, we need to celebrate. I bet all of us would leave this place with women by our sides if we could." Matthews cheered, already drinking a cocktail of some sort. He winked at me.

"Spencer, indeed it's a surprise to see you." James raised his head from his phone. His amber eyes were studying me closely. He had always been a complicated man. He got on better with Andrew than me.

"What about me, you fucker? I dragged that bastard here so he could have some fun before Maja breaks up from school," Rupert asked.

"You don't need to keep up with appearances, but Spencer

must keep a low profile. You shouldn't be here, especially tonight," James pointed out.

I didn't know what he was talking about, but he pissed me off.

He pretended he didn't care about my position and then he offered unsolicited advice on what I should and shouldn't do.

"What the fuck is your issue, mate? Is this about the housing policy in parliament recently? That's what you're pissed about?" I growled, frustrated.

James was also a businessman through and through, and sometimes, my party's stand on some policies made his life complicated, particularly when passed. He was always the first one to voice any concerns, but lately, he had been keeping his distance. Also, I couldn't see how a housing policy would affect him in particular. Of course, this was the one my own party opposed—I supposed he enjoyed the upheaval this created for me.

Rupert and Matthews lobbed their gazes between us, baffled. Then the pretty waitress came back with another round of drinks, so the tension eased up a little. I didn't know why he had such a problem with me being here.

"You hired the woman who showed up in your house as an escort as a nanny, Spencer." James lifted the drink to his lips but not breaking eye contact with me.

"What the fuck are you talking about?" Rupert and Matthews asked at the same time.

I was suddenly shocked, staring at his calm persona and

trying to figure out how he knew about Laura. Surely, he couldn't have known about this unless Jeremy had told him?

Fuck, this was bad. If the press got hold of that story, I was finished, and even worse, Maja would have a nightmare of a time at school. I couldn't do this to her.

I questioned Matthews with more suspicion this time. "What I'm trying to figure out is why Laura received a call from the Emperor asking her to come to my address when I didn't order an escort?"

"Wait a minute." He appeared perplexed. "Are you implying that your new nanny works for me?"

"No, it's all a misunderstanding. She got a phone call and then arrived at my private address only a few people know about, only to find out she had an interview for the nanny job," I clarified. "I normally use that house for you know what, but I didn't want to interview a potential nanny at Number 10. I wanted to keep this from Maja until I decided on the best candidate."

I had no choice. I had been planning to call him and ask about this whole mix-up, but it had slipped my mind. I blamed Laura for it, so I told them this story about her showing up in my house while I was waiting for my new girl. After I was done, Rupert and Matthews stared at me in disbelief while James appeared bored.

My gaze shifted to the dance floor, and my stomach dropped. Matthews spoke in the background, but his voice was nothing more than a distant hum. My gaze had latched on to the most hypnotic woman there. She wore an incredibly short dress that left little to the imagination for any of these sleazy perverts.

A surge of heat jolted down my spine and settled in my groin, as if someone had taken a match to my veins. It had been so long since anything like this had happened—at least until I'd hired my sexy nanny.

Suddenly, the girl with the red dress tilted her head in my direction, and my breath hitched.

Laura?

Chapter Fourteen

Spencer

"Spencer, you're a fucking beast. Please tell me you fucked her when she arrived on your doorstep?" Rupert asked.

His crude words crept into my consciousness and somehow irritated me.

My mind, though, was elsewhere, and I had no time to tell him to shut the fuck up.

This couldn't be another fucking coincidence, but my eyes weren't misleading me. She was here, dancing with some fucker before she'd called me. This wasn't the sort of place she'd frequent, but I reminded myself that I didn't know her all that well. She must have drunk way too much, then decided to call me, and for that I was already planning to punish her.

"No, I haven't fucked her and I'm not planning to," I finally responded, my tone gruff. "She's the nanny, plain and simple. She gets on with Maja very well, and I don't want to jeopardise this," I said, wanting nothing more than to get on that dance floor and drag her out of here. Every motherfucker downstairs was eye-fucking her. Shit!

"You should get rid of her. I can get you another nanny. This one is a liability, Spencer," James said.

I snapped my gaze back at him, sensing a warning in his tone. My brother was always a man of a few words, but today he was pushing it. He was also the fixer, the guy who hushed all the scandals and held some kind of leverage over the media. Normally I listened to him, because he was never wrong, but I wasn't planning to get rid of Laura. I just had to make sure I wouldn't do something crazy. Like have sex with her.

"No, James, I'm not getting rid of Laura. This thing with the Emperor was a misunderstanding Matthews needs to investigate." I stared at the man, who looked confused. "She's a good influence on Maja, and the whole family is going to meet her on Sunday. Mum insisted I invite her to dinner."

I glanced back at Laura again, hoping these fuckers wouldn't see me checking her out. It was bad enough that they all knew about that disastrous interview.

To make matters worse, some guy had already moved in on her. He was dancing with her, his fingertips grazing her hips possessively. Enraged, I felt dizzy. Without realising it, I leapt to my feet, shaking from barely contained rage. She shouldn't have gone out tonight. She clearly didn't know her own limits.

"Where the hell are you going? You still haven't told us everything. We need details, Spencer." Rupert tried to pull me into some sort of back-and-forth, but I was done. I was ready for blood, ready to destroy the guy Laura was now smiling at.

My voice of reason kept telling me to sit my arse down and just wait, but I was already on the move. It was none of my business that she was here tonight, but she had called me and she even confirmed that she wanted me. The sudden wave of jealousy that washed over me in that moment knocked me off balance. Laura was mine, and I was ready to break the hands of the guy who was daring to touch her.

Vaguely sensing my bodyguards following me, I stomped down the steps and blazed through the crowd of people on the dance floor. I didn't care if people would notice or recognise me. He needed to take his hands off her, otherwise things were going to get ugly tonight.

As I got closer, she ground into his cock, which, of course, meant I lost my fucking mind. Finally reaching them, I grabbed her wrist and yanked her off that arsehole.

"She's here with me, so piss off before I smash your pretty face and break your hands for touching what's mine." I got dangerously close to the prick.

The guy was obviously drunk, and when he saw me, he almost stumbled.

"Fuck off, will y—"

He didn't finish, because he must have taken a good look at

me, and his eyes widened in shock. It seemed like he'd recognised me, and so did a few other people on the dance floor. Damn it.

As I should have expected, my little mouthy nanny beat him to a response.

"What the hell do you think you're doing, Spencer?" Laura yanked her hand from my grip, truly pissed. She sounded a lot more sober than she'd been on the phone earlier on.

"What does it look like? I'm rescuing you, so now be a good girl and head over to the bar," I said, well aware that the idiot was already backing away.

Fuck, I was bringing too much attention to myself. Laura wasn't my girlfriend. She was my employee, and I shouldn't be acting like that, but I was too far gone at this point.

She must have noticed that people were staring, so she walked off while I pinched the bridge of my nose, reminding myself to breathe. I followed her, wanting to get a stronger drink. For some reason, I hated that this fucking wanker had put his hands on her. I was ready to castrate him.

I was just about to join my nanny at the bar when someone blocked my path. I only saw a mass of red curls and the face of a very pretty girl who was staring at me with daggers in her eyes. The very one who'd been dancing with Laura earlier on.

"Spencer Banks, where do you think you're going?" She stood too close and tried to be intimidating, but this would not work on me.

My brows drew into a frown as I glared at her. She was

small. I studied her further, and a feeling crept up on me that I had seen her somewhere before.

"Do I know you? Listen, I need to find someone, and you're in my way," I snapped at her and was just about to move past her, but she didn't seem to get the message.

"Listen, pretty boy, I won't move because I'm Laura's roommate and right now I'm looking out for her. You will not follow her." She moved even closer, probably because the music in this place was loud and she wanted me to hear her out, but then she poked my chest with her finger. "What the hell was that about on the dance floor?"

I gritted my teeth. My brother and the other guys were possibly wondering what the hell had happened to me. Besides, it was better that they didn't see me with Laura tonight. I stared at the famous escort roommate who worked for Matthews. She was stunning, but her resting bitch face wasn't doing anything to my cock.

"I was trying to protect her, and you shouldn't have left her with that sleazy guy out there," I ground out, still pissed off that I had to explain myself to this woman. "Laura drunk called me earlier on. She didn't seem happy that you had left her on her own."

She laughed before rolling her eyes.

"I've no idea what you are talking about. Why would she call you? Besides, Laura doesn't need my protection, and that guy was perfectly all right. I vetted him myself. Laura went out because she needs to pull and shag a hot guy. So, Mr Prime Minister, go mind your own business and forget about her until Sunday," she stated, still poking me with her finger.

Fuck me, she was pissing me right off. Surely, Laura couldn't have thought that fucking some random guy from the club was acceptable.

I smiled at her and grabbed her finger so she would stop with her jabbing. Over my dead body would I let Laura leave this place with another man.

"I'm the fucking head of the country and I can ruin your life with one phone call, so back off because you're getting on my nerves! Laura is my business. What she does may have repercussions," I growled.

Veronica showed no sign of fear. Her golden eyes oozed challenge, as if daring me to make good on my threat. I needed to be done with this altercation right fucking now, so I could find Laura and talk to her. This whole thing was ridiculous.

"I don't fucking care if you're the King of fucking England. Laura doesn't want to talk to you and that's final. Stop messing with her. She doesn't want you, but she needs this job—"

"Valerie? I mean, I should probably call you Veronica now right?" a voice behind me asked.

And Veronica's face suddenly changed. Rupert came into view, Matthews and James standing next to him. Veronica took in a sharp breath before she turned around.

Rupert scratched his head as he took her in.

"Oh, hi, stranger, long time no see. I guess you saw the video. It kind of went viral," Veronica said briskly, but her voice trembled. "What a nice surprise. What are you doing in here?"

"How the fuck do you know my brother, Spencer?" He sounded uncharacteristically enraged.

"Rupert, Veronica is one of my girls, and I think everyone has seen the video. It's raving with millions of views," Matthews explained.

His tone was worried, and I wanted to fucking scream. James watched all this unfold with an amused expression.

"Matthews, and you ... hmm, Rupert." She winked at my brother, then added, "Can you all give us a moment? I really need to finish talking to Spencer here."

"She works for you?" Rupert asked Matthews in outrage.

I grabbed this opportunity to leave them all to it.

I went around the club searching for Laura. Several agents followed. After circling the dance floor, I checked the toilets, wondering if she'd left without me. My thoughts were racing, and I could barely see straight. What would have happened if I wasn't here to interfere? She didn't know what any of these guys could do to her.

I came back to find James by the bar. He must have ditched Rupert and Matthews because I didn't see any of them around.

"Have you seen the tall blonde girl wearing a slutty red dress?" I asked him.

He sipped his drink and stared at me with a mix of disgust and pity.

"She's your fucking nanny, Spencer, so leave her be. Trust me. Otherwise, this will end badly for both of you," he said.

"I need to talk to her, that's all. She's my nanny, and that's all she'll ever be. Promise that I'm not planning to fuck her. Did you see where she went?"

James kept staring at me with a strange twinkle in his eye, and I was growing extremely frustrated with every passing second.

"When the shit hits the fan, don't come to me, because I've tried to warn you, Spencer. I saw her going out the employee exit to the right," he growled.

I took off, telling myself to stay calm. I found the exit and walked right through it. Laura stood a few metres from it.

"Stay here, I need to talk to her alone," I said to my detail while glancing down the dark corridor.

They nodded, understanding that I had to talk to her in private, and made sure that we weren't going to be interrupted.

"Leave me alone, I don't want to talk to you," she spat.

"Too bad, because I want to talk to you."

Chapter Fifteen

Laura

I thought I would finally have a moment alone, but then somehow, Spencer found me. My thoughts raced, and I wanted to get some air, but the other exit doors were locked. I was drunk earlier on when I'd called him. I hadn't planned it and then I'd sort of dialled his number by mistake when the girls had been dancing. Spencer had sounded so pissed off, trying to order me to send him my location. Good job I'd hung up, but now I was paying for that mistake. After the unfortunate phone call, I'd drunk a whole pint of water and then danced, trying to forget about him. Then Veronica had introduced me to that cute guy,

Julian, and before I knew it, we'd started dancing until Spencer Banks interrupted us.

I almost passed out when I saw him threatening Julian. I had no idea how he'd found me, but this time he'd crossed the line yet again.

Spencer had truly outdone himself on this occasion. Did he really think this was acceptable behaviour? God, I hated him so freaking much, and I wondered how far he'd go to make my life hell. Nothing about him would surprise me anymore.

"You used some kind of tech gadget to track me down all the way here? Didn't you? Are you out of your mind? What about Maja? Who is looking after her?"

He approached me, getting so close the heat radiating off his body warmed my skin. Before I could do anything else, he pushed me against the wall. His hard erection pressed on my front.

"Maja's with my mother," he growled. "Now, what you need to worry about is your arse, because it'll be raw once I'm through with you."

His voice sent a rush of blazing heat up and down my spine.

"I fucking hate you, Spencer!" I tried to inject as much venom into my voice as possible.

He chuckled in response.

Then he forced me to turn around, and my head spun. I gasped when his hand wrapped around my wrist in a vice and my cheek was plastered to the wall. He slid a knee between my legs, forcing me to spread them.

"Do you think you can just hang up on me after I specifically asked you to send me your location?" he whispered roughly in my ear. "Fortunately for you, I was in the same club as you, so imagine my surprise when I saw a girl on the dance floor wearing a slutty dress and acting all needy, allowing some fucker to put his hands on her."

The mixture of anger and desire that swirled inside me melted all other emotions until there was nothing left, except the pulsing throb between my thighs. My clit was swollen, and I was so wet.

"I can do whatever the fuck I want. You don't own my body," I bit back.

A few tense moments passed, and I focused on my shallow breaths. Then Spencer yanked my dress upwards, exposing my arse through the sheer tights, and the cool air made me even wetter. Veronica had talked me into wearing the sexiest underwear that I owned, and right in that moment, I was so glad I'd listened to her. The bottom consisted of a skimpy, lacy thong.

"You were mistaken, shortcake. We've owned each other from the first time you laid your eyes on my hard cock. There's something between us," he whispered.

I wanted to respond with something powerful and clever, but then he spanked me.

I yelped in surprise, releasing a soft moan as his large palm landed on my buttock. This wasn't a light or playful smack, but hard and painful. The searing pain left me breathless. He repeated the action at least five more times, and I groaned through clenched teeth.

My tights were also soaked through now. Done with his

punishment, he righted my dress and spun me around once again, so I was facing him. My back hit the wall, and his blue eyes devoured me. Arousal consumed me, but also rage.

"Next time you decide to disrespect my image with this outfit and hang up on me, I'll make you choke on my cock," he whispered, his eyes darting down to the impressive cleavage on display.

I had little to show off, but Veronica had loaned me a push-up bra, so my boobs appeared pretty huge with it. Although my desire had reached epic proportions, I couldn't stop myself from talking.

"I fucking hate you." I wanted to escape his grasp so badly, but his grip on my wrists remained steadfast; he held them above my head.

Our eyes locked, and he was so close that his heady cologne assailed my nostrils.

"Let's see how much you hate me, woman," he growled, then slipped his hand underneath my dress, running his finger over my sopping-wet tights and thong.

I had to shut my eyes tight and bite on my lower lip, stifling any noise that wanted to escape, refusing to let go of a desperate moan. Moving his hand up and sliding it inside my tights, he pushed aside the fabric of my thong and inserted one of his digits into my slit, tormenting me to the point of delirium.

"Your pussy is made for me, and you're drenched, which only tells me you must have enjoyed being spanked. You're such a naughty girl, Laura."

"Fuck you." I panted.

He kept running his fingers around my clit, delicately and slowly. Barely touching it. He only had to stroke me a few more times before I would break apart. It was pure possession, and with a single touch, he enslaved my body.

I ached for an orgasm so badly, but I refused to beg him for it. His pupils were dilated as he studied me with that infuriating smirk. He knew exactly what torment he was inflicting on me. Before I could form an insult or take a breath, his tongue swept across my lips, then eased inside, plundering, exploring my mouth and forcing out a desperate moan.

"All you need to do is ask politely and I'll make you come so hard you won't remember your name tonight," he said.

But I shook my head. This dickhead thought I'd beg him for pleasure? He was in for a rude awakening.

He withdrew his hand and stepped away then. I stared at him in confusion.

"What the hell are you doing?" I gasped, wired up and trembling, ready to finish myself off.

My legs felt weak, and my head was pounding.

"Tell me what you want me to do."

I opened and closed my mouth, too worked up and angry to express myself at that moment. I wanted him so much, but I couldn't bring myself to beg.

But my body was a traitor. Finally, I looked into his eyes—hating myself for it—desperation reaching new heights.

"Touch me, Spencer, make me come. I need your fingers inside me."

He was on me in a heartbeat, digging his left hand into my

hip while the other dived underneath my tights once again. In one swift movement, he ripped my thong off and tossed it on the ground.

"Fucking exquisite," he murmured, then went back in and shoved two fingers inside me with ease, looking directly into my eyes and finger-fucking me.

This man was a god, and I was at his mercy. I parted my legs and revelled in the feel of his fingers inside me. So close ... desperate for release.

"Spencer," I gasped.

He gently caressed my clit.

Intense pleasure rolled through me, and I let out a loud scream, climaxing, my head hitting the wall behind me. Then I grabbed his head with one hand and held him close. I shuddered from the incredible orgasm. The fire inside me erupted like a volcano while his fingers kept working their magic. We moaned together in wild bliss.

When he finally pulled away, I was utterly spent. My hips were still trembling, my legs quivering, and my breath came in ragged gasps. I caught sight of the visible bulge in his pants; he had not been able to come himself yet. My cheeks burned with embarrassment, but finally, I'd got what I had craved for weeks.

I refused to make eye contact with him as he picked up my torn thong and tucked it into his pocket.

"Thanks." I raised my gaze to meet his.

He was panting, too. Flustered. My tongue flicked across my lips and tempted me to act more on our animalistic desires.

"Just get out of here before I lose the last ounce of self-control I've and disrespect you by bending you over and fucking you against that wall," he said, his voice rough.

I quickly pulled my dress into place and hurriedly beat it through the door.

My breathing laboured, I searched all over for Veronica. I found her cowering in the corner, crying her eyes out.

"Veronica, what's wrong?" I enveloped her in a tight embrace.

Her sobs only grew more intense. She shook her head and wiped away her tears, gazing up at me.

"It's nothing. Let's just go home," she said, frantically scanning the club as though searching for someone.

She had never looked so vulnerable before, and I was worried about her.

"Let's go," I replied, then headed towards the exit with my friend.

We reached the club entrance, and I glanced back one last time. Spencer Banks stood on the balcony above the dance floor, his stare fixed on me. I gulped hard and dragged myself outside, his gaze lingering even after we'd left.

Chapter Sixteen

Spencer

"Are you sure Laura knows Granny's address?" Maja asked me for the fourth time today.

Jason, my driver, was taking us to my parents' house, and London traffic was once again horrendous. I was on edge, in a bad mood. Friday night had been such a mistake, but it was too late to take it all back now. I'd lost control and finger-fucked the nanny near the employee entrance where anyone could've walked in on us. I was such a twat.

"Probably, knowing Grandma, she already took Laura's number and has been bombarding her with messages." I attempted to pull myself together.

"Sir, we are here." The driver lured me out of my thoughts. Maja squealed.

"Daddy, come on. Laura is probably waiting for us inside." She dragged me away from the car.

My parents lived on the outskirts of London in a pretty good neighbourhood. My father was a retired politician. Two of my security guards who'd followed us in a separate car were parked behind us to discreetly watch the house. It seemed that Andrew was already there, because his own security agents were around, trying hard to melt into the surroundings.

My mother was standing in the doorway of her three-story Edwardian home, waving at us. This place brought back a lot of memories, some good and some bad, but I'd enjoyed growing up in this house. Maja ran to my mother and gave her a big hug, and then I followed them inside. I nodded to Jason, my main security agent, who was welcomed into the house.

"And how are you, Spencer? Your brothers are here." Mum gave me a kiss on the cheek.

"Is Laura here yet?" I asked, curious if she was being interrogated by my siblings.

That woman was going to be the death of me. I had been dreaming about her and her delicious pussy since Friday night. I'd texted her a few times during the weekend, asking if she was all right. The one-word replies told me she wasn't ready to talk to me about what had happened. She was my nanny, and I would not be with her, no matter how much I wanted to.

My father stood in the kitchen, cooking, and my brothers

were gathered in the garden where Maja started playing with Rupert.

"What's for dinner, Dad?" I patted him on the back.

Since my father had retired from politics, he enjoyed pottering around the kitchen.

Nine years ago, when Maja was born, I'd moved back to the family home so they could help me out. I had a job at the time that I couldn't afford to lose. I was grateful to have such supportive parents.

"You know, same old. Roast beef. I heard your pretty nanny is coming over, and Mum is going to match her with Rupert," Dad said with a gleam in his eye.

"Rupert needs to focus on finding his own girlfriend. Laura is too good for him, and I want her to stay, so that can't happen." I wanted to add 'over my dead body', but my dad didn't need to know I wanted her for myself.

"If you say so, son. I'm looking forward to this dinner. It should be interesting."

I took a glass from the cupboard, put some ice in it, and poured some scotch. I wasn't supposed to make this awkward, but after what had happened on Friday night, things were definitely complicated. The sounds of Laura's moans were imprinted on my mind. She'd nearly come when I'd spanked her ass. I had to stop thinking about her that way, though. My family had been trying to set me up with someone for years, and it never worked. The less they knew about my private life, the better.

Rupert was chasing Maja around the garden, and she was giggling like crazy. James was on his phone, as always, when Andrew spotted me standing on the patio. He might as well be my twin, because we had such similar features.

"Prime Minister." He mocked me, as usual.

My brother had started as a model, and then slowly he'd moved to the film industry. He'd started small, but then one of the directors had seen something in him and cast him in a small budget movie that blew up. Andrew had become famous overnight, and several big roles had followed after. His good looks definitely helped.

"So, how have you been? I heard you got a new nanny? Mother is already planning Rupert's wedding with that girl."

"Mother has been planning all our weddings since we left university." I sipped my drink as Apolonia materialised right in front of us.

She was Andrew's assistant, and she followed him everywhere, along with the entourage of security agents. I really didn't get why this beautiful and smart woman was still working for my dickhead brother, even after-hours.

"Spencer, you're looking sharp. How are things with you? I've been following the news, and I'm surprised that your party is refusing to back your new social reform. It's very progressive," she said, completely ignoring her boss and giving me kisses on both cheeks.

Apolonia had been in the UK for the past fifteen years, and her Eastern European accent was still pretty distinctive. She hated when my brother teased her about it, but she knew how to push his buttons. Both her parents were Polish. They'd emigrated when Apolonia was in high school.

"Apolonia, you were supposed to be playing with Maja. Why are you interrupting us?" Andrew rudely interjected.

If I didn't know my brother, I would have thought he had it bad for his assistant, but he always claimed they only worked together, and there was nothing between them. Apolonia was too smart to get involved with a player like Andrew anyway.

"We were having a girly chat when Rupert started chasing her around, so I thought I'd come over here and annoy you a little." She turned to face me once again. "The housing reform. What's up with that?"

"Nothing, but Jeremy is working on a few MPs, so it should pass in the next vote," I said.

"Does Laura normally come late? Maybe you should call her. How is she even getting here?" My mother carried trays with some canapés and other finger foods.

My stomach growled. I glanced at my watch. Laura was late by over twenty minutes.

"She's probably taking the Tube," I said.

"You didn't send a car for her?" She frowned at me.

"Mother, why would Spencer hire a limo for his nanny? She just works for him, so technically she shouldn't even be invited to this dinner," Andrew stated, then scrolled through his phone.

"I second that. She's the nanny, and she's used to taking the Tube," James chimed in.

My mother shook her head.

"Ignore him, Sue. He's just grumpy because he wasn't cast in the new James Bond movie." Apolonia gave Andrew a sweet smile.

"I should fire you, and you weren't invited either." He stared at her hand that was still gripping my arm.

"Well, your mother delivered the invitation in person when you were arguing with Sandra, so lay off with the attitude, boss." Apolonia popped a canapé into her mouth and gave us both a smile before she talked to our mother about something else.

"She has you by the balls." I chuckled while briefly staring at Apolonia's round arse, just to wind him up a bit more.

"She's the best, and she knows I can't afford to fire her," he muttered.

I was just about to tease him a bit more about Apolonia when I spotted Laura, who'd finally arrived. She was talking to Mum in the kitchen, but she didn't seem like herself. I instantly felt like something was wrong.

"My nanny is here. I should go say hi." I marched inside, clenching my fists. I paused when I took in her puffy red eyes.

"Hey, Laura, what's wrong?" I wanted to kill the motherfucker who'd dared to make her cry. Maybe I should have sent Range Rover over. The Tube wasn't safe in my opinion.

"Nothing, it's nothing. I'm very sorry that I'm late." She avoided my gaze.

"Darling, don't worry about it. Let me make you a cold tea. I always do regular tea when someone is upset, but today, it's too hot for that," Mum said.

Number 10 Affair

"What happened? You're not taking the Tube from now on. I'll make the car available." I wanted to take her in my arms and comfort her, but how could I in front of my family?

"No, it's nothing to do with that ... It's my mother. She's sick."

Chapter Seventeen

Laura

I shouldn't have come, but I didn't want to disappoint Maja. Before I left, I'd popped in to see my parents in Greenwich. Mum still worked as a teaching assistant, and my father was retired. I hadn't spoken to them since the last phone call when I'd told them that I'd started working for Spencer Banks and felt quite guilty that I had neglected them for so long.

Everything was fine until Mum served brunch. My father was silent, so I knew then that something was wrong because he was never so subdued. He liked talking and being engaging. He'd seemed so excited when I mentioned I was looking after the Prime Minister's daughter. Apparently, he'd voted for Spencer, which I found pretty funny because he normally voted for the other guys.

"All right, come on, tell me, what's the matter?" I'd finally asked.

"Nothing, honey, we are just tired. It's been a long and busy weekend. Tell us how you are getting on with your new boss, and Maja? I hope he's treating you well," my mother had said, avoiding my question.

"Everything is great. Maja and I get on really well," I'd replied, then prodded, "Mum, can you tell me what is going on?"

"We didn't want to worry you, but my liver is failing. The medication has stopped working." She'd dropped an unexpected bomb.

Now, I was standing in the Banks's kitchen, trying to keep it together, but how could I? I would have politely backed out from this invite were it not for the fact that Maja was excited for me to meet the rest of her family. Spencer's mum gasped and drew me in for a hug.

"How long has she been sick for?" Spencer questioned, his Adam's apple bobbing.

"She's had liver issues for years, but her meds aren't effective any longer and she's going into liver failure … Maybe I should just go. I don't want to ruin your family dinner." I wanted to disappear.

"No." Spencer and his mother caught me off guard.

"We would like you to stay, and I don't want you to worry about your mum. She's going to be all right. She's in London. I'll make sure that she's treated by the best doctor in the country," Spencer assured.

Just then, Maja made a run for me.

"Laura, you came! Come on. I want to show you my princess castle in the garden. Uncle Rupert built it for me." She was full of excitement as she pulled me towards the doors leading to the garden.

I mouthed 'sorry' to Spencer's mother and went with her.

I could still sense his eyes on me when I walked outside, following Maja and passing two other men who were eyeing me intensely. I suspected them to be Spencer's brothers; there were four of them altogether, and one of them, Andrew, was a famous actor. I smiled nervously, trying to get it together, but both of them gave off intimidating vibes.

The house was three stories, and the garden at the back was huge. Maja showed me her mini castle. She had two swings and a climbing wall, too. She was lucky. Downing Street Gardens were pretty impressive, but the playhouse at her grandparents' home seemed like every kid's dream. Lost in my thoughts, I nearly bumped into someone. He steadied me as I glanced at him, realising it was the guy who'd shown up with Spencer at the club.

"Uncle Rupert, this is Laura, the nanny. She came to see my castle." Maja tugged his hand.

"Hello." I smiled to be friendly.

"Maja, why don't you bring Laura the princess outfit from your room? Then you both can play inside," Rupert suggested, his gaze narrowed on me.

His body language showed that he was not happy to see me here at all. I wished I hadn't seen Veronica's viral TikTok video because now I was right in the middle of this drama, and I wasn't sure how to act.

"Oh yes, I've all the princess dresses upstairs. Let me get them." Maja left Rupert and I alone.

His expression remained cold and distant when he took a step towards me. He was as tall as Spencer, but he had olive eyes and lighter hair.

"So, Laura, you're Spencer's nanny, right?"

"Yes, I've been working for him for over two months."

"What exactly do you want from him, Laura? First, your roommate seduced me in Greece, and now she's trying to ruin my business by posting that video on TikTok. How convenient that you accidentally stumble into my brother's life as a fake escort girl," he spat.

"Veronica didn't know that this video would go viral when she posted it. She didn't seduce you," I explained. "And I've no idea what you think you know about me, but I had no agenda. I never claimed to be an escort. It was just one huge misunderstanding."

"Don't bullshit me. You came to him as an escort, but you got hired as Maja's nanny. You and your roommate must have planned this. I've to admit, it was a great plan, but Spencer isn't that stupid, and the sooner he realises, the quicker he'll get rid of you," he said.

"Planning what exactly?" Was this guy for real?

"You tell me."

"You're delusional. I've nothing to hide, and clearly, you're the one with issues." Why was I even trying to explain myself to him? "We have nothing else to talk about."

I turned around to leave, but he grasped my arm and squeezed it hard.

"Was it her idea? She orchestrated this whole thing because she wanted to have access to Spencer, right?" he asked.

"Let go of me right now," I snapped through gritted teeth. I didn't know what this man was even talking about and what Veronica had to do with any of it.

He snickered, so I grabbed his shoulder and kneed him right between his legs as hard as I could. Rupert released my hand and howled, going down on the ground. Then Maja walked back inside the castle, followed by Spencer and his two brothers. She frowned, staring at her uncle, who was still groaning with pain, rolling on the grass.

"Uncle Rupert, what happened? Why are you rolling on the grass?"

"What the hell happened to you?" Spencer asked, while the other two stared blankly at a moaning Rupert.

"Your brother acted like a total arsehole, so I put him in his place. Come on, Maja, let's go play," I said and walked out, heading to the kitchen, holding her hand. My whole body was shaking with fury.

Rupert really thought Veronica and I had orchestrated the whole thing because we were after their money? He couldn't have sounded more ridiculous.

It had been a mistake, a misunderstanding, and yet I was the one being called a liar.

Chapter Eighteen

Spencer

"What the fuck happened, Rupert?"

"She must have kicked him between the legs." Andrew chuckled, taking a sip of his drink.

James was impassively eyeing our pathetic brother, then shook his head.

I kneeled in front of him, wondering what he had said to make Laura lose control like that. He obviously must have insulted her if she'd reacted this way, which was pretty funny.

"What the hell did you say to her?" I pressed.

"Fuck off!" he growled.

"You can deal with him. I'm going to talk to Laura," I said and left them to it.

I didn't speak to Laura until later because my father drew me back to the kitchen, asking me to make sure the meat was cooked to our liking.

Rupert came out of the toy house looking awfully incensed, and I warned him to stay away from Laura.

"Are you going to tell me what happened over there?" I asked Laura, finally catching her by the downstairs bathroom.

Maja was playing with Rupert once again, who kept glaring at Laura from across the garden.

She folded her arms and hesitated for a long moment before answering.

"I don't know exactly what happened between him and my roommate on Friday night, but he accused me of orchestrating this whole thing—our first meeting when you believed I was … you know … so I could take advantage of your position."

I rubbed my jaw, making a mental note to tell him to stay the fuck out of my business. I could still hardly believe that the girl he wasn't able to get out of his head for two long years was Laura's roommate. Besides, Rupert claimed he didn't do relationships, and yet it seemed like he was after Veronica. This whole thing was pure fucking coincidence—it had to be.

"My brother is a bit of a dick, so did you really knee him in the crotch?"

"I lost it when he told me we were trying to scam you because of your position," she explained.

I chuckled. "So he deserved it, and I'll make sure he stays out of my business from now on."

"You don't have to do that, Spencer. I can take care of myself," she said with a faint smile. "Now, if you'll excuse me, I need a drink."

I followed her outside, practically like a lapdog. Bloody hell. My voice of reason kept telling me to forget about her, but I was already addicted to her wild response to my touch, and I wanted to have her in my bed.

Laura fitted into my complicated life perfectly, but only as long as I kept her at arm's length, so this whole thing wouldn't backfire.

I groaned inwardly at the thought.

Finally, around five, we sat at the huge table on the terrace where my father had brought out his famous roast beef. By that time, I was starving. Maja insisted on sitting between Laura and I, while Rupert, Andrew, and James sat across from us. The food was served, and the conversation flowed until my mother assumed the role of matchmaker.

My mother, unaware that Rupert couldn't stand Laura, and with me not having the chance to talk to her before dinner was served, it annoyed me that she thought Laura was good enough for him but not for me.

"So, Laura, did you know Rupert is travelling with Spencer to Sicily this summer?" my mother asked.

Rupert almost choked on his beef. He glared at me, then at our mother.

"The plans aren't finalised yet, Mum," Rupert grumbled.

"Do you have any plans for the summer, Laura? I'm sure Spencer would pay you a lot more if you help him out with Maja during the school holidays," my mother continued, staring at my nanny.

"Yeah, can Laura come with us on holiday? That would be so good!" my daughter shouted.

"Darling, what did I tell you? Don't talk with your mouth full. You're a lady," my father reprimanded her.

Maja apologised.

I gave my mother a look, but she ignored me. I had only agreed for Rupert to come with me to Sicily because he wanted some quality time with his niece. After all, he claimed he was her favourite uncle, and they truly had a great connection.

"That's a lot to take in," Laura said. "I really don't have any plans for the summer. I need to see how it will go with my mother. Knowing her, she would be too stubborn to agree to my help."

"Oh dear, that's terrible. I hope your mother gets the best doctors, but I know the NHS is in crisis," Mum added. "Anyway, if you get things sorted and the situation improves, think about spending the summer in Italy. The way time flies, it won't be long before the holidays are upon us."

My younger brother looked like he'd swallowed a fly as he kept glaring at me. I already knew he wouldn't come if Laura was joining us, but we still had a bit of time to warm up to this whole idea.

The dinner conversation flew once Maja teased Andrew

about his latest movie, and then James chimed in. Apparently, all her friends were asking her about him.

The dinner was delicious, and Laura kept praising my father for his amazing cooking skills. That earned her some serious points with him.

I was glad, though, that this whole family dinner was over by around eight. I had to get Maja home because she was tired and she had school tomorrow.

"I want you to sleep in the apartment, Laura, even though it's the weekend. I've missed you," Maja said to her when we were all saying our goodbyes.

Meanwhile, Rupert was still staring at my nanny.

And my mother was already pushing me to get help for the summer, as if she didn't trust me with Maja at all.

"All right, I'll do that for you, sweetheart," Laura replied.

My heart flipped. Maybe tonight I could finally talk to her.

"Just consider taking Laura with you. Maja will be delighted, and who knows, maybe she and Rupert—"

"Mum, Rupert isn't interested in Laura. He's interested in her roommate, Veronica, but you didn't hear this from me, okay?" The idea of Rupert and Laura being together made me want to commit murder. I wanted her for myself, even though I couldn't have her. No bloke out there was good enough for her. "Anyway, Jason is already in the car, so we need to go. Laura is staying over tonight, so she won't have to travel in the morning."

The drive back to Number 10 wasn't long, but my daughter was so worn out that she fell asleep on Laura's lap.

The silence was deafening and awkward between us. The

image of that fucking kiss and her wet pussy was still fresh on my mind, and I could hardly do anything to stop these intrusive thoughts. Laura Watkins was going to be the death of me.

"How is your roommate? I hope my brother didn't do anything to embarrass her yesterday?" I said, because I fucking had to break this silence that was driving me bonkers.

Laura was stroking my daughter's hair and glanced at me.

"They had an argument. Your brother isn't happy that she works as an escort. Also, this video must have complicated things a little because it went viral. But Veronica is tough. She'll move on soon enough."

"Understandably, my brother likes to be discreet, although he does change women as often as he changes his boxers. Still, he'd been talking about her since that holiday in Greece. He won't admit this, but he wants her." I felt bad that all I could think about was my predicament with Laura and not my brother's issues.

"Thank you for riding home with us. I know you like being in your own place when you're not working." I cleared my throat.

A small smile curved her lips, and I imagined her on her knees as she took my cock in her mouth.

"I feel more comfortable in your home than in mine, Prime Minister."

Chapter Nineteen

Laura

After dinner at his family home, things between Spencer and I were still pretty strained, and I had a feeling he was avoiding me again. I wanted to talk to him, even though I'd avoided him, too. In the end, we needed to discuss what was going on between us because I didn't think I could continue working for him when he was acting so territorial. I never told Veronica about that moment outside the club because I didn't really understand it myself.

As usual, Spencer had been on his best behaviour during the dinner, but then, on the way back, he stared at me like he was ready to consume me. This man was so confusing. When I was near him, I didn't know how to act. I had to get over this attraction.

Spencer left early in the morning, and as soon as I dropped Maja off at school, I made a call to one of the private hospitals. One of my friends had given me the number of a specialist who worked there, and apparently, they could see NHS patients. There was only a slim chance that this doctor could see my mother, but I had to try it, so I dialled the number.

"Hello, Medina's Practice. How can I help you?"

"Oh, yes, hi. I was just wondering if Dr Jonas has any appointments available. My mother has been well in the past few years, but after her regular checkup she got this unexpected diagnosis," I started.

"I'm sorry, but there's a two-year waiting list for him," the receptionist said.

A two-year waiting list? How was this even possible?

"Right, okay, never mind. Thank you," I said, disheartened, and then hung up. I stared at the phone for a little while.

Mum said that, apparently, she had the best doctors in the country, but she wasn't a priority, and we couldn't wait until she needed to have dialysis. That wouldn't end well.

"God help me," I murmured, wiping the tears stinging my eyes and staring out the window.

It was finally raining in London. I'd missed my hot yoga session today because I was too exhausted. Also, Veronica's friend had taken down the video, and we hadn't talked about Rupert since. She was clearly trying hard to forget about him.

I tried a few other clinics over the course of the week, but getting an appointment for my mother felt like an impossible task.

The Prime Minister kept avoiding me. He was leaving early and coming home when Maja was already in bed. This wasn't good because he was supposed to be spending more time with her, and she was missing him. I was angry with my own pathetic self, thinking that he actually would change and recognise there was something between us. I kept reminding myself that he wasn't the one for me, and I wasn't willing to settle for being his occasional fuck buddy.

On Friday afternoon, my phone buzzed with a message.

You have Friday night off. My mother is going to pick Maja up from school.

I was surprised but glad that I could go home early. Veronica had said something about going to the cinema, and I could use a distraction. As I was packing my stuff away, I wondered what Spencer was doing tonight. He was probably going to call an escort, and I told myself I didn't care. It was obviously a lie. I did care, and I was jealous—but maybe he had other plans. These things shouldn't surprise me. Spencer was a single father, and he'd made it very clear he didn't want a relationship.

"Veronica, are you home?" I called out.

The flat was tidy, and I was shocked to find my roommate in the kitchen, actually preparing food that didn't come out of a packet. Veronica wasn't very domesticated, so something must have happened. She only attempted to cook when she was stressed.

"I'm making fajitas. Brenda is coming over later," she replied.

I put my bag down and entered the kitchen. She was stirring the ground beef and seasonings on the stove, and the room smelled heavenly.

"Fajitas? I thought you wanted to go out tonight? Spencer gave me an evening off, which means I've the whole weekend to myself." I stared at her in total disbelief.

"Well, we changed our plan slightly because Brenda has this hot date tomorrow, so we need to discuss it tonight." She moved the pan like a freaking professional. "Anyway, what is Spencer doing tonight?"

I shrugged and went to the fridge to get a drink. Veronica had been busy lately, and I really wanted to tell her what had happened between me and Spencer in the club. I wanted a relationship with him, not a hook-up.

"No idea. We haven't spoken since the family dinner. I think he has been avoiding me," I told her, sitting on the chair.

Veronica turned off the pan and faced me, eyebrow raised. God, she always looked so gorgeous, even in a tank top and shorts, with her hair sticking out in various directions.

"Why not? What happened at the dinner? I thought you said it all went well."

"It's not what happened there, it's what happened before the dinner—at the club," I said and drank some water. Goosebumps appeared on my arm. The memories were raw, and even with him miles away, I still shivered at the thought of him.

"Come on, spit it out. We haven't got all day," Veronica encouraged.

"I didn't tell you this because you were so upset, and then you had to work, so we didn't discuss what actually happened that evening," I said, a little out of my comfort zone.

She wiped her hands and walked up to me with narrowed eyes.

"What did he do? I swear to God, if he hurt you, I'm going to cut his balls off," she fumed.

"Calm down, he didn't really do anything bad. I mean, it was pretty good." I wasn't sure why I was reluctant to talk about this with someone who had sex regularly with strangers. Veronica was my best friend. "I was hiding in this employee-only exit area, and he found me there. I was so angry with him, so I told him to fuck off."

"Let me guess, he didn't leave, and you two shared a kiss? Fuck, Laura, tell me he snogged your face off." She sounded more excited than me.

"Well, not exactly," I said. "Oh my God, he ... he pinned me against the wall, then turned me around, pulled my dress up, spanked my ass, and talked so dirty to me."

Veronica squealed, fanning herself with the magazine she'd snatched from the worktop.

"You're fucking kidding me, right? He spanked you ... oh my Lord, I think I might have to find a guy for tonight because this has me all hot and bothered!" she squeaked. "What happened after?"

I dropped my head in my hands and took a deep breath.

Then, I told her the rest—about him fingering me, begging him to continue touching me, and the most explosive orgasm in my entire existence.

"And then he just left me there, and I found you a bit later."

"That motherfucker made you orgasm in the space of a few minutes using only his fingers? Are you sure he didn't go down on you?" she asked, as though trying to figure out if I was telling her the truth.

I nodded, trying to breathe evenly at the same time.

"Yes."

"That's amazing! Spencer fucking Banks made you orgasm in under two minutes, while any other motherfucker out there couldn't do it in the space of two years. Hallelujah! Thank you, Jesus!" She looked upwards.

I rolled my eyes.

"That means nothing, because he has been ignoring me ever since. It's clear that he'll not make a move, and I'm okay with it. This whole thing is very complicated," I said.

"He's a coward, but he wants you—I can sense these things. He was furious when he saw you on the dance floor with that guy."

"He doesn't have a thing for me. He just wants to get into my knickers. That's all there's to it." I knew that deep down, I wouldn't mind having the wildest night of my life with one of the sexiest men I had ever laid eyes on. A man who, unfortunately, was also my boss.

Veronica grinned wide, putting me in mind of that scary clown, IT, for a fleeting moment.

"Darling, he definitely wants to fuck you, but he also wants you. I bet in a few weeks' time, you guys are going to be an item, and the press will go crazy over this whole story." She squealed with excitement. Her phone rang, and she excused herself.

While Veronica was talking, I checked on the taco beef, stirring it a bit more. As I was tasting the mixture, she hurtled in, looking flustered.

"What's wrong?"

"Nothing. I'm still processing what happened in that club. Anyway, change of plans. You're going on a date night. Everything is arranged, so let's pick out an outfit."

"Don't be ridiculous. A date? With who?"

Her eyes gleamed with mischief.

"A very handsome CEO who Brenda met the other day. You're free, and you need to have a good time. Trust me on this, girl. You need to go on a date to forget all about Spencer Banks."

Chapter Twenty

Spencer

"What about Africa? Have you ever been there? I mean, that's a silly question. Of course, you must have travelled there for business at least." Caroline took a sip of her champagne.

For the first time in my life, I'd let Jeremy arrange this date for me, and I had never been more bored. The guy was a sucker for romance, and in the past few months, he had been pestering me about my ratings that would surely go up if I indulged in dating. I wasn't convinced, but I hoped my relenting would get him off my back for a bit.

Caroline was blonde, beautiful, and sounded smart, too, but not for me. In an ideal world, I would have asked Tanya out on a date instead. She would have been more suited to me, and in the end, I would have been with her, too. Well, in a scenario where I wasn't the prime minister of a country, with a certain image and responsibilities to uphold, that might have worked.

"Travelling for work isn't the same. I never get to see anything because I'm always too busy with meetings, and also there's a security protocol." I looked around the restaurant.

We were seated upstairs on the first floor in one of the discreet rooms, so I didn't have to worry about being seen by other guests.

Jeremy knew exactly what I was after. He'd assured me that Caroline would be happy to satisfy me, and that was the main reason why I was sitting in front of her right now. I dragged my hand through my hair and took a sip of scotch, mulling over thoughts of Laura.

I'd purposely avoided her this week because I couldn't stop myself from thinking about her. I was suddenly so glad that she was not staying in the apartment. She'd actually texted me today, asked me to get my act together and start coming home for dinner, or she was going to quit. She made me feel guilty, hence why I'd gone ahead with the date. To forget.

How is that working for you, Spencer?

"Right, of course," she replied.

The waiter finally brought us desserts. I glanced at the door. No one could see us from where we were seated, but I had the best view of the whole restaurant. My men were sitting at the next table over, enjoying their steaks.

"Tell me about your social life. Lori has seen you at many banquets, you must enjoy the attention." She smiled.

God, she sounded so mundane, borderline rude and tacky, and despite her having a degree in political science, we had little to talk about. Maybe I just had to be straight with her and let her know this wasn't working. However, as I got ready to express my thoughts, something drew my attention to the restaurant entrance.

That something was Laura, who had just walked in.

For a moment, I thought there was something wrong with my vision. How was this possible—out of all the restaurants in London, she comes here? With some guy, too ...

Did she have a brother? No, he couldn't be, not with that smile and obvious possessive gesture, particularly with his hand on her lower back.

I ground my teeth.

"I don't like the attention, Caroline, and that is the main reason I chose this place." I wondered why the universe enjoyed messing with my head so much.

Laura and her companion were now seated in the middle of the main dining area on the ground floor, so I could see everything that went on. Who the hell was this guy?

She looked stunning in a flowing, stylish purple maxi dress. She laughed when he said something to her while they perused the menu. It was clear now they were on a date.

"Spencer, are you even listening to me?"

Caroline's voice brought me back to her. I hadn't even touched my dessert, and now, I really didn't want it anymore.

Even a messy, sexy session with Caroline in my fuck pad wasn't appealing.

I released a breath. She appeared annoyed while I was in another world, sweat beading along my forehead and nape.

"Sorry about that. I got distracted for a minute," I told her. The understatement of the century.

"Prime Minister, you can share what's bothering you with me. I'm a good listener," she encouraged.

And at that moment, I knew it was time for me to break this shitshow. She wasn't doing anything for me, but my obsession with my hot nanny was becoming an issue. I had to end this insanity, no matter what. The most important thing was that I couldn't do this to Maja. She loved Laura, and they got along well. If she was on a date right now, it was none of my business.

Why was I like this?

Caroline had flirted with me the whole evening, and she was obviously open to taking things further. At least, that's what Jeremy claimed. Apparently, she loved to collect notches on her bedpost.

I kept staring back at Laura and her date and wished I didn't have the perfect view. I felt so uncomfortable and I really didn't want to continue with this date.

Technically, I could excuse myself, tell Caroline that I had to use the bathroom, then I could find a way to talk to Laura somehow. But that would be crazy. I reminded myself that I was in a public place. Everyone had their phones on and everyone knew who I was, unless they had been living under a rock. I'd potentially ruin my entire career because I couldn't stand the fact that my nanny was on a date with another fucking guy. Madness.

Still, there was one thing I had to do. I had to tell Caroline that I had no intention of spending the night with her. It wasn't fair to lead her on.

"Listen, Caroline, I'm really sorry. I hate doing this, but ... You're right, something is bothering me tonight, and my mind is elsewhere. You're very sweet and beautiful, and I would love to get to know you better," I lied, "but not tonight. I'll bring a car for you, and I'll call you again soon."

This was the right thing to do. Jeremy had arranged this whole thing, and she had made the effort to come. I might not be attracted to her, and I might be a dick sometimes, but I didn't want to wilfully hurt her.

Caroline lost her smile, clearly shocked and surprised that this date was going nowhere. She was a woman, and usually, they could sense bullshit.

She was silent for a moment, then cleared her throat and wiped her mouth with a napkin.

"Are you sure this is what you want, Spencer? As I said before, I'm a great listener, and maybe I can give you some good advice regarding your issue." She worked overtime to salvage what could never happen.

I groaned inwardly. I could hardly concentrate on her, knowing that Laura was right downstairs. I did my best to not glance at her table and clue Caroline in on the real problem.

"I've never been more certain, Caroline. I sincerely apologise again. Please allow me to escort you outside." I itched to wrap this up.

I went to my bodyguards and told them what was going on, and to have another car brought here to take my date home. I walked with Caroline all the way downstairs where the restaurant manager was already waiting for us. He let us out through the back door, so that we were away from the public eye. He was discreet and honest, so I could count on him.

My pulse pounded when, several minutes later, the car pulled in. Caroline leaned over and gave me a kiss on the cheek.

"Take care, Spencer. I hope you sort out your issue soon," she said and then got into the vehicle.

I gave her a courtly nod, and then the driver took off. I was so fucking relieved, standing outside with my men. I knew what I needed to do next. It wouldn't do to attract too much attention and have the media involved, so I had to be both discreet and firm when I left the restaurant with Laura.

There was no way I would let her stay here with that arsehole.

"John," I instructed one of the agents in charge of my safety tonight. "I'm going to have a chat with my nanny in the main restaurant. Please arrange for our ride to meet us outside the main entrance and try to stay in the shadows. I don't want to bring too much attention to myself."

"Yes, sir," John said.

Then I went back inside.

I didn't fucking know how, but I had to convince Laura to leave with me. She was a smart one, so some lame excuse wouldn't do. As much as I tried to tell myself I should not get entangled with this woman, I could not ignore my fucked-up emotions. This whole thing had to be resolved somehow before I completely blew my sanity and career.

The manager showed me a different way to the main restaurant floor after I'd gone back inside. My palms were now damp with sweat as nerves took over, and I hesitated for a moment. Just then, I caught sight of Laura laughing at something this wanker said to her. Fuck, she was so stunning and relaxed in the company of that prick. Why wouldn't she act like that when she was with me?

At that moment, she was blissfully unaware that I was watching her. The restaurant was busy, so this complicated things for me because I couldn't afford to be seen doing something ridiculous.

But holy shit, I wanted Laura to laugh with me like that. She was mine, and I didn't want any other fucker to make any kind of claim on her.

Pull yourself together, Spencer. She will not cause a scene.

Pulling myself together, my men now back inside and standing discreetly in a secluded spot behind me, I strode purposefully through the restaurant, headed for their table while I focused on the fact that people were busy enjoying their meals and dinner companions. A couple of people might have noticed me, and I almost faltered, but I kept going. Laura must have sensed something and lifted her head towards me.

"Good evening, Laura." I nodded politely at her 'date', even though it took all I had in me to do so. I had to admit, he seemed well put together. Dressed in a tailored suit and expensive watch. I now realised I knew who he was.

"Spencer ... I mean, Prime Minister, what are you doing here?" Laura asked.

"I apologise for this intrusion, but I was dining upstairs in one of the private areas when I spotted you coming into the restaurant." I got straight to the point.

Laura's jaw was hung open, and she looked like she didn't understand any words that came out of my mouth. I glanced around, seeing that several people were giving us curious stares and whispering among themselves, so I needed to get her out of here as soon as possible.

"I just received a concerning phone call." I lowered my voice to a whisper. "It's about Maja. I'm afraid I need your help right now. "

"What happened to Maja?" She removed her napkin from her lap and placed it on the side of her plate.

"I'll let you know once we're on the way. The car is waiting outside. I apologise, Mr—"

"Mr Prime Minister, my name is Lucian Doherty, and I'm the CEO of Adius Energy Group. I believe we have already met a long time ago. Laura mentioned that she works for you," the man answered, then he stood to shake my hand.

"Mr Doherty, I apologise once again, but I need to steal Laura away. This is an urgent matter," I said. I turned to Laura. "Please?"

She nodded, seeming so concerned. I felt like shit for deceiving her this way, but I had no other choice.

"Lucian, I'm sorry. I'll call you tomorrow." She shot that wanker an apologetic smile.

Over my dead body, woman. He's not for you.

"It was a pleasure, Mr Prime Minister," he said before we walked away.

More people had caught on to my presence here, and I was glad I didn't have to hurry her along. She didn't even spare me a glance as we headed outside.

"The car is just over there," I told her when one agent who had gone ahead waved us over.

He opened the door, urging us to get inside. Laura got in first, and I was just about to do the same when someone approached.

"Mr Prime Minister, may I've a word, please?" A blonde woman, who I pegged to be around her mid-forties, smiled.

One of the agents pushed her away, but I stopped him, showing that I had this, so he backed off.

"I'm sorry, but I'm in a bit of a hurry," I said. "My agent will give you my secretary's number. She can arrange an appointment."

"Mr Prime Minister, I believe it will benefit you greatly to hear me out. I work for ITV," she explained with another brilliant smile, then showed me her card.

I swore under my breath, wondering how the hell she'd got to me so fast. Just my luck she'd been in the restaurant, too. I leaned inside the car, where Laura was sitting. "I'll be right back," I told her, then shut the door and moved away from the street.

My agents were not happy about this, of course.

"What is it exactly that you want, Miss—?"

"Porter. My name is Louise Porter."

"What can I do for you, Miss Porter?" I kicked myself in the rear for not letting my agents handle this a few moments ago.

"I overheard your brief exchange with your employee in the restaurant and I think I might have a story. Correct me if I'm wrong," she said innocently.

Fuck, how the hell did she even hear me? I thought I was speaking quietly. I glared at her, trying to think on my feet. This woman would not be easily intimidated, so I had to give her something, anything, just so I could leave.

"What exactly do you want?" I asked her, point-blank.

She brushed her hair away from her face. "An exclusive interview. I'm on the *Evening Show* staff," she said.

I exhaled sharply before dragging my hand through my hair. Christ.

"Please don't be concerned. I simply want to shed light on the human side of our country's esteemed leader," she added. "I believe the people are hungry for such news."

I hesitated, then sighed in resignation. "Fine, I can do an interview, but my advisor has to approve the questions first."

The journalist smiled once more, revealing her perfectly white teeth.

"We have a deal, sir. I'll call your office if I don't hear from you in the next week. Have a great evening." She then strutted away before I could say anything else.

I entered the Range Rover.

"Elm Street, Brian, as fast as you can," I said to my driver.

Laura turned to face me, her gaze questioning. She looked amazing in her beautiful purple dress, and my heart squeezed at the sight.

I was furious that she'd dressed up so nicely for that fucker. But now she wasn't buying what I was selling anymore. Sparks flew from her eyes. Uh-oh ... I was in trouble.

"What the hell is going on, Spencer? If you've made up this story about Maja to lure me away from my date, I'm seriously going to flip," she said as the driver eased the car into heavy London traffic.

"Take a breath, woman. We'll talk soon. I don't want anyone to hear what I've to say," I told her.

She continued to glower at me for several long moments before she folded her arms over her chest and sat back, staring straight ahead. The atmosphere in the vehicle was filled with tension, and that put me even more on edge.

It took us another twenty minutes to get to my fuck pad. Laura was quiet when I opened the door for her and she exited the car. She glanced around and instantly narrowed her gaze, recognising the place where we'd met for the first time.

I was relieved when she went inside without further discussion. I told Brian and the agents to stay put as I shut the door.

Tonight, two things would happen: I would either fuck the living daylights out of her or let her go, even though I wasn't ready for either. Definitely not for the second option.

Chapter Twenty-One

Laura

Even though I'd vaguely heard Spencer give the address to the driver, I was ready to blow up when the car pulled up outside the place where he normally met his escort girls. And the place we'd first met in a great big mix-up. This definitely wasn't home.

Spencer Banks continued to drive me crazy. I couldn't believe that he'd showed up in the restaurant, interrupted my date, and dared to bring me back to his fuck pad. I hated him so damn much.

My date hadn't been planned, but Spencer had given me a night off, and Veronica had set me up. She wanted me to have a good time, and frankly, so did I. I deserved it, and Lucian seemed like a fun guy. He was intense, probably because he was burdened by so much responsibility, but not as intimidating as Spencer.

"Of all the places on Earth, why would you bring me here, Spencer?" I asked when he followed me inside and we both entered the living room.

I remembered it all so damn well. Indeed, I'd never forget it. I still had dreams about it. He was pinning me with his gaze now but had still said nothing. Why did he have to be so incredibly good-looking and irresistible?

"So what's going on?" I continued. "Why did we have to leave? Is Maja all right?"

He gazed down at the floor, then back at me.

"Everything is fine. Sorry for that. I just wanted to get you out of that restaurant so we could talk in private," he said.

I clenched my fists, suppressing the urge to punch him. Shit on a stick. He was just ... awful. Infuriating. Aaaaaaaarrrrrghhhh.

"What? So you ruined my evening and made some lies about work-related stuff, then dragged me out in the middle of my dinner date just so we could talk? Are you out of your goddamn mind?" I shouted.

"I knew you wouldn't want to leave otherwise," he said. He didn't sound like he regretted what he'd done one bit. Of course, he believed it was okay for him to ruin my evening. "We need to talk, so I fucking told my date to leave. It wasn't working out anyway."

"Your date? You were on a date, too." I laughed nervously, in utter disbelief that he would go to such an extreme. He acted like he'd lost his mind. And he'd been on a date ...

"Unbelievable," I commented, because I didn't know what else to say.

"So really, Laura? You went out with that guy?"

I told myself to keep it together, so I closed my eyes and took several deep breaths. This somehow worked, so I opened them and stared at him. That riled me up again, so this time I tried to convince myself that violence wasn't the answer. I didn't want to act like the totally unhinged Spencer Banks.

"You have no right to ask me that. Why would you think it was okay for you to lie and drag me out here like this?" I hissed.

His silence only added to the ridiculousness of it all.

He took a step towards me, and I reversed until my back hit the wall. We had already been in this situation before, but this time I couldn't let him take control.

"I asked you a question. Why did you go out with that wanker?" he said, his eyes burning into mine. He placed his hands on either side of the wall, caging me in.

"He's Lucian, my date, remember, Mr Prime Minister?" I infused my tone with sarcasm. "Now, let go of me before you do something you will regret later. You're crossing the line again!"

Spencer had made it perfectly clear that there wasn't going to be anything between us, and I truly wanted to move on. I was ready to have a relationship with someone, and this fool here knew he would never be there for me.

"I'm not done talking to you. I thought you didn't date. This guy looks like he wants to take advantage of you."

Christ, he wouldn't let this go. He was also imagining things.

"What the hell is wrong with you? It is none of your business whether I date or not. You're only my boss, as you have expressed, so this ..." I waved my finger between us, "whatever this is, it's not real. And this attitude ends now. You have no right to dictate what I do and who I date!"

Spencer's nostrils flared. He brought his face so close to mine, our lips almost touched. I squeezed my thighs together because my body was already betraying me. *God, help me be strong.*

And he hadn't even touched me yet.

"Have you already forgotten how turned on you were in that club? How your pussy was soaked through for me, and only me? How your juices coated my fingers as you came ... So you are my business, Laura. From that moment on, you were always going to be my business." He leaned down, brushing his lips against my throat.

I closed my eyes, trembling with desire, his hot breath and crude words sending me weak at the knees. At the same time, I wanted to slap him, to hit him with all my strength. I rose onto my tiptoes and murmured, "You're so full of yourself. I'm still going to date Lucian if I want to. Now let go of me before I start screaming."

"Over my dead body, woman."

He fisted a hand in my hair, an unquenchable hunger in his eyes, then devoured my mouth with unrelenting passion until my lips burned, and I gasped out a broken and shuddering moan. That desperate sound only seemed to drive him further, to intensify the kiss until I was melting into him.

He tasted like the deep-blue sky mixed with scotch, mysterious yet tantalising. His tongue plundered my mouth, and I was lost in his embrace. My brain was screaming at me to push him off me, to fight, but my body ... fuck, my body had completely shut out my mind.

His hands moved through my hair, roughly tugging. He claimed me with a possessiveness I had never experienced before.

"You taste like you belong to me, so sweet, so fucking good. I can't stop touching you. What are you doing to me?" He pulled away slightly, breathing hard, his eyes now sparking unholy flames.

Then he spread my legs with his knees and moved his body between them. My heart was pounding, and I couldn't believe this was actually happening. He couldn't give me what I truly wanted, not now or ever.

"Get off me right now. You're no good for me," I said, tired of fighting him all the time.

But then, his mouth was on mine again, and he was pushing his hard erection against my stomach. He crouched a little and brought it to my core, proceeding to dry hump me against the wall. Damn, he felt so sinfully good, and I was aching for him.

He left me breathless as he kissed my neck, trailing his mouth down to my collarbone while he kept rubbing his hard cock on that perfect spot ...

I was slowly losing my mind.

"I can't ... I want you so fucking much," he rasped, his voice broken.

He was so hard, and only our clothes separated us. Without these garments impeding us, we could go all the way ...

Shit.

No.

It took everything I had to push him away from me and put some distance between us.

"You need to let me go. This can't ever be real. We are on different paths, and you can't give me what I want, Spencer. You know this," I said firmly, then closed my eyes because I couldn't look at him any longer or I would shatter.

I needed a break from all of this. From him. I didn't want to face reality and the fact that on Monday, I'd be back at Number 10, pretending once more that nothing had happened.

"I don't know what you want. Tell me the truth, Laura. Tell me how you really feel and how much you can't deny me any longer," he asked, attempting to cage me again.

But this time I was ready for him.

I raised my hand, pulled it back, then brought it up to his face and slapped him. Slapped him hard. One moment I was out of breath, pining for him, the next, I had reacted before I could process what I was doing.

Fuck, what did I just do? I'd slapped the Prime Minister of this country. My boss. *Jesus, I am in so much trouble.*

I brought my hands to my face and stared at him in horror. He took a few steps back from me. He seemed distraught, but there was no coming back from this. I did what I did.

"I ... I ..." I stammered, unable to utter a coherent word.

"Laura, I'm sorry," he interrupted. "I don't know what I've been thinking lately. Bloody hell ... I can't control myself when I'm around you. You're in my thoughts all the time, and I struggle to be around you without touching you. I want you so much. I don't trust women easily."

He swallowed hard, and I didn't have the heart to say anything at that moment. Then he stared at me like a puppy looks at its owner upon his return home from a long day of work, with heartbreaking adoration. "But I want to try with you."

I shook my head, telling myself not to listen to him. He was putting me in a precarious situation.

"I can," he insisted.

"I don't know what you're saying to me, Spencer. I can't be Maja's mother. You said several times you aren't interested in a relationship. You can't commit to me, and I'll not settle for less. This isn't good for your career either. You've invested so much in it. I see how committed you are to the nation ..."

I paused and glanced away. He was breaking my heart. "I don't want to leave Maja, but if you keep acting like a five-year-old who cannot get his way, I'll resign."

My threat hung in the air. He stared at me. I didn't want to do this, but it would be for the best if we parted ways now, before it was too late.

"You can't leave, Laura ... I'm sorry, and you're right. I'll do better," he assured me.

But I knew these were just empty words. He was losing his mind because of this simple infatuation. I didn't want to believe he'd fallen for me in such a short space of time. We were from different worlds and could never possibly be together.

I shook my head again. "I mean it, Spencer. I don't know how much longer I'll be able to stay in this job. And I'm sorry, but I've to go home. I can't do this right now," I said firmly—way more firmly than I felt—and then moved past him towards the door.

There was nothing else to discuss, and I'd definitely gone too far with that slap. I needed to put the brakes on the steamrolling emotions that were crushing us both. Maybe, if we both slept on it, Spencer Banks, my boss, owner of my most erotic fantasies, and the biggest thorn in my side, would finally wake up and see sense.

Chapter Twenty-Two

Laura

"Now I know why you set me up on that blind date on Friday night," I said to Veronica when I called her on Monday morning after all the chaos of Friday night.

Apparently, Veronica had an unexpected client that evening, so she wasn't at home when I'd returned to the apartment. I'd been too worked up to stay home on Friday, so I'd spent the rest of the weekend with my parents, making sure my mother was fine and had everything she needed. Meanwhile, Spencer had kept texting me all weekend, asking if everything was all right.

"I don't know what you're talking about, but tell me what

happened. Didn't you have a great time with that guy? You texted me to say he was very handsome. You know I wouldn't have set you up with some random man." She sounded concerned.

She only wanted what was best for me, and maybe I was overreacting.

"No, Veronica, everything was going well until Spencer showed up and told me he needed me because of some sort of emergency with Maja. I was so embarrassed and, of course, Lucian introduced himself to him," I said, remembering every single detail about that evening.

I wondered if Veronica had known about Spencer and his date, or maybe it was just a huge coincidence. That woman wasn't an escort, was she? Maybe I was being paranoid.

"Wow," she said. "So, what was he doing there?"

"He was also on a date," I said. The man had told me he didn't date, and suddenly he was out with a woman. I was so stupid, pining over him. "But apparently he cancelled the whole thing when he saw me coming in with Lucian, then he made this shit up about needing me and walked me out of the restaurant. By the way, Lucian was really sweet. He's obviously interested in me, even though I've no idea what to do about that yet."

Silence stretched out on the other side of the phone while the flashback of the slap kept playing on my mind. I couldn't believe what I'd done.

"Listen, we both know that you want each other, so he probably saw you, got a little jealous, and ruined your date. Men can be total children sometimes, and it doesn't matter how much power they have ... So what happened after that?"

I gripped the phone tighter. I didn't want to think about the slap, but I remembered the kiss all too clearly. The way he'd rubbed his body against mine ... Spencer Banks got me all confused and broken again, but I couldn't let myself go there. Besides, he'd behaved like an absolute prick, bombing my date and making me leave halfway through.

"He took me to his fuck pad because he wanted to talk to me and then he started drilling me on why I was even on a date in the first place. I was so angry with him, and after we made out, I pushed him off me and slapped him," I hissed into the phone, wanting to disappear at the same time. "I slapped the Prime Minister of the United Kingdom, Veronica."

She squealed like a child, and I groaned, walking into my bedroom.

"Oh my God, you didn't?" she cried. "I can just picture him. I bet no one has ever slapped him before, but good for you, Laura. Finally, you put him in his place, so now you can finally fuck his brains out."

"Hello? I think there's something wrong with you. I'm not getting involved with my boss, who also is the Prime Minister of this fucking country. He's arrogant and obnoxious. I hate his guts!"

"You will be banging like rabbits by the end of the week, and you will love every second of it," she declared, completely disregarding what I'd just told her.

"I'm hanging up now. My mum is calling me," I lied.

"Hold on, we need to talk about—"

"Bye, Veronica," I said and hung up because I was too angry with myself to continue to talk.

I searched around for my best pair of panties when I put the laundry away, but they were gone. What the hell? I was a hundred percent certain I'd left them there with the other folded clothing on my bed. Or maybe not? We had people to do the laundry at Number 10, but I preferred to keep my life as normal as possible, which meant I did all that myself.

Where were they?

Then it hit me.

No, he wouldn't have taken my best pair of knickers, especially not after what had happened on Friday night.

I left the room, trying to get on with my day after that. This evening I would probably see him—and a good thing, too, because he still owed me an explanation. My rational side was telling me to resign because he would keep taunting me until I gave in and we slept together, but more importantly, I didn't want to disappoint Maja. Spencer was an exceptional politician, and I knew his career was much more important to him than this thing he had for me. Today, of all the days, he would not avoid me like he had in the past few weeks.

He had to be the one to have stolen my knickers, and that annoyed me even more than the fact that he'd ruined my date. Miffed, I marched to his bedroom and stepped inside, a little apprehensive about invading his sanctuary. There were no personal items around. The walls were beige, and everything was neat.

God, I was crossing the line, but he had pushed me over the edge on Friday, and now I wanted to prove to myself that I was right. He was obsessed with me. I started searching, intermittently inhaling his scent on the pillows. Spencer Banks was everywhere; this whole room was so him. There was a book on the nightstand, so I picked it up.

"*Atomic Habits*," I read, instantly finding it a bit boring. I didn't peg him for one who'd read self-development stuff.

There was no sign of my panties anywhere, and as I moved I kept trying to remind myself why getting involved with Spencer was such a bad idea. I'd made up my mind. It was for the best that I wouldn't join him and his family for their holiday in Sicily. I had to give Maja as much time as I could and then simply resign. This was for the best.

I was just about to leave when I realised I hadn't checked the large polished wardrobe, only the two big dressers. I walked up to it and opened the door. Something told me I should stop this and leave the room because I was crossing the line, but curiosity won me over—especially when I saw a small box tucked between two shoeboxes. The thing was old, falling apart in places, but I had a tremendous urge to see inside.

The box contained some old photos of him and his family. In one of them he was so young but still very handsome. I kept wondering why he never talked about Maja's mother, because surely his daughter must have asked about her. I didn't know why she had left, or maybe it was Spencer who'd left her. Either way, I had a feeling he wouldn't want to broach that subject at all, especially when Maja was around.

Number 10 Affair

In one picture, he was posing with his brother, Rupert. The family resemblance was clear, though Spencer had cleaner features and darker hair. Rupert had a more rugged appearance, with tattoos peeking out. He was equally handsome but carried a rougher edge, fitting Veronica's type. I still needed to speak to my roommate and find out if she'd spoken to Spencer's brother at all since that Friday night in the club. This was such a freaky coincidence that we were both working for them. Apparently, Rupert had only just invested in Emperor, and Veronica found out on Friday night that he was going to be her new boss.

I had met Veronica shortly after I'd moved to London a few years ago. One night, I was strolling into a bar, trying to pull my life together, and she'd stormed past me in a huff, having just thrown her drink in some guy's face. We'd hit it off right away, and she quickly became like a sister to me. Well, as much as she would allow. She was like my family, yet a lost cherished one who I would probably never get to fully know.

I glanced through the rest of the pictures that were inside the box and then pulled another one of Spencer with a woman, or rather a young girl. The picture wasn't of great quality, and it was taken on holiday somewhere because the two of them were standing among palm trees, on a beach. My heart beat faster when I saw how Spencer had his arm around her and looked genuinely happy. I turned the photo around, and there a date was written, showing that this picture had been taken around eleven years ago.

The woman was blonde, slim, and beautiful. Even though the picture wasn't great, I could see the instant resemblance to

Maja. She had the same small beauty spot by her right eye like Maja had, too. I stared at that picture, thinking that there was definitely love between them. Eleven years ago, Spencer had been a different man. He wasn't afraid of commitment and he had wanted that closeness with someone.

I put the picture where I'd found it and then made sure to leave everything as it had been when I'd entered his room. I didn't like snooping around, but the compulsion had taken hold.

I still hadn't found my panties, even though I had no doubt he'd stolen them. Maybe I should call him out on it, but I had a better idea. Sooner or later, Spencer would regret that he'd started messing around with me.

Chapter Twenty-Three

Spencer

I obsessed over the whole Friday night incident throughout the weekend.

Laura had been on my mind the entire time, and my brain was in such a tangle, I even considered contacting my old therapist. I hadn't had a session for years, but I felt like I needed it because I obviously couldn't deal with my own demons. I had issues with commitment and women.

What an utter disaster. If I didn't stop pushing Laura like this, she'd end up leaving Maja ... and me. I'd officially crossed the line, and that broke me. When I finally got inside my empty home, I regretted sending my daughter to my mother's.

Christ. I was the Prime Minister of this country. If I couldn't get my act together in my own home, how could I make things better for my people in theirs?

I poured myself a glass of scotch and sat in the dark living room, thinking about Maja's mother. This was a bad idea, but I had these issues because Samantha had betrayed me. She'd vanished from our lives so unexpectedly, leaving me with a small child in the middle of the night. For days, I was unable to process the shock of the fact that she was gone. Maja didn't remember her mother, so we just hadn't talked about her after her initial attempts, which was wrong because my daughter deserved to know the truth.

It was foolish of me; I had fallen for someone who cared only for her own benefit and not for those around her. We hadn't been that young when the pregnancy occurred, unexpectedly. Samantha had never wanted children, but eventually after talking about this for a long time, we both decided that she would keep the baby. Unfortunately after Maja's birth, Sam didn't bond with her and left us eleven days after without a trace, and we hadn't seen her since. This completely shattered me, because in one moment I had a loving girlfriend and the next moment all that remained was a tiny baby who required constant care and attention. I had doubted myself, my insistence she have this baby. But I'd loved Maja long before she was born.

After this experience, I promised myself I wouldn't allow love to cause me such destruction again, so I'd steered clear of relationships ever since.

My mother had to step in, and I had to keep going and give Maja the best life she could have.

At the time, I was just beginning my political career, so it wasn't possible for me to hire a private investigator to look for Samantha. I'd changed forever, I had to grieve alone. On the plus side, love had altered me in positive ways, too, and I became devoted to raising my daughter as a single father. For some months, I'd held on to the hope that Samantha would return, because what mother could abandon her own child even though Maja wasn't planned? But she never had. Eventually, I'd stopped searching for her, and three years later, I'd started sleeping around to satisfy my needs, yet keep my distance from anything more.

I despised most women, I only used them for sex to fulfil my desires. Maja, my mother, and now Laura were the only females in my life I truly cared for and adored unconditionally—the others, I convinced myself, weren't worth my effort. Luckily, since Mum was retired, she was around a lot. She helped me when I returned to work, and when Maja finally started going to school, I hired a full-time nanny to relieve Mum a little, because she had her own life, too.

***

On Tuesday morning, I still felt bad that I hadn't apologised to Laura. I stole her pair of black lacy knickers after I got home on Friday night. It was a mistake and at some point I knew she would eventually notice. Also, for now, I was willing to ignore the fact that it ruined me because her scent was permanently ingrained in my brain.

Jeremy called just as Laura walked through the door on Tuesday morning, so I had to leave without talking to her. After the weekend, she normally came in early on Mondays because she had to get Maja up for school. I felt bad that I had to leave. I was determined to have a long and honest talk with her about Friday night. Just not right now.

I got on with my day as usual, with back-to-back meetings. I never complained about that because this was what I'd signed up for when I'd acquired this role. In the past few months, I had been away a lot on diplomatic engagements, and these kinds of trips were always tough on Maja who didn't like it when I was absent from home for longer than a few days.

This summer, things had slowed down a bit. However, Laura understood that this was part of the reason why I'd asked her to move in at Number 10, so she could be with Maja when an unexpected trip occurred. Around one in the afternoon, I headed back to my private bedroom because I'd spilled some coffee on my shirt and needed to change.

I sprinted upstairs, Laura still on my mind, as she'd been every minute of the morning. How could I make her stay? I hoped she hadn't made any decisions yet because I really needed her and I didn't want to break Maja's heart. Maja didn't do well with change, especially with my demanding schedule.

When I came downstairs, I bumped straight into Laura in the kitchen. She didn't even look where she was going. She seemed so distracted.

"Whoa, be careful. I would have crushed you," I said, nearly taking her down with me.

"I'm sorry, I was just heading out, but what are you doing here? I thought you were working," she asked, a worried expression on her pretty face.

Over the past few weeks, I had learnt how to read her, and I sensed if something was wrong.

"I had to change. I spilled coffee on my shirt," I said. "What's the matter? You look a little stressed."

She bit her bottom lip and finally met my gaze. I was fucking done, especially when she gave me that innocent and slightly anxious glance. I thought I had been doing so well lately, not walking around all the time with a raging hard-on.

"Nothing, it's nothing. I'll deal with it. I just had a call from Maja's school. Apparently, she punched some boy and they want to suspend her," Laura explained.

I was instantly on alert.

I frowned. "What do you mean, they want to suspend her? Did you ask why she punched a boy? Besides, she's only nine, so that sounds a bit extreme," I said, angry that the school hadn't informed me first. Technically, I wasn't supposed to be disturbed by any small matters that happened in Maja's school, but this sounded serious, so they should have called me.

"Spencer, I know it sounds bad, but I'll handle it. I don't know what happened yet. I just had a phone call and I'm heading to the school now, so please excuse me," Laura said.

I grabbed her arm as she tried to move past me.

"No can do, love. I'm coming with you and I'll deal with it.

Wait for me outside. I just have to make a quick call," I said, suddenly losing my focus because she was way too close.

Right then, I needed to handle this incident with the school and not entertain fantasies about what I wanted to do to my nanny.

"What? You don't need to do that. I've got this, Spencer, and I promise you I'll deal with it the best I can. I won't let them suspend her," she protested when I let go of her arm.

I shook my head and pulled out my work phone.

"Stop arguing with me for once," I snapped, dialling Jeremy's number.

He picked up right away, so I asked him to deal with whatever other meetings we had today as I had a personal matter to attend to.

"Well, that wasn't so difficult, right?" I said to Laura.

"No, but this isn't what I meant when I said not to go. I think it will be less stressful for Maja if I'm the one to go, since you're the PM, you know, security needs and whatnot, and everyone in school knows you," Laura explained, giving me a small smile.

"I don't fucking care. We are talking about my daughter here. I know she can be challenging, but her heart is in the right place. This isn't just any issue. She wouldn't punch anyone if there wasn't a specific reason for it, Laura. Besides, a visit to that school is long overdue. I haven't been to a parents' evening there since I started running for political office several years ago."

We walked outside, tailed by a number of agents who would accompany us.

Number 10 Affair

The distance from Number 10 to Maja's school was short, so I briefed the team on what would happen. They didn't seem too pleased with the idea, but they would work with it as they always did.

This felt strange, I had to admit. The Range Rover pulled over, and we headed there. It would have been so good to walk for once, as it was a nice day, but I wasn't allowed to do normal things like that without full planning.

Maja had attended Wycombe Academy since before my election, and she enjoyed it. This was an elite private school with very small classes that most of the upper-class kids attended. As we entered the building with my men, I felt a little guilty that I hadn't made an effort to be more involved in Maja's school life. She was only nine, and I had already missed so much.

The school receptionist nearly fell off her chair when she saw Laura and I approach, along with my detail. Parents who sent their kids to this school were wealthy and privileged, so I suspected she didn't see many of them actually coming to school themselves very often.

"Prime Minister ... sir ... we weren't expecting—"

"Please, can you let the headmistress know that we are here to see her? She's expecting us," I cut her off before she could make a fuss. Luckily, there weren't any other children or staff around, so I could get this sorted swiftly.

The woman's face went beet red, and she nodded frantically, dialling the number. Laura and I sat in the comfortable chairs to wait.

"I've to say that I'm quite surprised that you'd want to get involved, Spencer. Pleasantly so," Laura said after clearing her throat.

This was serious, but the fact she was comfortable around me at that moment made me feel better.

"Surprised that I can be a human being sometimes?" I asked.

She nodded.

What kind of monster had I become?

Thankfully, I had no time to mull that thought over. Several moments later, the door of the office farther down the hall opened up, and a woman stepped out. Her eyes widened when she saw me sitting there.

"Prime Minister and Miss Watkins, what a surprise. Please come inside my office and let's talk." Mrs Whittaker sounded very formal and uncomfortable.

I had learnt from Jeremy a while back that she had been running Wycombe Academy for years. I put my hand on Laura's lower back when we went inside. The touch instantly sent shivers down my spine.

"Thank you for seeing us, Mrs Whittaker. When Laura mentioned what transpired today, I was determined to be present for this meeting." I wanted to get straight to the point.

"Of course, I mean, this is pretty serious. Your daughter has been suspended, unfortunately, because the school cannot tolerate this kind of behaviour," the woman stated.

That pissed me off, and I suspected she either didn't fucking like me or my politics, or both. I just sensed it from the odd vibe

I was getting from her, because normally women behaved differently when I was around them.

She was a petite, older woman, probably in her mid-fifties, with brown hair and smooth features, and it was obvious she was a stickler for rules. Yet, she probably also had her 'pet students' and families.

"I'm rather confused, because surely, we need to ask Maja what happened first? She should be here, right?" I asked, already incensed because it didn't seem that she was interested in hearing both sides of the story.

"I don't think that's necessary. Maja knows that what she has done isn't right—"

"I insist. I want to know why my daughter punched a nine-year-old boy," I interrupted, and that shut her up for a bit.

Laura shifted in the chair next to me, and I wanted nothing more than to know what she was thinking. The headmistress' face flushed, flustered as she was.

"Well, the boy is fourteen, not nine, sir," she quickly corrected me.

My jaw dropped.

"What? Are you telling me that my daughter punched a fourteen-year-old boy and you want to suspend her before you get to the bottom of it all?" I snapped, my voice rising a little. What the fuck was going on here?

"Well, let me just call Maja in here." She picked up the phone.

Five minutes later, my daughter was brought in by the secretary. Her face instantly brightened up when she spotted me.

"Dad, what are you doing here?" she asked.

It hurt me that she was so surprised to see me ...

We all sat, and I turned to her.

"I'm here to find out what happened earlier today, Maja. Why did you punch that boy?" I gave her a reassuring gaze.

Mrs Whittaker was now staring at Maja with a cold and judgemental expression, arms folded over her chest. I didn't like how she and the school were handling this whole situation at all.

Maja glanced at me and then at Laura, who smiled so gently at her, then nodded. My daughter appeared to be so grown up, reminding me a lot of Samantha in that moment.

"I got angry when Mark asked me to go to the bathroom with him, and he kept asking other girls, too." Maja looked down at her hands.

Laura let out an audible gasp next to me, and I clenched my fists, but I had to stay fucking calm. I already knew where this was going.

"So that's why you punched him, because he asked you to go to the bathroom with him?" I repeated.

Maja's attention was on me, her eyes so wide and brimming with moisture.

"He said he wanted me to take off my shirt, to see if I'm a real woman yet," she stated. "Cora was crying because he said some nasty things to her, too, so I punched him. He made me really angry, Dad."

This time I was ready to smash something, and I gripped the chair so tight, I thought I might break it. I glanced at Laura, who instantly reached out to take my daughter's hand in hers. I faced the headmistress, whose blood had drained from her face.

"Did you know about these details, Mrs Whittaker?" I asked, already guessing the answer. "I'm aware of how you were happy to suspend Maja and sweep this whole thing under the carpet while you let that boy continue to molest younger girls." I spoke louder than I should, but the headmistress needed to fucking understand that she was being totally incompetent. "Are the exorbitant fees we pay not enough to protect all the students equally?" Blood was rushing to my ears, and fury blinded me.

"Well, no ... I mean, we were going to quest—"

"That's a lie and you know it. Whatever excuses you may come up with are rubbish. Do you realise that this little shit has made highly inappropriate sexual remarks towards my nine-year-old daughter and her friend, and just how serious this is? Why have the police not been called already?" I asked in disbelief.

The woman's eyes went as wide as saucers at my crude comments. Maja and Laura both appeared to be in shock.

"He should be lucky that Maja only punched him because he won't be able to stand once I'm done with him," I said.

"Mr Banks ... I mean, Prime Minister, violence isn't the answer! The school has to follow certain protocols, and you shouldn't be making any verbal threats," the headmistress said, her voice weak and breathless.

"Violence might not be your answer, but that boy will not have a prayer, a leg to stand on, or any future children if he dares to touch or harass my daughter again," I said through gritted teeth.

"Of course, sir, I promise I'll deal with Mark Chester, and he'll be reprimanded accordingly," the headmistress stated. She must have seen that I was close to really losing my shit. She was completely useless as the head of the school.

"And my daughter will not be suspended, because I'm taking her out of this school for a week so you have that time to sort things out before she returns. I mean it, Mrs Whittaker, because trust me, you will hear from me again if this situation isn't dealt with accordingly. And you won't like it," I said, then glanced back at Maja and Laura. "Come on, ladies. Time to leave."

Chapter Twenty-Four

Laura

I was looking at Spencer, thinking that maybe I had misjudged his interest in his daughter this whole time, because what he had just done was totally unexpected. And awesome. I had planned on having a peaceful day today, but then I had to deal with Maja facing unexpected suspension. When I was just about to leave for school, I'd bumped into Spencer.

He'd forced me to tell him what had happened and demanded that he join me. Despite my reluctance, considering the delicate situation, I had to relent. When I used to work for the Forresters, the young boy, Luca, was bullied at school and often came home crying, but his father refused to acknowledge it, and that had totally broken my heart.

Spencer had behaved the complete opposite, because not only had he gone with me to school, but he had also put Headmistress Whittaker in her place. I had to admit I didn't really like that woman. She was always so cold to me whenever I saw her outside the school, but after Spencer had wiped the floor with her, my ovaries exploded, or rather high-fived each other. After Friday night and this weekend, I'd decided the man was batshit crazy. I hated that he'd lied to me just so I would leave with him, but what he just did completely changed my perception of him, in a positive way.

He was a good father to Maja and he was going the extra mile to fight for his daughter's right to be safe, especially in school. In that moment, all I wanted to do was kiss him and bear his future children.

"Mr Banks, please, let's discuss this further. I apologise for this incident, but we all have to follow school policy." The headmistress walked out with us.

We finally stepped in the corridor. It must be breaktime because all the kids were milling around, hanging out in little groups outside the classrooms.

"We have nothing else to talk about, but I expect an update within a week or I'm pulling Maja out of this school and I'll be alerting the other parents if you haven't already done so," he said, this time more calmly as we kept on moving.

I glanced back at the headmistress, holding Maja's hand

tightly while my very core shook with the urge to jump Spencer's bones. Crap, I really needed to get a grip on myself.

"Dad, that's Mark over there, the one with spiky blond hair." Maja pointed at a boy who stood by the entrance to the toilets.

Shit, this wasn't good, because I knew Spencer would lose it. What that boy had said to Maja was totally inappropriate and wrong on so many levels. I dreaded to think what else he'd already gotten away with, but Spencer needed to keep his composure because we were still on school property.

Spencer's gaze narrowed on the tall boy who was now glaring at us. He was with another two boys, and none of them seemed intimidated by the fact that Maja was approaching with her father, who had to be recognisable.

"I'll be right back," Spencer muttered when we were close to the exit.

A number of kids were now staring at us.

Shit.

"No, please, I know what you're thinking. This will end badly. Let the school deal with it." I grabbed his arm.

Tingles spread through my skin as he stared at me. His blue eyes sparked with a mix of anger and ... something else.

"Laura, calm down. I'm not stupid enough to do anything here. I'm just going to have a word with this little prick, that's all," he said, and then he leaned down, adding, "Cross my heart. I'll be a good boy."

Fuck me ten ways till Sunday. My ovaries cannot take this protectiveness. I want to have your babies, Spencer. Now!

I truly had no idea what was going on with me then, but I had never been more turned on. Not even that time when he'd cornered me in the employee exit.

"Maja, stay with me," I murmured to her.

The girl had a huge grin on her adorable face. Sigh.

I looked around, making sure there weren't any other teachers around. Spencer marched over to the boy, and I followed, but I didn't get too close. I just needed to hear what he was going to say.

"Come here, Mark. I want to have a word with you," Spencer said, his tone brooking no argument.

The stupid boy smirked, then folded his arms over his chest. I could already tell from the way he was acting that he was an arrogant little prick. I didn't like to judge, but his parents were probably incredibly wealthy and he thought he could get away with anything.

"What happened? Did Maja run to her big, powerful dad to tell on me?" Mark puffed his chest like he wanted to show his friends that he was ready to take on a challenge.

Damn it, I already hated that boy and I wanted to beat the shit out of him myself.

Spencer smiled. He appeared completely composed, but I knew better.

"My grandfather told me this funny story. He had this hunting knife that had been in the family for years. In fact, I've it now …" He patted his trousers pocket. "Well, one day, he heard a rustling in the trees and thought it was an animal. Instead of a gun, or whatever everyone used, he threw the knife. And low and behold, it was his buddy, Paul, whose pants were now pinned to the tree at his groin. Close shave ... that knife would have sliced his balls clean off ... know what I mean, Mark?" Spencer said quietly, only for Mark and us to hear it.

I let go of an unexpected gasp.

"Want to feel the knife, Mark? Careful ... it's quite sharp, as I said," he added. "I keep it in a protective cover because I value my jewels, you know ..."

Spencer Banks, who was also the Prime Minister of this country, had just threatened to cut the balls off a fourteen-year-old bully with this innocent story, and I was bloody impressed. Nothing could ever top this.

Spencer became my personal superhero. He was a man who was ready to do anything to protect his own. I was slowly turning into a pile of goo.

And apparently, so was Mark.

I glanced at the little bastard who'd suddenly lost his smile and paled. He visibly trembled while my innards were scorching with fiery lust. Spencer patted Mark on the back and then winked at me.

"Come on, ladies. Let's go get some ice cream," he said.

A moment later, we left the school.

"I think you have the best dad in the whole world," I whispered to Maja, still barely able to walk because my libido was going crazy. I ached to drag this man back home and have sex with him right now.

Maja smiled at me.

"He's my hero, even if he's a bit grumpy sometimes," she admitted.

* * *

Two days later, I asked Veronica to meet me at the park since I had Maja with me. I had promised her we'd have some girl time together, and of course, she loved the idea.

After the incident at the school, Spencer had to go on a diplomatic trip to Sweden. But it was okay because Maja was still on cloud nine about her father's heroic stance with her headmistress.

I was now convinced Spencer was a good man, deep down, so I set our differences aside for a while. Particularly the incident at his fuck pad. I wanted him, but it could never happen because he was still my boss and a national leader.

"Hey, Maja, how are you doing? I'm Veronica, Laura's roommate. It's really nice to meet you." Veronica appeared out of nowhere and hugged us. As usual, she looked absolutely stunning in a yellow jumpsuit and several bracelets on her wrist.

Even Maja seemed impressed by her outfit.

"Wow, I love these. I wanted to wear some to school, but they wouldn't let me. You are so cool." Maja touched Veronica's bracelets.

My roommate laughed as she sat on the blanket next to us.

"Here, have these. I've several more at home," Veronica handed Maja some of her funky bracelets.

The girl's eyes went wide.

"Thank you so much. Oh! There's Bianca. Let me show these to her," she said excitedly, then stood and walked to her friend whom she'd spotted strolling close by.

It was a nice coincidence that Maja's friend was in the park, too. Bianca's mother was very sick, so Bianca didn't attend school full time. She was homeschooled during certain days of the week, so she could spend more time with her. It appeared that Bianca was there with her mother, who was waving to me now, so I waved back.

A couple of agents were watching us from afar. Their presence was slightly unnerving, but at least they kept to themselves for the most part, so we could be somewhat normal.

"Don't wander off too far!" I called out, reassured that the agents kept a close eye on her, too. They did blend well with the surroundings, I had to admit.

"So tell me, what did Spencer do this time?" Veronica lay down on the blanket I'd just spread out to soak up some sun.

It was boiling today, and I made a mental note to move into the shade soon.

I hadn't spoken to Veronica since our conversation about the disastrous Friday night saga because we had both been busy. But now that she'd brought it up, the memories came rushing back, and I felt myself blushing, thinking about how fierce Spencer had looked when he'd fought to protect Maja. I quickly filled Veronica in about the incident of Maja punching that boy at school and Spencer taking over.

"Wow, Laura, this is huge and totally unexpected. So he actually wiped the floor with that bitchy headmistress?" she asked as we both watched Maja and her friend who were talking by the tree.

I remained sitting, leaning back on my hands on the blanket, careful not to lose sight of my charge.

"Yes, and I couldn't really believe it myself, but he was so good at handling that! Afterwards, he took us to Harrods for ice cream. He really made a huge impression on me," I said with a sigh.

That afternoon, the three of us had spent an amazing time in Harrods. It was tricky to get security to work, but the store staff cooperated wonderfully. For a couple of hours, we sat in a private area and enjoyed a great time together.

She grinned, and I almost told her about how attracted I was to Spencer, but I held back. Besides, I needed to ask her about Rupert, since she was now working for him. Was she was planning to quit being an escort because of it? Spencer's brother had invested in the Emperor Club and became the silent partner right before that incident in the club.

"Now, tell me, how is work and Rupert? Do you actually see him often?"

"He comes in with Matthews, but we barely talk. He doesn't want me to work as an escort. He also knows that I'll never find a job that pays so well. Content creation takes time, and I still have to build my profile on Instagram," she explained.

After Veronica's video had gone viral on TikTok, she'd gained over a hundred thousand followers in the blink of an eye, and she'd started posting about other things. A lot of new brands wanted to work with her, and she told me that eventually, she really wanted to quit being an high-class courtesan. Yet, that was a huge decision she wasn't ready to make. I believed she could do whatever she wanted. Veronica was smart. She'd graduated in Media and Communication from one of the best universities, top of her class, too. She would take advantage of a great opportunity.

"So he hasn't tried to ask you out or anything? Oh, Veronica, I know you like him. You said it yourself that he was the best sex you've ever had," I reminded her.

Since she'd come back from Greece, she had never stopped talking about Rupert.

She rolled her eyes and twisted her head a bit to look at me.

"True, and he did ask me out a few times, but he was also rude and cold, so I said I wasn't interested. Rupert wants me for himself. He keeps saying he doesn't like sharing, but we aren't even dating, and he should know that he can't just dictate how I should live my life," she said, mindlessly picking at some grapes that I'd brought with us and popped one in her mouth.

"At least he's not ruining your dates and dry humping you against the wall. I think both of them need to see a therapist," I quipped, then lay down next to her when both girls started playing with a Frisbee next to our blanket.

"It's better to stay away from powerful and affluent men. All they give us is trouble. We are better off being single," she said.

I sighed.

"I couldn't agree more."

Chapter Twenty-Five

Spencer

I returned to London from my diplomatic trip to Sweden on Friday afternoon, the last one before the summer, totally exhausted. Jeremy was still on my case about showing up in public with a woman, and I kept making excuses to avoid it. The press was only waiting to get a juicy, scandalous story involving me. He didn't say a word about Caroline, and I hoped she hadn't called him to complain that I had cut our date short and sent her home last Friday.

Principal Whitaker contacted my office to clarify that Mark had been suspended. His parents assured her he would never act so inappropriately again. I was pleased with the outcome.

Maja normally didn't cause me any trouble since Laura had begun looking after her, and she wouldn't have lied about something like this, so I was glad I'd intervened.

Laura got on well with Maja, but the thought of dating someone like me was a whole different can of worms and brought a slew of problems to the table. So I wasn't surprised that she'd rather quit her job than deal with me. Besides, I still wasn't ready for a relationship, which was what Laura ultimately wanted. I couldn't give her the security and love she craved ... yet. At the same time, I couldn't imagine being with anyone else.

We hadn't had a chance to talk since the day I'd gone to Maja's school. I still had her knickers hidden in the bottom of my dresser drawer. I had every intention of keeping them. At least things with Laura seemed stable and we'd called a truce.

It was afternoon already, so after I had a quick shower and sorted out my work for the day, I texted her asking if she had any plans for this evening because I wanted to take her and Maja out for dinner.

Maja and I are heading to the water park now. I spoke to your security, and they said it was fine. They'll be with us.

I stared at the phone for several moments, wondering what to do, and then I texted her.

. . .

I'll meet you guys there.

Five minutes later, I called my security team and told them that they needed to take me to the water park. This would be a nightmare for them, but since last year, Maja had told me that a lot of kids from school were often there, so in the end I got my assistant to get me the club membership. Maja always enjoyed going. Since it was a private health club, I could occasionally accompany her. Now, with the sudden heat wave that had hit London, there'd be no better place to go to.

Most importantly, I got to see Laura. I hoped she had changed her mind about leaving the job. Maja needed her, and so did I.

I put on some casual clothes and got into the car. I felt optimistic and confident for some reason. I texted Craig, one of the security agents who had already made it to the destination to make sure everything was clear, to bring me some iced coffee. I'd never asked for it before, but as Laura liked it, I wanted to get it for her since I still owed her an apology.

As usual, my security team went inside first to sweep the whole place and made sure everything was in order. They also needed to warn the management and staff that I was going to be using the club. Today the whole place was a bit busier than usual because of the extreme heat.

I went inside with the iced coffee, sweat gathering on my forehead as a few other members noticed me. I didn't mind speaking to people, but I'd come as a private person who was trying to enjoy some time with my child.

I spotted Laura and Maja in the distance. My heartbeat increased. Maja was splashing around, having a great time with her friends.

Heat rushed to my groin when I saw my nanny in her swimming costume, and it took me a few seconds to realise that she wasn't alone. Laura was speaking to a man. They were standing very close to the main pool.

When I was close enough, a girl with bright-pink hair and lots of piercings spotted me approaching. She said something to Laura and then laughed when Laura responded. I had no idea what was being said.

Then the guy Laura was talking to turned around, and I nearly fucking tumbled with the coffee when I saw that it was the same prick—Laura's date from that Friday night.

"What a surprise, Prime Minister. I must tell you this was the last place I expected to see you today." He gave me an annoying grin.

"I'm here for my daughter. I thought this place was for members only?" I said, handing Laura the coffee, which she nearly dropped as our fingers brushed. An electric current shot through my spine, igniting my blood. I quickly turned my attention to the idiot, adding, "What about you Mr Doherty? Is this where the CEOs of big corporations have meetings these days?"

The girl with the pink hair laughed, and Lucian narrowed his eyes on me, obviously understanding my insinuation. I wished he would just piss off and leave us the fuck alone.

"I've been a member here for years and come here often." He stood his ground.

He was getting on my fucking nerves.

"Well, if you'll excuse us, I've a few things to discuss with Laura," I said firmly.

"This is a nice surprise, Spencer." Laura didn't seem happy. "Why don't you wait for me here? I'll wrap up my conversation. Maja is over there." She pointed. "I'll be back in a moment."

Lucian didn't seem to want to budge, but Laura pulled him away from the group.

"Pleasure seeing you again, sir," he said with an edge to his tone.

Maja hadn't even noticed that I had arrived yet, so I stood and kept an eye on her. Laura was officially defying me, and I was ready to spank that disobedient attitude out of her. It seemed whenever we took one step forward, we both had to take two steps backwards. She infuriated me so fucking much.

Several people who were lounging by the pool turned to stare as I sat on a lounger, away from the crowd. I took my shirt off, my gaze fixed on my nanny. My detail laid claim to a table close by, on alert.

I was dying for a scotch but I didn't move from my seat. No one dared approach because of who I was—my security would get involved. I watched Maja playing with the other kids and smiled, wondering what was taking Laura so long to get back. I would stay where I was, though, because I couldn't cause a scene.

"It was a nice gesture from your prime minister, bringing you your favourite iced coffee, don't you think?"

"Oh yes, it was quite the surprise."

Laura's voice, to my left. I craned my neck fleetingly to the side as though I had whiplash, then went back to watching Maja. Laura was talking to another woman I presumed was also a nanny as I'd recognised she was caring for the children of Nigel Stearne, a politician I'd known for years. She had mentioned this nanny before, but I couldn't recall her name. They must have met at the school gate, because Stearne's boys were attending the same school as Maja.

The pair had meandered over to the splash pad to keep a closer eye on Maja and the other children—conveniently within earshot of me. Since I was sitting in the shade, away from everyone, they weren't paying me any mind.

"That was very sweet of him," Laura added.

Sweet? Did she see me as fucking sweet?

"I think it was a very romantic gesture, especially since he's your boss. Why, my boss doesn't do any of that," the other nanny said, giggling.

Yeah, tell her exactly what's on your mind ... You have been cagey around me for days.

They both had their backs to me, but from this angle I had a perfect view of Laura's arse.

"We had some disagreements about some things, especially in the beginning when he promised me that he would be home to put Maja to bed, since she was missing him so much. Luckily, we managed to resolve this issue when I threatened him to leave, and since then his relationship with Maja improved. He's very protective of his daughter. There was this incident in school a week ago or so and I thought I would never say this but I was impressed by how Spencer dealt with this whole thing."

Laura didn't know this girl very well, otherwise she would probably have told her about the whole incident in detail. I didn't think what happened in school was a big deal at all, but I was suddenly glad that I impressed Laura.

"Nigel doesn't really deal with his sons school, he seems very stressed out with his work, but he finds time for his sons," the other nanny mused. "Okay, so tell me about the PM dating life? Apparently he hasn't been seen with a woman for a very long time?"

"Spencer doesn't date as far as I know," Laura responded, sounding annoyed for some reason.

This was true, but I was willing to change that rule for her, which wasn't a good idea.

"Really? So you haven't seen him with any women since you have been working for him?" the other nanny pressed. Obviously she wasn't done drilling Laura.

I wasn't even surprised, because people always liked speculating about my private life, whether I ever had any women in my life.

"Well that's not exciting at all. That man is super hot, and I can't even imagine how he would be in be—"

"Sarah, shh, someone might hear us. We shouldn't be really talking about this right here," Laura cut her off.

I was in a way disappointed that she didn't take the bait. I truly wanted to know if she wanted to jump my bones as much as I wanted her to.

"Oh, stop being so prudish. Every woman in this country is swooning over this man while their ovaries high five each other, unless you're being tight-lipped because you secretly know something. No judgement. If I were you I definitely wouldn't say no to any advances from his side," Sarah said, laughing.

She was smart, and she probably sensed the attraction between us, but Laura was too loyal to say anything.

"He made me swoon over him when he put the headmistress at school in her place, because at that moment I truly thought I could have this man's babies, but otherwise, no. I'm not interested in him that way. He's my employer, and that's all he ever will be," Laura snapped, more forcefully this time.

She seemed annoyed with herself, and I was officially done for. This woman was swooning over the fact that I was willing to protect my daughter. Fuck me, that was a huge surprise, but what woman didn't like an overprotective man? I guessed sometimes I wasn't that much of a prick.

"Ah, that's so romantic." Sarah sighed. "And the PM may act like a total arsehole sometimes, but he's definitely husband material. Don't you want to have kids someday? I know I want to have at least three at some point and I also want to be a stay-at-home mum," Sarah announced.

I did my best to blend with the shadows, because I truly didn't want to be busted listening to their private conversation.

"Yes, I want to have kids, but I've sworn off men. They're just too much hard work. I need stability." Laura sighed.

Oh, woman, I can definitely put a baby in you.

Fuck, where did this idea even come from? I was almost forty, and I'd never thought about having more kids until now.

Truth was, I would gladly have another one with Laura. She would be a fantastic mother, not like Samantha ...

But that also meant I would have to settle down with her.

"Can you imagine if you were pregnant with the Prime Minister's baby? That would be the scandal of the century, and I bet he would be so overprotective. I can see it already."

I didn't hear what Laura said because they got out of the splash pool and walked away while I finished my drink.

Oh dear. The thought of getting Laura pregnant before the summer ended to ensure she would stay with us forever popped in my head and stuck there. Swirling and swirling around.

It was a good plan. Wasn't it?

No, it was an arsehole move—my inner voice answered for me.

Chapter Twenty-Six

Laura

Maja and the twin boys had a great time splashing in the water. When I'd come back from seeing Lucian off, Spencer was nowhere to be seen, and my friend, Sarah, didn't know where he'd gone either. I suspected he was angry with the fact I was hanging out with Lucian again. Not that he had any right to be.

My conversation with Sarah left me a little unsettled. I had always wanted to have children, but the idea of being pregnant by Spencer made absolutely no sense, especially when he'd been clear that he didn't want commitment of any sort.

"I can't believe that Spencer let you come with us. What did you tell him?" I whispered to Sarah an hour later when we were all getting inside the van.

I was in a way glad that we'd met at the school gates, because otherwise I would never share such private details about the PM with her. She was nice, and we were on friendly terms, but she could technically sell everything that I told her to the press, so I reminded myself not to be so forthcoming.

The boys who Sarah was looking after were called Samuel and Jack. They were currently whispering something in Maja's ear, and she couldn't stop giggling.

Today's outing was a total success in Maja's eyes. She was so happy when I told her that her dad wanted to spend the rest of the day with us and that he was back from Sweden.

"Nothing much, but I may have mentioned that MP Stearne had said several times he wanted to set up a meeting with him, maybe invite him over for dinner." Sarah winked at me.

Maja didn't have many friends as she tended to keep to herself, so this would be good for her. Sometimes I wondered if Spencer was pressuring her too much with all the extracurricular hobbies and tutoring.

"Lovely," I said with a smile. When I glanced at the rearview mirror, I caught Spencer staring back at me with fire in his incredible blue eyes.

He had decided to sit near the driver who had come to pick us up, which wasn't really done, to accommodate the extra people in the van.

I wanted him so much, but the situation was too complicated. I never saw things happening between us.

After the summer, I'd need to make a serious decision about my future with the Banks family because I didn't think all of this tension was healthy. I was close with Maja, but maybe finding another job was the answer for everyone's wellbeing.

Sarah and the boys stayed for a few hours, playing in the garden, and Maja asked her dad if they could come back on Saturday. I didn't work weekends, but apparently Sarah did.

I wasn't sure what I was going to do next weekend yet. I needed to check on Mum since she was getting treatment, so that would likely take up the majority of my day.

While Spencer hung out with everyone in the garden, I snuck upstairs to his bedroom to look for my lost knickers again. I had a feeling he'd been the one to take them and I would find them if it was the last thing I did. The idea of searching through his things, especially when I was sleeping in his bedroom while he was away, had not crossed my mind since the last time I'd snooped. But today, after our brief interaction, I started thinking about it again.

I slipped inside and glanced around, wondering where he would have hidden them.

First, I searched through his pillows and then I beat the quilt, but I got nothing. After going through the bedside cabinets, I looked under the bed from where I pulled out a pair of pink handcuffs with little hearts on the side. What the fuck? My face instantly heated, and warmth spread through my body. Why would he have these here? Of course, he must have had a woman here before, even though he said he normally saw them at the other place.

God, he was so gross ... Well, no, he wasn't. He was freaking hot, and I was already picturing him handcuffing me to the bed.

Growing hot and bothered, I went through his clothes to distract myself because, clearly, I had lost my freaking mind. First, I went through the wardrobe, then the dresser drawers containing an obscene number of boxer briefs. My thoughts raced, and my stomach knotted when I paused for a minute and listened for noises outside. Who knew what Spencer would do to me if he caught me in here, going through his things?

My fantasies were already going wild, because the idea of him spanking me wasn't in the least unpleasant ...

"Aha!" I said, pulling out my pair of sexy Victoria's Secret knickers.

Now I needed to get out of there before he came upstairs, but at the same time, I couldn't just take them because he would know that I'd gone through his things.

Hastily, I took the pair that I was wearing and replaced them with the other ones. Damn, this wasn't very hygienic and downright disgusting, but Spencer would definitely sniff them, and the trade-off was worth it.

I was getting wet just thinking about it. I shoved the pair I'd come in with into the drawer and put the other ones on. "It's game on, Prime Minister, and I know you won't say anything, but you're so going to enjoy this," I muttered and put the handcuffs back where I'd found them.

I rushed back downstairs, just in time to see Spencer and Maja returning to the living room. Sarah and the boys were gone now. It was late, and Maja needed to go to bed soon.

Spencer had on a white t-shirt and blue shorts, so informal, just like the average dad. Only he wasn't average. My heart went a mile a minute. Lucian was handsome and charming, but I longed for the obnoxious Spencer who'd spanked me in the club corridor and made me come in minutes since my break up with Jake. Damn it.

"Sarah is great, isn't she? And Maja obviously got on well with the boys," I said, trying to make small talk.

He cleared his throat while Maja changed channels on the TV.

"Can we talk in the kitchen for a minute?" he asked.

I nodded because I couldn't very well refuse, could I?

Shit, why was he being so polite?

In the kitchen, Spencer went to stand by the island and folded his arms, staring at me, but I couldn't read anything from his guarded expression. Yet, all I could think of was how damn sexy he looked in his casual clothes. I definitely needed a fan.

"What do you want to talk about?"

"I know I've already asked you about your summer plans, and you said you were going to think about it," he began.

I let out a breath, glad that he wasn't planning to discuss our incident in the club.

"But I think it would be a good idea if you accompany us to Sicily. I rented a villa, and we will have a chef and a cleaner while we are there. There will be plenty of space for all of us. It's got a private beach, and many celebrities have stayed there, it's got added security. There you'll get to meet the Italian side of my family, too. Maja would really love that."

This all sounded amazing, and I had always wanted to visit Sicily, but there were a lot of other things I needed to consider.

"Your brother really doesn't like me. How long are you going for?" I asked, catching him staring at my lips. Distracting me. How could I handle this tension and not screw up?

"We will be going for six weeks as we do almost every year. My father is half-Sicilian. Maja loves spending time with her cousins, and I think you will absolutely love the island once you see it. Rupert is coming along, but he's going to do his own thing, so you wouldn't have to worry about him."

Spencer walked up to me, closing the distance between us. I didn't know what to think, but the look in his eyes gave me pause. Was it regret I saw there? Maybe he'd realised that actions had consequences. My skin prickled with awareness at his proximity. He was giving me whiplash. The man was cold, obnoxious, and rude on one hand, yet hot, thoughtful, and polite on the other. There was no in-between.

"I really want you there with us because I like it when you're around. It feels like we are a real family."

I suppressed a gasp at his admission because I didn't know what to think. I loved Maja, we'd bonded, but hearing Spencer say these words felt good. Clearly, he thought I was doing a great job of helping him raise his daughter. What Spencer was truly saying was that he respected me, and that was crucial.

Yet, if I joined him on his annual holiday, first I needed to set some clear boundaries.

"All right, let's just say I go with you and Maja to Sicily. What about us, Spencer? Are you going to cause a scene when a man starts talking to me? Are you going to act like a jealous, crazy arsehole like you did on Friday night?"

Veronica had been right. Spencer wanted me, but that didn't mean he was going to move past his issues.

His eyes darkened, bringing out the storm in his blue irises. He was exhausting, and frankly, I didn't think I could ever relax around him when he stared at me like he wanted to devour me.

"Is that what you want? To go on holiday with us so you could flirt with other men?" he growled.

Was he really that possessive of me, or was I just imagining things?

"It's a hypothetical situation, Spencer, because I'm going with you as your nanny, not your girlfriend or fuck buddy," I said, frustrated that he wasn't focusing on what was important. I wasn't planning to flirt with other men, but even if I was going to, I shouldn't feel bad about it. There was nothing between us.

"You need to understand that it's hard for me to trust women," he said, dragging his eyes away from me and taking a deep breath. "I want more, Laura, but I'm afraid you might get overwhelmed and then leave when things get complicated. Maja would be devastated, and I don't want her to remember you like this—like another woman her father drove away."

I was not expecting this at all. I thought he would want to talk about Friday night, that maybe he would apologise and acknowledge that he had acted badly, but no ... instead, he was showing his vulnerable and broken side. An emotion—pride, relief?—swelled my chest when I realised I'd been right about him. The attitude was an act he put on because once upon a time, a woman he loved so much, probably Maja's mother, had betrayed him, and he couldn't let that go.

Giggles came from the living room, breaking our moment. Spencer's expression changed, growing tense and serious once again. He took another step towards me, his ripped, muscular body towering over mine.

"Spencer, I'm not planning to go on holiday with you and then flirt with other men. Also, I'm not planning to leave. I couldn't do it to Maja," I admitted.

"Good, because you know I care about you, and I can promise you I'll be on my best behaviour," he said.

His lips were only inches away from mine, and I didn't think I could resist ...

"Even when you are close, I promise you I won't try to tuck your hair behind your ear like this."

My breath hitched when he moved a wayward lock behind my ear, sending a tremor down my spine. I parted my lips as he leaned closer, brushing his cheek with mine. I shuddered.

"What else won't you do?" I whispered. I was playing with fire, but I needed to hear more, feel more, discover more.

"And I won't say that I want to peel your little bikini off you with my teeth when we are alone at the beach, then make you scream my name while you ride my face all night long. No, I won't do any of those things because you're still my nanny and I'm your boss."

Chapter Twenty-Seven

Spencer

Laura rushed out of the kitchen, all flustered and breathless. She'd pushed me again, and I'd shared some things with her about myself that no one else knew. She needed to understand what she was doing to me, but at the same time we couldn't cross that line, at least not just yet.

After the conversation in the kitchen, Laura and I fell into a new routine. I could no longer avoid her, so we had dinners together while I watched her, indulging myself by just being in her presence. We talked, laughed, and argued as it was easier this way, even though I was dying inside when we accidentally touched or if I caught her staring at me.

The conversation between her and Sarah, the crazy pink-haired nanny, kept playing on my mind throughout the whole week. I didn't think I was ready to have another child, but if that meant that I could keep her with me, then perhaps this was a good plan. A mad plan, to be sure, but one that seemed plausible in my twisted mind. Because still, the thought of being in a committed relationship had me sweating with anxiety.

On a personal level, I was so messed up.

On Saturday, late afternoon, after spending a few hours with MP Stearne and his twin boys at his home, I felt at ease. We had only interacted briefly before, and he was much younger than me, and quite new to politics. He came across as a nice guy, and most of all, Maja enjoyed being around his sons.

Afterwards, I dropped my daughter off at my mother's, then went straight home. The school term was ending next week, and I needed to pack our bags. I had staff for this but enjoyed doing it all myself; it helped me feel normal after a year of schmoozing and politicking.

We were leaving for Palermo on Friday morning on a private flight, and I was looking forward to this holiday. First, because I could finally relax and get away from my stressful life in London, and second, because I was ready to seduce my infuriating nanny.

She'd become my new obsession. She wanted me, too, so we both needed to get each other out of our systems. This was going to be easy. I had promised her I'd be on my best behaviour while we were away, but my desire for her was destroying the last bits of resilience I had. I was ready to burn the whole world for this woman, if that's what it took to make her mine.

This heatwave wasn't helping my sexual frustration, so once I got home, I had a cold shower because the image of Laura on her knees during that first night we'd met kept invading my memories. Still, I remained semi-hard when I walked back, naked, into my bedroom.

I opened the drawer and looked through my boxers when something caught my eye. I lifted a pair of red knickers and brought them up to my face, thinking that surely there must have been some mistake.

"She wouldn't," I whispered, staring at her knickers. This wasn't the pair I'd accidentally ruined with my cum the other day. Instead of that, she'd left me her red, sexy-as-fuck thong.

Damn it ... of course. She'd figured out I'd stolen her knickers, which meant that she'd come into my bedroom and had gone through my things or maybe she'd done it whilst I'd been away in Sweden. My heart pumped more blood into my dick. I brought them up to my nose and inhaled deeply. Fuck, these knickers had been worn. She smelled incredible, and I remembered her every moan and every move from that time I'd made her come in that dark, empty staff corridor. The only time I'd lost control, the only time I'd had my hands on and in her.

My cock was now rock-hard. Laura was playing a game with me. So I'd play along.

I went to bed and wanked myself off. When I came with a grunt and made a fucking mess everywhere, I only felt good for a few moments because this only took the edge off my dark mood. It wasn't Laura, and after a while, the yearning returned.

I was completely alone on Saturday evening, and me sitting in bed, sniffing my nanny's worn knickers was undeniably pathetic. I was the fucking Prime Minister and good at my job, yet I was so fucked-up personally that I chose not to have a relationship with a woman who could take care of me. This had to change.

She will be mine soon.

* * *

The summer holidays kicked in, and Maja was brimming with excitement about our upcoming trip. We would take a private flight to Sicily, accompanied by my usual security staff. This trip had been meticulously planned for quite some time.

"Daddy, will Uncle Rupert be waiting for us at the airport?" Maja bounced up and down as we drove to the small airport where our jet waited.

Laura gazed out of the window, and I was in a good mood knowing she was coming along.

London's temperatures kept soaring, and Cefalù promised to be even hotter. That didn't matter, though, because I looked forward to reuniting with my family on the island.

"He should be. He has been excited about this trip for a long time." I checked my phone. It was refreshing not to see hundreds of missed calls and text messages from Jeremy, who himself was preparing for his family trip to Florida next week.

When Laura came back on Monday, she'd told me she'd decided to travel with us and said she'd keep taking care of Maja as long as Rupert was all right with her tagging along. I didn't give a fuck what my brother thought, I trusted Laura. He needed to get over the fact that she lived with Veronica at the weekends.

We didn't bring up the subject of stolen panties. I still had her worn pair hidden in my chest of drawers at home and I wasn't planning to give them back unless she called me out on it. This morning she'd showed up on a red summer dress that reached her knees. When we went outside and the wind blew a little, I caught a glimpse of her tanned thighs. The sight made me so insanely hard, it wasn't even funny anymore.

Around half an hour later, we were dropped off at the private airport and taken to the VIP lounge where an additional security team that would travel with us was already waiting. Rupert was there, too. When he saw Laura he didn't look happy at all, so he ushered me to the side to complain.

"I know exactly why you're bringing her along, Spencer." Rupert stood in front of me in a white t-shirt and designer sunglasses.

I watched as Maja showed Laura something she had in her bag.

"So she can look after your niece if we both decide to go out, Rupert. You said it yourself—you won't be with us all the time. Maja was really happy that she was coming, so I don't see the issue?" I glanced at my watch. We would be boarding any minute.

"This isn't about that, Spencer. It's about the fact that you want her. I can see it in your eyes. I know I'm not in a position to give you advice, but you should really think about this before you make your move. You said it yourself. She gets on with Maja, but I doubt very much that Laura is ready to be her mother," Rupert followed my line of vision.

He was right. It was a big step, so I had a lot to consider. This was nothing new.

"Exactly as you said, this is none of your business, little brother, so get off your high horse and just enjoy this break while you can," I said, then quickly added, "Did you speak to her roommate, Veronica? How are things with the woman you have been obsessing over for the past two years?"

"I don't fucking want to talk about it," he snapped.

I laughed, then slapped him in the back. "I thought so."

He walked away then. I knew he was worried about me, but I had never felt this way about anyone else. Rupert wouldn't understand because he had never been in a serious relationship before.

Once we'd boarded, I headed to the back of the plane where Laura was seated. I spoke to the pilot for a few minutes before take-off, to make sure everything was all right. He was the same one who'd flown us to Sicily last year, and it was good to see that familiar face again. Maja sat in the middle with Rupert, who was setting up a card game for her, probably so she wouldn't get bored.

I sat next to Laura even though there were plenty of other

seats around. The security personnel took up space at the front of the aircraft. Laura was reading.

"What do you want, Spencer? There are plenty of other seats available, and I don't like being disturbed when I'm reading." She stared at me with her beautiful green eyes that haunted me in my dreams.

"What? I want to sit next to you, and trust me, I don't have any hidden agenda." I smiled, then grabbed the book off her and glanced at the title. One of those steamy romance books she liked.

"Hey, give it back. You're not the target audience." She tried to get it back.

But I was busy skimming over a few interesting passages. I was shocked at how graphic they were.

"What the hell are you even reading? Porn? I pegged you for a thriller-loving kind of girl." I read a very graphic part where he was thrusting into her from behind.

"I enjoy reading steamy romance when I'm travelling, thank you very much," she said, still attempting to take the book off me.

I skimmed a few more pages and then came across a word that made little sense.

"All right, so what does this mean? STFUATTDLAGG? Is there even a word like that in the English dictionary?" I pointed at it on the page.

Laura finally managed to take her book back and quickly closed it, looking flustered.

"Nothing that you should concern yourself about," she said. "Only romance readers and BookTokers know what it means."

"Come on, tell me now. I'm curious." I pulled out my phone.

Moments later, when the captain switched off the seat belt sign, she got up and unceremoniously went to sit a few seats away from me, crossing her incredible legs. From my vantage point, I could stare at her with no one noticing.

"Figure it out yourself, because I really want to finish reading this scene," she said. "Please don't talk to me for the rest of the flight."

I decided to go spend time with Maja then and didn't actually get the chance to Google the term until right before we landed. That was a bad idea, though, because I was so fucking turned on by what I discovered I had to adjust myself on the seat a few times. Also, I didn't want to disembark the aircraft with a raging hard-on. That acronym literally meant: shut the fuck up and take that dick like a good girl. Of course, I was already picturing Laura on her knees while she was choking on my cock.

Fuck, these romance novels were lethal. I was planning to read some to see if I could become one of the heroes from her favourite book. The next six weeks seemed promisingly intense ...

Chapter Twenty-Eight

Laura

Once in Sicily, a driver waited to take us to our villa in a limo. Just before leaving the UK, I'd received a call from Mrs Forrester. She shared that the family was contemplating moving back from the States, as the children weren't happy. This unexpected development left me speechless. Mrs Forrester enquired about my new job and urged me to consider returning as their nanny if they moved back around November. I promised to think about it, and she mentioned calling me again in September.

What timing. While I loved Maja, I had to consider my own needs. Perhaps, if I took another job, I could contemplate a relationship with Spencer. Right now, though, I would focus on enjoying the holiday.

My excitement peaked as we reached the villa after a long drive. Spencer had chosen an incredible place for us to stay on the side of a hill. It overlooked the sea and boasted an amazing infinity pool.

The massive property was fully equipped and surrounded by lemon and orange trees, and even had a playground for Maja. I couldn't believe this would be my home for the next six weeks.

"Wow, this place is so much nicer than the one we had last year. Dad, you've done well," Maja said, glancing around the villa, captivated by its charm.

Spencer remained outside, engrossed in conversation with his security team.

"Your dad did a great job choosing this place. We'll definitely have fun here," Rupert commented.

"I'm going inside to see if I can find my room." Maja broke away and a moment later ran inside.

Rupert followed me until we reached the barbecue area.

"I think we should clear the air between us since we'll be living together for the next six weeks. I'm proposing a ceasefire." I turned to face him.

Removing his sunglasses, Rupert studied me for a moment. "What are your plans with Spencer? Are you aiming to make him fall in love with you?"

"Make him fall in love with me? Do you realise how ridiculous that sounds? I'm here to help him care for Maja. There's nothing going on between your brother and I, and there never will be," I stated firmly.

"There's nothing between you two for now, but who knows? It's hot in here, and I know Spencer. He wants you badly, and he'll drive you crazy until you give in," Rupert asserted.

Warmth suddenly spread throughout my body.

This was precisely what Spencer had been doing over the past few weeks—driving me crazy. Rupert went on to reveal Spencer's fear of commitment after Maja's mother had left him abruptly, nearly causing him to lose everything. He shared intimate details about Spencer's past. I listened and realised why Spencer often wore a mask. Despite everything, Rupert obviously cared about the wellbeing of the people he loved.

"There's nothing going on between us. I've been in the spotlight before, and it ended badly. I'm trying to be professional around Spencer. Also, I'm not sure if I'll even stay in this job after the summer." I felt compelled to be transparent, too.

He scrutinised me as he ran his hand over his jaw. "I knew it. So you're planning to bail on them. Do you realise how much this will crush Maja?"

"No, it's not like that. The family I worked for before might be returning to the country. I got a call a few hours ago. Nothing is set in stone, Rupert. Mrs Forrester wasn't certain they were coming back, which is why I don't want to talk about this right now. I don't want to risk Spencer's career. This type of scandal could ruin him. We started off on the wrong foot, and I'd like to change that for his daughter's sake," I explained, regretting that I had even mentioned anything.

Despite the uncertainty, Spencer was a complicated man. He avoided commitment, and whilst I had never been more attracted to anyone, I didn't want to get burned again.

I extended my hand, wanting to bury the hatchet between us. After a moment's hesitation, Rupert finally shook it.

"I get it, but whatever you do or don't do, don't let him get too involved if this goes beyond ... whatever. Spencer wants you, and trust me, he always gets what he wants," he added before walking to the villa.

I took a deep breath and wiped the sweat off my forehead. Rushing back to the house, I found Maja, and we took a thorough tour of the villa. We had a quick lunch after we unpacked, and then, finally, we were all able to relax outside by the pool. Rupert had gone out to make a phone call, and Spencer was still in his room, so Maja and I hung out.

We jumped into the pool, splashing and laughing until Rupert showed up and took over from me. Exiting the pool, I yawned, realising I was pretty tired after the flight.

Veronica had insisted I pack only sexy bikinis in order to drive Spencer crazy. She must have put a few of her swimming costumes inside my bag when I wasn't looking, because when I was emptying my suitcase earlier on, I couldn't find anything that was appropriate to wear. Everything was skimpy or barely covered my boobs. I was pretty skinny and had no boobs, so there was nothing to show off really, but these scraps of material I now had on didn't leave much to the imagination. I also found a box of my birth control pills that I thought I'd forgotten to bring. I stared at it for a long moment, trying to figure out if Veronica had put them in for me. She must have, because I always forgot a ton of stuff when I was going away somewhere, and I was suddenly glad she'd put them in my luggage. I went to the doctor a week before we'd left. I knew nothing would happen between Spencer and me, but as a precaution I'd decided to start taking birth control pills. We were going to be away in paradise, it was going to be hot, and I definitely didn't want to get pregnant just yet, so I wanted to be in control if anything did happen between us.

I glanced up at the second-floor terrace, catching Spencer sitting on a chair and staring directly at me, undressing me with his eyes. Swallowing hard, I raced to the lounger and wrapped my towel around me. Oh my God—how was I going to survive this?

I tried to focus on my book, and when he finally showed up, I was too turned on reading my spicy novel to look up at him without his shirt on.

Dear God, give me strength.

I was drooling over his muscular, oiled body. Spencer was an exceptionally handsome man. He reminded me of a Greek god, and I imagined he couldn't possibly be bad at sex. A man built like Adonis would worship my body. The truth was that at this point, I was convinced I could orgasm by simply staring at him.

My phone rang, and Spencer jumped straight to the pool, and when I glanced back at the screen I saw it was Veronica. Rupert, Spencer, and Maja were all splashing in the water, so I thought it was safe to talk. Also I had to thank her for the birth control. Veronica was a godsend.

"Hey, girl." I waved at her in the video call.

It looked like she was at a pool party with our other friend. They seemed tipsy.

"Ah, hey, Laura, how is it going? We want to know everything. How was the flight and how is the villa?" she asked.

"The villa is absolutely gorgeous. It's scorching hot, and we have the most amazing view. What can I say? I'm in paradise." I took my sunglasses off.

"God, we aren't jealous at all. Come on, turn the phone so we can see everything." Veronica giggled.

I bit my bottom lip, wondering what to do. I hadn't told her that Rupert was here with us.

"Later. Spencer is playing in the pool with Maja, and I don't want to pry too much," I said. "I'll speak to you guys when there's no one here."

"No, come on, show us Mr Prime Minister. We need to see if he's as gorgeous without his shirt on as he's in his suit," Veronica insisted.

Then Jess grabbed the phone.

"Dear Lord, Laura, we need to see him right away! Do you understand I might never see this man without his shirt on ever again?" she said.

Luckily enough, I sat quite far from them, so they wouldn't hear me.

"Stop it! This is really not a good time," I pressed.

"Laura Watkins, show us the hot Prime Minister. Otherwise

I'm going to book the first available flight to Sicily and surprise you there!" Veronica danced to the music.

Fuck, she would not let this go, so I swapped the screen, and they both had a view of the pool.

"Get closer. I can't see anything from this angle," Jess shrieked.

I shook my head and walked around, hoping the men and Maja would not notice because this was truly embarrassing.

"I'm zooming in, just calm down," I said.

"No, just get closer," Jess added.

I couldn't help myself and rolled my eyes.

"This is the view from the villa. It's absolutely breathtaking, and we haven't even been out yet." I tried to distract them both.

"Fuck the view, Laura. Where is he? Just zoom onto him so we can get a proper look," Jessica said.

I sighed and slowly turned around, not realising that Maja must have gotten out when I was showing the girls the view. Then I zoomed just when both Spencer and Rupert were coming out of the pool.

My heart thudded, and my breathing hitched as I stared at Spencer. Everything was suddenly happening in slow motion. Water dripped down his body, past the trail of hair and over the swimsuit, leading to his ... cock. I was in a trance, unable to take my eyes off him, while Veronica and Jess went radio silent.

"Laura, what are you doing? Are you filming us?' Spencer brought me back to reality. He had noticed me standing there, of course, holding my phone up.

"Jesus, Laura, why didn't you tell me that Rupert is there, too? What the hell?" Veronica said.

"Who the hell is Rupert? Oh my God, he's gorgeous!" Jess commented.

"His brother is much better-looking. Now get out of my way," Veronica snapped.

I pressed on the screen to flip it back to me, but the buttons weren't working.

"Veronica, is that you? So, are you spying on me now?" Rupert got close enough to notice who I was talking to.

Shit, I needed to switch off this phone as soon as possible, but then he snatched it and stalked away.

"Damn ..." I said to Spencer, who towered over me, still dripping wet. "Why are you staring at me like that?"

"What? I'm admiring your gorgeous body," he replied with a smirk. "But you really have to do something about that bikini because I'll be walking around with a permanent hard-on if you keep this up."

A flush crept over my cheeks. I reminded myself to keep breathing. I was too turned on to think straight, especially when he was standing so close.

"What do you suggest I do in this heat? Wear a coat?"

"I suggest that you stop looking at me like that if you're not planning to do anything about it," he growled.

Despite how flustered I was on the inside, I tried to play it cool, so I placed my hands on my hips and stared at him.

"And how am I looking at you?"

His nostrils flared, and his frown deepened. We were

standing way too close to each other again, while Maja was still splashing in the pool—she must have jumped back in. I was so glad she couldn't hear us.

"Like you want me to stop being a real fucking gentleman and demand that you sneak into my room late at night, so we can finally fuck each other's brains out." He sounded like he had been thinking about this for a very long time.

I swallowed hard, staring directly into his prominent blue eyes. Speechless.

"And what would happen if I did sneak into your room late at night?" I whispered when I found my voice again. I should back off, but Spencer had put a spell on me, and my body was rooted to the spot.

"I'll make you moan my name while you ride my face," he whispered back. "So please, woman, stop acting like you don't feel this incredible pull between us and let me in, or I'll wait outside your door every night until you do."

Chapter Twenty-Nine

Spencer

This was going to be so fucking hard because Laura's tiny bikinis were going to tip me over the edge of my obsession. I wanted to peel them off her with my teeth and then taste her dripping-wet pussy.

That evening, after Rupert had cooked our evening meal, we sat at the table. Maja had been chatting animatedly throughout dinner while the three of us maintained an awkward silence, occasionally stealing glances at each other. I didn't know what Rupert had said to Veronica, but he'd nearly thrown Laura's phone into the pool. The details of what was going on between them remained a mystery.

The idea of cutting the holiday short crossed my mind. I wasn't sure if I could deal with blue balls all the fucking time. Laura kept peeking at me, pretending to eat but barely touching her food. Eventually, she excused herself to take Maja upstairs.

I was tired, too. I had promised my daughter a tour of the coastal area and towns beyond the city of Palermo. Another day, we'd be heading to Mount Etna, too.

I was exhausted and ready to head to bed, but I wanted to know why my brother was acting so strangely when it came to Veronica. The opportunity finally arrived when, in the evening, he brought beers and we sat outside on the terrace. We chatted about mundane things until I point-blank asked him what was going on between him and Laura's roommate since they'd finally been reunited with each other.

Rupert had been talking about a certain red-haired woman from the moment he'd returned from Greece two years ago. He had tried to search for her in London, with no luck.

He took a swig of his beer, looking defeated. "Nothing at the moment. We talked, but I can't get over the fact that she lied to me."

"How did she lie to you?" I probed, recalling the night I'd mistaken Laura for an escort.

Massaging the back of his neck, he hesitated before saying, "When we met at that bar in Greece, she told me she worked as an air hostess. We got a bit wasted before going back to my hotel. The sex was incredible, mind-blowing."

It didn't surprise me that Veronica had lied to him. She was an exclusive escort, and honesty wasn't her forte. "And you found out what she did for a living when you saw her with Laura in the club after that video went viral?"

"Some guy showed me the video, and I planned to call her. I had already invested the money in Emperor before I knew she worked for Matthews. When he mentioned her exclusive clients, I felt betrayed. I told her to take the video down, and we argued," Rupert explained, his disappointment clear. "I know I told you not to mess with the nanny, but I think you should go for it now."

"What? Earlier you said it was a bad idea."

"This tension between you two is getting to me, man. Just fuck her and get it over with."

"Why the sudden change of heart?"

He continued staring out at the view, the sunset so pretty with lights coming on as far as the eye could see. "She might not stay with you ... Listen, if I tell you this, it has to stay between us."

"Fine," I replied through gritted teeth.

He hesitated before dropping a bombshell. "She said her old employers might be coming back from the States, and they're pressuring her to go back to work for them again."

I got up, running my hand through my damp hair. This couldn't be happening. "And she told you she's going to leave us? When the fuck did she say this, Rupert?"

"Calm down. If she leaves, it won't happen until November. Laura has made no decisions yet, but she's considering it." He tried to placate me.

"That's why you want me to fuck with her, because you

know she'll be gone by the end of the year?" I asked, incredulous.

"Well, yeah. You guys sleep together with no strings attached, and then she'll be gone. If you want to keep dating her, you technically won't be her employer anymore so it won't be inappropriate. Think about this, Spencer. It's a good option. Laura believes she's controlling the situation. No one will get hurt, and you can avoid a scandal. It's a win-win if you ask me."

I exhaled, still grappling with the shock that Laura was considering leaving. In a way, my brother was right. Sex could ease the tension between us. But I couldn't fathom her leaving Maja. I wanted her more than I'd admit, and the thought of her moving on was unsettling.

"I'll think about it, brother, and I appreciate you telling me this," I said.

"I'm going to hit the sack. Your daughter has tired me out, but I'm looking forward to tomorrow." He patted me on the back before walking away.

I remained seated on the sunlounger, gazing out at the breathtaking view of the island as I recalled the promise I'd made to myself a year ago: to have a woman willing to be the mother of my daughter and share my passion. Last year, I was afraid to take that step and I was so fed up with fucking around, but now I finally had a chance to change my life.

* * *

I was in touch with a few of my cousins already. Fabio, one of my second cousins, was taking his family on a cruise, so we planned to see each other once they came back. The next two weeks were very active, with security managing the planned trips admirably, but I made sure that we had a few relaxing days when we did nothing.

The day after our arrival, we all went sightseeing in Cefalù, a small but touristy town in the north. I had a feeling Laura was slowly falling in love with the island. She was amazed and really enjoyed visiting the towns and historical sites. Things between us were still unclear, and I thought sex might complicate everything further. I was the one being hesitant, not wanting to ruin things, so I made sure to be on my best behaviour.

Over the next two weeks, we visited Palermo, La Kalsa, Vucciria, Il Capo, and Albergheria. Sicilian culture fascinated Maja. This wasn't the first time we had been to Italy, but the other night she'd told me that so far, this was her favourite trip because Laura was here with us. On top of that, the food was incredible. We had a full-time housekeeper, and I had to admit, her homemade food tasted out of this world. Throughout the day, when we travelled, we stopped at traditional restaurants that had been vetted beforehand and offered a private area for our group.

We stayed clear of busy places. I was having a great time with my family, and I wasn't willing to disturb our dynamic. It seemed like even Rupert was enjoying himself.

Today, we were sunbathing on a tiny private beach near Syracuse. One of my security personnel, who was actually from there, had recommended the place. It was operated by a small hotel and not open to the public. This meant we didn't have to worry about crowds, and we were able to secure a few hours of private bliss.

Marco, my security guy, had arranged it all. We entered the hotel through a VIP entrance and were led right out to the beach area. A true paradise. In the distance, I spotted at least three lifeguards and several staff members who were walking around with trays. It was a perfect spot for an afternoon chill-out in this heat.

"Spencer, this is truly amazing." Laura sighed and touched my arm when we stood on the sand, looking out at the crystal-blue waters.

Even Maja seemed impressed.

Laura's touch sent a jolt of heat through my groin. I was trying to remain calm lately, but that didn't stop me from checking her out everywhere we went. She was so sexy ...

"Come on, Daddy, I want to get in the water," Maja said, yanking me out of my thoughts.

Laura smiled at me, then glanced at my arm as if she'd only just realised she had her hand on me, and quickly pulled away.

"Ladies first," I said. "Just make sure you watch your step, Laura, as there are rocks in the water."

She nodded, then followed my brother and Maja.

This was going to be so very hard.

Chapter Thirty

Laura

I was drowning! Water was getting into my nose and mouth. Panic crushed through me as I tried to reach the surface of the water, throwing my hands around and kicking my feet. This was pathetic, I didn't want to die like this. Of all the places in the world, I would end my life on this beautiful island. I didn't even realise how strong the current was, and the waves were pushing me farther up. I'd swum all the way here because I thought I'd seen Maja for a second.

Another waved crushed over me, and then a split second later someone was pulling me towards the shore. I was so disorientated that I was certain that for a second I must have blacked out, because it felt like an eternity before my feet moved through the sand, then a voice was saying to me, "Tieni duro, bella, adesso ci sono io."[1]

I didn't understand anything that was being said. I glanced to my right, focusing in on the most gorgeous man who was carrying me out of the water. He had his arm hooked around my waist while I was coughing, completely disorientated.

"Laura ... fuck, are you all right? I'm here, I've got her now," another familiar voice said as I collapsed onto the warm sand.

Soon after, Spencer was kneeling next to me, looking scared. I had never seen him so terrified.

"I thought I saw Maja in the water and I panicked," I said, still coughing while Spencer was touching me everywhere like he wanted to make sure I wasn't injured.

"Bella, you must be careful, the sea is dangerous," the lifeguard that was smoothing his tar-dark hair said, staring at me with concern, too.

Then he kneeled next to Spencer, and I suddenly felt better, being protected by the two most gorgeous men I'd ever laid my eyes on.

"I tried to get to you when I heard the screams, but luckily *bagnino*[2] here managed to pull you out," Spencer said and glared at the lifeguard who was smiling at me.

I tried to wipe the water out of my eyes and calm down my racing heart. At least I could breathe now, but that was scary. I'd swum way too far, panicking because I thought a girl around Maja's age was her, and when I realised that this child was fine, I'd lost control a little.

"Are you sure you're all right?" Spencer asked. "I'm going to get security, and we'll take you to the hospital just to be on the safe side."

"It's okay, I'm all right. I was swimming too fast," I said, all of a sudden overwhelmed that Spencer was so worried about me. "No need to go to the hospital."

"No ... no hospital, Bella is fine, really," the lifeguard said in a thick Italian accent.

Spencer shot him another irritated gaze, probably because the lifeguard had got to me first. It was so sweet of him that he was trying to rescue me. Maybe he did truly care about me after all.

"I'm really sorry. This won't happen again, and you don't have to worry. I'm really fine," I said, feeling like a complete idiot.

"What's your name, *bella*? You are very beautiful. You from England, yes?"

"Il suo nome e Laura, e siamo tutti riconoscenti. Adesso ci penso io a lei,"[3] Spencer replied quickly for me.

And of course, I didn't understand a word he'd said.

The lifeguard shot Spencer a surprised look, then he muttered something to himself and suddenly stood.

"What did you just say to him? I hope you weren't rude, and I had no idea you could speak fluent Italian," I asked him.

"He's done his job, so I thanked him for saving your life," Spencer explained and added, "I should have been in the water before him."

"He's husband, yeah?" the man asked.

Spencer shot him another glare. God, he needed to calm down. The man was probably just curious.

"Sì, sono suo marito, e siamo tutti grati per il tuo aiuto, ma adesso ci sono io,"[4] he said, his tone dismissive.

"*Ma quelle buone sono sempre prese.*[5]" The lifeguard sighed. Then, with a typical exaggerated hand gesture, he walked away.

"What did you tell him?" I asked.

"First I thanked him once again that he saved you, and then I confirmed that you were my wife," Spencer replied.

I slapped him on the chest.

"Your wife? What the hell? Spencer, he's a lifeguard and he was only doing his job, you didn't need to be so abrupt with him."

The sun was burning my neck. I had hoped this was going to be a calm and relaxing day, but as usual, shit had to happen. He was so close to me that it was unnerving, but he was making me feel safe and protected, which I wasn't really expecting because he was always so guarded.

"I got distracted and I should have paid more attention to you in the first place," he said and then skimmed his hand down my arm. "He was right about one thing, you should have been more careful. You could have easily drowned."

"Can we drop this now? I panicked a bit, but I'm fine, so you don't need to worry about me anymore, Spencer," I said, more forcefully, because he was making a huge deal out of this when he didn't need to.

The same lifeguard strolled past us again, and he winked at

me. I flashed him a thankful smile, because I felt bad that Spencer had been so short with him just a moment ago.

"That lifeguard was hitting on you," Spencer said, looking between me and the lifeguard who was now heading away.

Damn, did he see the wink?

"He wasn't hitting on me, he was just being nice," I said and then added, "And what if he was? This shouldn't be any of your concern anyway."

I appreciated that he was worried about me, but we weren't together. I was still working as his daughter's nanny. Besides, the lifeguard was the only other man here. Well, apart from the hotel and security staff.

"When you're with me, you're working, so I won't allow another fucking guy to hit on you, Laura. You know I'm working through my issues. I want you only for myself. Nothing has changed since that last time at my place, and I told you I'll be exclusive with you," he said. His clear-blue eyes darkened and clouded like a brewing storm.

"No, I don't know how you feel about me because you have never actually told me. Besides, we aren't doing this right now, not here," I snapped, suddenly really pissed off that he was acting like he owned me. "And in this moment, I'm not working for you. Maja is with your brother, therefore, I'm on holiday and I can do whatever I want. That includes flirting with whomever I wish. So watch me, because I'm going to do exactly that!"

I stormed away, fuming. What was I to do? Get far away from Spencer, that's what.

The man was super protective and caring—granted, he

ticked all the right boxes for panty-melting material—but he was also an insufferable arsehole.

Finally, I spotted the familiar face of the lifeguard again. Spencer Banks was a pain in my backside, and I was so done with him acting like a jealous wanker. He'd had a chance to make a move so many times, but he'd chosen not to. I wasn't his therapist or personal assistant. He knew exactly what I wanted, and I was done waiting.

I was just about to shout and wave to the hot lifeguard when a strong force lifted me off the sand, threw me over a shoulder, and carried me like I weighed nothing more than feathers.

"Spencer Banks, put me down right now or I swear to God I'll scream!" I shouted, pounding on his back.

But he ignored me. He sprinted up the steps.

"Spencer, where the hell are you going, man?" Rupert called out.

"Take care of Maja and tell security down there I'll be okay and will meet the others at the villa. I'm going to take Laura home. I think she has sunstroke! Will send the car back so you can get home later," he said while I pummelled him hard on his back.

"I don't have sunstroke. Put me down right in this minute!" I roared.

But he just chuckled.

"Signore, a sta donna non piace essere trattata in sto modo, stile uomo delle caverne."[6] someone commented. It was probably one of the older Italian guys who worked for the hotel.

"Sto portando mia moglie a casa. Che problema c'è?"[7] Spencer stopped for a moment.

The man raised his hands in a gesture of surrender. "*No, nessun problema, signore, anche se non sembra molto felice in questo momento.*"[8]

"*Non si preoccupi, quando arriviamo a casa, sarà la donna più felice del mondo!*"[9] Spencer sounded thoroughly amused.

Fucker, I wanted to kill him, especially when laughter sounded at my expense. I lifted my head, catching sight of two men in uniform using dynamic hand movements, pointing at us with an open hand or making a thumbs-up gesture like he was showing approval and enthusiasm.

"Put me down. Put me down right now! You're going to injure yourself carrying me in this heat!" I yelled.

But he didn't take me seriously at all. "You weigh next to nothing, and I'm quite enjoying having your arse next to my face," he growled.

Although I could tell that he was struggling to walk. These steps were steep, and it was a hell of a trek back up.

The comment about my arse infuriated me more. Spencer eventually put me down. He must have asked one of the agents to grab my clothes, because when we finally got back to the road, Spencer handed me my dress and barked at me to put it on. I snatched it off him, feeling like I was going to lose it with him if he didn't calm down, but I put it on, because I didn't want to parade around in my bikini in front of his security personnel. Then he instructed his two agents who'd stayed to get the car ready, to take us back to the villa.

I was too angry to even look at him.

"I can get a taxi. I don't want to be anywhere near you right now," I spat.

Lorenzo gestured for me to get inside, but I folded my arms over my chest and refused to move. I was too furious to be told what to do.

"Get in that car right now or I'll shove you inside myself, then strip off that fucking thing you call a bikini and spank you hard on the back seat while poor Lorenzo and my men watch!"

Did he just say what I thought I heard him say? There was no way he'd do something like that, but his gaze openly dared me to defy him, so I got in.

My palm was itching to slap him, so I closed my eyes and counted to five in my head. We spent the rest of the way home in complete silence. There was so much I wanted to tell him, though, because Spencer Banks drove me absolutely batshit crazy. And today, he'd finally crossed the line.

If Mrs Forrester called me again today and asked me to come back, I wouldn't even hesitate. I would hand Spencer a week's notice and then leave. I knew this would upset Maja, but I could no longer tolerate her father.

When we arrived, I got out of the car and ran back to the villa, wanting nothing more than to lock myself in my room, but Spencer was right behind me, following me into the kitchen. He dismissed his men, and they headed to their rooms.

"You have no right to treat me like this. Do you fucking understand? I'm not yours and never will be!" I poked my finger into his chest as hard as I could.

He stared at me with his usual quiet intensity, as though waiting for me to finish my tantrum.

"That's debatable, woman, because when I say that you're mine, you are fucking mine, so don't even try arguing with me," he said.

I gasped. We were standing so close, our faces only inches away, and the air was crackling with rippling energy.

"I'm done playing games. I know you stole my knickers, but this ..." I stepped away from him and pointed between us, "is ending today because I can't take it anymore. I'm going to ask Lorenzo to drive me to the airport right now. I've had enough of you acting like a horny, teenage caveman, but not actually having the maturity or guts to say what it is you want. We have nothing else to discuss, Prime Minister. We are done!"

My God, it felt good to finally be able to get that off my chest. I turned around, heading towards my room. At least that was my plan, but it seemed Spencer had other ideas.

"Not so fast." He gripped my elbow and abruptly spun me around. His eyes were again stormy blue, reflecting raw, unhinged desire.

I felt it from my core to my toes—he was untamed and completely feral as he groaned.

"Fuck this, it's been long enough."

My brain struggled to register the sudden turn of events, but my instincts understood.

Spencer seized the back of my head and crashed his lips into mine in a fierce and passionate kiss. There was no going back from this.

Chapter Thirty-One

Spencer

I had been waiting for so long to have her and I had been picturing this perfect moment for what felt like eternity, so because of that I was planning to take my time with her, draw it out as long as humanly possible.

I wanted to savour this moment forever.

Laura tasted like midsummer rain, a raging storm in the ocean, and sweet like vanilla. Her scent dominated all my senses.

She was right. I was so fucking done with being so close to her and not doing anything about it. Absolutely fucking done.

"I'll say you're right because I'm finally going to do what I meant to do when I had you pinned against the wall in that club." I pulled away briefly as I could barely catch my breath. My lungs were burning as I stared at her slender frame and those stunning green eyes that were filled with fire for me.

She was mad at me, but she had no idea how bat shit crazy she was driving me when she was annoyed.

The moment I picked her up and threw her over my shoulder, I knew that today we would finally fuck each other's brains out and nothing was stopping me from fulfilling that promise. That kiss blew my mind, but it wasn't nearly enough. Her swollen lips were like a new drug–fresh and addictive. I was already imagining my life where she was mine and I was hers.

Laura was breathtaking, especially when she was furious.

"Do what exactly, Spencer?" she asked, staring at me with her swollen lips and flushed cheeks.

"Don't ask any questions right now, because I am extremely mad that I waited so long to have you. I want you, I crave you, I wanted you from the moment I laid my eyes on you in Elm street and today I am going to feast on your pussy like my life depended on it," I stated.

Before she could argue or talk about this, I gripped her waist and lifted her onto the kitchen worktop, slamming her arse on it. She gasped, staring at me with those eyes that melted every doubting thought away. "Spread your amazing legs for me."

She obeyed, after the merest hesitation, her gaze wide. I helped her take off her dress then removed my t-shirt straight after, I didn't think I could do it fast enough. I needed her naked so I could worship her beautiful body.

At last, we were skin to skin. She was right in front of me, wearing only a pair of tiny red bikini bottoms. I was completely lost. Everything about her was soft and delicate, she was like a blossoming flower, her nipples perky and firm. Fuck, I went hard instantly, ready to suck on them.

"Kiss me again," she pleaded.

I groaned because I was going to do so much more than kiss her. It was too hard to hold any kind of restraint that I had in me not to worship her body.

"I'm just about to ruin that pussy of yours. I have been wanking myself silly, sniffing your knickers every fucking night because I couldn't stop thinking about you spread in front of my face, your cunt dripping wet for me." I ripped off her skimpy red bikini bottoms, then I trailed my hands over her hips, moving my fingers over the delicate skin on her stomach until she took a quick sharp breath.

"Touch me, kiss me, do something before I lose my mind," she whispered, giving me a look that totally made me want to drop to my knees for this woman and do anything that she asked for.

"Sweetheart, I'm going to do a lot more than that," I promised, then grabbed her chin and pulled her towards me to kiss her slowly, devouring every inch of her smart mouth. She plunged her tongue into my mouth, her fingers sliding into my hair, while I caressed her side. I moved my hand to cup her left breast, then played with her nipple while kissing her with urgent need.

Slowly my fingers dropped down to her stomach, feeling her

delicate skin, then lowered it further and moved it over her drenched slit. She flinched on the marble worktop as though my fingers burned her.

"Fuck baby, you're soaking wet for me already," I murmured, slowly rubbing her clit gently at first while I kissed her neck and her collar bone before moving further down and taking her right nipple into my mouth.

"Spencer, shit, this feels amazing," she moaned as I sucked on her nipples like it was the most luxurious sweet.

We found a steady rhythm, but it was not enough ... it never seemed to be enough. I found her mouth again and we kissed, our tongues dancing, while we clawed at each other's bodies.

I wanted to fucking admire her for a second, take my time like I promised myself to, with my forehead on hers, I had the perfect view down her glorious body. I took a few calming breaths, but Laura seemed to be impatient, trying to grab my cock with her small hands.

"No so fast, I know you want me, but I have been waiting months for this moment, so let me admire your beautiful body for a little while longer," I told her. She bit her bottom lip, the flush on her cheeks spreading further. She was so fucking cute when she was shy.

I took a step back, my eyes roaming over her body. I wasn't sure about how I was managing to control myself right now, because I was seconds away from fucking her until she couldn't walk.

"Spencer, I'm so wet, please fuck me," she pleaded, making me insanely hard. I dragged my hand over my chin.

"Lie down. I'm going to have a feast first," I ordered and she obeyed me instantly. "I am starved and I want to eat you out until you can't take it anymore."

I drew her closer to me and bent down so her pussy was right in line with my face. She was perfect. I inhaled the scent of her drenched sex, digging my fingers into her hips, she smelled exactly like I thought she would–absolutely fucking perfect.

I started kissing her soft, supple legs, moving quickly up to her thighs, biting and nibbling, until my mouth was on that intimate spot. I dragged my fingers over her slit, seeing that she was soaking wet for me until she moaned, urging me to use my mouth to make her come.

"Impatient aren't we?" I teased her and before she could respond, I dived in, licking her clit in a slow rhythm. She tasted fucking delicious. My pre-cum leaked down my cock.

Laura moaned, as I kept moving my tongue over her slit, slowly circling her engorged clit. Her juices were smeared all over my face as I stuck my tongue into her hole, fucking her until her cum was dripping down my chin. Her loud muffling noises were driving me crazy with need.

She was ready to come for me, but I was trying to prolong it, stopping and slowing down a little. I wanted to tease her for longer, because she tasted so fucking good, and I was addicted to her delicious pussy.

I continued to lick, nibble, and suck on her clit, holding her thighs steady on either side of my head. I pulled away for a second to look at her, spread on the kitchen counter, breathing hard and trying to comprehend how I got so fucking lucky. This woman was incredible. I dived back in, sucking intensely on her clit until her whole body tensed, and her back arched as I teased her with my tongue, plunging in and out of her.

"Fuck, Spencer! I'm so close," she moaned.

I paused for a moment to catch my breath and steady my erratic breathing. The sight of her parted lips and stormy green eyes greeted me. My heart pounded in my ribcage. I wanted her, I craved her and I finally had her, that emotion alone made me feel fucking invincible.

"Why are you stopping?"

"You will come when I allow you to," I growled, then eased two fingers into her sex.

She dropped her head back and let out a keening moan and I swore under my breath as her cum dripped down my hand. She was so ready for me, I could feel her pulsating sex as I stretched her out. Her nipples were so hard, and I couldn't wait to tease them again. Meanwhile, I sped up my pace with sucking her clit fast while fucking her with my fingers.

She was so responsive, moaning, and urging me to go faster. I couldn't fucking wait to thrust my cock inside her tight pussy.

"God, I hate that you're so good at this," she moaned.

"Shut up and come for me now," I ordered and that was all it took. Laura's thighs and hips trembled, and she gasped for air. I felt her orgasm slam into her like a storm rippling through the ocean. This was exquisite, watching her come apart for me and only me. Soon, her body convulsed as the waves of ecstasy surged through her.

"Spencer! Shit ... Spencer!" She looked so stunning when she came.

I slowed down a bit, but she continued to ride my face. Her pussy throbbed, and she tugged on my hair, and I lost my mind.

"I'm nowhere near done with you yet," I murmured. "Taste yourself on my lips."

Her pupils dilated when I drew her to me and kissed her deeply. I planned to fuck her for hours, make sure that I took my time testing every inch of her body, because she needed to be worshipped. She needed to be fucked until she could barely breathe, until she was so fucked that she would never think of another man, until I was her entire universe.

Moments later, she pulled away from me.

"Wait, what if Rupert comes home with Maja?" she said, glancing around the kitchen. The scent of sweat and sex was intense, wafting around us. I was itching to make her come one more time.

"I'm going to keep my promise and fuck you until you beg me to stop, so go upstairs and wait for me in my bedroom. I will send Rupert a quick text, tell him to take Maja somewhere for the rest of the day," I told her. There was no fucking way that I could keep this short, I needed more time and I hoped my brother would get the message to stay out of the villa.

"If you want me to be obedient, then you have to ask nicely, Mr Prime Minister," she cooed.

Oh, she was so positively fucked. I didn't think I would ever be able to prepare food here ever again without a smile on my face and the memory of her exploding as she rode my face.

I put my hand around her throat and squeezed it hard. I wanted to punish her, I wanted to see the fear in her eyes and experience my torment that I went through in the past few months. Her smart mouth still drove me crazy.

"Do you remember that romance book that you read on the plane?" I asked, releasing the grip so she could breathe again. Her eyes widened.

"STFUATTDLAGG," she whispered and I nodded smirking.

"Shut the fuck up and take that dick like a good girl," I said, letting her know that I had done my research, that I knew she had tested me then. "You're going to do what I say. Fuck, your smart mouth makes me so damn hard."

She grabbed my hand and put it between her legs, smiling.

"I really want to have your cock in my mouth Spencer, you're so beautiful, so handsome," she said as I started rubbing her clit with my thumb. I smirked, it had taken her long enough to admit that she was attracted to me. I knew from the moment I saw her that us ending up together was inevitable.

Fuck, this woman was everything I'd ever wanted. She was going to take my cock like a good girl, but not yet, not right now. First I needed to thrust my cock into her pussy, feeling her come all over it and scream my name because she belonged to me, no other man would ever have her. Moments later, I stopped touching her and lifted her off the island. She was light as a feather.

"Go upstairs, wait for me there. Don't make me repeat myself," I ordered, then licked her juices off my fingers. Laura's pupils dilated as she stared at me with a coy smile, watching how much I was enjoying the scent of her cum.

"Of course, sir, anything for you," she teased, gathering her clothes, then she quickly ran upstairs.

This was it. I couldn't go back from this, even if I tried, because I'd already tasted her. Laura's throbbing pussy was forever ingrained in my memory.

I dragged my hand through my hair and exhaled. This had only been an appetiser—I was starving for so much more. After sending a quick text to Rupert telling him not to hurry, I climbed the stairs.

In the bedroom, I found her sprawled on the bed, naked, flushed, and ready for me. I wanted to be rough with her, to punish her for months of torment, but the temptation of going slowly was too intense. I didn't even think that one evening would ever satisfy me, because Laura was like a new drug–addictive, always craving more.

"On all fours. I don't think I will ever let you leave this room. You're staying where you fucking belong." I shut the door behind me.

She obeyed me right away ... and that fucking arse, God, I was the luckiest guy in the world. I stared at her, my eyes roving over her perfect body, stiff nipples and dripping cunt. I was already hard as a rock.

"What are you going to do to me Mr Prime Minister?" she asked with a smile.

"I will fuck your brains out until you will be begging me to stop because your pussy is sore and swollen," I growled, taking off my boxers and climbing on the bed. I felt her shudder when I placed a kiss on her spine.

"Sounds divine, have you got any condoms?" she asked.

I slapped her arse and my cock glistened with pre-cum. She moaned in response while my palm itched to punish her some more.

"I want to feel your bare pussy coming all over my cock. I'm clean." I leaned close to her cheek. The warmth from her body spread into my cells. The fire in the pit of my stomach made me feel like I was high.

"Okay, I'm on birth control, just so you know" she replied.

Not for long sweetheart, soon we'll be a real family.

Now where did that come from?

"Good to know." I knew that at some point we would have to talk about what was going on between us, because this was a groundbreaking moment for me. I had never allowed myself to feel anything other than pure carnal satisfaction without the emotion. I had never felt more connected to anyone else.

 I nudged her dripping entrance with my cock, ready to ram it into her, but I held off.

"Spencer, I haven't been with anyone for a long time. I don't know if I can meet your expectations," she suddenly stilled, biting down on her lip nervously.

I froze, and quickly pulled her towards me. She avoided my gaze: this wasn't a good sign. I couldn't understand what the hell was going on. She was fucking perfect and I was ready to worship her.

"What are you talking about, Laura?" I grabbed her chin and tilted it up so that she would look at me.

"You must have been with many experienced women before me, and I can't compare—"

"Don't you fucking dare think that you're not enough! Laura, you've changed me in ways none of those other women ever could. You made me open myself to you. With the others it was just sex, only sex and nothing else, but with us, it has never been about that alone," I said, more vulnerable than ever before, but she needed to know that I had never felt emotionally connected to any other women after Samantha. Laura was the only one that made me feel human again, she taught me how to feel. I couldn't stand it that she thought she wasn't experienced enough or good enough for a prick like me. "And trust me, you're driving me fucking crazy. Now, let me fuck you because I might actually die of blue balls if I wait any longer."

She laughed and pushed me onto my back, straddling me.

"God, you're so hot," she muttered and eased herself onto my cock. "Let's do it this way."

I knew that this time I needed to let her take control. She felt self conscious and she didn't have to, because she could never fail me. I rubbed her tits, moving my thumb over the perky nipples as she was sinking deeper onto my shaft. Fuck, her pussy was ready for me. My cock gave another convulsive twitch, and I felt a hot flow of moisture flow from the tip. She was going to be the death of me. I was ready to explode inside her, and I didn't want to. I needed to fuck her slowly, but this task felt impossible.

I gripped her hips tightly, bringing her tits down to my face. This position was perfect because I had her hard nipples right where I wanted them—near my mouth.

"Fuck, you're so tight but so perfect," I said as she rocked over my hips, willing myself not to come just yet.

I was in heaven. She rode me at a languid pace, staring into my eyes. This woman was my goddess, the light at the end of a long, dark tunnel. I licked her left nipple, then drew it into my mouth, sucking it deeply. She picked up the pace and I let her. Those slick, tight inner walls clamped down on my aching cock as I impaled her on it. My vision went a little blurry as her pussy milked my erection with an explosion of tentative ripples.

"Spencer ... oh God, I'm coming again!" she screamed.

I gripped her ass cheeks and thrust up deeper, moving harder, whilst small droplets of sweat appeared on my brows. There was so much I wanted to do to her, but we were going to take this slowly. I willed myself not to come even as she writhed on top of me, but it was impossible as the rush of heat overtook my senses. My balls were so tight, so full and I needed to release my seed.

I squeezed her boobs, pinched her nipples, and pushed my hips harder, falling into the oblivion of ecstasy, coming apart right with her. The orgasm shattered me, breaking me to a million pieces. Laura kept riding me, using my body to shamelessly prolong her own release. Beads of sweat broke over my forehead and back as I tried to fight for control. Both our bodies were vibrating from the orgasm.

"Please can you fuck me again, but this time on all fours?"

she pleaded, looking at me with those wide green doe eyes after a long moment of heavy silence that was broken by our heavy breathing. I smirked, feeling a rush of new energy, so I pushed her off me. I couldn't bloody believe that she was ready to go again. I thought I had great stamina, so I never expected her to challenge me in the bedroom.

"Hold onto the headboard," I ordered as I lifted myself to my knees. Laura's eyes sparkled with mischief and she got on all fours like I'd asked her, then put her hands on the headboard.

"Christ, you're going to be the death of me and this time I am going to fuck you so hard, that my whole security team won't ever look me in the eye again," I told her, situating myself behind.

"Please Spencer, fuck me so hard and deep that I have to think about you every time I have to sit down or walk anywhere," she begged. I was still trying to gather myself, but my breathing was ragged. My pulse was pounding in my ears.

I closed my eyes, ordering myself to calm fucking down, because this time I needed to meet her expectations.

Once I could catch my breath again, I spread her legs, and adjusted her hips until the crown of my cock was aligned with her wet pussy. I pushed my hips forward, seating my entire shaft to the root inside her in one thrust.

She screamed loudly and I brushed my fingers over her spine, then down to the crack of her ass while I waited to regain control of myself. I eased my shaft out then thrust my cock way back into her. I slid my palms up to cup her small breasts as I began to fuck her tight, drenched pussy.

Laura was already on the verge of another orgasm. I could feel her walls contracting, her pussy throbbing around my cock. All she needed was a little pressure in exactly the right spot. I kept pounding into her harder, deeper, then released my hand and dove down between her legs.

"Spencer, I–"

"Hush, you're such a good girl," I praised. "You're so ready to explode all over my cock, aren't you?"

"Yes, but I want it in my mouth, please let me suck you off," she said, surprising me even more. I laughed, then pinched her clit and buried my cock to the hilt until she cried out with pleasure.

"Now come for me baby," I ordered and then she did exactly what I told her. Split seconds later, she fell apart, her whole body convulsing around my shaft, then I was coming with her, ejaculating fiercely, the scorching heat rippled through me in waves as we were both coming apart simultaneously. My release wrenched free, my own pleasure enchanted her own.

It was the most memorable fucking session I'd ever had, yet I already wanted more, needed more.

I must have fallen asleep because when I woke up, it was already dark outside. For a moment, I lay there alone, disoriented and feeling like I was coming down from an unbelievable high. Laura's scent lingered on the pillow, and I stared at the celling, wondering what the fuck I'd just done.

I brushed my hand over my face, trying to gather my thoughts, when voices floated up from outside. I climbed off the bed and went over to the window.

Laura was sitting with Rupert and Maja by the pool.

My cock was fucking sore. I had taken her several times in various different positions. She came hard every time, and now she was downstairs, still playing the role of the dutiful nanny. Now that I'd had her, I had less than four weeks left of the holiday to enjoy my time with her.

After that, there was no way we both could go back to being mere employer and nanny. I was too addicted to her. I wanted to chain her to my bed and never set her free.

I had exactly four weeks to make her fall for me, because I didn't think I could ever let her go, especially not after fucking her ten ways till Sunday. I knew that one time was not enough. It was never going to be enough, no matter how many times I kissed her, touched her, and made love to her, because all these things were never enough. She was the shining star in my gloom, and I would be lost without her if she ever left.

Chapter Thirty-Two

Laura

"Veronica, that man is insatiable. He's like an animal, and I'm exhausted."

I sighed, quickly moving my phone away from my ear as Veronica screamed so loud, she nearly burst my eardrums.

A week had passed since my first explosive sexual encounter with Spencer on the kitchen worktop. After he'd fucked me senseless, he'd fallen asleep, so I'd slipped away when Rupert and Maja had returned from the beach. Spencer had looked so peaceful when I'd left.

"Oh my God, I can't believe this. You finally shagged. I

think I'm going to cry. I'm so emotional," Veronica said, pretending to sniffle.

I rolled my eyes.

I was in my bedroom, drained after engaging in yet another day of tourist activities with the Banks family. Sicily was truly wonderful, and we had visited so many breathtaking beaches and sites.

Almost every night, Spencer snuck into my room and made love to me until dawn.

Every single day, I felt hungover.

Some days, he tackled me in the garden, too. That man was everything and more, and I could barely keep up with his overactive libido.

"Stop it. This will not work long-term. Once the summer is over, we are done. It's too risky to carry on fucking each other's brains out once we get back to London," I whispered into the phone. We were only having fun while on holiday. I couldn't allow myself to fall for him.

He was trying to show me his sweet side—he'd become less curmudgeonly—but still, I wasn't ready to officially date him. He was the Prime Minister, and the press would be all over this if they caught even a drift of this story. The man worked too hard to keep his reputation intact, and he was known as the eternal bachelor. I was not keen on being in the limelight again either. I was the opposite of Veronica.

"Oh, whatever. You turning up at his home and him mistaking you for an escort was the best thing that ever happened to you," Veronica said with a sigh.

She was right, but I still had nightmares about that day.

"Maybe, but that doesn't mean this can go on forever. I don't think Spencer is ready for a relationship." I shook my head, dreading the thought of going back to London. "How are things with you?"

"We are travelling around, visiting the most incredible places this summer," Veronica replied vaguely, and then someone shouted something in the background.

"Where exactly are you? You should come to Sicily for a visit."

"Oh, I'm not sure we'll manage. Anyway, I've got to go. I'll fill you in later. Oh, and don't let him break your vagina, sweetie."

"All right, bye," I said, then hung up.

Spencer, Rupert, and Maja were downstairs preparing dinner. Spencer wanted to grill the steaks himself tonight.

I went to the bathroom to take my birth control pills and suddenly I was so glad Veronica had slipped them into my suitcase, because I would have been screwed now. I took the packet and started looking at the days, seeing that a few of them were missing, which was impossible. It had been a week and I had definitely been taking them unless ... fuck ... no, he wouldn't do that.

I told Spencer that I was on on the birth control pills, so he must have knew I had them somewhere in my room. I stared at the packet for several long moments and then decided to place them somewhere else to test my theory. I didn't think Spencer was capable of stealing my birth control, because he didn't want any more kids, but then we didn't use any protection.

This was a little reckless of me, because I didn't want to get pregnant right now, but maybe Spencer was planning to trap me after all. I really had to talk to him about this, rather than make assumptions, because if that's what he was doing, did I even want to be with a man like that? I didn't know what Spencer thought was going to happen between us once we returned from Sicily, because every time I broached the subject, he was all over me, distracting me from the topic.

"Laura, what are you doing upstairs? Dinner is ready," Spencer called out.

I left the pills in another spot and told myself I would count them again in a couple of days, so then I would be sure. Deep down, I hoped that he wasn't trapping me into staying with him by me getting pregnant.

"Coming!"

I went downstairs, knowing that he was a good guy and he wouldn't do that to me. Spencer was dressed in a white polo t-shirt, setting up the massive table outside. He gave me a once-over and licked his lips, eyeing me hungrily, so soon I stopped thinking about it

"We need to talk to Maja. I can't do this anymore," he grumbled.

Rupert was pouring wine into a large glass jug, and Maja was laughing, watching something on her iPad. He had been going out a lot more lately, and sometimes he hadn't come back to the villa at all. Spencer had mentioned that he'd met someone, but Rupert wouldn't tell him who it was or whether it was anything serious.

"What are you talking about?" Rupert asked.

"Talk to her about Laura and I, because I've to keep reminding myself that I can't touch her when we are all together, and I can't fucking stand it." Spencer grunted.

Thankfully, Maja had headphones on so she couldn't hear.

Rupert had teased me relentlessly since he'd caught me leaving Spencer's bedroom early one morning. We were careful, and I told Spencer that this wasn't a good idea, but he had been in my bed almost every night since we'd started having sex.

"Let's wait until we get back to London," I whispered, placing the bowls of food on the table.

"Laura, I'm playing *Roblox* with Robbie. He's in Mexico." Maja showed me the screen of her iPad and took her headphones off.

"Oh wow, but since we're having dinner now, can you please put your tablet away." I sat next to her.

Spencer placed a huge bowl of pasta in front of us and joined us.

"What about Uncle Rupert?" Maja asked.

I glanced at Rupert, who was on his phone, smiling.

Spencer leaned over the table and snatched the phone out of his hands.

"What the hell? Give that back," Rupert snapped.

"We are about to have dinner, and from now on, no electronic devices at the table," he declared.

"Spencer is right. We should be having a conversation with

each other during our meals. We are in Sicily, and the food is so fresh. You will enjoy it more if you are conscious of what you're putting into your mouth." I smiled.

"Don't go all Mummy on me, Laura," Rupert grumbled.

"She's not, but she's right, we are having a meal as a family." Spencer gave his brother a stern look.

I was so glad that he'd backed me up.

Rupert cheered up a bit later on when we talked about our plans for the rest of the trip. Maja was excited about finally seeing her cousins. She kept saying she missed them, and I was curious about this side of Spencer's family. He kept sending heated glances my way throughout dinner, and I felt so lucky. After Jake, I really didn't think anyone else would find me attractive, but at the same time I reminded myself to guard my heart. Spencer Banks was a complicated man, and only a few weeks ago he'd claimed he wasn't willing to commit to any relationship, so something must have changed recently. He must have overcome some of his issues since we'd come to Sicily and he was much more relaxed than when he was in London.

"The food is getting cold, and I still want to fuck you on the beach before Rupert disappears for God knows how long," Spencer whispered in my ear, abruptly pulling me away from my intrusive thoughts.

"That will not be happening," I said loudly.

"Whatever, woman, keep telling yourself that. You know I get what I want. Always," he said while shoving a huge piece of steak into his mouth.

The rest of the evening passed with no incidents.

I carried the plates into the kitchen, wondering how Maja would react if Spencer finally revealed that we were together as a couple. I kept thinking about every possible scenario, because I didn't like surprises and I cared about her more than I realised. She'd become really attached to me, and I didn't want to screw anything up.

Spencer came up behind me and took the plates from my hands. He was trying hard to be careful with me when he was around Maja, and in a way I was glad about that, because our relationship or whatever was happening between us was still sort of unclear, since we hadn't discussed the logistics. I didn't want him to rush into any hasty decisions. Maja was his daughter, and we both needed to protect her.

"I'm so happy that you got that phone call that day and you showed up at my house." He helped me to load the dishwasher.

I raised my left eyebrow. "Why?"

"Because we would have never met otherwise. I'm really glad that you're my daughter's nanny, Laura. It's because of you that Maja and I've a much better relationship," he said.

A sudden, inexplicable tug resonated within my chest, a silent testament to the emotions stirring within me.

"You were right all along, but I was too stubborn to listen to you at the time. I should have spent more time with her, but work took priority and it shouldn't have."

I stared at him, unable to form any words, very touched that he was willing to admit that he was in the wrong. I wasn't a therapist, but I thought this was a groundbreaking moment for both of us, because he suddenly acknowledged the fact that he was wrong in how he parented Maja. I felt emotional.

"I'm truly glad that your relationship has improved now, and you don't need to thank me. I just nudged you," I said.

Then he leaned down and kissed me.

It was just a simple and soft kiss, but my skin was burning in a thousand different places, igniting my blood. He was a good and honest man, but he didn't let other people see that side of him very easily, he only showed them the flaws. I didn't think he was always like that, but over the years he'd let this arrogance rule him.

Then a moment later, when I was just about to tell him that he made me very happy, Maja appeared behind me. However, before I could ask her if she needed anything, she put her arms around me and squeezed me tightly.

"Laura, I love that you're here with us, I'm having so much fun with you, Uncle Rupert, and Dad," she said, closing her eyes.

I glanced at Spencer, overwhelmed by these unexpected words that hit me hard in the feels. He was staring at Maja with a smile.

"Oh, sweetie, I love being here with you, too. We are having such a wonderful time together," I said, my voice breaking a little.

She opened her eyes and looked up to me.

"I love you, Laura, and I wish you could be my mum someday," she added.

I gasped, my heart exploding and pounding loudly. This

was a totally wholesome and sweet moment for all of us, and I felt like I was part of their family. I wished I could stop time, because I wanted to stay in this moment forever.

Spencer parted his lips, appearing to be completely shocked by his daughter's admission. Tears swelled in my eyes as I wrapped my hands around her.

"I love you, too, darling, you're such a smart little girl, so don't you ever forget that," I said, my voice really wobbly at this point.

It seemed that Maja sensed her father had changed for the better. I attributed this to the sunshine and the fact that he wasn't so stressed out like when he was back in London, but also to the fact that Spencer was making an effort to change for me.

Maja nodded and then went back to her iPad. Spencer was still staring at her, emotions filling his handsome features. Then he looked at me, and I could recognise so many different emotions in his eyes: pride, admiration, and love, too. The electricity was zipping between us, and blood was drumming in my ears. I was proud of myself, proud of how far I had come to get to this moment.

"Maja has just confirmed everything I said earlier on," he said.

I smiled. "Yeah and what's that?"

"That you're the most heartwarming and wonderful person, Laura Watkins. We are lucky to have you," he replied and then added, "I've been with many women before, but I've never felt like this with anyone else."

"Care to elaborate? How exactly do I make you feel?" I

asked, and I knew that maybe I was pushing him a lot at that moment, but I wanted to know if this was going anywhere, so I could be prepared.

I continued to breathe, waiting for an answer. Spencer wasn't telling me that he was falling for me, he was thanking me. We had a lot of time to discuss, mainly the logistics of our relationship and where it was going, but maybe not today. Maja's declaration made my heart whole. I was happy that I'd managed to make her safe and loved by me.

"It feels right to have you by my side, and I want you to know you're important to me," he stated, confident.

I glanced down at the place I was wiping, thinking about my stormy relationship with Jake. This felt different, but I still felt a bit insecure when I was around him.

"Hey? Where did you go?"

"No other guy I've dated has said anything sweeter," I admitted.

Spencer wiped his hands and touched my chin, lifting my head, so my eyes met his.

"Because they were fucking idiots. None of those guys have ever deserved you," he snapped, sounding angry. "You're wonderful and you're enough. I want you to remember this whenever you doubt yourself again."

I nodded, forced to swallow my tears, warmth spreading through my chest. He was right, I was intelligent enough to know that there was nothing wrong with me. Jake was the one with issues. I didn't do anything wrong.

"Yes, Mr Banks, I'm enough," I replied.

His eyes darkened.

"And always remember that," he said and then winked at me, before he walked away, leaving me with my own thoughts.

I sighed loudly, feeling grateful and lucky that somehow, the universe had my back.

Chapter Thirty-Three

Spencer

I was nervous and I wasn't sure why. I was squeezing Laura's hand as Lorenzo drove through the long Sicilian roads. We had one more agent in the front and a few others were following us in the van. It had been a few days since our conversation in the kitchen, and this was my only opportunity to take Laura out on a real date. Of course, I didn't tell her where we were going and what I had planned for us to do. I just wanted to surprise her, so this was a perfect opportunity. I was also motivated by the fact that my daughter had already accepted Laura as my partner, maybe not literally, but figuratively.

After Maja had told Laura that she wished she was her

mother, I'd called Cath back in the UK and asked her to arrange something really special for this evening. Cath was a good assistant, and she didn't ask many questions, although I could tell by her tone she was surprised by what I'd asked her to do.

I'd doubted myself in the past, and I was worried how my relationship with Laura could impact Maja, but now my daughter had reassured me that Laura was right for our little family. I truly wanted Laura to fall for me and I knew I had to show her the real Spencer Banks.

Rupert had already given me the heads-up; he was planning to leave soon for Europe. Apparently, a few of his mates were meeting in Greece, and he needed a little break from us, which I understood, although I was sure he was bullshitting me about meeting his mates. He was probably seeing a woman, and I didn't understand all the secrecy.

"Are you going to tell me where we are going?" Laura asked, her eyes sparkling with mischief.

I didn't know what was happening to me, but she was in my head all the time. The sex was mind-blowing, and there was no denying that we were crazy about each other, but I wanted more.

This scared the hell out of me, but everything about Laura Watkins felt right, and tonight I wanted to make sure I was making the correct decision.

"No, it's a surprise, and you will love it, right, Lorenzo?" I asked the diver.

"Si ... si, it will be fantastic, Bella," the driver shouted back, making a typical Italian gesture in the air.

Laura narrowed her eyes at me and then glanced at our entwined hands. Even if she was concerned, she didn't say anything, and we stayed like that until we arrived at the private car park that was situated by a hotel on the outskirts of San Vito La Copo. I hoped Cath had managed to pull everything together as I'd asked, because I needed it to be perfect.

I took Laura's hand, and we strolled inside the hotel lobby. The Italian woman at the reception nodded at me as we passed, and I quickly turned around. Giovani, the head of security on the island, understood the signal.

"What was that about?" Laura asked.

We walked through the stylish lobby, then the restaurant, heading towards the exit. By this point, she'd probably figured it out that my security detail wasn't following us anymore.

"Nothing for you to worry about, my dearest," I replied. "It's all part of the surprise for this evening."

Then another hotel employee directed us through a set of double doors. We stepped outside and moved down the steps. The view from this hotel was absolutely mesmerising, and Laura gasped when she saw it, standing still and looking all around us. The tiny voice of angry Spencer whispered that this was too much, over-the-top romantic, but I tried to block him out.

My security would be fairly close by, I couldn't make them go away, but they would watch us from as much of a distance as they could give us. Finally, after several long minutes of walking, we stepped into a private garden. The sun dipped below the horizon, casting a warm, golden glow over the private garden nestled on the cliff of the hotel. I led Laura through an archway of entwined vines, guiding her into a secluded haven of beauty. The scent of blooming flowers filled the air, while a gentle sea breeze whispered through the leaves of ancient olive trees. A wrought-iron gate opened to reveal a small, elegantly set table adorned with crisp white linen, delicate china, and polished silverware. Laura was speechless, trying to take all this in, her eyes darting around until I nudged her, pulling her chair out for her.

She finally took her seat with a view that stretched beyond the cliff's edge, unveiling the breathtaking expanse of the Mediterranean Sea. The table was adorned with flickering candles, their warm light dancing on the polished surface and casting a soft, intimate glow. We settled in, and I gestured towards the musicians discreetly arranged in a corner. A trio of talented men, dressed in refined attire, tuned their instruments under the dappled light of a strategically placed lamppost. The sound of a violin, a cello, and a piano filled the air with a melodic anticipation, promising an evening of enchantment.

The musicians themselves were seated on ornate wrought-iron chairs, positioned in a semi-circle to allow for a harmonious blend of their classical instruments. Their faces were veiled in the shadow of night, creating an air of mystery as their fingers delicately traced the strings and keys. This whole setup was absolutely spot-on; I couldn't have asked for more.

"Spencer, I ... I don't know what to say, this whole thing is simply perfect," Laura said, her voice a little wobbly.

I smiled at her and then poured us both a glass of Sicilian

wine, the rich aroma mingling with the fragrances of the garden. The distant murmur of the waves crashing against the cliffs made me feel a little nostalgic. Sicily was my second home, and I hoped that one day it would be for Laura, too.

"It's only perfect because I'm here with you. We both know that we needed this," I said. "I hope you don't mind that I ordered for you. We have squid as a starter and then the best pasta in Sicily. This restaurant is Michelin star, and I know the chef personally."

"No, that's wonderful, thank you," she replied.

A moment later, the waiter showed up with our starters, asking me if everything was all right, then he drifted off again.

"I wanted to do something special for you, Laura. Besides, we haven't even been on a real date yet, so I thought I'd quickly rectify that," I told her, and maybe I was acting crazy for thinking this, but I needed to tell her that she was mine. I was done fucking around, acting like this was just sex and nothing else. Laura had turned my views and life upside down.

She was staring at me with her lips slightly parted, still looking like she was in shock. She didn't need to say anything. I knew she was afraid of the future. I had been a serial bachelor until now. I was allowed to change my mind and have a relationship, and maybe our relationship would cause a sensation, but I was done sneaking around. It was bloody exhausting. The media would go crazy for a few weeks, but after that, things would settle down and we could officially be a couple.

We started eating, and Laura moaned when she tasted the

squid while the musicians were playing. That sound went straight through my groin, hardening my cock again.

"My mum loves classical music. I need to bring her here one day. My parents have never been to Italy," she said, once the waiter had collected our plates.

I wiped my mouth with a napkin, relaxed. I realised for the first time since being in Sicily that I felt happy, content, and at peace with myself, because I had her next to me.

"We will be coming here every year, so don't worry, we can bring them next time," I said.

Her left eyebrow lifted.

"Spencer, this whole thing is wonderful, but you told me yourself that everything between us is only physical," she said, sounding wary.

I reached for her hand across the table. My heart was thumping loudly. I was a cold motherfucker most of the time, but with Laura I was back to being a normal guy.

"I don't want this to be only physical. I know I told you that I couldn't commit, but you're making my world brighter, Laura. I allowed Samantha to break me all those years ago, and I haven't been able to trust any other woman since, but with you it's different," I said, unable to actually say what I fucking wanted to. I didn't even know why I was suddenly so nervous. "These past few days have been wonderful, and I've never been so relaxed. When we get back to London, I want to let people know that I've someone in my life. I want to make this fucking official, if you'll let me."

She gasped again, and for a long moment I could only hear

the music. I didn't want to make this decision without her, she needed to tell me that this was exactly what she wanted, too.

"There will be a media storm, and we'll both be in the spotlight then," she said.

"As long as you're okay with all this then I'm happy, Laura. No more hiding. We are both adults, and I'm the PM. I'm single, so wanting a relationship shouldn't surprise anyone."

"Yes, Spencer, I'm scared, but I think it's the right step, but let's wait until we get back to London to discuss this with Maja. She's having such a great time here, and I don't want to ruin anything," she said.

I nodded, then sipped the wine. I wasn't too happy about this arrangement, but Laura was right. This whole thing was very fresh and still fragile, so we had to take it slow. My daughter needed to be protected.

"I think my parents are going to freak. They supported me so much when I was with Jake, but all the attention and press got to them later on."

I growled with anger when she brought that wanker's name up. She had to forget about him.

"I'm going to talk to your parents at some point. We'll arrange for them to come to Number 10 and have dinner, so they'll see that I'm not fucking around," I assured her.

The waiter appeared before Laura could say anything more about my idea, followed by another two bringing us the main course. It was pasta with seafood, and it smelled absolutely divine. I waited for Laura to taste it first, and when she did, she let go of another moan.

"I think you were right, this is the best pasta dish that I ever tasted," she exclaimed.

I was suddenly glad that the food distracted her from questioning whether it was a good idea for us to go public or not. We continued to eat while listening to the music, and by the time our plates were cleared, the musicians played another classic. I kept staring at Laura. She seemed lost in her own thoughts with this view, so I took another sip of my wine. She was beautiful, and my heart pounded as I took her features in, trying to picture her as my wife. Fuck, I didn't know where this was even coming from, but she dominated my thoughts.

"Penny for your thoughts?" I asked.

She finally looked at me.

"I was thinking about my sister," she admitted.

I had no idea how I didn't know about this. Laura had been vetted, but there was nothing in the file about a sister.

"Your sister?"

She glanced down at her hands.

"You probably already know that I was adopted. I never managed to find my biological parents. I've a sister, she's a few years older than me, but I've no idea what happened to her. I don't even remember her. She must have been adopted before me," she explained, sounding sad.

"Have you tried searching for her?" I asked.

"Yes, my dad started helping me, but we didn't get anywhere, and I never had enough money to hire someone who could find her," she explained. "I was born in Poland, and it was never easy to find anything. We needed to hire a translator and a private detective."

Then the waiter arrived again as I was going to ask her more questions, yet again enquiring whether everything was all right. I told him in Italian that nothing could ever be more perfect than this moment. After that, we fell into another conversation about Laura's education, but the subject of her sister remained in my thoughts. That evening, I made a decision to find the woman for her. I had all the means and resources, and this would make her happy. She didn't know her real parents, but it would be good for her to be reunited with her sibling. I kept listening to her, believing that Laura deserved all the happiness in the world, and I was willing to do anything for her, because I was slowly falling for her.

Chapter Thirty-Four

Laura

I was falling for this man, for my boss, for the Prime Minister, and there was nothing I could do about it. Spencer Banks was not the man I thought he was. Behind the hard, intimidating, and arrogant exterior was the man who needed to be loved. He was kind, romantic, and caring, but he didn't want anyone else to see that side of him. He acted all cold and obnoxious because that was his coping mechanism—at least that's what I believed—but that exterior had started slipping whilst we were in Sicily. At first I only got glimpses of it, but now he was truly showing me his vulnerable side, and I couldn't resist him any longer.

The surprise, the concert with the most romantic dinner, it

all blew me away. I truly hadn't expected any of it when he'd said earlier on that we were going out for a drive. Rupert was staying in to look after Maja, but something was going on with him, and I had a feeling that this whole thing had something to do with a certain red-haired beauty who was also currently travelling around Europe. I was certain she was somewhere near Italy now.

I watched Spencer when he was talking in Italian to the waiter. He was so relaxed and fun when he was not under pressure. The waiter said something, and Spencer laughed. Each note of his laughter soothed my worries, enveloping a sense of joy within me. I wished he would laugh like that more often.

He wanted to have a relationship with me, he wanted to make things official between us, and I was apprehensive. I was happy he was including me in this decision-making process, but after what had happened with Jake, I wasn't sure if this was such a good idea.

"You will absolutely love the dessert we're having," he said after the waiter had gone and we were left alone again.

There was another tune being played, and for a moment, I listened to it, so incredibly grateful that I was here. It was so good not to worry that anyone would see us here, especially when security stayed behind and we were finally in solitude. I'd felt a little self-conscious after the beach, because I thought his agents gave me funny looks sometimes, but Spencer told me I was just being paranoid.

Then he asked about my sister and was a little sad that I wasn't able to track her down. It had been so many years, and I often wondered if she had a family of her own and if she'd ever tried to search for me. She must have remembered me, because she was a few years older than me.

"We have to thank the chef later," I said, drinking the wine as he stared at me with smouldering heat. "I should have become a politician myself when I had the chance. It seems that this job comes with a lot of perks."

Spencer narrowed his eyes, and in the dim lights around us I thought he was so handsome, wearing a crisp white shirt, and since we had been in Sicily for over two weeks, not only did he have a glorious golden tan, his jet-black black hair was a bit longer, and he had more facial hair, too. I liked that new rugged appearance more than the polished one since he was not in the office.

"So why don't you go back to it? I read your file. You graduated and you were on the right path towards a career in politics until you weren't?" He looked at me intensely.

A slight pinch twinged in my lower stomach, but I ignored the pain.

"I've been asking myself the same question for years," I responded, thinking about my jaded past.

Things had been going well for me after I'd started working for one of the MPs, but then I'd met Jake. He hadn't wanted me to work, and after a few months it was clear to me that I couldn't continue being with him and try to climb the political ladder. He wanted me to be with him all the time, he said I was like his anxiety relief pill, and then he asked me to go on tour with him.

I'd wasted two years of my life with a guy who'd ended up screwing me over.

"I couldn't go back to that life after everything that happened. I thought no one would take me seriously when my name was splattered all over tabloids, so I ended up studying child psychology after that," I explained, and I knew Spencer was probably aware of it, because he'd vetted me himself.

"You're smart, strong, and you would have made a great politician. I would have hired you," he said.

I laughed.

"You are biased, no one would hire me then. People were stopping me on the street telling me that they were on my side, but that's where the support stopped," I said and bit my bottom lip. "Besides, Jake shattered my confidence. I truly loved him, but after everything that happened, I couldn't even look at myself in the mirror. I lost myself being with him."

Spencer growled, and then he took my hand, squeezing it tightly. His eyes were stormy blue, and I didn't know what he was thinking in that moment.

"You were always good enough, so don't you ever dare think that any of this was your fault. That guy was an arsehole, and he didn't deserve you," he said, giving me that intense stare.

Butterflies rioted in the pit of my stomach.

"You're beautiful and intelligent, you make Maja and I very happy, and I want you to think highly of yourself. And I'm sure, one day, you will go back to politics and kick arse, because I believe in you."

"Thank you." I felt like I was going to cry. He would really do this for me? Give me a job so I could go back to politics? It would have been a dream come true, but I didn't want to leave Maja just yet. We had bonded so well since I'd started working as her nanny.

Just then, the waiter arrived again, this time with our dessert, and I was grateful for the distraction. The food here was out of this world, but by the end of the night I was so full and a little tipsy from the wine, because Spencer kept topping it up.

"I need to go to the ladies." I got up, and then a sharp pain razored through the pit of my stomach. I hissed, trying to control my breathing, touching my stomach.

"What's wrong? Are you okay?" Spencer asked, suddenly appearing next to me.

Another painful cramp, and then I realised why and groaned with anger. I was getting my period, but it was too soon, I had several days left of my cycle. I groaned, thinking that this couldn't have been happening tonight.

"Nothing, it's fine, don't worry." I tried to keep a brave face, but then the pain multiplied, and I had to sit back down.

Spencer's eyes darkened as he kneeled next to me.

"This doesn't seem like nothing. What's going on, Laura? You know you can tell me anything," he was asking.

I tried to breathe through the painful cramps.

"I think I'm getting my period, which is strange because I should have another few days. Anyway, sometimes it's really painful, not always, but when it is I'm out of commission for a day or two." I felt bad that I was ruining our date. Why did I have to get my period right now, damn it?

"All right, we are leaving. Do you want me to carry you to the bathroom?" he asked.

I looked at him like he had lost his mind.

"What? No, I'm fine for now, I just need to get to the ladies', and you're not carrying me," I said sharply and then forced myself to get up.

"Why the hell not? You're in pain and you weigh next to nothing," he said.

I shook my head and encouraged myself to keep on walking, not wanting to hear another word about this. Somehow, I'd managed to convince him not to carry me to the bathroom. His security was waiting for us in the lobby after I took care of the problem for now. I'd started bleeding a little, but luckily I was always prepared, however, the pain was getting worse.

Around twenty minutes later, I was so glad that we were back in the limo and I was in his arms, breathing hard and trying to think about something other than the pain.

"How bad is it?" he asked as I moved my hands to my stomach.

"I'll survive, but I'm sorry that I've ruined this magical evening. It was wonderful, and you did so great with all the details, but tell me about Samantha." Him talking about Maja's mother was a good distraction for me.

He dragged his hand over his chin and then exhaled.

"There's nothing to tell. We were young when we met and we were together for a few years. I thought we were compatible. She supported me in my career; she always said that I was going to be powerful one day." He put his palm on the top of my stomach. "Then she got pregnant, and everything went to shit. Sam never wanted to be a mother. It was an accident, we didn't plan it, but eventually we both mutually agreed that it was best if she kept the baby. We fought over it for a long time, and ultimately after talking about it for days, we felt like we could do it. Sam started to get excited, and I thought everything was all right."

"What happened after that? Did she leave when Maja was born?"

"Yeah, eleven days after. I think she didn't realise how much hard work is required to raise a baby. She must have panicked and decided that motherhood wasn't for her, so she left. It was a Sunday morning, and we were in bed. I didn't think she'd ever bonded with the baby, she was exhausted because of the lack of sleep. She'd insisted on driving to Starbucks that day. I didn't really think she would leave, but she just didn't come back. Later that day, I found that all her things were gone. She must have packed her suitcase when I wasn't home; she must have been thinking about it for a long time."

We were silent after that, and I was so shocked. I couldn't comprehend how any woman would ever leave their newborn. This must have been so devastating for Spencer, and he must have loved her.

"It must have been hard for you, especially since Maja was so small," I whispered.

"I was in shock for a few days. Maja was crying, and I didn't know what to do, I thought something had happened. I kept calling Sam, but she must have thrown the SIM card. I went to the police. They filled a missing person's report, but they couldn't track her down. Several weeks later, I had a text saying not to look for her. Don't get me wrong, I tried calling the number, but it got disconnected straight away. It seemed that Sam didn't want to be found, so I had to accept the fact that she wasn't planning to come back and be in Maja's life. Then I called my mother, because I didn't know what to do with a newborn. Sam had refused to breastfeed, so at least that worked in my favour," he admitted.

And just then, we both realised that we had arrived at the villa, because the car had been stopped for a little while.

"We are here, sir," Giovani said when he opened the door for us.

I stood and nearly collapsed from another shooting pain. My knees went weak, and I groaned when a moment later someone was lifting me off the ground.

"I've got you, Bella, let me take you to bed," he said.

I didn't want to protest. We were in the villa, and it was late. Maja and Rupert were probably already in bed, so I nodded. Spencer carried me inside, then upstairs, and went straight to his bedroom. He laid me on the bed while I was trying to focus on him, not the pain, although the cramps were the most painful I had ever experienced.

"I'll be right back, don't move," he said and then vanished into the bathroom.

I closed my eyes and tried to breathe. Several moments later, he came out looking positively glowing.

"I ran you a bath, and I'm going to undress you, so you can relax," he said.

I was so touched but unable to form a coherent response because I felt suddenly overwhelmed by my emotions and pain. Spencer helped me to strip into my underwear, and then he pulled something out of his pocket.

"I Googled that lavender oil helps with the period pain and I managed to get some from the hotel reception when you were in the loo."

Then he spilled a few drops on his hands and rubbed my stomach gently. I stared at him, tears welling, but I told myself I couldn't cry. He was so sweet, and his warm hands on my skin instantly relaxed me. He was massaging my stomach, making the pain more bearable.

Sometime later, I opened my eyes, and we were staring for a long moment, our gazes holding each other. I lost my ability to breathe when he was looking at me with such intensity, stripping all my layers of self-control away.

"Come on, let's get you into the bath and then into bed," he finally said with a smile.

"Thank you, Spencer, that really helped with the pain. You have very skilled hands," I said and touched his face.

He kissed my palm and then carried me to the bathroom. It was too much, over the top, but I couldn't tell him no, because he was a wonderful man, and I was so lucky to have him.

Chapter Thirty-Five

Spencer

Laura Watkins had shaken my world, even though not everything was going according to plan. Our date was perfect, despite the fact that Laura ended up soaking in the bath. I was falling for this woman hard and fast. All these new feelings and emotions terrified me, but I couldn't imagine not being with her. She made me a better man, and I wanted to change for her.

Luckily, the next day Laura seemed in much better spirits. She stayed in bed most of the day but by the evening she was back to being her perky, normal self. Rupert seemed grumpier than usual, and he didn't want to say what was wrong with him.

We spent the next few days chilling in the villa as we had

plenty more places to visit over the next three weeks. The weather was glorious, and for a change I was happy, because I'd made the right decision. Laura wasn't going anywhere, and Maja already loved her, so the future looked bright and sunny.

I promised Laura and Maja a movie marathon later on in the evening, but before then, I took Laura to the beach. Rupert didn't mind babysitting, and he didn't say anything when I told him I was taking Laura for a walk.

The villa was situated on the cliff, and the view was absolutely mesmerising. We didn't have to worry about privacy, because there weren't any other properties around us and this bay was very secluded. Besides, the sun was just about to set, and I wanted Laura to enjoy the magnificent colours in the sky.

"What do you think is going on with Rupert? He has been acting very strange," Laura mused.

"He's seeing someone, but he's tight-lipped, so I can't get anything out of him," I explained, knowing that sooner or later Rupert would spill his secrets.

"I don't know, maybe, but I truly thought he was right for Veronica. She has fallen for him. She won't admit it, but I know she has," Laura said.

I wasn't sure if she was right. My brother was clear, he didn't like sharing and he'd given Veronica an ultimatum.

"Rupert is a complicated man. He was voted one of the most eligible bachelors in the country by some of the papers over the past few years. I don't think he would commit," I said.

Laura wanted them together, but I didn't think my brother believed in love. He was a cynic.

"Really? Well, I'm not surprised, your brother is handsome and he's a billionaire," Laura added, and when I glanced at her surprised she added, "However, I don't like the way Rupert is looking at us."

"And how exactly is Rupert looking at us?" I asked when we walked down the steep steps.

She turned to me, frowning.

"Like he knows exactly what you are doing to me behind closed doors," she huffed.

I laughed, and she glared at me.

"This isn't funny, Spencer. Once the press finds out, they will eat us alive."

"If they find out, that is. Besides, you're worrying too much about insignificant details. I'm a bachelor and not doing anything wrong, so we will deal with things in our own time. Now, come and stand by this rock. You have been distracting me all day," I told her as we reached the bottom, surrounded by cliffs. This was the perfect place for us to fuck, because no one would interrupt us and the steps that led back up to the villa were steep. "These past few days have been excruciating for me. I was trying really hard to act like a gentleman and give you some space. It was especially hard when you wore that red dress to dinner last night."

"I'm sorry about our date, I knew you were hoping for a different outcome at the end of the evening, and I was too, but I got my period early," she admitted.

"Don't worry, shortcake, we have plenty of time to make up for it," I said, already thinking about the ways I could fuck her here. The views were mesmerising. I needed to keep her here for a few extra hours so I could remind her who she belonged to. The sweet scent of her pussy was like a rush of a new drug in my bloodstream.

Laura smiled and tossed her hair behind her shoulder. Laura's heart was wholesome, so much that it twisted my own heart when she'd said she thought she was broken, because no other guy after that fucking pop star could make her orgasm. She had mentioned that her ex-boyfriend told her she was a terrible lay. What a wanker! She was the hottest sex I'd ever fucking experienced, and every single day, I would never have enough of her. She was also kind, smart, and headstrong, which made me walk around with a semi hard-on when I was supposed to respect her space.

"You're being terribly bossy today, and what if I don't want to have sex? After the last time, you nearly broke my vagina," she complained, then turned around and dipped her toes in the water.

She stared at the sunset. I put my arms around her and inhaled her perfume while the sky glowed with orange and yellow hues.

"Were you sore, baby?" I asked, now feeling guilty that maybe I'd pushed her too far. She probably realised that I was ready to fuck her all the time, especially from behind, but I loved it when she straddled me and took control of how deep she wanted to have my dick inside her.

"A little, but I'm fine now, and I'm horny again," she mused, turning to look at me, her tits pressing against my chest. "And I would like to do it against this rock, because your dirty talk is turning me on so much right now, Mr Prime Minister."

I pulled her to me and placed my hands on her buttocks squeezing them hard.

"Hmm, I believe that we need to do something about it, don't we?" I said and then kissed her, claiming those lips like I was a starving man, her low moan heated my blood, and my raging hard on pressed over the zipper of my shorts. I needed to have her here and now.

"Please Spencer, touch me," she pleaded when I stared directly into her eyes. I smiled.

"I like when you're begging me baby, did your needy cunt miss my cock?" I asked, stroking her hair away from her face. Her eyes widened when my other hand slipped under her dress and stretched her knickers aside. I hummed, finding her drenched. I grazed my finger over her slit, then rubbed her clit slowly, while her whole body trembled for quick release.

"Keep doing that," she said and I eased one finger inside her, finding her completely and utterly soaked for me.

"Are you going to take my cock here and then come all over it like a good little slut?" I asked, thrusting my finger in and out slowly until she started panting. I wanted that mouth around it too. I withdrew my finger and then slapped her arse. She groaned with disappointment.

"I need you Spencer. Now!"

"And you will have me. Bend over by that rock, baby. This won't take long ..."

She gasped and obeyed me. I smacked her arse again,

drawing a giggle from her. After dragging her panties down, I glanced around to check my surroundings. Laura stared at my pulsating cock and then swallowed hard. There was so much more that I wanted to do with her, but I didn't want to rush it.

"Don't you want to wear a condom?" she asked.

I lifted her dress and smacked her arse harder this time. She hissed, releasing a loud moan.

"No, I need to feel you in all your natural glory," I growled, then pulled out my rock-hard cock. I truly couldn't get enough of her.

After days of being with her, living with her in true paradise, I felt different, and I was glad we had established that she was mine and I was hers. I wanted to commit to her, and even if the thought of her being my wife still terrified me, I was willing to make her mine in every sense of the word.

She moaned when I entered her. Laura was so tight, so fucking perfect.

"Spencer." She struggled as I moved inside her while rubbing her clit.

One thrust, and I was ready to explode. Sweat gathered on my forehead as I pushed myself to ease into her slowly, but it was impossible. She felt absolutely perfect and I was already on the verge of my own release.

"You feel incredible. I never want to be apart from you," I whispered in her ear. "Your pussy is made for me baby, only me. Do you understand me?"

Gripping her hips, I sped up the pace.

"Yes, only for you," she moaned and panted for air. I wrapped my hand around her throat and squeezed it.

"Fuck you're so tight," I growled, aware that I was pushing things a little too far, not letting her take another breath. Her eyes widened with panic as I thrust harder and faster. "Tell me you like my hands on your throat shortcake?" I released my grip enough for her to reply.

"I missed – oh God," she moaned and I put more pressure on her windpipe, her breathing now constrained to tiny gasps of air. I kept fucking her, seeing the panic seeping in slowly as I squeezed her throat tighter, cutting her oxygen off.

"That's my good girl," I whispered. "Now come all over my cock!"

I released my grip, then placed my hands on both her hips, thrusting to the hilt and in a way I was glad that we were alone and far from the villa because she came undone, exploding all over my shaft. I pounded into her, feeling invincible; my own release was close.

"Does your greedy pussy like when it's milking my cock, my slutty nanny?"

She convulsed and writhed around me.

"Yes, oh God, yes!"

Colours burst behind my eyelids like fireworks. Every inch of me participated in this collision of ecstasy. I came hard, filling her with my cum. This woman was going to be the end of me, and nothing was going to change between us once we returned back to London.

I dragged my hand through my damp hair, trying to calm my erratic breathing. Laura looked positively fucked.

"I think you might have broken my vagina permanently, Spence, and we really need to get back now. Rupert is probably waiting for us," she said. When I glanced at her, I saw red marks on her throat and I suddenly felt a little guilty. Maybe I'd pushed her a bit too far, too soon.

I pulled up my shorts and took off my t-shirt, then I walked up to her, stroking her face.

"Are you okay? I didn't hurt you right?" I asked, as my gaze roamed over her throat and chest.

"I have never been better, you don't need to worry, you can't break me so easily. I like when you're being rough with me," she said with a smile.

"You are full of surprises," I said, drawing my fingers down between her breasts. "Now, let's go for a swim."

I was ready to fuck her again, she was so fucking perfect, but I jumped into the water instead to push that thought away for now, because we really needed to head back. My head kept spinning, and the water felt so refreshing. I imagined owning a villa on the island. Maja would love it, and then I could invite the family here, too.

Laura hesitated for a split second before stripping off and getting into the sea.

She dove underwater then emerged, smiling at me. I brought her closer, and we floated, taking in all the sensations of the moment.

"I needed this break, so thank you for convincing me to come along." She touched my cheek.

We locked eyes, and I shuddered, drowning in those green depths. My heart raced, and the realisation hit me like a bulldozer. I was falling head over heels for Laura, hard and fucking fast.

My own heart was jackhammering inside my chest at the unexpected realisation, but I held her close as we both drifted over the surface of the water. We stared at each other for a long time, silently communicating and knowing what was suddenly forming between us. We didn't need to say anything and deep down that petrified me a little, because I never had this with anyone else.

"Glad to be of service," I replied, though I wanted to say something more meaningful and romantic. It was the fear of the past, old limitations and insecurities that turned me into a robot —how did I turn it off? "Come on, princess. As much as I want to stay here with you for the rest of the night, I don't want you to be eaten by a shark."

She laughed and kissed me. I cupped her head, devouring her mouth. Feeling her to the depths of my soul. When we parted for breath, her eyes screamed thousands of unspoken words.

I knew this love was either going to be my end or my beginning.

Chapter Thirty-Six

Laura

"Let me see if I've this right. Francesco is your second cousin, right? He's married and has four kids?" I questioned Spencer on the way to Trapani to visit his Italian family.

Spencer's security team was following behind in a separate van, and there was one more agent sitting in front beside the driver.

"Uncle Francesco is so funny, and Catarina, Domenico, and Pierre love playing with me, but they only speak a bit of English," Maja shouted from the back.

Rupert had gone out and never returned home last night. I didn't know what was going on with him, but apparently,

Spencer had spoken to him over the phone this morning. He had no idea where he was because Rupert didn't want to tell him anything, which made me wonder if maybe he was secretly seeing Veronica. But how? She'd said she didn't have time to visit Sicily, and if she did, she'd tell me, right?

"Don't forget about little Luca, I think he's almost two now," Spencer said to his daughter.

This was our fourth week on the island, and I was looking forward to meeting Maja's cousins. She was so excited and had barely stopped talking about them, although I wasn't sure how she would communicate with them. Spencer mentioned she'd taken Italian classes before, but she only knew a few phrases.

A couple of hours later, after a very fun drive with the three of us joking and laughing, we finally arrived in Castellammare del Golfo, near Trapani, and Lorenzo parked in front of a large house on a hill. We all got out of the car, and I quickly pulled Spencer aside. The security team parked next to us, and a moment later, the agents started getting out. One of them nodded to Spencer before following the others inside.

Maja jumped up and down in excitement when a tall Italian man greeted her with an outpouring of affection and slightly broken English. Spencer grabbed my hand and walked me towards the gate where his cousin stood. The sun was blazing, and sweat was already dripping down my body. Spencer had on a white polo t-shirt and blue shorts. I always thought he was hot, but then he was like Adonis, especially when he was so tanned.

An old woman embraced me, speaking in rapid Italian while

squeezing me tightly. After she finally let go of me, she took my face in her palms and gave me two kisses on both cheeks.

"*Zia Sofia, st'è la tata di Maja e la mia ragazza,*"[1] Spencer said.

I really had to take lessons because I couldn't understand a thing.

"*Finalmente ti sei trovato una donna. Ma questa è solo pelle e ossa. Dobbiamo ingrassarla un pò,*"[2] Sofia pointed at me.

"So you must be Laura. Spencer can't shut up about you. My name is Beatrice, and I'm Francesco's wife." Another woman appeared out of nowhere and finally freed me from Sofia. She cradled an adorable toddler in her arms.

"Yes, hello, it's so nice to meet you. Maja has been so excited to see her cousins." I touched the face of the cutest curly-haired boy I had ever seen.

Shying away, he hid against his mother's chest.

After exchanging pleasantries, we strolled towards the house.

"Francesco invited a few of his friends so everyone will be very loud, speaking mostly in Italian. Don't be scared, okay? I'll try my best to translate everything," Beatrice said.

"I kind of know what to expect." I laughed nervously.

We chatted, and it turned out that Beatrice had lived in London for years, studying economics. She'd met Francesco when he came to close some sort of deal with the wholesaler she worked at. Apparently, it was love at first sight, and then he immediately moved to England for her, leaving behind his whole business.

Spencer had me sit next to him at a large table, where at least twenty other members had gathered. The kids were running around, playing by the smaller pool, and Maja was with them. Luca was placed in a high chair, and Beatrice fed him plain pasta and vegetables.

"Who are all these people? Is this your whole family?" I asked Spencer.

"Yes, mostly family. Francesco has five brothers, and some of these men are his cousins. They always invite the extended family if we are visiting." He placed his hand possessively on my thigh.

"Stop it. We are in public. You need to go back to being nice and gentlemanly, Spencer Banks, because this is highly inappropriate," I said, then smiled at an older lady who put a huge plate of something that appeared to look like antipasto in front of me.

"*Mangia, mangia, carissima,*"[3] she muttered and walked away.

"What did she say?" I asked.

"That you should eat," he said.

The cold cuts were delicious, and after I finished the course, Sofia kept bringing more and more food, still talking to me like I understood everything she was saying. At some point, I had to stand and paced for a bit because I could hardly move, I was so full. I went to the pool and watched Maja and her three cousins splashing around.

Spencer had mentioned that Francesco had a vineyard somewhere close. After Beatrice had graduated, they'd all gone back to Sicily to start a family, and nowadays, he was in the export business, dealing particularly in wines.

Spencer's father, too, was half-Sicilian, and he came to the island almost every summer. That's how he spoke fluent Italian. Several moments later, the kids got out of the pool, and I got some towels to dry them, then they ran towards the garden. Maja shouted that her cousins had a playground farther down, by the lemon trees.

"*Ciao, bella,* what's your name?" Someone startled me.

I turned around and nearly tripped upon seeing a hot shirtless Italian man who had sat at the table earlier. I suspected he was one of Francesco's cousins who'd been invited today. Beatrice had told me everyone's name, but I couldn't remember all of them. The man handed me an icy orange-coloured drink and gestured for me to try it. I didn't know what to do, so I tasted it.

"It's Aperol spritz. You like?"

The drink was slightly bitter yet sweet at the same time. It was quite refreshing.

"*Grazie,* it's good. My name is Laura," I replied.

"*Bellissima,* you Spencer family? Came with him?" he asked in a thick accent.

He came to stand a tad too close to me, so close that I could smell his overpowering cologne. His shorts were drooped below his waist, exposing the top of his pubic hair. My cheeks flushed. Oh dear, these Italians didn't give a damn.

"I take care of Maja. I'm her nanny." I had no idea if he understood me or not, because his eyes were now focused on my chest.

In a sudden move, he took my hand and kissed it, then leaned over like he wanted to whisper something into my ear. I was not used to another man touching me like that, especially without my permission, and I didn't like it.

"*Credo che ti devi prendere una pausa, ragazzo. Questo non è un bel modo di comportarsi.Questa donna non ti capisce, quindi scusati con lei. Mentre ora scusati con me per aver toccato cio' che e' mio.*"[4] Spencer appeared next to me like a shadow.

Whatever Spencer said made my new companion angry, because he took a step towards Spencer and snapped, "*Ma mi ha appena detto che è solo la tua tata. Allora le posso parlare, no?*"[5]

"*È la mia donna e ti stai fissando sulle sue tette, allora sparisci prima che smetto di essere cordiale,*"[6] Spencer replied with a growl.

I could sense that he was already agitated. He was also a little drunk.

"*La tua donna? Ma piace pure a me. Forse vorrà scegliere u veru omu sicilianu,*"[7] the man said.

I was just about to tell him that I needed to use the restroom because I truly didn't want to witness any altercation during the family dinner. But then, Spencer growled something incoherent and pushed the guy into the large adult pool. I gasped, freezing. Once more, he was overreacting. When a few members of his family started laughing and talking all over each other, I wanted the earth to swallow me whole. The man finally emerged from the pool, shouting and waving his fisted right hand at Spencer, splashing water everywhere. I was too stunned to react.

"Let's go. That's enough of socialising for you today," Spencer said as he grabbed my hand and dragged me away.

"Wow, hold on. Where are we going? We can't just leave your family like that." I pulled out of his grip. "And why did you push that guy into the pool?"

"That's was Gennaro, one of Francesco's black sheep cousins, and he wanted what's mine. Come on, Laura, I need to show you something in the bathroom." He took the stairs.

"Spencer, wait, we were only talking!" I hurried after him.

He stood by the sink, washing his hands, so I shut the door and folded my arms over my chest. I was hoping that Spencer hadn't told his whole family that we were together. I knew he was acting all territorial and jealous when other men were eying me up, but we had agreed to take things slow, at least until we got back to London, because of Maja.

"It drives me crazy when other men look at you, Laura, and that guy touched your hand and then put his filthy mouth on it. You make me lose control so easily," he said, his voice dropping a single decibel as he stared at me with the same intensity and heat.

"I admit, he shouldn't have touched me, but you don't have to be jealous. I can fight my own battles," I told him, intimidated by his hard and deep stare through the mirror.

"Fuck ... I don't want to act this way. I hate myself when I'm losing control, but when I'm around you and another man touches you, I feel like I'm ready to commit murder, because you're mine," he said.

I swallowed hard. He was probably sharing more with me in this moment than he'd anticipated.

"I'm falling for you hard, and it fucking terrifies me to the point that I feel like I'm spiralling out of control because normally I fucking crave all the control, and these new emotions feel raw. From now on you need to understand that you're mine and no other man touches you. Not only will I break every single bone in his hands but also advertise the fucking consequences."

I wanted to jump into his arms, suddenly happy that he was showing me the most vulnerable part of him, because he cared a lot about me, but I couldn't move. I was paralysed and so turned on by his possessive words, by him showing me his true feelings.

He was truly falling for me?

I didn't know how to react, but warmth fluttered inside my chest when he acted like that, and this wasn't right, but for some reason I liked seeing him so wound up over something so insignificant.

"Spencer." I was getting wet thinking of all the possibilities; my panties were probably drenched by this point. "I'm falling for you, too, but you need to stay calm because I'll be around many other men who may or may not find me attractive." This wasn't only about sex and lust, because we were together as a couple. We were in an actual relationship, and he was having trouble processing that.

He turned around and walked up to me, his eyes heavy on me.

"I'm willing to burn the world for you, but before that I

want to roar at the top of my lungs that you belong to me and only me," he said, his voice husky.

"I'm yours and I'm here to serve you, Prime Minister." The atmosphere between us had shifted, and the air became charged with electricity. I was so turned on, my thighs were clenching with arousal.

His eyes narrowed into slits, and he inhaled sharply.

"Get on your knees, woman," he ordered.

Chapter Thirty-Seven

Laura

I shuddered at his order. Even though he'd manhandled me in front of his family, I was so turned on, ready to do whatever he asked.

As we stared at each other, we understood that neither of us could deny the energy vibrating between us. So I knelt on the cold tiled floor, already imagining sucking his cock, wanting to be in control.

Spencer's shorts strained with a giant bulge. At that moment, he eyed me like a hungry wolf.

"You're such a good girl. I'm going to let you taste me because I can't wait to see you choking on it," he said, low and deep. My chest expanded at his praise, the urge to please him filling me from the inside out.

I reached out, unzipping his shorts and tugging them down

to his knees. He pulled down his boxers, and my mouth watered at the sight of his cock. I needed him too, but this wasn't about me. I wanted to give him a sweet release.

"I thought your cock was beautiful when I first saw it," I said softly.

"I could tell you liked it from the way you were staring at it, baby."

I licked the glistening tip of his salty pre-cum, and Spencer let out an approving growl. After that, I leaned in, my mouth parting as I sucked him between my lips, my jaw stretching to accommodate him. His hand moved down to tangle in my hair. My tongue began swirling around the flesh and when the tip of my tongue found the ridge on his head, I flicked it. Spencer groaned, his hand on my head pushing me further into him.

"This feels so good, baby. Lick it slowly. I don't want to damage your filthy mouth just yet."

I weighed his balls in my palms and sucked his shaft, getting wetter with every passing moment. God, what was he doing to me? I was ready to do anything to please this man. Maybe, deep down, I wanted him to do dirty things to me, to punish me, to tie me up and use me in whatever way he wanted. His dick pulsated; he pushed it so far into my mouth until my vision went blurry. He tugged on my hair, holding my head in place. The vein on the underside of his shaft pulsated on my tongue, and I moaned, a rush of desire surging through me.

"Fuck, you're going to make me explode." He ensured I took his cock all the way to the back of my throat.

I gagged.

His movements were painful, and my jaw ached; he smashed into the back of my throat, thrusting his cock in and out.

"Are you going to swallow me whole, woman?" His voice sounded husky. He was nearing his climax.

Warmth trickled down the back of my throat.

Spencer grunted, his cum filling my mouth. I swallowed it quickly and then tried to get some air into my lungs. He was leaning over the sink, breathing hard and staring at me with a mad gleam.

"Look at the fucking mess you made. Now, I think your pussy needs a little attention."

He wiped the side of my mouth with his thumb. Then he grabbed my face and lifted me to my feet, then kissed me, catching me off completely guard. His tongue pried my mouth open and I lost myself to this feeling, releasing all my emotions and pouring them into him. That kiss was anything but tender. Spencer's kiss turned dangerously toxic and I craved more of his lust on my lips.

"You tasted good, Mr Prime Minister," I said, as I pulled away for a moment.

"Good, because now I'm going to fuck you hard. Try to be quiet. We don't want anyone to hear you coming all over my cock." He twisted me around. "Lean over the sink and spread your legs for me."

"So demanding." I placed my elbow on the sink and did as he asked.

Spencer lifted my dress, then pulled down my knickers. His

hard cock nudged at my entrance, and he thrust into me, my breath hitching. I quietly cried out as he fucked me from behind. Our breaths mingled in the space between us and when he started to slow his movements, his lips skimmed my spine with every thrust. His cock pressed deeper and the thrusts felt even more intense.

Spencer swore when his phone rang suddenly, and he paused for a moment.

"Hello?"

I turned to look at him in horror, wondering if he had lost his mind. He didn't just answer the phone while he was having sex with me in his cousin's house. I was dreaming right?

"Yes, Mother, everything's fine. Maja is doing great, and the family loves Laura," Spencer said.

I tried to wiggle away, but he held me in place. He was still inside me whilst talking to his mother. I shut my eyes, trying to calm my pounding heart because he thrust languidly and it felt so damn good.

"Rupert is doing his own thing ... Yes, I'm taking care of Laura. We are having a fantastic time." He was still fucking me, going painfully slow. Oh God! "All right, see you soon. Laura, say bye to my mum."

I widened my eyes in shock when he handed me the phone.

"Bye, Mrs Banks," I choked out.

He moved faster.

"Bye, dear, take care and enjoy the holiday!" she said and hung up.

"What the hell, Spencer—"

"Stop talking, Laura, you're distracting me." He fisted my hair and tugged on it as if trying to make a point.

He quickly made me forget about the phone call and his mother when the pain seared through my scalp. I was lost in the storm of pleasure and pain.

"Spencer, I'm going to come!" I cried out.

He went deeper and harder. This was intense, fast, and almost brutal, but soon, I let go and came. Waves of pleasure spread through me. A familiar blaze of heat swept from my toes to the roots of my hair. I felt like this man commanded the powers of hellfire, his scent was still all over me as the orgasm detonated inside me. Colours burst behind my eyelids like a fireworks display. I was trembling from the aftershocks, each more satisfying than any previous orgasms that I'd ever had in my whole life.

A moment later, he sealed his mouth over mine, kissing me so deeply that my toes curled. When he finally pulled away, he smiled.

"Come on bella, let's get back to the family," he said, looking very smug, probably knowing that he just gave me the best orgasm of my life.

Spencer got dressed and told me to fix my makeup. I could hardly walk straight. I looked thoroughly fucked, and my hair was a total mess. This house was huge, and we had locked ourselves in the farthest bathroom upstairs, because I didn't want any family members to overhear our antics. Besides, the children were still around. I felt a little guilty thinking about it.

I waited a while before I joined everyone in the garden to make it less obvious that Spencer and I had been away together.

Spencer smirked at me as though letting me know he still wasn't done with me yet. I had never had this kind of sex before. It was so rough, and my jaw still ached.

Beatrice came back after putting Luca down to sleep, and we chatted until late. By the time we got back to our villa, Maja was fast asleep in the back seat of the car. Once we'd carried her inside and settled her into bed without waking, we tumbled into bed and I nodded off with Spencer snuggling into my side.

* * *

The last two weeks passed quickly, and Spencer's family visited us a few more times at the villa. Spencer told Francesco to limit the number of cousins and brothers he was bringing when he was in Italy. Maja couldn't stop talking about her cousins, and I got close to Beatrice, babysitting Luca and the other kids while she went out on a date with her husband.

Spencer had changed into a new man—kind, less obnoxious, and caring when he was relaxed. Spencer opening up about his past made me feel reassured that he trusted me and that our relationship was strong. Sam had wounded him badly, and that was the main reason why he didn't trust women. Apparently, he'd been through therapy a few years ago, and he had attempted to have relationships, but since none of them had worked, he'd gone back to just sleeping around.

We didn't see Rupert at all in the last week of August. He

told Spencer he was somewhere in Croatia and he'd meet us back in London.

Maja, Spencer, and I developed a new routine. In the last week of our holiday, Spencer told me he wanted to cook for us. The housekeeper wasn't too pleased with this new arrangement because I caught her walking around muttering and grumbling in Italian when he'd informed her of this. We were all used to security that seemed to follow us everywhere, although when we were in the villa, they stayed in the background, giving us some privacy. I didn't know if I was ever going to be used to this lifestyle, and if I dated Spencer, I would probably have my own security, too.

"Maybe we should slow down a little when we get back."

We sat on the plane, returning home. It was the beginning of September, and school was restarting next week.

Spencer had his hand on my thigh, and he was reading a book.

"What do you mean? Do you want me to stop making love to you? Is that what you're saying?" he whispered.

He kept his voice low, and in addition, Maja had headphones on and she was sitting two rows in front of us in the small aircraft, so she couldn't hear him. Thankfully.

The man was a sex machine. He was almost forty, and I wondered if he was ever going to leave me alone because he was constantly all over me.

"Yes, Spencer, because we are going back to the usual routine, so we won't be able to have sex all the time." I leaned closer. "My body needs a break from your giant dick. Besides, I'll be due to get my period again soon."

"You love it, so stop moaning, and I don't mind getting dirty when I go down on you later at Number 10." He winked at me.

My jaw dropped.

I closed my eyes, trying to breathe when the image of him on his knees in his private office flashed through my mind.

"Spencer, I'm serious. We have to be careful. You're too much, and you know what will happen if the press finds out about us. There won't be a moment's peace," I said as he moved his hand discreetly upwards, right under my dress.

"Trust me, they won't find out. Besides, what if they do? I'm a single father and not doing anything wrong. I told you, you're mine, and we both agreed to give this a real shot. I want to tell the whole world about us," he said.

When the plane touched down in London, it was raining. It felt good to finally feel the cool air. Jason took us home, and by late afternoon, we were settled in the living room in Number 10, ready to jump into the new routine after the weekend.

"Thank you, Spencer. I had the most amazing time, and I know I said I wouldn't catch any feelings, but I think I'm falling in love with you," I whispered, breathless. We were snuggled together in his bed. This was a bad idea, but he had proven to me he was serious and I wasn't just another fling.

I waited for him to respond, and when I leaned over to see why he wasn't saying anything, I saw that he was already fast asleep.

Chapter Thirty-Eight

Spencer

We came back from Sicily several days later, and as soon as I stepped onto the English soil I felt a little sad that it was time to get back to reality. Maja had just gone back to school, and I still hadn't told anyone what was going on between Laura and I because she was adamant that nothing should change right now. I had to talk to Jeremy and my parents, before I announced it to the world, but things had been so hectic. There was yet another crisis in parliament that I had to deal with.

It was Friday evening and I was still in the office going over some paperwork for the budget. This evening one of the advisors brought me the Chancellor's Red Box. The box was used by ministers to carry and transport official ministerial papers. Tonight, I was supposed to go over some budget details with Jeremy but he'd vanished twenty minutes ago and hadn't come back yet.

My mind kept drifting back to Laura. She was probably in the flat upstairs or maybe in the kitchen since it was pretty late. I was just about to pick up the phone and ask her if she wanted to have dinner together when there was a knock on my door. I frowned, glancing at the clock, knowing that I wasn't expecting anyone. Cath had cleared my schedule for this evening.

"Dad."

It was Maja, she peeked round the door, looking hesitant to enter. I got up and walked up towards her, wondering what she was doing here.

"What's up Maja? Where is Laura?" I asked, a little concerned that Maja was able to come straight in here and none of the security agents had stopped her. I knew they were around, even if they were not right outside the door. Maja always managed to sneak past them somehow.

"She went to check on dinner, so I decided to come see you," Maja said, and then placed her hands on her hips, giving me an intense look. "We need to talk Dad."

I couldn't help but smile, because my daughter looked so serious when she meant business. I was instantly curious to find out what she wanted to talk about.

"All right young lady, sit down at my desk and let's talk," I said, knowing that this conversation was long overdue. I had been meaning to tell Maja that I planned to marry her nanny.

My daughter looked a little surprised, but she marched over to the desk and sat down anyway, while I took the seat opposite her, acting like this was a very important meeting. It still amazed me that she was so confident at such a young age. Maja's eyes settled on me, she was still in her school uniform.

"I want you to marry Laura, Dad and I don't want her to be my nanny anymore. I'm almost ten and I can take care of myself," Maja fired out, catching me completely off guard. I cleared my throat, trying to hide my smile, not expecting her to say anything like that. I thought that she'd come here to talk about us getting a dog, which she knew we couldn't do. She had been nagging me about a pet for the past two years.

"Well, I have been meaning to talk to you about what has been happening between Laura and I since we returned from Sicily, but first of all, I think I owe you an apology," I said, wanting to clear the air between us and put everything that had happened in the past, behind us.

I had done a bit of reflecting over the last few days and I realised that Laura was right all along. Maja had been craving my attention and since I'd taken on the position of the PM I had neglected her. I felt guilty that I'd treated her like she was an inconvenience to me this whole time.

My daughter looked so grown up and she was the spitting image of Samantha. It scared me sometimes, just how much the two of them looked alike, even if I hadn't seen my ex in almost ten years.

"You want to apologise for what?" she asked, looking wary like she thought this was some sort of test.

"I'm sorry that I was selfish about our time together. You are a very smart girl and you know that my job is important to me, but I have to admit that I have worked too much. This shouldn't have happened, I should have come home to have dinner with you, so for that, I need to apologise and from now on it won't happen again. I love you more than you can imagine Maja, and I want us to be a real family, you me and Laura," I said, not even knowing where this came from, but for the first time in my life, I allowed myself to speak exactly what was on my mind. I hadn't told Maja that I loved her often enough and that needed to change. Maja looked totally shocked for several long seconds, while I started to sweat, wondering if maybe I'd gone a little too fast.

"Dad, I love you too and you're my best person in the whole wide world," she finally said. She jumped off her chair and started hugging me tightly. I released the breath that I didn't know I was holding, because for a second I thought she wouldn't accept my apology. She already said that she loved Laura back in Sicily, so I didn't have to worry about her accepting her as her new mum.

"Yes, I am pretty awesome aren't I?" I teased.

"So, are you going to marry Laura?" She asked, giving me the same intense look to make sure that I was serious. I laughed, I couldn't help myself, Maja definitely had my character.

"Of course I'm going to marry Laura. She is very special to me, but only if you give me your permission," I said, lifting my hands up like I was surrendering. I wasn't entirely convinced that we needed to rush things with Laura. I still had no idea how she felt about me and such an unexpected conversation about marriage could spook her, so I had to take this slow. I knew I fucking loved her, but I was too anxious to share my true feelings with her.

"Yaaassss, I am so happy, I really want her to be my mum," Maja said again, jumping up and down with excitement. Moments later, there was a knock at the door and Laura appeared by the door.

"Maja, your grandma is here, we should get going," she announced.

"All right, see you later Dad!" Maja shouted and before I could say anything she flew from the office and vanished behind the door. I stood up, staring at the woman that drove me crazy most of the time, a little confused.

"I didn't know my mother was taking Maja out tonight," I said and Laura smiled mischievously, my cock rising to half mast.

Shit. Did she arrange this so we could have an evening together?"

"I'll explain everything later Daddy," she said and then she quickly shut the door behind her, leaving me completely and utterly speechless. Laura calling me Daddy had unleashed the ripple effect of raw lust through my whole body, and in that moment, I wanted to drag her back into the office and fuck her until she couldn't walk straight.

I forced myself to take control of my reactions while I waited for her to come back. I sat back down and fidgeted in my seat, waiting for her drove me fucking bananas. I was ready to release my cock and start myself off, but somehow I restrained myself, I just needed to be a little more patient.

"All right, I am heading home, we can finish the budget talk tomorrow." Jeremy interrupted my line of thought, walking in unexpectedly. I swore under my breath, wondering what the hell was he still doing here. I thought he'd left ages ago. I lifted my head and glanced at him. I had been snapping at people all day and I knew it had to stop. I didn't want to be the old Spencer anymore.

"I thought you went home earlier, so get the fuck out before I tell the security to escort you out" I said, knowing that Jeremy always worked too hard and he looked exhausted. I wanted him gone before Laura came back, because I had so many dirty things on my mind.

"All right, all right, I'm going now," Jeremy muttered and then he shut the door behind him, finally leaving for the day. I knew that my security was still around, they could never leave as long as I was in the office.

I felt a little bad that I didn't go out to speak to my mother, I blamed Laura for my temporary lapse of judgement. She'd caught me off guard with that mouth of hers, so I would let her deal with it .

My cock started pulsating against my zipper. I was rock hard, and I needed my nanny here, I was planning to fuck her on this desk the moment she stepped inside my office. Quickly, I poured myself a drink. The Scotch burned my throat as I swallowed it in one go.

Several moments later, she finally came back and this time

she didn't knock. She walked straight in and then she locked the door from the inside behind her, without even breaking eye contact with me. Blood started to pound in my ears, because just like my daughter had, Laura meant business. I desperately needed to be inside her right fucking now.

"Good evening Prime Minister," Laura said, standing in front of me, wearing a long khaki jersey dress with long sleeves.

"What fucking took you so long and what the hell are you wearing?" I barked, ready to storm towards her and show her exactly how much her calling me Daddy had affected me. I was pissed, horny as fuck and on edge because she'd left me hanging here. She knew I hated waiting. I didn't think that anything hotter could have come out of her smart mouth. Laura's blond hair was tied up in a messy bun, but one single lock of hair fell onto her face. I inhaled sharply, noticing that she was wearing a pair of high heels.

Was she trying to kill me?

She smirked, then slid her arms inside her jersey dress and slid it over her head, letting it fall on the floor. My eyes took her in and my heart made a somersault in my chest. My whole body went rigid as I stared at her standing there wearing a black and white maids outfit, looking so fucking sexy. I was already burning with anticipation of tonight's encounter. The skirt was really short and barely covered her thighs, exposing her amazing slender figure. My cock was raging hard, pulsating and moistening with pre-cum. Every minute I wasn't inside her was a new level of hell for me.

"Fuck, you're going to be the death of me," I muttered, my voice hoarse.

"I've missed you Spencer, so I asked your mum to have Maja for tonight. I said I wanted to do something special for you and she instantly agreed," Laura explained, still not moving while I was dying to touch her, hold her. "And then, just before I walked in, I overheard your conversation with Maja and my heart melted a little, because you were so sweet Spencer. Maja was so happy when she left, and I was so glad that you finally realised that you'd made a mistake, so after your mum and Maja left I decided to change into this outfit to surprise you."

"That conversation was long overdue sweetheart, but I don't want to talk anymore, because right now, every fibre of my being is forcing me not to bend you over this desk and fuck you so hard until my whole security team hears you scream my name while you're coming all over my cock," I said, clenching my fists so hard that I almost drew blood. My jaw started to ache as I realised I was clenching my teeth trying to keep control of myself. She looked exceptionally beautiful and when she smiled I felt like the whole world was a better place.

"There is no one standing outside this door, most of the agents are further down the hall, Daddy," she replied, taunting me again. Her voice held unfulfilled promises and I was hanging on a thread, ready to do so many filthy things on that desk, but then I had an even better idea.

My cocked throbbed painfully against my zipper as I thought about it for a few seconds. Laura was my queen, and since she was so willing, I was ready to make her my plaything.

Her eyes locked on mine. Her gaze was filled with emerald fire that burned through my skin like someone had placed a hot iron on it. I took off my suit jacket and hung it on the chair, pushing it over to the wall. Laura was watching my every move as I carefully rolled my sleeves up then settled myself on the edge of the desk.

"Take off that slutty dress," I commanded, my voice held the rough edge of frustration. Laura obeyed me instantly, there was no moment of hesitation in her eyes this time, she was willing to do anything to please me. She slipped off her dress, letting it pool at her feet on the floor and stood by the door, wearing only the heels, black lacy panties and matching bra. My cock throbbed more intensely when I said. "Good girl, now crawl to me."

The silence stretched on and the tension between us mounted, the air grew heavy. My slutty little nanny loved this challenge for dominance, I could already see the conflict in her eyes.

"As you wish Prime Minister," she responded and then dropped to her knees. If Laura thought this would be degrading or humiliating, she didn't seem to care. I bet that her pussy was weeping for me.

She began to crawl, my office seemed to stretch forever and I was rigid watching her crawling slowly towards me. My breathing grew erratic as I watched her body sliding closer and closer, her eyes taunting me with desire until she was right by my feet.

"You serve your Prime Minister so well," I praised her as she fixed her eyes on my popping erection and then licked her lips. I knew she wanted to taste me, to take out my raging cock and lick it but I was too turned on to allow her to exercise her control over me. My need to sink into her wet cunt and stay there for the rest of my life was exhilarating.

Laura released a sexy moan and brought her hands between her legs, but I didn't want her to touch herself, so I yanked her upwards by her wrists and captured her mouth in a hard passionate kiss.

She had to understand how much I wanted to have her in that kiss, how much I was willing to give up to see her come apart for me. I was ready to get on my knees for this woman and beg her to be my wife, no matter what it took.

"Spencer, I wanted this evening to be special, but right now I need your beautiful cock in my mouth," she responded breathlessly when we stopped kissing. "I want to swallow you whole, I need you in my mouth."

"And you shall have it, but not right now, because I am going to make you orgasm until you see stars. I want you to remember you belong to me, always and forever, understand?" I asked, holding her tightly in my arms. I was ready to fucking scream that I loved her, but this wasn't the perfect moment that I had pictured, in my mind. Instead I let my eyes, my body, my touch speak for me. She could break me so easily and then I would be the one on my knees in front of her, begging for more. We didn't need the words to understand how profound this moment was for both of us.

"Spencer, I–"

I didn't let her finish what she wanted to say, instead I pulled her to me and with one swift movement I pushed the stuff off my desk. Papers, pens, figures and everything else crashed to the floor, along with the Red Box. Laura gasped when I undid my zipper, letting my raging hard cock spring free. The tip was glistening with pre-cum.

"No talking now my Queen, because I need you to be quiet, I don't want my agent to think that I am murdering you in here while I fuck you so hard that you walk like a cowboy tomorrow," I said, exhaling a sharp, shuddering breath, I roughly parted her thighs, then yanked her knickers down. The memories of me having her for the first time on the kitchen counter etched permanently into my brain as I thought how much I wanted to prolong this very moment.

I skimmed my fingers through her soaking pussy and then shoved them in her mouth, forcing her to taste herself, to see how ready she was for me. Laura's eyes were wide and filled with raw fire.

She must have understood what I was planning to do, because she laid back on the desk. I pushed my cock inside her, then drove home with one powerful thrust of my cock.

She screamed out, lifting both of her thighs upwards to give me better access to her needy cunt and I slammed my hand over her mouth.

"Fuck, my Queen, you feel incredible, and your pussy belongs to me now, only me," I rasped, already on the verge of my release. I couldn't even move yet or I would be done for. Laura let out some muffled noises as I pushed myself into her harder, fucking her fast, the whole desk was shaking. I slowly began to release the heat and tension that had accumulated inside me over these last few minutes. I inhaled the scent of her sweet pussy, pounding into her like a mad man. Split seconds later, Laura was coming, her body shuddering with ecstasy. I fucked her long, hard and voraciously until sweat broke over my forehead and I was panting. I released my palm until she screamed again as my own orgasm brought on another of hers. A shower of lights burst behind my eyes as I held my hand over her mouth as we orgasmed simultaneously. I wanted to ride on this release forever, but I already wanted to go again and make her come even more intensely next time around.

"Spencer, that was incredible," she mumbled when I pulled my hand off her mouth. Then in one swift move, I spun her around, so that now, she was bent over my wooden desk. My phone was buzzing somewhere in the background. It was a total mess in here. The air smelled of sex and scotch.

One hand gripped the back of her neck, the other rested on the curve of her amazing arse, my fingers flexing into the flesh.

"I'm not done with you yet, we need to christen this desk properly," I growled, moving my hand over her arse and stroking it gently. Fuck I wanted to ruin her whole body, fuck her both holes at the same time. I needed more time to prepare her for this. She arched her head and moaned loudly, her thighs quivered when I eased two fingers inside her. She was soaked right through, dripping for me.

"Then own my pussy with that dick, so I can never stop feeling it," she said. I was rock hard again, as soon as she said that. I loved that she was spread out in this position in front of me, ready to take my cock again, begging for it.

"Gladly," I said, and then I thrusted into her with no warning, burying myself in her flesh, deep stretching her to the max. I felt her muscles rippling around the head of my dick and I groaned through my teeth.

"Breathtaking and all mine," I rasped and she was taking my cock so well, moaning and begging me to fuck her harder. I worshipped her scent, peppering kisses over her back as I slammed myself home again and again, powering my hips into her until my balls slapped rhythmically against the back of her thighs.

"Spencer, I'm coming," Laura screamed and I thrust harder, faster. Her entire body seized around me. My cock was locked inside her as thousands of tiny muscles gripped me. I held her as her pussy rippled up and down my cock. She was trembling as her release rolled on.

As she was done, still trembling and loosening off her grip on me, my own goddamn orgasm shattered through my soul like a storm – hard and violent. I ejaculated inside her, being buried deep in her core, filling her up with my sperm. My shout scorched my throat as I branded her with myself, making sure that she remembered this moment forever. I pushed into her until my balls were empty, but my heart was full of love for this woman.

Chapter Thirty-Nine

Spencer

"Sir, your brother, James, is here to see you," Cath said when I picked up the phone.

"Send him in, thank you." I adjusted my tie. My brother's visit was long overdue.

Moments later, the door opened up and James entered. He was dressed in a black suit, and he was immaculate. James was taller than me and broader, he was built like a brick shithouse. Maybe that was the reason he went into the forces as soon as he'd graduated, because even in this office he looked pretty terrifying, especially with that stone-cold expression. His jet-black hair was styled in a short, cropped back and sides.

"Prime Minister," he mocked with a slight bow as he sat on the sofa.

He had a file in his hand, so I instantly knew he had what I'd had asked him to get.

"Let's skip the small talk, James," I said, not even knowing why I was suddenly nervous. Things were going well with Laura, and my brother was good at what I needed for her. I didn't want him to get involved, but he was the only person who could track down Laura's sister since she couldn't find her. "Do you have what I asked for?"

James kept staring at me intensely with his usual detached air. He'd been through a lot in Iraq, and when he'd come back he was not the same guy as before.

"Yes, it took me a little longer to track down the name, because it appears that Laura's sister didn't want to be found, but everything is in the file," he said, then he stood and buttoned up his suit jacket. "I told you that your nanny was a liability, and she still is, Spencer. I now understand why you are so infatuated with her."

"What are you talking about?" I stood, and then I snapped the file out of his hand. I opened it and scanned through the text, suddenly feeling like my entire fucking world had crumbled beneath my feet.

This is not possible. No fucking way.

I glanced back at James whose face was still completely devoid of any emotions. His perfect poker face was getting to me.

"How could I've been so fucking blind?" I stared at the

picture from over twenty-five years ago. There was only one, but the resemblance was striking.

"You were thinking with your dick, not your brain, that's for sure." James sounded bored, then he absentmindedly adjusted his cufflinks.

Blood was drumming in my ears. It had been nine fucking years, and she had never reached out to me, not even once.

"I need you to find her for me, I've to speak to Samantha." I wanted to punch the wall. My thoughts were suddenly racing. She had set me up, and I was so blinded by my attraction towards Laura that I hadn't seen it.

"No need, she's already back in London, and she's probably going to pay you a visit soon," he said. "I presume you can take it from here?"

I had no idea how come James was so fucking calm while I was shaking inside, but it was in his nature now. He kept all his emotions tightly bottled up.

"Yes, I'll take care of it," I snapped and then went back to my desk.

Laura was going to freak, and I had no fucking clue how to deal with it. What was Samantha after?

James walked towards the door, but just as he was about to leave, he stilled, then turned around.

"Spencer, your nanny is still a liability. Stop thinking with your dick and use your brain. End things with her, before she costs you your career," he said, and before I could reply, he left the room and quietly shut the door behind him.

I held my head in my hands, reminding myself to breathe,

but the fact that Samantha had turned out to be Laura's biological sister made me question everything that had happened in the past.

James's words rang in my head, but I still had no idea what his problem was with Laura. Me being Prime Minister and dating my nanny would cause a bit of a wave in the press, but I was a bachelor, I could date whoever I wanted at the end of the day.

I looked through the papers, and my head was still fucking spinning. I was uncomfortable with this whole situation. Why would Samantha do this? She was not interested in Maja. I had full custody, so why did she have to get Laura involved, too? I knew for a fact that I had to share the truth for her today.

Moments later, I picked up the phone and told Cath to clear my schedule for the rest of the day. Jeremy wasn't going to be happy, but this matter was much more pressing.

Laura deserved to know the truth, and I had to be the one to break the news to her.

Jeremy barged inside. He must have run all the way here, because his face was beetroot red and he was panting heavily.

He shut the door quickly and ran over to my desk.

"The photo! Someone has leaked it online, and the press secretary is already getting phone calls from journalists about it," he said when I lifted my head.

I told myself to breathe, because there couldn't be another crisis.

"What photo? You're not making any sense, Jeremy," I said.

Then he handed me his phone, and I swore under my

breath. Someone must have taken a photo of Laura and me when I had lifted her and carried her over my shoulder back in Sicily.

"It was a private area. How did the paparazzi find a way to get in?" I said, not even hearing my own voice.

"Spencer, we need to do a press release. Maybe you can say that you had a temporary lapse of judgement while you were on holiday, but now—"

"Jeremy, what the hell are you even talking about?" I cut him off. "I didn't bloody have a lapse of judgment. Laura means everything to me, I love her, and I'm not going to end things with her."

My heart was pounding as Jeremy stared at me with his eyes wide. I loved her, and I didn't know why I'd only just realised that, but I loved her so much that it hurt.

"Don't be a fool, Spencer, she's just your nanny," Jeremy fired out.

"No, she's not just my nanny, she's going to be my fucking wife," I barked back at him and then got up.

"Where are you going?"

"Out, and don't follow me, I'm taking the rest of the day off."

* * *

I decided I was going to talk to Laura about Samantha first. I was worried about the leaked photos and the media backlash, they could paint me as a playboy bachelor all they liked. Sure, this whole thing was inappropriate, but no one knew how we'd met. As long as the majority of this stayed out of the press, then I had nothing to worry about.

Laura was in the kitchen, reading a book and eating an apple. She was so fucking adorable, and for a moment I just stood by the door, gazing at her and wondering how she was going to take such shocking news.

"Spencer, what are you doing here? Is everything all right?" She put the book down.

I took a deep breath and dragged my hand through my hair.

"Yes and no. I need to tell you something, and you need to sit down for this," I told her.

Her blonde hair was tied up in a messy knot, and her green eyes were studying me intensely. I handed her the file that James had brought me.

"I asked my brother, James, to track your sister down after our conversation back in Sicily, and he just brought me this," I said when she opened the file and started scanning it.

"This can't be right," she said, skimming through it, the frown on her forehead deepening.

"Samantha, Maja's mother is your biological sister, which means that Maja is your niece," I explained, still pretty much in shock as I stared at Laura.

She lifted her gaze to me, paling instantly. Her mouth gaped open in disbelief.

"How? I mean, I don't understand, and I don't believe in such a coincidence, Spencer," she said, her voice trembling.

I sat next to her and wrapped my hands around hers.

"I don't think it's a coincidence at all. James found out that

Samantha was actually the one who called you. I mean, she used some sort of device to change her voice. She wanted us to meet, I've no idea why, but I'm going to find out." I hoped I could get to the bottom of this quickly.

"I can't believe this, Maja is my niece? This is truly unbelievable," she whispered, but then a small smile appeared on her lips.

We were both trying to process this, and it wasn't going to be easy.

"Hold on, how are you going to find her?"

"James told me she's back in London, so it shouldn't be too difficult. I need to figure out what she wants," I added and then took another deep breath. I didn't want to be the bearer of bad news, but Laura needed to know about the photo, too. "But that's not all. Right before I came here, Jeremy barged into my office. Someone snapped a photo of us in Sicily when I was carrying you and posted it online."

Laura brought her hands to her face, releasing a horrified gasp. This wasn't good, but it was something I had to deal with head-on.

"Oh my God, what are you going to do, Spencer?" she asked.

I smiled and pulled her up to her feet, then I wrapped my hands around her body, hugging her tightly. I inhaled her scent; fuck, I didn't want to lose her. I had never been more sure of anything.

"Don't worry about this for now, I'm going to deal with it, but I'll ask someone from security to get Maja from school today and then you probably should stay at home for a few days. This whole thing will blow over soon," I said, already formulating a plan in my head of how I was going to tackle this whole scandal.

"I should go back to my apartment, and we should probably not see each other for a little while," she started saying.

I grabbed her face, suddenly feeling like I might lose control.

"No, this isn't happening. I want you to stay right where you belong, Laura, you're not going anywhere. I'm going to fight for us, no matter what. I told you, I want to tell the whole world about us." I looked directly into her eyes.

"All right, Spencer, I trust you," she said.

I smiled at her before I kissed her, not knowing why I couldn't just tell her how I felt about her.

Chapter Forty

Spencer

"We are done for, the photo is all over the news." Jeremy flopped down on the sofa and buried his face in his hands.

It had been two days since the photo had been leaked online, and now everyone was gossiping about the fact that I was screwing my nanny. This was not what I ever wanted, it was a PR mess, but I couldn't say I was overly surprised. I still hadn't tracked Samantha down, and that was a real worry, because I knew she was planning something.

She was the one who'd left me, so I didn't understand her motivation for what she'd done to me, but that didn't change the fact that I needed to speak to her.

"Are you all right, Jeremy? You really should try to avoid all this stress, you have high blood pressure," I told him, still thinking and talking to all my advisors about how to solve this whole saga.

"Spencer, you're my good friend. I think you should call a press conference. People will want to hear your side of the story."

I was just about to tell him no when the door opened and Cath stood there appearing harassed.

"Sir, there's a Samantha Morrison here for you. She's not on the list of approved visitors, but she said she's family," Cath explained.

I jumped up, a wave of anger rippling through me. Of course she'd decided to show up when things were blowing up. I should have found her much earlier; now everything was getting so complicated.

"Send her in," I said and then turned to Jeremy. "It's Maja's mother, and I've to speak to her, so can you give us a few minutes?"

Jeremy was surprised.

"Sure, but we should talk about this later," he said and then he stood. He passed the woman who had left me out of the blue, almost nine years ago, in the doorway. He glanced at her for a few seconds before he shut the door behind him.

I released the breath that I didn't know I was holding, staring at Maja's mother, not quite believing she had actually shown up after so many years of no contact.

"I've been expecting you," I said and stuffed my hands in my pockets.

I couldn't believe she was really here, in my fucking office, acting as if no time had passed at all.

I took a few deep breaths and counted to ten, but it didn't work to calm the rage building within me. I had hoped Samantha wouldn't show up here and suddenly decide that she was going to be Maja's mother again.

I went over to my desk, but I couldn't sit. I was too worked up staring at Samantha's wavy blonde hair. The resemblance was striking, and I did notice it before, but I hadn't really connected the dots back when I first met her. I was too busy thinking with my dick rather listening to the voice of reason. Laura was more beautiful, and her features were more natural, but they still looked so much alike. Samantha had changed little over the years. She was dressed immaculately, still wearing designer clothes.

"Have you? I thought I'd surprised you, but obviously I didn't plan it properly." She smiled and brushed her red nails through her long hair. "I came to rescue you, of course. I see there's trouble in paradise." She pulled out a brown envelope from her bag and tossed it on my desk. "There's something very interesting inside. I hope it will help you piece all the clues together, my dear Spencer. You should have vetted your nanny before you let her into your bed."

I sighed loudly, telling myself to stay calm, but I was on the verge of losing my shit. She had always been cunning and manipulative. It had been years since we'd last seen each other, but since I'd found out she was Laura's sister, I was piecing everything together slowly in my head.

"And how are you going to rescue me? Are you going to join the press conference and act like nine years have not gone by? Pretend that you didn't just abandon your daughter and never looked back?" I wondered what I had ever seen in her. We were young, and she was my first ever big love. "You came because you must have found out that Laura is your biological sister. Tell me, did you know when we were together that you had a sister?"

If Samantha was surprised that I'd figured out her game, she didn't show it. She placed one long leg over the other one, appearing comfortable.

"I knew I had a sister, but I never felt obligated to search for her. I wanted to forget about that part of my life, but things changed. I started looking for her two years ago," she said. "I came back because you would need my help and, cards on the table, I need some financial assistance."

"Bullshit. I know you well, Samantha. You came back because you saw an opportunity. All of this is your doing. You didn't come here for Maja—you still don't even care about your child," I said. Samantha thrived on drama. Indeed, she lived for it. "Maja doesn't need a selfish, absentee mother, and I don't care what is in the envelope. Leave before I call security."

A smile played on her lips. Her eyes were devoid of any warmth as she gazed at me.

"No, Spencer, I'm not leaving until I get what I came here for," she said firmly. "Maja was a mistake. You knocked me up and you didn't want to hear about abortion. Sure, you manage to persuade me to have her, but I was hormonal and so young back then. I should have never made that decision."

Maja didn't deserve this. She was such a good child.

"We don't need to dwell on the past now because we can come to an agreement. I've some very interesting photos of Laura. She has betrayed you for money. Here is a screenshot of her bank account."

I stared at her, blood thrumming in my ears. I didn't want to believe her. Sam had become bitter and angry. I couldn't figure out why she hated Laura so much. The two of them were sisters by blood.

She took the envelope from my desk and then opened it. Laura would never betray me. She had been with me since the beginning of the summer, and I'd paid her well.

There was a screenshot from her bank and one transaction that Sam or someone else had highlighted showing over two hundred thousand pounds being deposited. My heart drummed faster.

"I'm not going to explain to you how I got that information, but I wanted you to see for yourself that Laura is a liar and she has been using you since the moment you moved her into Number 10. She was the one who leaked the photo of you two from Sicily to the press and started this whole drama. Check the envelope, because all the evidence is in there, besides, you should go and ask her yourself. Tell her that you want to see her phone," Samantha explained while I clenched my fists. "Also, I've an idea of how we can fix your image with everyone talking about you and the nanny."

"I'm all ears. Tell me what's on your mind?" I asked, but deep down I still didn't believe her. Laura couldn't have betrayed me. She was kind and had a good heart. It wasn't in her character to do something like that.

"We go in front of the camera and we tell the whole world that we reconciled. You fire Laura and tell the press that she was the one who seduced you and that she was trying to take advantage of your position. I've given this a lot of thought and realised it should be me next to the Prime Minister, not my so-called sister. It's not fair. Of course, just as Laura is being paid to be your *nanny*, I won't do this for free. Your whole family is rich, and I was stupid to leave without severance pay, but we live and learn. Once you've given me a sufficient amount, I'll go away and have the life that I deserve. You can show the nation that you're a family man with values and you care what your voters think about you."

I dragged my hand through my hair, trying to think. In a way Sam was right. People weren't going to be too impressed with the fact that I was fucking around with my nanny, however, it wouldn't ruin my career. This whole thing would have been different and immoral if I was a married man with children, but I wasn't. I had been single for years and I had the right to date any woman I wanted to, including my nanny.

"Just get the hell out of my office, Sam, we are done here and we have nothing else to discuss," I snapped at her, having had enough of her dictating how to get out of this mess to her benefit.

She got up, staring at me intensely. Finally, the sly smile vanished.

"I'm doing this for you, Spencer, because I care about you. I know this is going to hurt, but your nanny has betrayed you," she added and then tossed the brown envelope on my table before she marched towards the door.

I snatched the envelope, breathing hard and trying to control my anger, but I was ready to smash my fist against the wall. When the door finally slammed shut, my mind raced, thinking about what I was going to do next.

I took the paperwork out of the envelope and stared at the photo of Laura and Lucian. I wasn't sure where these were taken, but Laura was standing on the street with him. They were smiling. What the fuck? The next picture had Laura, Lucian, and Louise Rogers, the reporter, in it. Blood drained from my face when I saw Laura was typing something on her phone while the reporter woman was showing her the screen of hers.

Was Laura taking her number?

Was it possible that Laura could have leaked that photo online because she needed money?

I trusted her with all my heart. She couldn't have betrayed me like that. In fact, I refused to believe she had. Those pictures didn't prove a thing, really. I should sit down and have a talk with her.

In truth, there were times I wanted to tell the world about us, and as I'd told Laura, that kind of press leak didn't faze me much.

Why would I be disappointed then?

Maybe the possible deception ... the going behind my back ...

Jeremy barged in, and he looked totally distraught.

"I just got a phone call from a guy at the BBC, and he shared some disturbing news with me," Jeremy said, shutting the door.

He paced while I stared at the photographs, attempting to make sense of them.

"Jeremy, I need to be alone to think for a moment," I said calmly.

He slapped his hands on the desk, getting my attention.

"Listen to me, man, and listen to me carefully. Your nanny is a liability. She sold you out. A huge sum of money was deposited into her account a few hours ago. Apparently, Louise Rogers from ITV has convinced her to do an exclusive interview. Now pull yourself together and let's figure out how to deal with this before it's too late," he said.

So ... she did do it for money? Was I a terrible judge of character? Had I just imagined her caring, her love for Maja? I put my head in my hands, leaning over the desk and wanting nothing more than to shut the world out. How could she? There had to be an explanation for all of this. If I lost faith in Laura, too, my whole life would fall apart. How could I ever trust another woman ever again?

"She's not like that. She ... she couldn't have done it," I murmured, ready to fucking throw up. I wasn't angry anymore, just broken. Disappointed. Laura couldn't be after my money, but the proof I had showed otherwise.

Perhaps I didn't know her at all ...

"Listen, man, I'm sorry you had to find out this way, but we have all the evidence. Besides, there were some other things from her past that didn't add up. You need to fire her while I get the press conference ready," he stated. "Is Maja's mother still here? She could help us if we play this right. If you show a united front—"

"No way. I'm not going anywhere near that woman. Come up with an alternative," I said.

"Are you fucking kidding me? What will the nation think if their prime minister lets himself be duped by his own nanny?" he argued. "Everyone will suddenly think you can't keep control in your own household. Therefore, how can you lead their country?"

"I'm not giving in to Sam's blackmail. She came back because she wants to suck me dry, you know. She's not doing this out of the goodness of her heart, Jeremy. She just wants money out of me. She's evil," I said. "Now, I'm going to speak to Laura, whether you like it or not. I'll be back later."

Chapter Forty-One

Laura

"Why are you so sad?" Maja asked while we were watching a Disney movie in her room upstairs.

More people were arriving in the press room, and I didn't know what to do. Spencer had told me to switch off my phone and wait for him. He also said he was going to track down Samantha, but it had been a few days since I'd learned the truth and he hadn't managed to find her yet. I was wondering what she was planning.

"I'm not sad, just a little worried about your dad," I explained, on edge. I couldn't believe someone had leaked that photo online, and now it felt like the whole world was talking about me and Spencer.

"Are you going to break up with my dad and then I'll never see you again?" Maja asked.

I glanced at her, wondering where this was coming from. She couldn't have known what was going on.

"What? Why would you say something like that?" I asked.

Maja was perceptive, though, and she'd seen me when we were surrounded by reporters outside her school. She could have easily put two and two together.

"Because he upset you, and you don't want to be my real mum. I overheard Melissa saying that my dad is in big trouble because of you," she stated.

I sighed and stroked her hair, trying to figure out how to explain the situation. Moments later, I heard the door downstairs, and Spencer called up for me.

"I promise I'll explain everything after I speak to your dad, all right?"

"Fine," she replied but didn't seem too convinced.

Spencer stood in the doorway. I could instantly tell he was very stressed out.

"Maja, I'm going to talk to Laura downstairs. You'll be okay here for a minute?" he asked.

Something had happened—he was not himself. I could sense it.

I followed him downstairs, all the way to his private office, each step urging more panic to rise in my chest.

"What is going on, Spencer?" I asked nervously.

He leaned against his desk, his arms crossed over his chest. "Have you got your phone on you?"

"Yes, but you asked me to switch it off, so I've," I told him.

He dragged his hand through his hair, and only then did I notice he wasn't wearing a tie. He had dark circles under his eyes. Pulling out his phone, he scrolled through it and placed it in front of me. On the screen was a picture of me standing in the street with Lucian and the reporter lady. I had bumped into them a few days after we'd come back from Sicily. I had no idea what they were doing together, but when Lucian had introduced us, I'd told him we already knew each other.

"What were you doing with them?"

"I bumped into them outside the coffee shop. Lucian introduced me to this woman. She asked for my email address—apparently, she wanted to write an article about people who work closely with public figures, but I turned her down, of course," I said.

"Why are you lying to me? I know you were the one who leaked our photo online. I also know about the payment posted in your account, Laura. You don't have to pretend, but at least tell me why you did it," he said in a flat tone.

Yet underneath it all, I sensed the pain.

I stared at him, unable to form a single word. An awkward and painful silence stretched for some time.

"Are you serious? You think I leaked that photo of us online to make money? Do you even know how ridiculous that sounds?" I finally found my voice. I turned my phone on.

"Log in to your internet banking. I know the money is there,

Laura, so you can stop lying to me right now and tell me why you have betrayed me—*us*," he said.

My mind was trying to process what he'd just said.

I handed him my phone, hurt that he was saying these things to me, as though he no longer trusted me. He scrolled through it, and I could practically feel the tension in my body.

"See, there's nothing there, Spencer, and I think—"

"An unknown number sent you this late last night." He handed me back the phone.

I glanced at my messages, and there was indeed one that I must have missed last night. A picture. I opened the photo and gasped, realising that someone had snapped a picture of Spencer when he'd picked me up off the sand in Sicily and thrown me over his shoulder. The timing was perfect, and the photo of us was pretty good.

I opened my mouth to tell him that there was some kind of mistake because I hadn't seen that message last night. Besides, the text arrived at nine p.m., and I was with him then. My phone was in my room.

Then he handed me back his phone—a screenshot of my bank statement, showing a transaction for two hundred thousand pounds. I gasped and then quickly logged in to my internet banking. My heart was going a hundred miles an hour as I tried to breathe; I couldn't get enough oxygen into my lungs. It only took several seconds, and when my balance revealed that I was loaded, I widened my eyes in terror.

"I honestly don't know where this money came from, Spencer, and I hadn't leaked that photo. I swear to God, I have no idea what is going on right now. Please believe me! This is absurd," I shouted, tears streaming down my cheeks. Someone was setting me up, but the way Spencer was staring at me in that moment felt like he was plunging a blade into my heart.

"Unfortunately, Laura, I have to let you go. You cannot be Maja's nanny any longer because I don't trust you anymore. All the evidence is here, right in front of you, so you can stop lying already. I'll send the car, and the driver can take you back to your apartment," he said.

But I wasn't listening to him anymore. I kept shaking my head, ready to get on my knees and plead for him to listen to me and believe that he was wrong about me. About this.

"I've more important things to deal with. I've a press conference to attend, and it's better if you are no longer associated with the Banks family anymore. You have done enough damage as it is."

"Are you seriously firing me?" I asked in complete shock. I was shouting at this point. My whole body was shaking, and I kept telling myself that this wasn't happening for real.

He stared at me with a detached and cold expression.

"What did you expect that I would do?" he asked, his voice low. "Cath will send you the confirmation by email. You can collect the rest of your things later."

"No, I'm not going anywhere. We need to talk about this, please. Why would I leak that photo to the press? You were paying me well enough, I didn't need that money. This makes little sense," I said, quickly wiping the tears away from my face. In his eyes, I was the woman who'd taken advantage of his situation, pretended that she cared and then betrayed him. I thought he was different from other men, different from Jake in assuming the worst of me, but ... that money in my account was pretty damning.

"I don't know anymore, Laura, but I'm taking Maja to Sarah's, and she's going to stay there for a little while until this whole thing is settled," he said. "And I don't want you here when she comes back. I know she's going to be devastated, but I've to protect my family and my reputation."

"So this is it? Are you going to dig more into this? I'm telling you, I've been framed. And you know me well enough to know I don't care for status or money. Does it not appear a little odd to you? After what we've been through?"

No answer from him. Just a stiff jaw and impassive face.

Regret and resentment took root in my very soul. He really did believe I'd done this.

I took a deep breath and briefly closed my eyes, bracing myself. Doing my utmost to not break down in front of him. "If I go now, Spencer, that is it. Maja will be the one to suffer, not you or your fucking over-the-top ego. This hurts me so much. She and I've a bond, and I don't want to leave her, but you have crushed my dignity. I'll not beg because it's obvious you don't believe me. You don't want to give me the benefit of the doubt, even though things look bad. You talk about trust, but that goes both ways! I didn't do this," I said, my voice rising a little at the end. I was dying inside because this man had lost faith in me.

I was nothing to him.

"Maja is strong, and I'll find a great nanny for her ... and whatever happened between us will never happen again," he said through gritted teeth.

This hurt so much more than I could imagine. Not the fact that he'd made the decision that we were over, but the fact that he didn't even care about his own daughter's feelings. Maja was my niece, and she was only nine. This would upset her, but Spencer was blinded by his own ego, so nothing else mattered to him anymore.

"There's no us because according to what you've just told me, there never was. A relationship where trust is so fragile that it can break at the drop of a hat? It doesn't exist. We claimed to feel so much for each other, but it appears we were only fucking after all. But I tell you this: once I prove I had nothing to do with that picture, it will settle this matter and that will be the end of it," I said and marched out of the office, swallowing my tears. There was no way I would cry in front of him. I wouldn't give him the satisfaction.

He didn't follow me out, of course. All the evidence pointed to me being the culprit.

My heart shattered with every step I took. I went to my room anyway, because I had some personal items that I needed and I truly didn't want to go back to this apartment ever again, even though this would truly break Maja's heart, but it was for the best. I would try to talk to her at some point, but I was in no shape to face her right then.

I asked the driver to drop me off right outside my flat. I ran upstairs, knowing that Veronica was home, and dropped the suitcase on the bed. From the moment I switched on my phone,

I'd received countless messages from my parents and other concerned friends.

But now that I was alone, I broke down and cried my heart out.

I cried and cried until there were no more tears left.

Veronica burst into my bedroom when I was wiping my face, trying to get a grip.

"Laura, oh my goodness, what's the matter? I saw what happened and I'm so glad you're home, thank God," Veronica said.

She cradled a mug of tea. "Oh dear, sweetie, you're really not okay." Sitting on the bed next to me, she pulled my head gently onto her shoulder. "Please don't cry, baby. Everything is going to be all right."

When Spencer had told me about Samantha, I'd called Veronica immediately, dropping this bomb on her. She couldn't believe it herself, but after everything that had happened, it made sense. We'd talked on the phone for an hour, trying to figure out what to do next, because I really wanted to speak to Samantha. I needed to know why she'd pushed me into Spencer's life and when she had actually found out about me.

"He didn't believe me, not at all, and I'm not surprised, but I'm shocked that he had such a low opinion about me," I said.

"Spencer Banks is an arsehole. He doesn't deserve you, and the sooner he realises the better," she said.

I wanted to cry harder, but what was the point? I had to be positive.

"I think I should talk to Rupert."

"No, please, Veronica, don't talk to anyone. All the evidence is there, and I just need some time to figure out what to do next for the best. It's not worth it. Spencer hurt me, but he will destroy Maja, because this will break her little heart. She wanted me to be her mother, and now I won't be able to even see her."

"All right, don't worry, I won't talk to anyone, but I'll help you. We will clear your name together and figure out who framed you." She allowed her warmth to seep into my cold bones. "I'll make you a mug of hot cocoa. That always cheers you up. Extra marshmallows."

"Why would anyone hate me that much, Veronica? There's two hundred grand in my account, and someone sent that picture of us in Sicily to my phone last night before it went to the media." I told her what she already knew, because I couldn't stop talking about this. Spencer had fired me like I meant nothing to him, and this hurt so damn much.

She rubbed my back, her hands moving in slow circles, and I had to admit, on some level it was quite soothing.

"I don't have any answers right now, but I promise that we will figure it out together. How about that hot drink first? If that arsehole really believes you would do something like this, then he's not worth your time. He's never been worth it." She squeezed my arm.

I didn't respond, but she was right. I was in love with him, but he was never worthy of this love—ever.

Chapter Forty-Two

Spencer

I watched her leave, and my heart turned to stone. It was pounding, and my palms were damp with sweat.

I stood in my kitchen, holding a cup of tea in my hand, although I was ready to down a whole bottle of scotch. My heart fucking burned, and the pain was spreading. We were done, and she was never coming back. I had no fucking idea how I was going to break the news to Maja.

I had never felt more distraught and let down than I did in that moment. It took me a while to get to a point where I could face others. I should be trained for this in my position, but nothing had prepared me for what had happened.

When I was somewhat ready, I headed over to Maja's room, knowing that my own daughter was going to hate me for it. Laura was her aunt, and maybe at some point in the future I would allow them to see each other again, but not over the next few days or maybe even weeks. Laura had betrayed me, and I didn't want to be associated with her any longer.

Maja was on her iPad when I walked in, but she instantly put it down, frowning.

"Where is Laura?"

I sat on her bed, not even knowing where to start. Maja was smart, but I couldn't tell her what had happened, especially since she'd bonded with Laura so well over the past few months.

"I asked her to leave, because she has betrayed my trust and she's not coming back." I got straight to the point.

Maja jumped off the bed, staring at me with her eyes wide.

"No, Dad, you can't, Laura is the best nanny that I ever had, you have to bring her back, right now!" Maja folded her arms and was quite angry.

I wasn't really sure what to say next.

"I'm sorry, hun, but it's not possible. Laura isn't coming back, and I know you love her, but I cannot trust her anymore. Sarah is going to be here soon, and from now on she's going to be looking after you. It's only temporary until I find another nanny." I felt like the worst father in the world.

Maja's face went red, and she pushed my chest with her tiny hands.

"No! I don't want Sarah, I want Laura back. She's the best, and you're the worst. I want you to call her right now!"

I grabbed her wrists, trying to stay calm as my stomach felt like a churning cement mixer. Maja sobbed and hit me with her fists. I couldn't take it. I knew I was the cause of her pain, but she had to accept that sometimes we just didn't get everything we wanted in life.

"I'm sorry, hun, but I didn't want to lie to you. Come on, calm down now." I took her into my arms while her little body shook. I felt so helpless—how was I going to fix this? Her room suddenly felt so small, and Laura's scent was still lingering in the air. The whole residence reminded me of her, and I had no fucking idea how I was going to move on.

"W-why did you have to let her go? What happened?" she finally stammered.

I released a heavy sigh. I couldn't tell her everything, but I had to give her something.

"She revealed information about me to the press, and that really upset me," I explained with a heavy heart. I was squeezing her tightly, hoping that maybe she would understand this.

Then she pushed herself off me and got off my lap. Tears were still streaming down her cheeks.

"She made a mistake, and everyone makes mistakes sometimes, but you can still call her, please, Dad, please," she was saying.

I stared at her while my heart was jackhammering loudly. My shirt stuck to my back while Maja was still begging.

"I'm sorry, sweetheart, but I can't. Cath will take you to Sarah shortly—"

"I hate you, I hate you so much and I never want to see you ever again, not until you bring Laura back!" she screamed.

She was hysterical at this point, and I got up and went to bring her closer, but she moved.

"Maja, darling—"

"No, don't touch me, you're the worst father in the whole world, and I hate you. Leave me alone, leave now!" She continued to shout and started pushing me out of her room.

I didn't know what to do, how to act in this situation. She was going crazy, and I didn't want her to hurt herself, so I left the room. Maja slammed the door and then continued to shout that she hated me.

Why had I done this to her? What if Laura really didn't do this and I'd blamed her so quickly? My thoughts were suddenly racing so fast. I marched all the way back to the kitchen, feeling like the whole world was crumbling beneath my feet. Blackness obscured my vision for a split second. I grabbed my phone and called my mother. She agreed to help instead of Maja having to go to Sarah, and I was suddenly so grateful that my mother was coming to stay with us for a while.

It was just the beginning of a long and stressful week.

* * *

The next few days passed in a blur, and I remembered little of what had happened. Some members of the opposition party were expressing their concerns in interviews, but I didn't worry about that. My performance was immaculate, and I never did anything wrong. Still, the public had to be appeased.

"Sir, this is a very serious matter, and things might sort themselves out if you make a public address. The press knows that you fired your nanny, and people are talking," George Farleigh, one of my cabinet members, told me over the phone.

"Don't worry, George, I'll take care of this. I'm working on the press release as we speak," I told him, but deep down I wanted to tell him to go to hell. This was my private life, and the media shouldn't interfere.

Over the next few days, I only saw darkness and I felt miserable. Maja was not speaking to me. She kept kicking me out of her room and slamming the door in my face. She kept saying she hated me. I tried to console her, but she was even more stubborn than me.

"Spencer, you have to give her time. She really loved Laura," Mum said.

We chatted until late in the kitchen after she had temporarily moved in.

"Are you certain she was the one who leaked the photo? I might be a bit biased, but I don't see why she would do such a thing."

"It doesn't matter, I fired her, and that's the end of the story. I know she's technically family now, but I don't trust her," I said, calmly, because I was done with shouting and barking at people.

My mother rubbed her hand over my back.

"All right, let me make you a camomile tea, you shouldn't be drinking right now," she said and then put the kettle on.

I finally began to appreciate the fact that my mother was willing to drop everything and help me. Sometimes I was too harsh with her, because I was putting on the angry mask that belonged to the other Spencer Banks.

Moments later, I got up and went to embrace her, feeling like the worst human being in this world.

"Thank you for being here and helping me with Maja," I told her.

She pulled away, stroking my face, smiling.

"You have a good heart, darling, and everything will be all right, Maja will come around," she assured me. "But you have to let her see Laura. I know you don't trust her, but this poor girl is her aunt. Trust me on this, Spencer."

I didn't want to agree and I didn't want Laura back in my apartment, because I would be a wreck if I even sensed her smell, but Maja was miserable.

"Fine, but you will have to arrange it so Laura visits her in your house. I don't want her here," I said, well aware that I was fucking in love with her, no matter how much I tried to deny it.

"Yes, I'll make sure she goes there," Mum said, sounding happy.

Laura's soft laugh kept haunting me, but that wasn't the only thing that kept me up at night. Sam had called me a few times, although I only spoke to her once, hoping she would eventually get the message and stop bothering me. She was still after my money, but I firmly told her she wasn't getting a penny from me, so she changed her tune and said she wanted to see Maja. I nearly broke my phone, but then I hung up and told Cath to call my lawyer. Samantha was a leech, and I was still having trouble processing the fact she was Laura's biological sister.

The next day was the day I allowed Laura to see Maja. I just didn't have the heart to separate the two any longer, so my mother arranged for her to go to her house. It was easier and safer that way. The press kept occupying the whole street outside Number 10, and my father said that reporters were outside my parents' house, too.

It was nearly four o'clock in the afternoon, and I had a meeting coming up that I couldn't miss.

In my head, I kept replaying all the good times Laura and I had together in Italy, rehashing memories of a woman who'd turned my life upside down. I missed her like crazy, and I could barely function because she was constantly on my mind. Maybe she was telling the truth that she was set up. Maybe I'd reacted too impulsively. But the money ...

I dragged my hand through my hair. I could smell her in my bedroom, bathroom, kitchen, and, of course, in Maja's room. I never thought I would get attached to her, but she'd gotten under my skin so fast. There was no point in lying to myself anymore. I cared for her in a way I'd never cared for another woman. Even Samantha.

I got on with my meetings and then headed home for an early night. Then, Mum called, asking me to come over for dinner. I knew what she was doing. She wanted me to talk to Laura, and I was too exhausted to argue with her, so I told her I would think about it.

I desperately wanted to see her again.

I pottered around the apartment for a while, trying to find something to do, but I was restless. If I didn't see her, I might lose my mind because her absence drove me insane.

She was my weakness, but she'd wounded me.

Had she, though? I never gave her a chance to really explain.

In the end, it didn't matter. I was thoroughly fucked.

I called security and asked them to send the driver over, and he took me to my mother's.

"Thanks," I said to him when I got out of the car.

My mother opened the door for me with a smile.

"I'm so glad that you could make it, Spencer," she said after I embraced her. "Dinner should be ready soon. Maja is playing with Laura upstairs. I don't know what you have done to that poor girl, but I'm begging you to fix it. She looks like she's lost at least ten pounds."

I sighed and rubbed my chin, feeling as though someone had broken a piece of my heart into even smaller pieces. We needed to talk. Fuck, I wanted to forget about this nightmare, but I knew I couldn't.

I went inside and stayed in the living room for a bit while my father was rambling about the foreign policy and the conflict in the Middle East. Nothing was working, I could barely listen to him, because Laura was so close, she was only upstairs, and I suspected she didn't expect to see me here. This was her time with Maja.

"All right, Spence, I'll distract Maja in the kitchen for a little while and you can go speak to Laura. Oh, and Rupert is coming for dinner, too," Mum added, calling Maja.

Several long minutes later, Maja ran downstairs. She still refused to talk to me and frowned when she saw me, so I was very surprised when she spoke to me.

"Be nice to her, Daddy. I don't like seeing Laura upset." It was a clear warning on her part while my stomach hollowed out.

I fucking missed her and I truly wasn't planning to upset her again.

"All right, sweetie. Go help Grandma in the kitchen," I said.

I rushed upstairs, my chest heavy, but the moment I saw her, my whole world crumbled. She was picking up toys from the floor but instantly stiffened, probably sensing I was near.

She wore a long pastel dress I'd bought for her in Sicily. When she finally turned around, her eyes widened, and she swallowed.

"Spencer, oh, I didn't know you were going to be here," she said.

Indeed, Laura had lost weight. She looked fragile, and for a split second I wanted to take her into my arms and tell her I had made a terrible mistake, but suddenly I couldn't move.

"I better go."

She passed me in the doorway, so I grabbed her elbow, the touch stinging me within.

"Stay. We really need to talk," I said, longing to embrace her but keeping away. I'd hurt her, but all the evidence against her was there, right in front of me …

"Let go of my arm," she snapped.

I did.

She was right. I had no right to touch her or even think about her. We were done with each other, she'd betrayed me. But why did I feel like my heart had been crushed with a sledgehammer? She backtracked into the room as I leaned against the doorframe, wallowing in my misery. I shouldn't have slept with her. It was a mistake, and now I was paying the price.

"How are things with Maja?" I asked.

"We are fine. She kept asking me why you were upset with me, so I told her that I released some information about you that I shouldn't have. She was very persistent, but I managed to distract her with something else," she replied. "What do you want? Dinner is probably ready, and I've somewhere else to be."

"Please, Laura, I've something important to say. Can you listen to me for a moment?" I begged. I had never done this before, but my skin was on fire. I felt anger, lust, sadness, excitement, disgust, and love for this woman. I needed to have her close again, even if my mind roared at me to stay back.

"Why should I? You didn't listen to me when it mattered. We really have nothing to talk about," she said.

"I'm trying to figure out where the money that you received came from," I told her. I'd asked James to look into it, and so far he had no leads.

"I've no idea, someone framed me," she replied with anger.

"James said that whoever did the wire was a professional, but he's going to get to the bottom of it," I assured her, not even knowing why I was saying this. She was right, I'd presumed that she was guilty, so what had changed?

I'd fallen in love with Laura because of her kindness and affection that she'd showered Maja with—her niece now. Fuck, the wall between us was so thick, and I wanted to smash it until my hands bled.

"It doesn't matter, you don't need to do it. I told you I'm going to clear my name, so James doesn't need to investigate this at all," she stated. "Is there anything else you wanted to tell me?"

She wants to leave, which means she doesn't want you; she doesn't love you. Isn't it obvious?

"I want to believe you, Laura, but Jeremy has evidence against you. He said that you sent the photo from your phone."

"Then we have nothing else to talk about. Leave me alone and don't contact me again."

Chapter Forty-Three

Laura

It had been another week since that photo had been leaked online, and I could barely sleep. This afternoon, I went to my favourite bookshop where they had the cutest coffee shop inside, so I could browse the romance books and have a bite to eat. I needed the distraction because my life had fallen to pieces and I still wasn't sure how I was going to figure out who'd set me up.

For the first few days, I was apprehensive about going out because reporters had found out my parents' address, and that complicated everything. Mum was in the hospital, so she didn't know what was going on. Her new doctor said she was responding well to medication, so for now, I didn't have to worry about that, at least. I was planning to talk to my parents after this whole thing blew over. They had enough on their plate, and I didn't need to worry them further.

After I settled in, ordered a coffee and their delicious pistachio pastry, I browsed through social media. A video of Spencer leaving Number 10 caught my attention. My heart tugged as I stared at the screen, wondering what had happened to us. We had never been so far apart, and now, since I'd found out Maja was my niece, I missed her even more. There was a clear resemblance between us, and I had no idea how I hadn't seen it before. This was very bizarre, and despite what was going on, I promised her I would figure out a way for me to see her again. She missed me, too, but what had happened between Spencer and I was still raw. It was going to take me a very long time to even consider seeing him again.

I returned my attention to the screen.

"Prime Minister, can you tell us whether you were ever romantically involved with your nanny?" one of the reporters asked the dreaded question during the latest press conference that I was now watching on my phone.

"My private life remains private. Are there any other further questions relating to the latest foreign policy?"

"He's very charismatic, isn't he?" someone asked, standing behind me, startling me.

I glanced to my right, seeing a woman who decided to make herself comfortable right next to me. She sat beside my table, smiling at me.

"Samantha, I've been hoping that we could talk at some

point, but I didn't know how to find you," I told her, locking the screen. I was perfectly calm, but nevertheless she'd surprised me. My heart was pounding loudly. I stared at my real sister. We had both been born in Poland, and I'd had great difficulty trying to investigate what had happened to us. When I'd spoken to my mum and dad, they'd told me that they'd only found out I had a sister after they'd brought me back to London.

Samantha raised her left eyebrow. She was truly beautiful; she had distinctive features that were very similar to mine.

"Let's skip the small talk, it's obvious that we are related because we have the same taste in men. Spencer can be difficult, but he was always wild in bed, don't you agree?" she asked with a smile that instantly brought on nausea.

"Why are you here? I'm sure you didn't track me down all the way here to talk about my sex life." I wondered what exactly her game plan was. She didn't want anything to do with Maja, that was for sure, so I didn't understand what she was trying to achieve.

She was blonde, had blue eyes and immaculate makeup, dressed in elegant designer clothes. Despite the makeup, her Slavic features were very prominent like mine, but it seemed that Samantha was trying hard to conceal her true roots.

We were very much alike, but she was the complete opposite of me in the way she dressed and carried herself. I always knew I wasn't Spencer's type, and now I understood why. I could never be like Samantha.

"No, I'm not, but I must admit your romantic track record is pretty impressive. I bet Jake was a beast in bed," she mused.

A shudder of disgust rushed through me. I couldn't believe I was related to someone like her.

"Anyway, I'm here because I've a very generous proposition for you."

"Just hurry up and tell me what you want?" I'd got tired of her games.

"I think we should do an interview together. This unbelievable story will make us a lot of money. Poor Polish girls who were separated when they were children, now involved with the same man—the Prime Minister of the United Kingdom."

This conversation was just getting worse and worse.

"It's obvious that you don't know me, otherwise you'd know that I genuinely care about Spencer." I glanced around the coffee shop and made sure no one else was looking at us. I wouldn't be surprised if Samantha had someone recording the whole thing.

She placed her bag on the table and pulled out a lipstick and a small mirror.

"Too bad, because I'm a little low on funds and I could really use your help. Besides, if it wasn't for me you would have never met Spencer." She opened the mirror, staring at her reflection and quickly reapplying her red lipstick.

"I still don't understand why you would do something like that? If you wanted to get back with him, you should have just come back," I said, still trying to understand why she was pushing me into Spencer's arms so much.

She was watching herself in the mirror, pouting her lips.

"I never really loved him. I thought he was the one, but we

had different goals and aspirations, and even after so many years, I still believe in love. I don't want Spencer back. I mean, I considered coming back when he became the PM, but I truly don't have the motherly instinct," she explained. "I've been searching for you for years. I even hired a private investigator in Poland, because I didn't want to travel to that horrible country, but I gave up after he turned out to be a scammer. You were too small to remember me, but I always planned to find you. When our mother passed away, we got adopted, but then that family decided that they couldn't take both of us, so I was unexpectedly sent to another family in Wales ... God, they were such losers."

"Poland is a beautiful country," I said, suddenly angry that she was so dismissive of where she'd been born.

"Around two years ago, I found out that you were adopted by a loving family in East London, the family that I should have had, so I started putting my little revenge plan together. It wasn't fair, I ended up with absolute arseholes who exploited me in every way they could."

"I still don't get what you have to gain with me working for Spencer, taking care of Maja." I wanted to empathise with her situation, but I didn't know where to even start.

"I've good friends who have worked for the Emperor Club in the past, and we kept in touch. When I found you, I accidentally discovered that Veronica was your roommate, so I figured it was the best time to put my plan into motion. I've been wondering how could I get you two together since I learnt that you were my sister, and then the universe unexpectedly answered my prayers. I arranged for her to see Spencer. I knew he didn't ask for the same woman twice, and after that, I decided that you should meet. He didn't date, and you had experience with children, so why not send Spence someone who would take care of Maja well? Obviously another perk was that you were her aunt. Despite what you may think of me, my daughter needed a good mother and I didn't want Spencer to settle with someone else. Luckily, you didn't ask questions because you were desperate for work at the time. I didn't know if my plan would work, but I was hoping for the best. But you obviously made an impression on him, since he trusted you with our daughter." She sounded so proud of herself for this whole plan.

I wanted to tell her that Maja wasn't hers because she had never been in her life, but I was still trying to process the fact that this woman had set me up. She was the one who'd called me that night, and I had fallen into her trap, without question.

"Why would you do this?" I asked.

"Ah, so you're one of those women who doesn't care about her social status, and that's the main difference between us, dear. It's a huge story, and the fact that he acted upon his desires when you were working for him is inappropriate, but he won't lose his position. Technically, he was a single father who fell for his nanny, but if you give an exclusive interview revealing the ins and outs of your relationship, we both get rich. I've a few debts with some dangerous people, and let's just say, desperate times call for desperate measures." She chuckled.

I felt physically sick that she was doing this purely for the money. Deep down, She must have cared about Maja a little, even if she claimed she didn't.

"Spencer is never going to forgive me," I said, suddenly gasping because I'd just realised something and I couldn't understand how I hadn't figured this out sooner. Samantha was the one who'd set me up for everything.

"No he won't, especially since he thinks you leaked that photo from Sicily to the press." She grinned at me.

"Why did you set me up? And where did that wire even come from?"

Samantha didn't respond. She waved at the waitress and ordered a coffee for herself. Sweat gathered on the side of my brow.

"I thought that my plan was solid, and despite what's happened between us, I assumed Spencer still cared about me. He loved me so much before, and I wanted to believe he would ask me to help him to hush up the scandal," she replied quickly. "And it's better if you don't know where this money came from. I've been formulating this plan for years, and I've had help. Now, unfortunately, I'm in a bit of trouble, so the financial reward is very important to me."

I hid my face in my hands, trying to breathe.

This woman was unbelievable, cunning, manipulative, and determined to do anything in order to achieve her goal, but she didn't know who she was dealing with.

"Listen, we may share blood, but I'll never consider you to be my family, because my real sister would never have done anything so despicable. You've ruined my life and driven

Spencer and I apart. Do you really think that after all this, I'm going to play along with your game?"

She snickered, pulling out her phone and sliding it across to me.

It was a photo of me and Spencer outside Elm Street, the night we'd met when he'd mistaken me for an escort. Then a photo of me from the bedroom upstairs on my knees.

"There are many leaks and rumours of how you two met all spreading around in the media. It's just a matter of time before everything is revealed and Spencer's reputation is ruined. No one will turn a blind eye to a PM who used an escort service. People will be outraged, so rather than having your relationship exposed in such a damaging way, you can make the sensible decision to address the situation honestly and openly. That way you can control the narrative and minimise any negative impact on Spencer and his career," she said while I was having a mini heart attack.

She was smart and she was right. If I decided to do the interview, I would minimise the damage and protect him, but then he would definitely never forgive me. I knew what to do instantly. There wasn't any other option, I had to sacrifice my love for him in the process.

This was the woman who Spencer had almost married? God, she was a truly evil bitch.

"So let me get this straight. You want to ruin Spencer's life, even your own daughter's life, because of money and social status? Think about Maja. Don't you have any conscience?"

Samantha sighed, tossing her blonde hair behind her.

"I never wanted to be a mother. Maja ruined all my plans for the future I wanted, and Spencer was useless. He didn't even want to hear about an abortion, and I don't even know why I agreed to keep the baby. Spencer was so invested in having a real family back then, so I thought we would be happier if I said I wouldn't get rid of it," she explained.

But that didn't make me feel any better.

"I know you won't understand, but I'm very ambitious and I always get what I want. I scheduled that interview, and you had better show up or you will never work with children again."

Spencer and Maja were going to hate me, but I had to protect them. I didn't see any other way out of this. I felt so hopeless, so depressed that things were so complicated. Spencer would never forgive me, but I couldn't let Samantha ruin his career and his reputation, so I had to do the interview because I was in love with him.

Chapter Forty-Four

Spencer

"Daddy, have you talked to Laura? I want her to come back to the flat, I miss her," Maja asked for the fourth time while we were watching TV.

I ran my hand through my hair, trying to figure out how to answer this question and not make her lose control again. The past few days had been extremely stressful, and tomorrow was going to be a challenging day.

The *Daily News* exposed the Winter's document which showed that shadow chancellor, Craig Winter, was involved in a supposed plot known as "Project Mercedes" to out me as a leader and place me with Jason Brown shortly after the next election. I couldn't believe it when Jeremy handed me the papers and told me that this would be an interesting read. On top of that, one of my other MPs from my party, Aaron Reading, was caught with an escort girl by his own wife and apparently she tried to kill him, so the media were going crazy over this story. This had hit too close to home, so I had to deal with it.

Over the next few days, both stories were all over the tabloids, and journalists were camping outside Number 10, trying to get me to comment on the scandals. I had to do several press conferences to make sure that the issue had been dealt with as soon as possible. Recent scandals that involved my party members would distract people from my personal issues, but I was still worried about Laura.

"Nothing changed since we last discussed Laura, Maja, so please can you drop the subject for now?" I asked.

She'd started speaking to me again after she had been allowed to spend some time with Laura at my parents' house. James was still trying to figure out where the money that Laura had received came from. He kept telling me he was close to the truth.

After tonight, I'd lost complete faith in her. Jeremy had informed me that Laura had agreed to do an interview with Louise—the reporter I had met at the restaurant.

Laura claimed she was innocent, and I'd wanted to believe her until I'd found out about the interview.

Maja looked at me as if I had lost my mind and jumped off the couch.

"I don't want another nanny. I want Laura. Why won't give

her another chance?"

Here we go again. I tried to bring her closer, but she stepped away from me.

"Maja, please, we have talked about this. Laura has done a few things that really upset me, and I can't forgive her," I explained.

"You're a terrible father. She's good and she loves you so much. I hate you," Maja shouted, tears streaming down her cheeks as she ran out of the room.

"Maja," I called out in vain.

Something wasn't adding up here. If Laura was planning to go live on air to talk about our relationship, then she knew it would damage my reputation if she decided to tell the world how we'd met. Fuck, I really hoped this wasn't the case.

I felt terrible, and I fucking missed her like crazy. My heart beat only for her, but none of this mattered anymore; Laura had shattered me. After meeting Jeremy, I went to see Rupert, hoping that he'd know something, but he could hardly believe it himself. I still needed to have a chat with James.

"I'm sorry, man, but I've no idea what is going on. Veronica hasn't said anything. Let me call her," Rupert said. But he couldn't get hold of her either.

It was close to seven, and the programme was going to air in about an hour. I took out my phone and scrolled until I got to her name. I hesitated, but I had to talk her out of doing that goddamn interview. She knew exactly what would happen if the news about me using an escort came out. I would be totally crushed. If Laura needed money, then she should have asked me and I would have happily given it to her, but the way she was going about it just didn't make sense.

I didn't want to beg, but she couldn't do that to Maja, to herself and to me.

I got up and dialled the number. She was probably already in the studio, getting ready for her big moment.

"Hello," she answered.

When I heard her voice, I gripped my phone tighter.

"Laura, don't do this," I said in a quivering voice. Fuck, I didn't realise that this was going to be so difficult.

There was silence on the other end of the phone, and so many unspoken words passed between us. I listened to her uneven breaths while my heart was spiking, thumping. I wanted to know what she was thinking.

"Spencer, it's not that simple. I don't have a choice, please, I need to go."

She broke me again, thrusting a knife into my chest.

Fuck, that hurt.

I fucking loved her.

"If you go through with this, my career will be over and you will destroy us, Laura. Maja will suffer because of you, and I won't allow you to see her ever again." I clenched my fist. "It won't be long before the press will put two and two together—me using escorts and the fact that Veronica is your roommate."

"You don't get it, there's no us, there never has been. We

were never going to make it from the start. The world was against us," she said.

And she was crying. I could hear it in her voice, but I didn't get it.

"Laura ... I couldn't believe that I was good enough for you, but now I do, please—"

"Don't, Spencer, don't do this. I've to go, I ... Goodbye," she said, and then the line went dead.

I squeezed my phone, wanting to destroy it like Laura had destroyed us. Just then, a knock sounded on my door.

I took a few deep breaths, trying to calm myself down. I was so disappointed, so fucking angry. I had lost everything because the woman I loved chose fame and money over all else. Fuck, and all this time, I'd thought she was different.

I opened the door, staring at my bodyguard, Jason.

"Sir, your brother, James, is here to see you," he announced.

I exhaled with relief, suddenly glad James was here.

"Yeah, let him in." I stood and buttoned up my suit jacket. I hoped James had something that would help me unwind this nonsense, otherwise I would have to prepare myself for the shitstorm that would hit tomorrow morning after Laura's interview aired.

Jason nodded and James walked in, and right behind him there was another tall man, carrying a briefcase. He was dressed in a black cardigan and black trousers. My eyes widened with shock, because I was not expecting him here at all.

"Dexter Tyndall, what a fucking surprise. It's been years, man." I embraced him in a hug, suddenly remembering everything from our shared past.. That fucker was handsome, and he knew it. We'd studied law together in Edinburgh but hadn't seen each other in at least seven years. "What are you doing here?"

"I called him while I was looking into Samantha, and it turns out that Dexter's wife, Sasha, knows Samantha," James said with his usual calm demeanour.

I had never seen him lose control or show any kind of emotion. That guy had the best poker face I knew.

"I'm all ears," I said as I pointed at them to sit.

Dexter and I had lost touch years ago, after I'd moved back to London with Maja and he'd stayed in Scotland.

Dexter was wearing a wedding ring. I couldn't fucking believe that he was married. That guy had fucked every woman on campus back in the day, and he'd vowed he would never settle. That was surprising.

"I've been trying to follow the money trail, but I was getting nowhere until I got some very interesting info on Samantha after I figured out that Laura was her biological sister. For the past nine years, Sam has lived in Poland, and she found out about Laura around two years ago. Several months ago, Samantha got engaged to a businessman, and they were meant to get married, but then she caught him cheating on her," James said, still sounding bored while I was trying to process all this information.

Samantha had never talked about her family before. She was adopted, but I had no idea that she was born in Poland.

"Samantha didn't work, and it appears that her ex-fiancé,

Kowalski, left her without money. Funnily enough, he was arrested a few weeks later for embezzlement."

"All right, but what's that got to do with Laura and I?" I asked.

"Samantha has been formulating her revenge plan for years. A few months ago she was set for life, invested in her fiancé's company's shares, and then lost everything, so she got involved with some dodgy people to ruin her ex-fiancé," Dexter injected. "She called my wife about a month ago. She was hoping to borrow some money since the two of them used to be friends."

"I don't know what happened exactly, but Samantha made some kind of deal with the Polish mob," James continued. "They offered to give her the money with a high-interest repayment. These people wired the money to Laura's account, and afterwards, things got significantly more complicated for Sam. I believe the Polish mobster who goes by the name Vic, became quite annoyed when Sam started avoiding his calls. She's in big trouble, and I believe that she has some photographic evidence from the night when Laura and you first met."

Fuck, this sounded unbelievable, but I knew Sam. She was capable of anything, and now that she was desperate for money, there would be no limit to her scheming.

"The money was wired from an offshore account. Sam directed all her hurt and anger to her sister and used her as the scapegoat out of spite," Dexter said.

I was still trying to process the fact that Laura was clearly innocent, just as she'd claimed.

"Dexter, James, I appreciate your efforts, but this is over," I said, glancing at my watch and then shifting in my seat. I didn't know how they thought they could help me. That interview was going to be aired soon. "In around fifty-five minutes, my former nanny is going to tell the world about our relationship, and then the whole nation will be aware that I used an escort service. There's nothing much that any of us could do at this point."

Dexter shook his head and opened his briefcase, pulling out files and photos of Samantha and Laura.

"Man, I'm sorry to be the one who has to break this to you, but you have fucked up. Samantha was hoping that you'd lose your mind over your hot nanny. This was her plan all along, and she was right." Dexter paused and then glanced at James before he leaned forward. "By the way, if I weren't happily married, I would have lost my fucking mind for that nanny, too, probably much quicker than you. However, I love my wife, so forget I said any of that."

"I fucking fired her, I accused her of leaking that photo ... after everything that's happened—"

"Spencer, for fuck's sake," Dexter snapped. "Stop wallowing in self-pity. It's pathetic, so get it together. The point is, Samantha was envious because Laura got two loving parents after their separation, and Sam ended up with some real fuckwits all the way in deepest darkest Wales. She wanted to use Laura to get to you, so she framed her. Made it look like she'd leaked the photo and got paid for it. Then she came to see you, thinking you'd do exactly what she said. She truly believed she had you where she wanted you, but you told her to go to hell, so her entire plan was ruined. She didn't have the money to pay off her debt with the mob, so she became desperate."

"So Laura is completely innocent?" I wanted to punch the wall again.

"Correct. Sam was behind this from the start, so she told Laura that she was going to ruin you if Laura didn't do the interview. I believed that Sam already gave some sob story to ITV and made a deal with them." Dexter made me feel like a complete dickhead.

I should have known that Sam was behind all of this.

I exhaled and then glanced at my brother, who was, as usual, perfectly calm and collected. I hated him at that moment.

"I've to go and stop Laura before she goes live on air," I finally said, and then glanced at my watch briefly. Time was running out.

Dexter laughed, then shook his head. James appeared bored again.

"I thought you were more intelligent than that. Obviously, I was wrong," he said dryly. "I'd rather be doing more interesting things on a Saturday night, but your position has certain benefits, so let's fucking go before I change my mind."

"I love you fucking, too, brother, and I'll pretend that I didn't hear what you just said." I stood, then I went to Dexter and shook his hand. "Thanks, man, I really appreciate that you reached and helped James. It's been fucking years, and I hope we can catch up at some point before you head back to Scotland," I said, although I was wasting time right now, but Dexter was a good friend.

"I'm staying in the city for business anyway, but I bet Sasha would love to finally meet you. I also have a four-year-old who is a handful." He quickly added, "Anyway we can catch up later. Now fucking go so that all my efforts don't go to waste or I'll be really pissed off."

Chapter Forty-Five

Laura

"Are you ready, sweetie?" Carla, one of the producers, asked as I stared at the clock.

I had ten minutes before we went live.

"Yes," I replied. I wanted to scream at her that I didn't want to do this fucking interview, but Samantha was outside. She was on set, and if I pulled out of this, she wouldn't hesitate to leak the information about Spencer using escorts. I didn't care about my own reputation, but this wasn't just about me. Other people close to me were involved. Veronica had already quit working for Emperor, but Rupert was still a partner. I couldn't risk it.

Veronica had gone into hysterics when I'd told her what I

was planning. I hadn't said anything about Samantha and her blackmail because I already knew what she would say about that. She would have urged me to stand up to Samantha, but there was too much at stake. Veronica wouldn't understand my reasons. I loved Spencer very much and I was willing to protect him and Maja even if that meant that I had to sacrifice our love.

"Come on. Let's go. Everyone is waiting for you," she said.

I stood and glanced at myself in the mirror, ensuring I was decent enough. My family and my friends would hear about the intimate details of my relationship with Spencer, all because my sister wanted her five minutes in the spotlight.

I walked out of my dressing room on shaky legs. Louise was already waiting for me. This was her show, and she was going to get a big promotion afterwards.

I pushed my legs to move onto the set, and my stomach churned. I took a deep breath, and then someone shouted.

"You can't go in there, it's not allowed!"

There was a commotion in the corridor that led to the studio.

"Please step aside, it's the Prime Minister of this country, so show some respect," another voice stated calmly. It was James, Spencer's brother, but what was he doing here?

Then my heart stopped because right behind him was Spencer himself.

"Prime Minister ... sir, this isn't a good time. We are just about to go live."

Two men from the television crew tried to stop him. Samantha and Louise also noticed as they were approaching.

"Unfortunately, there won't be a show tonight." James adjusted his cufflinks.

I fixed my gaze on Spencer, trying to snap out of the shock.

"What's going on here?" Louise glared at them.

"Laura, come on, let's talk. I've something important to tell you." Spencer moved towards me.

"I can't, I've to do—"

"That's right, Prime Minister. She's just about to do the interview, and don't stop her, because you won't like the consequences." Samantha placed her hands on her hips and gave him a severe look, but he ignored her.

He stared at me, his eyes burning into mine.

"Sam, please, I don't like this as much as you do, but you're going to want to hear me out in the room next door." James turned towards Samantha.

Spencer grabbed my hand and dragged me away.

"Spencer, what are you doing? This is really not a good time—"

"Be quiet, Laura, I know everything. I know that Samantha blackmailed you to do this." He cut me off, suddenly coming close, cupping my face and gazing right into my eyes.

I parted my lips, wanting to ask him so many questions, but then he kissed me, devouring my mouth with so much passion and urgency, like it might have been his last chance to do so. I was frozen as he held the back of my head and brought me in closer. He sent my body into a spiral of sensations, tasting like pinewood and scotch. I could hear nothing but the drumming of my blood in my ears. I felt nothing but the softness of his lips and the tingles of heat beneath my skin. I let go of a moan, and he groaned into my mouth. Pulling away to catch our breath, we stared at each other with melting desperation.

"Spencer, she's going to tell the whole world how we met. If I don't do the interview, then she'll leak the information about you using the escort service." I tried to catch my breath and slow down my frantic heart.

He held me close, still staring at me with that hungry look.

"Don't worry about Sam. She's in huge trouble as it is, and soon, she'll be very busy with her own affairs. She won't dare to release any evidence against me. Let's go home now. Maja is still pretty mad at me, and she wants you home." He dismissed my concerns.

I shook my head, retreating.

"I'm not going anywhere until you explain everything."

He dragged his hand through his hair and muttered something incoherent.

"James has been trying to figure out where the money that was deposited into your account came from, but he was getting nowhere. Then, out of the blue, our old mutual friend reached out to us," he began and told me about Dexter and Samantha's troubles with the Polish mob.

I thought my legs were going to give out on me when he mentioned that Samantha had been living in Poland all this time. I thought she truly hated being born there. By the time Spencer was done, I gawped at him in complete disbelief.

Louise barged inside the room, pissed off.

"Prime Minister, I've no idea what is going on, but Laura is needed in the studio. It's too late to cancel the show. This will cost the station a lot of money," she snapped.

"I apologise for stopping it so late, but Laura will not do this interview. However, once things settle down, we will give you an exclusive one. We'll talk about our love, and our life, to make up for what's happened here tonight." Spencer intertwined his fingers with mine.

I was too shocked to speak or do anything, while Louise stared at him, dumbfounded.

"That's right, Laura Watkins. I fucking love you, I've loved you from the moment I saw you outside my door all those months ago, but I was too much of a coward to say that to your face." Spencer took another step towards me.

"All right, all right, let me give you a minute, guys," Louise mumbled and then left us alone.

There was a long moment of silence while I tried to process what he'd said to me. Did Spencer Banks just admit to me he loved me? I wanted to laugh and cry at the same time. I didn't think I believed him. He was apparently in love with me this whole time.

I swallowed hard, then I pulled my hand away from his. I needed to put some distance between us and breathe for a moment. This whole thing was overwhelming, so many things had happened. I needed some time to think about my own feelings and the roller coaster they had been on.

"So, you just realised that you're in love with me?"

"Well, no ... I knew I loved you back in Sicily," he admitted.

I laughed, shaking my head. I suddenly felt so betrayed and

angry. He loved me, even when he'd called me a liar, fired me, and accused me of being the one who'd leaked that photo of us in Sicily. He wasn't there for me when I needed him the most. He'd upset me too much to make me forget how badly he'd treated me.

"And what now? What exactly are you expecting me to do?" I glared him, tall and confident. I was done being intimidated, done believing in his admission of love and actions of betrayal. Jake had claimed he'd loved me, too, and then he'd slept with two women at the same time. I couldn't compare these two incidents, but I still felt betrayed both times. Spencer hadn't believed me when I'd said I didn't leak that photo, then he'd tossed me away like rubbish.

"Can we talk about this? I'm sorry, Laura—"

"Save it, Spencer. I don't want to hear your apologies. I'm not going to simply throw myself into your arms, act like you didn't fire me, and pretend that you didn't believe in me, believe in us," I cut him off.

His eyes darkened, and he frowned.

"I've made a mistake, a huge mistake, and I know you're angry with me and you have every right to be, but we could finally be happy together. We don't have to hide anymore, and I want to be with you," he whispered.

"Of course I'm fucking angry. You didn't believe me. You thought I was the one who leaked that photo," I shouted, tears streaming. He had wounded me so much and now he was fucking sorry. "You didn't trust me and you pushed me away. It broke me, and I won't forget that because you just realised that you have feelings for me and someone else told you that I was innocent. You should have believed me in the first place!"

He took a deep breath, looking at me like a wounded puppy. Spencer Banks was a good man, but he was also arrogant, obnoxious, and selfish.

"Please, let me make it up to you, Laura. I know I've been a selfish prick, but with all that evidence, everything told me you were guilty." He put his hands in his pockets.

"I'm going to leave to digest what's happened here tonight, but that doesn't change the fact that you hurt me and you broke my trust. I need some time to think about this," I told him and left the room, fed up with the drama, but I was glad that this whole thing was finally over.

* * *

"I love your jewellery. I think I need to ask my daddy to take me shopping, so I can get some, too." Maja touched Veronica's impressive set of bracelets and earrings.

It'd been another long week for me, and I felt so exhausted with the constant drama. I thought that after talking to Spencer, this whole thing would be over, but the press was still talking about us.

I was certain I was coming down with something. Spencer kept calling me after the fiasco, not respecting my need to have space.

I wasn't ready to see him just yet, but I missed Maja, so he'd arranged for her to be dropped off at my place today. It was

Saturday, and we were planning to hang out, just the two of us, but then Veronica's plans got cancelled, so she'd stayed over.

"You can have this bracelet. It will match with your outfit today." My roommate handed Maja her favourite piece.

Maja's eyes widened, and she smiled brightly.

"Thank you, I love it. Laura, look." She giggled, showing me her wrist.

After I'd left the studio on Friday night last week, I'd gone straight home. Veronica had screamed, then danced, then screamed again after I'd told her everything. It was a long and exhausting evening.

"It's so amazing."

He had been on my mind a lot in the past few days. He'd sent flowers every day with apologetic messages.

"No, you aren't going to just forgive him. That guy has to grovel after everything that he's put you through," Veronica had said, once she was calm enough to speak again.

She was right. Spencer had broken my heart and my trust. I loved him and missed him, but I didn't think I was ready to walk right back into his life like nothing had happened.

"This came for you," Veronica said, handing me a thick envelope.

I opened it and pulled out an invitation.

"What is it?" Maja asked.

"Your dad wants to have a romantic dinner with me," I replied, wondering what Spencer Banks was up to this time.

Chapter Forty-Six

Spencer

"My darling, Laura will not forgive you, and if I were her, I don't think I would either. You need to do something special," my mother said as we sat around the table for dinner on Sunday afternoon.

Mum had insisted on an emergency family meeting, because she'd said I needed to plan how to win Laura over. My brothers were there for moral support, too. Rupert smirked and shook his head.

"Mum, give it a rest. Laura will never forgive Spencer. That woman has him by the balls," he said.

Maja giggled.

"Rupert Banks, language." She gave him a stern expression.

She had made another roast lamb today, and it was delicious, but I couldn't eat, because as always, my mother was right. Laura was a tough nut to crack, and I had truly fucked up.

"Don't worry. I've something in mind, but right now, I'm done talking about it," I said, eyeing everyone around the table. "Just make sure you all keep an eye on the news on Tuesday."

"Just don't do anything inappropriate," James said, not even looking at me. "Or even romantic."

"I thought you said you wanted me to fix it?" I cleaned my mouth.

"Fix it but not compromise your position further. Use your intelligence," he said dryly.

I was planning something that could go two ways. I would either have to resign, or they would remember me as the most ridiculous Prime Minister in the history of this country.

"Thank you for your advice, I'll keep that in mind," I answered.

"Whatever you're planning, it has to be romantic. Laura is strong and smart. So far she was the only one who was brave enough to call you out on your crap, right, Apolonia?" Andrew turned to glance at his assistant who just glared at him.

I didn't know what that was about, but she was like family now, and I wouldn't be surprised if Andrew married her, eventually.

"Dad, you're so silly. Laura wants to go back to Sicily." Maja shoved carrots into her mouth.

"If I were her, I would dream about Sicily, too, shortcake." Rupert chuckled.

I threw a brussels sprout at his head.

"Bumble bee, how do you know Laura wants to be back in Sicily?" Dad asked Maja.

"Because when I went to visit her on Saturday, I heard her tell her friend that she wished she was still with us on holiday in Italy."

"Spencer, that is an excellent idea. You should take her away for a weekend in Sicily," Mum suggested. "That would be so romantic, darling. Make an effort and show her how much you love her, then she'll forgive you."

They needed to stop interfering in my love life.

Samantha had left London a few hours after James had spoken to her in the studio. I didn't know why I'd asked him to do what he did, but I would sleep better at night knowing that the mother of my child wouldn't end up with a bullet in her head. This would complicate things for me, so I decided to pay Sam with my own money, so she could settle her debt with the Polish mob, and leave the two hundred grand in Laura's account, so she could decide later what she wanted to do with it. I should have left Sam to fend for herself, but after all, she was Laura's sister. She was part of the family whether I liked it or not.

I wasn't sure how Laura felt about her yet, but as soon as we were back together, I would chat to her about it. I had been trying to talk to her, but she'd only texted me back if it involved Maja, otherwise she was ignoring me. She was driving me crazy again, so I thought long and hard about my plan to win her back, and part of it was already set in motion.

"Why are you letting Maja spend time with Veronica? I know she quit working in the club, but that doesn't mean she's a good influence on Maja. Veronica shouldn't be around her at all," Rupert growled later on after dinner as I was getting ready to leave.

Laura was already back at work, taking care of Maja, but I had other plans for her.

I glanced at my brother, who clearly still hadn't resolved his feud with Veronica. This has gone on for long enough.

"Maja can't wait to hang out with them again." I tried to speak quietly because Mum was in the kitchen, wrapping more food for me to take home. "Maja likes her, and you like her, too, so you might as well ask her out."

"Be careful, Spencer, Veronica is bad news. She cannot be trusted around a child." He sounded angry. Something had happened between him and Veronica that had driven them even farther apart, but he was tight-lipped. He refused to discuss her with me.

I wanted to say something to him but decided against it. Rupert was more stubborn than me, and he needed to figure things out for himself.

"I'm leaving and I'll not tell you what to do, because you won't listen to me, but I want you to know that you may regret this in the future," I said, then I went to talk to my mother about the next few days to make sure everything was arranged. Laura was going to be mine, whatever it took.

***

On Tuesday morning, Laura walked into the kitchen and stopped when she saw me standing there, attempting to make a coffee for her, but my machine wasn't cooperating. She point-blank refused to move back into Number 10, but it was just a matter of time before she was back in my bed again.

Fuck, she looked so beautiful, wearing a fitted purple skirt and thin top. It was still warm outside in September, and I instantly wanted to rip those clothes off her and fuck her right there on my kitchen worktop.

"I thought we agreed you weren't supposed to be here." She glared at me with suspicion. She was annoyed with me, but it didn't matter, because after this afternoon, we were going to be inseparable.

"Don't worry, I'll be leaving soon," I said, heat rushing down to my crotch, especially when she bit down on her bottom lip.

Her hair was styled in a messy bun, and I wanted to grab it in my fist so damn much. *Fucking focus, Spencer*, my inner voice chastised.

"Can you come to my office at twelve, please? Cath will give you the details. We need to pick up Maja from school early."

"And why do we have to pick her up together?"

"It's for publicity reasons," I said. I hated lying to her, but she had a good heart, and even though she didn't want to see me right now, I knew she would want to help me.

"All right, whatever," she said.

"Thank you. See you later," I said and walked out of the kitchen.

I headed straight to my office and then threw myself into my busy and hectic work schedule. Around half past eleven, Jeremy showed up, appearing tense.

"Why are there reporters gathering upstairs? Are you going to do a press conference?"

"Yes, in half an hour," I said.

"There's nothing on the agenda. What are you going to discuss?"

"I'll talk to you later; I need to make a phone call."

Jeremy hesitated for a few seconds, but he eventually left the room.

I followed him out of the office a few minutes later, nervous. Laura was likely already waiting for me upstairs.

Jeremy and probably the rest of the staff would lose their minds, but this was my life. I was the one in charge, so they had to get with the programme if they wanted to keep working for me.

The woman who brightened my day showed up, looking uncertain as we were waiting to go in front of the cameras. My team was there, and my publicist and a few other people were talking quietly behind me.

Cath was carrying the red box, and Laura was right behind her, appearing slightly confused. I'd instructed my assistant of what to do earlier on, so she knew what to expect, and she was grinning from ear to ear once I shared with her my plan of getting Laura back.

"Spencer, what's going on? It seems like you're just about to do a press conference. I'd better go." Laura gazed around, luckily not noticing how nervous I really was.

A moment later, Cath handed me the red box.

"Yes, come on, we don't have a lot of time." I pulled her out of the back room so that we were both standing in front of the cameras.

Laura paled when I winked at her and then opened the red box right in front of her. Then I picked up a pair of rose-pink handcuffs that someone had once given to me with the engagement invitation and handcuffed Laura to me in front of all the reporters who had gathered in front of us. She was too stunned to react. Then I handed the box back to Cath, who appeared ecstatic.

"Ladies and gentlemen, I apologise for the confusion with the Chancellor box, but I wanted to make sure that this woman here wouldn't escape, so the box served a different purpose for today, so now let's begin."

Everybody looked very, very confused, but a few people laughed, and the room buzzed.

"What the hell, Spencer? Have you lost your mind?" Laura glanced around.

"Yes, I've lost my mind for you," I muttered and sent her a wink. My heartbeat was unsteady, and I was sweaty, but I finally had her attention, so I could relax, because in a second the whole world would know how serious I was about her. I walked with her right towards the microphones while she was trying to stand back.

I picked up the paperwork and passed it over to Cath, who gaped at us.

"Thank you all for coming. Unfortunately, we won't be discussing the budget today, but my private life," I began and lifted my hands. "You all probably know Laura. She's my daughter's nanny, but unfortunately, for her, this is her last day, because I'm firing her, effective immediately."

Laura gasped, and a few whispers moved through the crowd of reporters. Laura parted her lips like she wanted to say something, but she remained silent. Tension filled the room, thick enough to suffocate as I tried to gather my thoughts. Almost everyone in the room had their phones on, pointing at me like they were forgetting that we were broadcasting this whole thing live.

"I'm a single father, and Maja's mother was never in the picture and probably never will be. A few months ago, this woman ..." I paused and smiled at Laura, who looked like she was just about to pass out. "Showed up to my house, and I mistook her for someone else, so we didn't have the best start, so much so that she absolutely hated my guts and told me that to my face, knowing that I could fire her anytime."

Laughter echoed in the room.

"Anyway, I wanted to give her a chance because I was desperate for a nanny. My daughter had driven all her previous nannies away, and it was my fault. Then Laura stepped in, and things changed. Needless to say, I realised that I was falling for her. My position of power and my charismatic personality has not impressed her whatsoever, and frankly, I'm surprised that she hasn't run away, because I've not treated her as well as I should have. I've upset and hurt her, so that's why I'm standing in front of all of you today, trying to apologise. My heart belongs to her. I love this woman and I'm not ashamed to admit it. She's the love of my life, and I never wish to be apart from her ever again."

Chapter Forty-Seven

Laura

This was completely unexpected, so I told myself this was a dream and I would wake up soon.

Spencer stared at me with eyes full of love.

"Ladies and gentlemen, I, the Prime Minister of this country, have fallen madly in love with my nanny. You can call this whatever you want, but I'm not prepared to step down from my position just because I choose to fight for true love."

I didn't know where to look. I wasn't equipped to deal with these emotions in public, then tears filled my eyes.

My chest felt heavy with raw and painful love for this man. I wanted to tell him to stop, but the cameras were rolling and people were still listening. Spencer was taking a huge risk; he could ruin his career if this was taken out of context.

"Unfortunately, I betrayed her trust when a photo of us from our holiday in Sicily was leaked online, and that is the reason I brought her here today. Laura needs to see that I'll do whatever it takes to get her back, even if I've to stay handcuffed to her for the rest of the day. I'll remain in the office as the leader of this country with this wonderful woman by my side. I hope you will all accept it. Thank you for listening, and that will be all for now," he said and then he paused, gazing at me for a long moment, before he pulled me in front of him.

Seconds later, he went down on one knee, and I gasped.

This is not happening, this is not happening, he can't be serious. My inner voice was screaming at me. I was having a mini heart attack. Spencer smiled up at me, and then he reached into his jacket pocket and took out a small black box that he opened and presented to me, which wasn't that easy since my right hand was chained to his.

"Laura Watkins, will you marry me?"

Gasps and whispers echoed all around me while I stared at the most beautiful ring that I had ever seen, unable to make any coherent response. I was completely stunned. I didn't know how long I was silent, but at some point Spencer muttered:

"Laura, please put me out of my misery. I'm trying to impress you."

His voice brought me back to reality, and I smiled, because I couldn't say no to this man. I didn't want to. I loved him so much and I wanted to be his wife.

"Yes, Spencer, I'll marry you," I replied. Tears spilled down my cheeks, and in that moment, the whole room cheered.

The reporters screamed and shouted as he got off his knee and kissed me. Then, before I could react or say anything else, he tugged me towards the other door, where all the reporters behind us were still going crazy.

"Prime Minister, sir, when is the wedding?"

"Is she going to become the next UK's princess?"

"Do you think your daughter will accept her as your new wife?"

More and more reporters were shouting, but we were already walking away, vanishing through the back door.

"Spencer Banks, do you realise what you've just done?" someone roared.

We stopped midway. A furious Jeremy stormed towards us.

"Yes, I told the whole country that I love my nanny, and then I asked her to marry me." He gave me a heated look. "And I'm a lucky fucker that she said yes, because for a second I wasn't too sure if she would agree."

"You are ruined, you buried your career. People will demand for you to resign from your position!" Jeremy shouted.

"You don't know what is going to happen to me for certain, but I decided to trust my gut," Spencer stated. "It's up to the public now to decide."

Jeremy widened his eyes in shock.

"You're making a huge mistake," he said.

"Maybe, but it's my mistake. I'm tired of being that guy who is constantly miserable and angry. I don't want to be him anymore, Jeremy, and I suggest you get used to the new me."

"And what if I don't? Are you going to fire me?" he asked.

"No, but you have to ease off sometimes." Spencer laughed, and then for the first time, Jeremy smiled at me.

He was relieved in a way, and I was so glad that he was willing to stand behind Spencer.

"All right, have fun, kids, and don't do anything that I wouldn't do," Jeremy said and then sent us a wink.

Spencer turned around, and we walked away. I had to go with because I was still handcuffed to him.

"Slow down, you're going to give us bruises," I said.

All his security staff tagged behind, and I wondered what they all thought about this whole situation. Spencer stopped and looked at me.

"Sorry, shortcake, but I feel exhilarated." He appeared flustered.

I thought it was the first time I'd seen him so out of control.

"Good, but the handcuffs have to go," I told him. "My wrist is starting to hurt."

"No can do, Laura. We have to go," he said. "Come on, I need to grab our bags."

"What do you mean? Where are we going?" I tailed him all the way to the living room.

There, he picked up a small suitcase and winked at me.

"You will see." He smiled.

My thoughts raced when I thought about all the people who

had just watched us on live TV. My phone pinged like crazy, and I didn't even want to check it.

"No, Spencer, I'm not going anywhere until you uncuff me!" I shouted.

He chuckled.

"I'll but you have to come with me or I'll carry you out of here if I've to," he threatened.

"Fine, I'll walk."

As soon as we entered into the working part of Number 10, Spencer was surrounded by his team of advisors. They were all talking, asking questions, but he ignored them all. He quickly rushed us outside, pushed me into the car, and then we drove off, leaving the staff behind, but of course, his security team followed, as usual. Two of the agents were with us in the car. I had no idea where he was taking me.

We got out of the car in an underground car park and then we were in a lift, going to the thirtieth floor with two of his other agents. I was too embarrassed to say anything, so I kept quiet, watching as we went higher and higher. Then when the door finally opened, I was shocked to discover that we were on the rooftop of a building, and Spencer was dragging me towards a helicopter. Jason and two other agents ran with us towards the door, and then Spencer helped me get inside. He put headphones on me, and we took off. My stomach filled with butterflies. My ears popped, and my heart pounded like crazy.

"Are you okay?" Spencer asked.

It was only then that I realised I was squeezing his hand painfully hard.

"Sort of. So you handcuffed me and now you're kidnapping me?"

"I had to get your attention somehow," he said and then reached into his pocket.

He showed me the key, and I felt better after he uncuffed us.

"Are you going to tell me where we are going?"

He took my hand and rubbed my slightly bruised wrist.

"No, not yet. I want it to be a surprise," he replied and then held my hand which was very comforting.

I rested my head on his arm, and eventually, I must have fallen asleep because later on it seemed that we had to stop to refuel. Some time later, we finally reached our destination, and when I glanced out of the window, I gasped. A familiar Mediterranean island in the middle of the sea looked spectacular, and it instantly warmed my heart.

"We are going to be here for two days, no press, no Maja, just the two of us," he said in my ear.

His voice sent shivers down my spine, and his eyes told me more than his words ever had. He loved me. He had risked his reputation and his entire career to make me happy, and he'd asked me to marry him, so I could forgive him. I still wasn't sure what people were going to make of it, but I had to give him another chance.

"Spencer, I've no words," I breathed out when we finally stepped out of the helicopter into what seemed to be a private airport.

"Say nothing else, just tell me you forgive me," he said with that cheeky smile.

I slapped his chest, overwhelmed with emotions. Everything had happened so fast that I couldn't think about us, him and me together as an official couple.

"Hmm, I don't know, I've to think about it for a bit longer." I wanted to tease him for a another few hours.

"Are you going to make me grovel more? Christ, Laura, I don't know what else to do." He turned me around and brought me into his body.

"Of course, I wouldn't have it any other way." I smiled.

"Come on, let me show you where we are going to stay." He pulled me along and inside a car.

"Bella, welcome, welcome, come stai?" a familiar voice shouted.

"Lorenzo! Oh my Lord, it's so good to see you." I stared at our Italian driver, who'd taken us everywhere on the island. I glanced at Spencer, embracing him quickly towards me, and kissed him.

"You're the best."

"I know darling, I know."

Chapter Forty-Eight

Spencer

This time around, I'd rented a cosy apartment in Cefalù that overlooked the sea, and Laura loved it. We didn't want to be too far out of town, and since we were only here for one night, I wanted her to feel special. My security team was set up in the apartment right next door, making sure that everything was in order.

The apartment was tiny, but it was gorgeous, stylish. When we arrived, I took her straight to the balcony and opened a bottle of wine.

It'd been weeks since I'd held her in my arms, so I kissed her, telling myself that she was mine again.

"I'll be right back," she said when her phone rang again.

I should have thrown her mobile out into the sea because all these phone calls irritated me. Soon, she returned, pale.

"What happened?"

"I can't believe you were the one who got my mother that appointment in Royal London with the best doctor in the country." She stared at me with tears in her eyes.

Damn, how had she found out about this?

"You weren't supposed to know, and please don't make a big deal out of this. It was just a favour that one of my old friends did for me."

Laura was still staring at me, appearing very emotional as tears streamed down her cheeks.

"I hope you're not mad at me. You were upset, so I pulled some strings."

"Oh, Spencer, this is too much. I can't believe you have done this for her, for me." Laura hugged me tightly.

I rubbed my hand over her back, indulging myself with her scent.

"Don't even mention it, and as far as I know, your mother is doing well now. She might even make a full recovery," I said.

She finally let go of me, and I wiped her tears with my thumb.

"Thank you, Spencer. This means a lot to me," she said. "Hold on. How do you know she's doing better?"

"Because I kept in touch with the doctor on a weekly basis."

"I can't believe it, thank you. This is so thoughtful." She held my hand.

"Anything, my love. Let's go out. I've planned a romantic dinner by the sea," I said.

She brightened up.

My security team had found a small restaurant on the outskirts of town and arranged for us to have a private dinner there. End of September was warm, and the town was still pretty busy.

"You look beautiful tonight, and I can't wait to fuck you again," I said after the waiter had brought our starters.

Laura nearly choked on her wine. It'd been too long, and I wanted her so fucking much.

"You're very sure of yourself, Prime Minister. How do you know that I've already forgiven you?" She shifted on her chair.

I knew she was wet for me, and tonight, I was so glad we would not be disturbed, because I was planning to make love to her all night long until she couldn't walk.

"You don't have to say anything. I know you can't wait for me to thrust my hard cock into your tight pussy. And if you keep biting that bottom lip, then I might lose control and take you home right now," I said.

She went shy on me again, but her eyes were full of fire.

"Spencer, you're terrible," she said.

I chuckled, already imagining bending her over the table and fucking her until she begged me to stop.

Laura

. . .

"Morning, sleeping beauty." I stretched and then I leaned over to kiss Spencer, his morning wood already poking my behind.

We'd had the most incredible night. The dinner turned out to be delicious, and afterwards, an old Italian man arrived to serenade us with his guitar.

Then we went back to the apartment, and before we got through the door, Spencer was already undressing me. He tore my dress and tossed me on the bed. The sex was mind-blowing. Explosive. Intense. Slow. When I fell asleep in the early hours of the morning, he pulled me on top of him again. That man was a total sex maniac, and I freaking loved it.

"More like sleeping monster," he growled and then rolled me over so I was on my back and he was lying on top of me.

"I think it's time to check the news. Let's see what the nation thinks about your little stunt with the handcuffs and unexpected proposal, of course," I said.

"James rang me last night when you went to the loo. So far, no one has called for my resignation." He held me so tightly that I could barely breathe.

"Oh, and what about the press?"

"They're calling you the UK's princess. Now I guess I just have to tell my mother that she can start organising the wedding," he added, kissing me.

We stared at each other for a long moment before he smiled.

"You know she lives for this stuff."

"I know, but let's slow down a little. This whole thing is happening too fast," I said and then felt a little nauseated. "Now, I need to go to the bathroom."

I went to the hall, wondering when I'd had my period last. Fuck, the past few weeks had been so exhausting that I had forgotten all about it.

I glanced at myself in the bathroom and then took a few deep breaths. I unwrapped the pregnancy test that I'd stashed in the cabinet yesterday.

After I peed on the stick, I placed it on the side of the sink and waited, wondering if Spencer was going to freak out.

Later, I walked out of the bathroom with a positive test. It was official. I was pregnant with his baby.

He was making us a coffee in the kitchen while the TV was on. He was so sexy without his shirt on, and I got butterflies again.

"Are you okay?" he asked, turning to face me.

I placed the stick on the kitchen worktop in front of him. He seemed baffled at first until he figured out what it was he was staring at.

"It looks like your wish has come true after all, because I'm pregnant," I said and then bit my bottom lip, quickly remembering that I'd thought Spencer was stealing my pills back in Sicily. It seemed that I was a little crazy. "I think I must have missed a few of my birth control pills when we were in Sicily, because I was so relaxed and happy. And for a moment I thought I was going a little crazy thinking that you were stealing my pills."

A myriad of emotions flashed across his face before he rushed up to me and lifted me off the floor.

"I'm glad that you were distracted enough, and yes that has

crossed my mind a few times, but that would be malicious, plus I can't make that kind of decision for you. We are in it together," he said, still holding me tightly.

"I decided to go on the pill right before we left the UK, but then I thought I forgot the packet, but then I found them in my suitcase days later. Veronica must have slipped them in when she was sneaking in all her tiny bikinis that barely covered anything," I explained. We should have had discussion about protection back in Sicily the first time.

When I glanced back at Spencer I saw that he looked ecstatic and there was that mad gleam in his eye.

"Well, it seems that I've to personally thank Veronica, because she's the one who made this all possible, especially with these things that you call a bikini. Christ, I was walking with permanent hard-on every day since you changed into these," he said, shaking his head. "Besides, it seems that everything has worked out for the best. The universe has followed through with my intention."

"Hold on, what intention? What are you talking about?" I asked, confused, as he put me down.

He smiled mischievously.

"Rupert told me you were planning to quit when we were all in Sicily before." He grinned. "I wanted to keep you so badly and thought it would be good if you unexpectedly got pregnant, so that's why I didn't insist on condoms as much."

"Oh my God, you're terrible, but it all makes sense now," I said and I was a little angry with him, because he should have said something—it was also *my* choice whether I became pregnant or not. I wanted to blame this pregnancy on him but couldn't. After all, I was the one who forgot to take the pills and I should have pushed to have conversation about him using not using condoms.

"I didn't want to risk losing you, and it seems that the universe was on my side. I still can't quite believe that we are going to have a baby. It feels surreal but so right," he admitted. "I love you, Laura Watkins, and I can't wait to spend the rest of my life with you."

Combusting happiness swelled my emotions, and I cried. Damn hormones.

"I love you, too, Spencer Banks, even though you're obnoxious and possessive and the craziest man," I replied as he pulled me in for a scorching kiss.

"Good, because you wouldn't have it any other way."

Bonus Scene

Number 10 Bonus Scene

Spencer

It was Christmas Day, and I was so fucking excited to see Laura's face when she opened my present. I knew she'd always dreamed of going away for Christmas, but over the past few years, my busy schedule hadn't allowed us to fully enjoy the season. This year, though, I was finally making her dream come true.

"Spencer, darling, how are you getting on with the turkey?" my mother shouted from the living room for the fourth time today.

Christ, she had no faith in my cooking skills.

"Fine, Mum, as I already said before, I've everything under

control. Don't worry," I shouted back and then opened the oven to baste the delicious bird a bit more.

Both mine and Laura's family had gathered at our home in North London for this year's Christmas dinner. James and Andrew were not here yet, they were usually both late, but I expected them any minute now. Tosia was sitting on Rupert's lap, singing to herself. Her name was Antonia, but we called her Tosia, and it fitted her perfectly well. I was surprised that my little devil of a child was actually paying attention to her uncle for once. Normally, she'd be running around, trying to get everyone to play with her. My daughter was almost three, and she definitely had my fiery personality. Laura and Sam didn't keep in touch. After two years, Laura had tried to reach out to her, but without luck, so eventually she gave up. My wife decided to donate the money that Sam had wired to her account to charity, and I supported her with that decision.

"Are you sure about that, Dad, because last time you burned the potatoes and then Tosia ruined my dress with her new slime?" Maja said, leaning against the doorframe, giving me a judgmental look and observing how there was currently no space on any of the kitchen worktops—I was a messy cook.

"No, I didn't. Your uncle Rupert was in charge of potatoes," I corrected her. "But don't worry, my dear child, soon you will have the best Christmas dinner of all time. Everything will taste absolutely delicious."

Maja was thirteen now, not a little girl anymore, but a teenager with a snarky attitude and a highly challenging personality. Her colourful social life was driving me up the wall, but luckily I wasn't the Prime Minister any longer, so I didn't have to worry about the media's reaction. I still had security around the clock—apparently these guys were going to stay with me for life. After four years in the office, I stepped down from my position to focus on my family. It had been an honour to serve the country, and I'd remained active in parliament. Stepping down and becoming an MP suited me. This kind of lifestyle wasn't as fast-paced as the top job in government, but it was satisfying.

Maja got on swimmingly with Laura, and after Tosia's birth, the two of them had bonded even more. I was worried because Maja was slowly transforming into a stunning young woman, and I wasn't ready to accept the fact that she was suddenly interested in boys. I told Laura that she would not date until she was at least thirty, but that didn't change the fact that my daughter was slowly driving me to an early grave.

Maja was smiling, staring down at her phone while I continued to baste the turkey.

"Go and see if your mum needs any help upstairs," I muttered, already knowing why Maja was in such a great mood. She was probably talking to another boy through Snapchat or whatnot. When she didn't react, I quickly grabbed the phone out of her hands to get her attention.

"Hey, give it back. That's unfair," she complained when I held the phone above my head so she couldn't reach it.

"Did you hear what I just said? See if your mum needs help. I don't want her to be stressed today. I've a huge surprise for all of you later on, and I need you to behave at least tonight," I said to her before handing back the phone. My comment instantly piqued Maja's interest.

"What kind of surprise is it? Please tell me, Dad?"

"You will see when the time comes. Now go, and please, for once, do as I ask," I said.

She made a face and then finally vanished from the kitchen.

The past four years had gone by so fast. After Laura and I had returned from Sicily, the nation didn't ostracise me and I remained in office as Prime Minister. As it turned out, British people were quite romantic, and they admired my determination in pursuing the woman I loved.

I was so fucking in love with her, I'd handcuffed her to me and asked her to marry me. After that, Laura had given birth to Tosia, my second daughter. Of course, the wedding took place in Sicily—a small and intimate ceremony, surrounded by our closest family and friends who came to celebrate our special day with us. Apparently, all the social media influencers called my proposal the most ridiculous, stupid, and yet utterly romantic thing that any politician had ever done in the public eye, especially during a live press conference. Months later, Laura had also said that a lot of videos of the handcuffing scene went viral on TikTok and BookTokers were going feral over it, comparing me to their favourite book boyfriends.

I couldn't fucking believe how lucky I was to have her by my side. Our life was perfect. Sam had stayed away, and a few months after the wedding, Laura decided to go back to university to finish her BPTC and became a barrister. Of course, I supported her as best I could. After she completed all the training and qualifications she was able to work as a solicitor and she had never been happier.

We had been resisting the urge to hire a nanny, but after Tosia had been born, Laura had agreed we needed additional help. She had her hands full looking after Tosia and Maja while I worked, especially when she was also trying to finish her studies and start a promising career.

I headed to the dining room where Veronica and my father were almost done setting up the table.

"How is the meat, Spencer? Is it moist enough?" Laura's former roommate whispered, following that with a giggle.

Dad glanced at us, shaking his head. Veronica hadn't changed much. She was still crazy, but very much in love with my brother, Rupert.

I still wondered how the fuck Rupert had managed to tame that woman. She was so wild, but she no longer worked as an escort, and that was the main reason why the two of them had ended up being together.

"You will not get enough of it once you taste it, and trust me, it will be the best fucking Christmas dinner you ever had," I said, filled with confidence and gratitude that I had everyone I loved around me this year.

Just then, my brother appeared behind me and clapped me hard on the back.

"You said that last year, bro, and then you burned the potatoes," he muttered.

Veronica laughed.

"No, you were the one in charge of side dishes, but then you got so freaked out about your secret proposal that you forgot to keep checking on them," I countered.

Last year, Rupert had finally popped the big question. Those two had gone through so many ups and downs together, and at one point, Laura told me she couldn't see Veronica ending up with Rupert at all. Things had certainly turned around.

Luckily, Rupert didn't get the chance to argue further with me because a second later there was a knock on the front door, so he left to answer it.

Several moments later, James' voice was echoing in the hallway. Then a few security agents marched through the house. I sighed, wondering what the fuck they expected to find in here as my house couldn't have been more secure. Besides, I already had my own security that was always around. James should have told them to stay back, but apparently this was the new protocol since my brother was now engaged to Princess Evangeline Romanov, who was the only remaining heir to the throne of the Sovereignty of Bellavista—a small Eastern European country between Poland and Russia. I couldn't fucking believe it when, several months after being away in Europe, he'd come back to London with a bloody royal in tow. Mother was obviously thrilled. This was a huge shock to all of us, but Evangeline was a very sweet girl, and she hated being called anything other than Evangeline.

My oldest brother and his new girlfriend—the princess— came through several minutes later, after Evangeline's private security detail had finally left, passing me in the corridor and apologising for all the fuss. James gave me a wink. Andrew and Apolonia were right behind him. I still didn't fucking know if Andrew was dating Apolonia or not, or whether she was still only his assistant. That fucker didn't want to say anything about it, but I had a feeling there was definitely something going on between them.

"All right, everyone, let's gather around. Spencer, call Laura. It's time to open the presents!" my mother announced.

This was a big house, but the living room still looked crowded. A giant Christmas tree, that Maja had insisted on getting this year, stood by the fireplace. Laura's mum and dad were sitting next to it, chatting with my father. Laura's mother was going through treatment, and she was doing much better, but she was still on heavy medication, so she only worked part-time at the school. Laura and I had tried to persuade her to give it up, but she said she loved being busy and missed the kids too much to quit.

"Presents, Daddy. I want my presents!" Tosia pointed at a huge wrapped package she had been desperate to open since five this morning.

We had let her open a few smaller presents, but she was determined to see what was in the biggest box.

"What's going on in here? Who said that you can open the presents now?" My wife appeared next to me.

She looked stunning in a black fitted dress, revealing her incredible legs. My cock went rock-hard at the sight.

"Me, me! Santa came, and I want to open all the presents

now," Tosia shouted. She ran up to Laura and started tugging on her dress.

My wife stroked her hair.

"All right, go on. I think you can open the big present now, sweetheart," she said, smiling at Tosia.

"Come here, woman, sit on my lap so I can touch you up a little," I murmured in her ear as Tosia finally tore the paper on the big present apart with sheer determination.

I flopped into the chair and pulled Laura down with me. I couldn't get enough of her, even after so many years. Tonight, I had to have her. I needed her. The past few days had been so hectic, we had struggled to make time for sex. I vowed that the situation would be promptly rectified.

"All right, Tosia. After you finish opening your present, you can pass one to everyone else," my mother said.

Tosia had already torn most of the wrapping paper and screamed when she finally saw that Santa had brought her the pink scooter she had been badgering us for over the last few weeks. Laura squirmed on my lap, rubbing on my dick that was now painfully hard and throbbing.

"I love you, and after you open your gift I'm going to drag you upstairs so I can have my dessert before the main course," I murmured while everyone's attention was on our daughter who was now pushing Rupert to put her scooter together.

Laura's green eyes peered back at me, a playful smile spread on her gorgeous face.

"What dessert?" she asked, confused for just a moment before her eyes widened—she must have felt my erection pressing against her arse. "Are you out of your mind, Spencer? We still have a million things to do, and everyone is here now."

"Love, I've been fucking patient enough, and I'll not sit at the dinner table until I feast on your pussy first and make you see the stars," I whispered back, shifting on the chair and showing her how much she affected me.

I glanced around at my family, seeing that for the first time, James's entire attention was fixed on the petite woman who was sitting next to him. They'd only just started dating; he used to be her bodyguard. My brother didn't like discussing his private life too much, but after he'd returned to London, he'd revealed that the two of them had met when he was forced to step in when one of his best men had suffered a skiing accident right after he was assigned to protect the princess. Apparently, she'd hated him from the very beginning, which was pretty ironic considering how I'd met Laura.

"Ah, Laura, this one's for you," my mother's voice interrupted my train of thought. "Tosia, hand it over to Mummy, will you?"

Tosia grabbed the big, fat, red envelope from her grandma, stared at it in confusion for a few seconds, then marched over to Laura, who shifted forward. My dick swelled even more. Damn it!

I fantasised about getting her pregnant again. Perhaps we'd have a little boy this time ...

"What is it, Mummy? What did Santa bring you?" Tosia jumped up and down while Maja was talking to Veronica about her new horse-grooming set that she'd got from me.

"I don't know. Let's see ... I think this is going to be very special, because Mummy has been very good this year," she said.

I swore under my breath, wanting to fuck Laura so hard until she was too exhausted to move.

"Indeed, Mummy has been very good this year," I said out loud.

Laura blushed, and Rupert and Andrew laughed.

Laura opened the envelope, pulling out a pile of tickets, along with some leaflets describing the resort in Lapland.

"What is it?"

"It's plane tickets for four people to go to Lapland." I smiled.

"Oh my God, Spencer, this is amazing!" Laura cried in excitement before turning around and hugging me tightly.

"Guess what, Tosia? We are all going to see Santa in a few days." I grinned at my little devil of a daughter, whose expression changed from perplexed to pure joy when she finally understood what I'd said.

She and Maja screamed, and Laura grabbed my cheeks and kissed me hard.

"Thank you, you're the best husband ever! You know how much I've wanted to visit Lapland, and both Maja and Tosia are going to love it there, too." She rubbed her nose against mine.

"Of course, but now, Mrs Banks, I need you to get up and head straight upstairs. I'll be there shortly," I whispered.

She stared at me for a few seconds, probably contemplating various ways to defy me, but then she got up and quickly left the room.

No one was paying much attention to us anymore because Tosia was excitedly helping the others to open their presents, throwing the wrapping paper all over the place. I excused myself to check on my bird again and make sure everything was still on track for later. I still had around twenty minutes to kill before it would be done, at which point I'd need to usher everyone back into the dining room, while the turkey sat on the worktop for a few moments, absorbing all the juices.

I dashed upstairs to our bedroom in record time and shut the door behind me. Laura was already sitting on the bed, waiting for me. The memory of that day, four years ago, when I'd mistaken her for my escort, flashed in front of my eyes. However, this time, Laura didn't seem nervous at all.

"I've changed my mind. I want you to get on all fours. I need to fuck you hard and fast. I don't think I'll have time to feast on you just yet, but there's always tonight ..." I said as I locked the bedroom door.

Tosia had a habit of walking into our bedroom whenever she felt like it, and right now, I really didn't want to be disturbed.

"Spencer, you're out of your mind. We had sex only a few days ago," she said, but there was a gleam in her eye that told me she was looking forward to this as much as I was.

I would never stop loving this woman.

"Exactly, a few days ago, and I've been walking around with a hard-on since yesterday—because this is what you do to me. You're driving me crazy with need, woman." Getting on the bed, I helped her get on her knees. Then I tugged up her dress, happy to see that she was wearing my favourite thong. I pushed my face into her pussy and inhaled sharply.

She gasped.

"Oh, Spencer. I need you inside me now. Have you got a condom?" she asked.

I slapped her arse hard, laughing.

"Fuck the condom. I'm going to put another baby inside you," I growled before pulling out my hard cock. I pushed the thong out of the way and thrust my cock into her warm and soaking sex.

"What? Spencer, no. I don't want to be pregnant again just yet. What about my career?" she asked, barely able to speak as I moved inside her.

Fuck, she felt so damn good, but I paused for a moment.

"We'll manage everything together, and we have Kasia to help us too. The big question is: Are you ready to have a third child?" I asked, knowing that I couldn't make this decision for her, not to mention that it may not be the best moment to discuss this.

Laura glanced up at me; she looked flustered and was probably frustrated that I'd stopped fucking her to pose the question.

"You know that I've always wanted a big family, Spencer. I know we have lots of support, and yes, I'm ready, " she declared, smiling coyly at me.

"I know you do, but I wanted to make sure you were ready. I'd love for us to have a son, but another daughter will still be a blessing, too. I really want to see your swollen stomach again. You being pregnant with my child is such a turn on" I growled.

Grabbing her hips, I pounded into her again, hard and fast, just the way she liked it. "Let's get to work on making this baby boy."

This woman was everything to me, and I could never get enough. I fisted her hair and pulled on it while a scorching wave of heat burned through me. Laura gasped and panted. She loved it when I was rough with her. She loved being fucked hard.

The tiny voice in my head played around with the idea that nine months from now, I could be holding a son in my arms, even though that was not guaranteed. We would just need to keep trying. Either way, I didn't care because I would get her pregnant again, and trying was the best part ... because she was the love of my life, and we were perfect together.

Sneak peek from Rupert and Veronica's story

Viral Love Chapter One

Veronica

"Come on, let's go in here. I'm not drunk enough yet to head back to our Airbnb, Clara," I said, pulling my bestie into a swanky bar in Ornos, on the island of Mykonos, Greece.

This was the holiday of a lifetime, and since we'd spent most of our money, it was a good thing this was our last night on the island. Tomorrow morning, we were flying home. It was the end of August and scorching hot. My white top was sticking to my body. I didn't mind. I loved the heat, and this climate suited me.

"All right then, but I'm only having one. Remember our flight is early in the morning. I don't fancy flying back home and being hungover to fuck," Clara, my travel companion, stated.

I waved my hand, and a moment later, we walked into a busy bar in the centre of town.

I had been working as a stripper in London over the past few months. In doing so, I'd saved a bit of money for this summer, and Mykonos was our last stop. Tomorrow, I was going back home, back to the reality of the strip club and my apartment in Camden Market. Unfortunately, my life hadn't turned out how I had imagined it would when I was growing up, but I kept telling myself that as long as I was having fun, nothing else mattered.

My other best friend and roommate, Laura, was currently away in America. She was working as a nanny for a wealthy English family, but it wasn't her dream job either. She had gotten herself involved with a famous pop star who'd turned out to be a real arsehole in the end. He'd cheated on her with two women while snorting cocaine. After that incident, Laura was too afraid to go back to the corporate world of politics, so she'd settled on being a nanny, telling me that her quiet and ordinary life suited her better than being constantly in the spotlight.

"What can I get you?" a cute dark-haired Greek barman asked when we finally squeezed through the crowd of drunken people having the best time of their lives.

I really didn't want to leave the island yet, but Clara and I had been travelling since July. It had been a long, eventful summer, full of laughter and fun. We had met a fair amount of guys during this time, but so far I had avoided sleeping with any of them.

We were both young and single. None of us were looking for a real relationship, but after going through so many arseholes, I had given up on the idea of no-strings-attached sex.

Tonight would be my last attempt to finally hook up with a handsome stranger on this trip. I didn't like sleeping around, but it had been so long since I'd let my hair down that I was up for some steamy action. Tomorrow, this fairy tale would end, and life, as usual, would resume.

"Two mojitos, please, and keep the tap open." I handed the barman my silver credit card.

"Coming right up," he said with a smile. His gorgeous eyes twinkled.

He was my type, but he was working, so he probably wouldn't have time to sneak out to the back to satisfy a girl like me.

"I'm going to take some pictures. This is our last night, and we need to go back to London with good memories." Clara pulled out her phone and took a zillion selfies of me and her.

Then the drinks arrived, and I sucked on the straw, very turned on all of a sudden.

I had been craving sex for so long, but I didn't have that urge to sleep with random guys, whereas Clara had done it in every new country and island visited over the past two months.

Every guy who showed an interest in me turned out to be an arsehole, so I always ended up in my room alone and miserable. All right, maybe I wanted something more than just a guy who was extremely good-looking and funny. I wanted him to hold a meaningful conversation for at least a minute, and he needed to be smart, too. I didn't want to go to bed with just any random idiot. Yeah, it was just one night, an hour of passionate sex, and we would never have to see each other again after that. Still, I was craving a little something extra from the interaction, so that was the main reason I had been holding back.

"All right, I'm going to dance. You coming?" I asked Clara, who was scrolling through her phone, not noticing the two guys eyeing us from their seats in the corner.

"Nah ... my legs are aching, and I need to message my brother back. He's worried about me," she replied.

I shrugged and went onto the dance floor alone, leaving Clara alone to fend for herself. The music was loud, and I swayed to the rhythm, holding my drink, surrounded by people. I closed my eyes for a moment, trying to immerse myself in this atmosphere, and then peered back at Clara. It looked like she was taking a video because she was waving at me to keep dancing.

I sipped on my drink and continued to dance for several long moments, enjoying the feeling of surrendering to the beat. There was something in the air, an electrifying energy that made me feel alive. Full of desire for something ...

"Hey, beautiful, do you mind if I join you?" a sexy and sultry British-sounding voice asked.

I instantly turned my head to see a tall guy standing behind me. He was handsome, and I was now certain he was British. I glanced back at my drink, wondering if I was hallucinating, because surely, no one could be this good-looking. He had black hair, pale-blue eyes, and a beard that hadn't been trimmed in a while. The heat from his stare sent shivers down my spine.

"You want to dance with me?" I eyed him with reservation.

He was standing so close, and the air between us crackled

with electricity, stealing my breath away. Normally, at this point, any other guy would just stare down at my cleavage, then let his gaze trail brazenly down my body—but not this one. The man in front of me was looking directly into my eyes, as though he was suddenly captivated by me.

"How about we go outside to get some fresh air, so we can talk?" he asked.

I nodded without thinking, because I wanted to get to know him. He took my hand and walked me through the crowd of people until we stepped outside into the heavy, humid air.

"My name is Rupert. What's yours?"

"I'm Valerie," I introduced myself with the fake name I always used.

He gave my hand a firm shake. I didn't want to give him my real name just yet. We stared at each other for a few beats, but during that span of seconds, it felt like time stood still and the world ceased to exist around us. It was as if a spell had been put on me because I had an inexplicably strong attraction towards this complete stranger.

"It's really nice to meet you, Valerie. Have you been on the island long?"

"Yes, about two weeks, and you?" I asked, immediately knowing that I was going to spend the night with this guy.

"I only just got here this evening and wasn't planning to go out at all, but my brother told me he was meeting some girl here, so I tagged along," he explained, staring down at my lips. "I hope you don't mind me saying so, Valerie, but you're so beautiful. The moment I saw you, I couldn't take my eyes off you."

What was happening to me? This guy wasn't like any other I'd met on my travels around Europe. He seemed so down to earth, well-spoken, and he wasn't too forward with me. All the previous guys I'd met in the bars or clubs were instantly all over me, trying to kiss me or hold me, but not Rupert. He was close, but he wasn't in my space, and he wasn't trying to touch me.

"Thank you, that is sweet of you. So, are you going to tell me where you're from? You have a proper London accent," I asked, unsure whether I was right or not. I was attracted to him, there was no doubt about it, and at that moment, all I could think about was kissing him, just to prove to myself that I could.

He laughed. "Yes, I'm very cliché. I'm a businessman from London. So what is it that you do, Valerie?"

I licked my lips and told myself to fuck it. This was my last night, and this guy was polite, handsome, and sexy as hell, so I had to make the first move. He was wearing a white cotton shirt, and his two top buttons were undone, revealing a tanned, muscular chest. I took a step towards him, a slight breeze wafting on my neck.

"I work as a flight attendant," I replied quickly and then added, "I'm going to kiss you now, Rupert, and I want you to know that I normally don't do that with guys I just met, but I feel like we have a connection." I stared directly into his pale-blue eyes, then I drew his mouth towards mine and stood on my tiptoes to do what I'd said I would.

The moment my lips touched his, I was lost. Rupert pulled me closer, grabbed my face with his large hands, and kissed me back with incredible passion and roughness. Fuck, I had never been kissed like that. His lips were so soft, and as he devoured my mouth, a rush of burning heat gathered between my legs. He was kissing me like he couldn't get enough, and he tasted incredible.

By the time he eased away, I was breathless, flustered, and my nipples were hard.

"Damn, Valerie, you are something else. I want ..." He took a deep breath. " I want to hear you moan my name when you come for me. I want you in my bed, and I know this may sound crazy, but I normally don't sleep with women I just met." He dragged his trembling hand nervously through his hair.

I smiled but screamed on the inside. I couldn't believe that this was happening for real. Rupert's words filled me with longing—I couldn't have asked for a better person to spend my last night in Greece with.

"I want the same thing." I leaned into him. "Take me to your hotel room," I said confidently, never more sure of anything in my life.

A huge smile broke over his handsome face. "Come on then, it's not far from here."

He took my hand again, and we strode together through the streets of Mykonos, heading to Rupert's hotel. I texted Clara quickly, letting her know I wasn't coming back with her tonight. She'd probably already met someone in the bar, as usual; that was how things normally rolled with her.

Rupert wasn't lying when he'd said that his hotel was very close. It was one of those stylish high-end boutique places in the heart of the island. We entered and got into the lift with other people. He held my hand while my heart thumped loudly.

It had been over a year since I'd slept with anyone, and now I wasn't sure what to expect. I just had to hope I'd be enough for him, because he was so ... different. People assumed I'd be easy because of the job I had, but nothing was further from the truth.

The lift arrived at his floor. We got off and walked down a short corridor to his room. He opened the door and gestured for me to come inside. A gentleman, too ...

Once in the room, he closed the door behind us.

"Wow, this is very nice." I looked around and spotted his enormous bed. The room was decorated in calming colours and tasteful art. A bouquet rested on a small table by the balcony window.

He turned to me and bent down to rest his forehead against mine, his thumb drawing small circles on the back of my hand. "Are you sure you want to do this, Valerie?" He stared at me with hunger in his eyes.

From the obvious bulge in his trousers, I knew he was holding back.

"Because once I've you in my bed, I won't let go until everyone in this hotel hears you screaming my name."

I swallowed hard and told myself to keep it together. Rupert wanted to make sure I was all right with us sleeping together tonight. He wanted me, and he was waiting for me to say yes to him. Damn it, I had never met a guy who acted like that. He was nothing like the men who hung out at the club or those I came across on my nights out. He must have had some great female influence in his upbringing

"Yes, Rupert, I want you, too." I moved to look up at him, mischief taking over. "Don't hold back. Fuck me like you mean it." I peeled off my shirt so that I stood in front of him in my lace bra.

His gaze moved down to my neck, then to my chest, and then back up to my lips. Then he grabbed my neck and kissed me hard, until I was gasping for breath, needy with desire, moisture pooling between my legs. Suddenly, his mouth was everywhere, kissing and nibbling at me until I was moaning loudly. He traced his lips down my neck, while his other hand squeezed my breasts.

"I'm so hard for you. I need you to tell me exactly what you want me to do to you right now." He kissed my collarbone and proceeded to unclasp my bra.

I was so wet for him, so ready and throbbing, but I had never been very expressive in the bedroom, so I wasn't really sure what to say.

"Touch me between my legs … oh!"

I cried out when he licked my left breast, his tongue circling around the hardened nipple, then he sucked on it hard, sending me crazy with need. That felt so good, but I wanted and needed more. No other guy had ever asked me to tell him what I liked in bed.

"No, not good enough. I need you to tell me exactly what you want me to do to you, in specific detail," he growled before pushing me down on the bed.

I stared at him as he took off his shirt, and then a small gasp escaped me when I saw his perfectly chiselled, muscular chest. He must work out a lot because he was shaped like one of the Greek gods.

"I want you to touch me there—"

"No, no, no, I said to be specific," he insisted.

Oh God. I swallowed. "I want you to touch my pussy, my clit, until I go crazy ... and then I want to feel your cock inside me. I want to come all over it," I said, not knowing where this was all coming from. I wasn't in the habit of talking dirty in bed, but this was special. I was not in my usual environment, and I felt so free.

"Good girl. So your soaking-wet pussy wants my throbbing cock?" He eyed me intensely and approached the bed. He took off his shorts and quickly got rid of his boxers, too.

God, I stared at his enormous cock, wondering how it was even going to fit inside me. I was suddenly apprehensive about this whole thing.

"Yes," I replied in a shaky voice.

"Remove the rest of your clothes and spread your legs for me, you dirty, dirty slut."

His rough voice sent a shiver down between my legs. I had never been more turned on in my whole life and I quickly got rid of my shorts and knickers. The bed was huge and very comfortable.

"So fucking beautiful. I'm going to ruin your wet cunt and arse tonight, and you will love every second of it." Rupert climbed onto the bed, leaning over me. His eyes were penetrating mine.

He turned me around swiftly, so I was on all fours, and I squealed. His words were a real turn-on, and I was desperate for him to touch me. His hands caressed my arse; I gasped and quickly followed through into a groan when he suddenly eased two fingers inside me.

"Christ, your pussy is soaking for me. Do you want me to touch your throbbing clit?"

"Yes, Rupert, yes, please touch me there," I pleaded, desperate and so needy.

I felt the rising heat in the pit of my stomach; he kept moving his fingers inside me, before he lowered himself and his tongue lapped on my clit. Fuck, this felt so amazing, and my thighs were trembling. He sucked on it like it was a lollypop.

"So wet and ready, fuck, I'm going to explode inside you, but don't worry, I'm not planning to go easy on you. I've all night to play with you and make sure you remember my cock ramming into your cunt every time you even think about fucking another guy," he said, and then he pulled away.

I cried out for more. I was ready to beg him to fuck me. I was already so close to climax, he just had to keep that filthy mouth of his on my clit and I would have come, but it seemed Rupert had other plans. I protested loudly, and he slapped my arse hard, not once but several times, and then rubbed my clit again in slow, torturous motions. The skin on my arse was burning, and my juices were rolling down my inner thighs. He was behind me and sounded like he was putting a condom on.

"Rupert, it's too big ... I can't—"

I stopped talking and suddenly thrust his enormous cock inside me, before I could react or beg him to take it easy. He was so big, and this was so painful. I stopped breathing for a second; he stretched me inside.

"Shut up and take it. I know you can take it all. Fuck, you feel incredible." He groaned and eased himself out and back into me.

He entered me fully. I screamed his name and begged for mercy. Then, he gathered my hair in his fist and pulled it hard which tilted my head back and arched my back farther.

He then leaned down and whispered into my ear, "Remember this, you dirty red-haired whore ... you will never forget this night, and even if you fuck someone else, you'll always be disappointed knowing that that guy wasn't me. From now on, you will always and forever be mine."

I was losing my mind, feeling this intense pain and utter pleasure at the same time as Rupert pounded into me. He definitely delivered on his promise, fucking me until I couldn't move or even breathe. He came quickly afterwards, and then after a short break, he was ready to go again. I had never had sex like that in my life. Around midnight, I had a feeling that he'd let me sleep for a little while, but then I woke up, finding his head between my legs. He licked and sucked on my clit once again. He ate me up like I was his last meal and then continued to fuck me a few more times.

Rupert was intense, rough, and he fucked me in every position through the night, into the early hours of the morning, until

I'd cried and begged him to let me rest. He was totally obsessed with making sure that I came every single time, and I wasn't sure if I was even going to wake up the next morning.

I didn't really remember what happened after that, but we both must have finally drifted off to sleep from exhaustion. A noise from the road outside woke me, and when I opened my eyes, I realised it was already light outside. I grabbed my phone and checked the time; I cursed silently, sore and achy all over. I just knew I had to get out of that room, otherwise I would never make it back to London. My plane was leaving in two hours. Rupert was fast asleep on his front so I couldn't catch a final glimpse of that beautiful chest of his. My legs felt wobbly when I stood, and my head spun. This epic night was etched in my brain forever, I was certain of it.

I quickly picked up my clothes, got dressed, and snuck out of his room, knowing I would probably never see that wild, sex god of a man again, and maybe it was for the best.

It was the most incredible night of my life. It was exactly what I'd needed, and even if I could barely walk, I knew it was worth it.

Rupert was something else, and I felt sad walking out of that hotel room, believing that nothing this amazing would ever happen to me in the real world.

Newsletter

If you enjoyed it, please considering leaving a review.

Get Signed Paperback and Signed Special Edition Hardback with bonus content on my website.

Join my newsletter for release updates, special previews and giveaways exclusive to my subscribers:

Click here to get started

Notes

Chapter 30

1. Hold on, beautiful, I got you.
2. lifeguard
3. Her name is Laura, and we are all grateful. We don't need your help now. I've got her
4. Yes, I am her husband, and we are all grateful for your help. There is no need for anything else. Now she is with me.
5. The good ones are always taken.
6. "Sir, this woman doesn't seem to like being carried. Why are you treating her like a caveman?"
7. "I'm taking my wife home. Is there a problem?"
8. No, there's no problem, sir, even though she doesn't look very happy right now.
9. Don't worry, once we're back home, she'll be the happiest woman in the world!

Chapter 36

1. Auntie Sofia, this is Maja's nanny and my girlfriend.
2. Finally you found yourself a woman. But this one is only skin and bones. We need to fatten her up.
3. Eat, eat, my darling.
4. I think you need a break, buddy. This is not the way to behave. This woman doesn't understand you so apologise to her. Now apologise to me for touching what's mine.
5. But she just told me she is only your nanny. I can talk to her then.
6. She is my woman and you're staring at her tits, so leave before I stop being polite.

Notes

7. Your woman? But I like her too and perhaps she'd want to choose a real Sicilian man.

Printed in Great Britain
by Amazon